W9-BDR-596

"Destruction spread across the colony? A restaurant awash in its own comestibles? Armed felons tied up in service corridors for innocent civilians to come upon unawares? Destroying valuable equipment in the most elegant hotel in the sector?" Admiral Podesta paced back and forth.

"We had no choice, sir," I said, patiently. "They were dangerous criminals. And none of the ones we left tied up were armed. Besides, we didn't do any of the damage to the ballroom. That was all done by the pirates."

Podesta met me nose to nose. "It was not your job to apprehend them. It was your job to inform me, and let me decide what action to take."

My emotions got the better of me. "Admiral, they might have gotten away!"

"That would have been correct. You were unprepared. You were to review the local militia."

"I did that, sir. They prove to be loyal, effective soldiers."

"They were brave, that's certain. Having to put up with you, I would also give them commendations for patience." The admiral continued, "I have received bills for almost nine hundred thousand credits' worth of damage to that dining establishment, the hotel, and all the other station facilities. The *Wedjet* itself had to abort its patrol to arrive as quickly as possible."

The admiral was correct. It was my responsibility. "I cannot express to you how very sorry I am, sir."

Podesta sighed. "So am I, Ensign. Especially when you leave me no choice but to ... commend you."

BAEN BOOKS by JODY LYNN NYE

View from the Imperium
The Grand Tour
School of Light
Waking in Dreamland
The Ship Errant
Don't Forget Your Spacesuit, Dear

License Invoked (with Robert Asprin)

With Anne McCaffrey:
The Ship Who Saved the World
The Death of Sleep
The Ship Who Won
Planet Pirates (also with Elizabeth Moon)

VIEW FROM THE IMPERIUM

JODY LYNN NYE

VIEW FROM THE IMPERIUM

This is a work of fiction. All the characters and events portrayed in this book are fictional, and any resemblance to real people or incidents is purely coincidental.

Copyright © 2011 by Jody Lynn Nye

All rights reserved, including the right to reproduce this book or portions thereof in any form.

A Baen Books Original

Baen Publishing Enterprises
P.O. Box 1403
Riverdale, NY 10471
www.baen.com

ISBN: 978-1-4391-3430-6

Cover art by David Mattingly

First paperback printing, April 2011
Second paperback printing, July 2012

Distributed by Simon & Schuster
1230 Avenue of the Americas
New York, NY 10020

Pages by Joy Freeman (www.pagesbyjoy.com)
Printed in the United States of America

To Bill, with love

❧ PROLOGUE ❧

The ions stopped exploding off the surface of the ship as it emerged from ultra-drive and the rift in space sealed behind it. The long vessel's self-effacing dark blue shell continued to repel in glittering sparks the few microscopic particles that had previously occupied the portion of space that the ship now possessed. Four broad fins of a wedge-shaped cross-section ran the entire length of the solid tube shape. At the propulsion end, the fins widened out to form a traditional landing pattern. At the navigation end, the top was contained in a repulsor net of energy that allowed the sensors within to operate without being ripped off or irretrievably dented by space junk. Its light weapons emplacements lay in the angles. Except for the minor fireworks and the glimmer of the net, the ship *Little Darling* was a narrow bar of darkness across the greater darkness spangled with pinpoints of diamond light. One star stood out among the others. Portent's Star, a medium-sized blue-white, shone fiercely, its light only faintly bent into the distance by the black hole only half a light-year away that separated the rest of the Castaway Cluster from the vast Imperium. The red light of a stationary navigational warning beacon glowed like a lantern at the doorway of an ancient inn, welcoming the ship and its contingent to the system.

"Good, th'un's out there," Captain Iltekinov stated, more for the benefit of the row of distinguished visitors standing behind him on the bridge than for the crew. He received no reply. He pressed his broad back into the tattered, glossy, oxblood-colored padding of his chair and peered over his shoulder. All five of the Councillors, clad in the long yellow robes of the Yolk system, were engrossed in the row of shallow viewscreens attached to the handrails.

"When's reception return?" Ruh Pinckney, the senior diplomat, demanded. He smacked the side of the display with the flat of his hand.

A blare of sound and a blaze of light made everyone jump.

"There it is," Tam Quelph announced, pointing at her screen, as the rapid data transmission resumed. The woman peered at the time-coding running along the bottom. The backlit image threw colored lights that blurred her white-blond hair and the elaborate wave patterns of pink on her face with blobs of black, blue and white. "Damn all, we've missed over five days of discussion during the transit!"

"Y'can get archives from the First Councillor when y'land," Iltekinov growled. It wasn't the first time he had made this observation.

"We're hopelessly behind," Quelph complained. "We caught up with a more current stream, and it only shows how late we are!"

"Y'could ask 'em to stop talkin' 'til you gets there," the captain suggested. He was tired of the endless grousing and whining of the embassy from the Yolk system. An independent businessman who plied his trade among the inhabited planets and stations within the Castaway Cluster, he normally hauled cargo, mostly dry goods and produce. It all stayed quietly in its containers in the hold and didn't wear his ears out unnecessarily. He still had a whole ear on one side, but only half an ear on the other. The scar, the result of a fight in a Dree station bar over thirty years before, ran across his face to his nose, digging a ruddy furrow among the dark blue angles and crosshatches of his clan tattoos that covered his cheeks and the bridge of his nose. After thirty years and more plying the spaceways, his least favorite load was politicians. Lucky for him, a full, in-person council meeting was a rare event.

Pinckney, a heavyset man whose dark-green and yellow facial tattoos vanished into the rolls of fat under his swarthy chin, made a sound of outrage at his suggestion. "We have not been introduced to the board yet!" he said. "Our views cannot be noted until we are presented—in person—and been welcomed by the host delegation!"

"Dunno why," Iltekinov muttered to himself. "Waste of time. Traders don't bother with face-to-face. Entertainers don't bother with face-to-face. *Law enforcement* don't bother with face-to-face . . ."

Pinckney overheard him. "We will do these things properly, as our governments have done them for two hundred years, Captain," he said, stiffly. "Representational and in the proper order. We will have to speed-review all of the minutes taken thus far so we don't delay the others any more than we already have."

Iltekinov yawned. Once again, Pinckney was trying to blame him for their tardiness. The captain shut out the criticism. He had warned them when they'd first contacted him for passage to Portent's Star that space travel wasn't like running a light-rail system in a city. It had been too much to assume that the politicians would pay the least attention to what he'd said, let alone retain it. He was a good Yolkovian, and he had been willing to carry the negotiators to this very important conference on Dree for no other fee than fuel replenishment, in spite of the trip's interrupting his usual rounds through the Cluster.

Worse yet, the diplomats' luggage, for five human beings intending to spend less than a month in a location where food, shelter, entertainment and, if necessary, toiletries and clothing would be provided, took up almost a third of his cargo bay, making him leave behind that much of his payload on Yolk 5, also called Setria, the home planet in the system. The councillors could have made up for it by being pleasant, but no, they went on and on about how an ion storm prevented him from picking them up on the day that he had promised, as if they knew anything at all about the rigors of astrogation or physics, for that matter. How in all of nature did the five biggest complainers in the galaxy end up being named as representatives for the entire system of Yolk? He grumbled to himself and started to turn back.

The lone Wichu on the council, Ferat Urrmenoc, looked up from her screen and tipped him a sheepish grin and a wink of one of her big round eyes.

The nonhumanoid with the thick, black-tipped white fur was the only one who picked up on what he was thinking. He grinned back at her and settled down in his seat.

A side screen on his personal console ran what they were seeing. The Yolkovian contingent was receiving the minutes of an extended meeting of the advisory council of the Cluster system. He had his screen muted so the transcribed text ran along the top of the image instead of playing audio into the implant in the portion of skull over his left ear. While the combined vid featured visuals, graphics and historic videos in an attempt to liven it up, the content of each learned and lengthy discourse was such boring stuff he wouldn't bother to listen to it even if he was on a fifty-year sublight haul all the way to the Core Worlds of the Imperium or the center of the Trade Union and had lost his entire collection of action shows and pornography in a database crash, and everyone in the ship he might play basketball with was in a coma, and hidden somewhere in the press of information was the directions to a planetoid full of cut jewels and wanton, willing women. The download wasn't even good for inducing sleep, since every so often one of the delegates would break into a screaming diatribe, probably out of frustration that he couldn't strangle all the others.

The Yolkovians ought to feel grateful that they had the rapid data transmission system at their disposal. True, it wasn't as satisfying as being in the room with your conversation partner, but it was a fast conveyance of information. The system had become vital during the founding of an interstellar community, and evolved greatly over the course of history as that community had evolved. The distance between two planets once meant a nine-hour gap in between sentences. Digital high dispersal transmission had shortened that to nine minutes. Once the FTL border had been broken on energy transfer, one could carry on a conversation between *stars* with a lag of mere hours, far better than communications carried by the first human ancestors to traverse space, but nothing ever seemed fast enough for people in a hurry. Like the council.

"Now they're talking about government structure," Pinckney wailed again.

"Calm yourself, Ruh," Quelph said. "They cannot make any decisions without us."

"They might form opinions," Pinckney insisted.

"Oh, they have plenty of those," Urrmenoc laughed with the grunting breaths of her kind. "So do we. But listen: they're saying the same things they were five days ago. We just heard those same arguments. They are not likely to change before we get there. How long now, Captain?"

Iltekinov turned his head around, no longer having to pretend he wasn't eavesdropping.

"Matter of two shifts," he said. "We can't resume ultra-drive within the solar system. Too much disruption might distort the orbit of a planetary body; 'course, you know that. We've got to take sublight, runnin' about point-one-five C. By late third shift."

Ignoring the grumbling, the captain nodded to his navigator to get *Little Darling* under way. Natalia Poldin nodded back. She was an old-time spacer, gray eyes crinkled at the corners from ages of staring out ports at the stars. Her clan tattoos were shaped like small teardrops on their sides so they resembled schools of fish swimming toward the bridge of her nose. None of them needed explicit instructions on how to do their job. Iltekinov changed the view on his screen to monitor movement of the asteroids and stray bodies in the belt of debris.

Out here on the edge of the system lifeless rocks the size of small planets rolled and tumbled in a complex pattern that would have made a fine screen-saver. The banging sound that came from the bow of the ship was an artifact, not actual strikes, made by rocks too small to dodge as they met the pure energy of the protective net and exploded into harmless dust repelled by the shield.

There'd been movements over the centuries to urge ships to enter star systems at a beacon set above or below the plane of ecliptic, in order to avoid potential collisions when coming out of ultra-drive, but there was no doubt that it made getting one's bearings just that much easier to aim for the geographical marker that was the ring of stone and ice around nearly every star's purlieu. Even longtime spacers were more comfortable having a solid goal than a nebulous point in space one could only see on scope.

The danger of being struck by one of the gigantic rocks was microscopic compared with, say, having a collision with another vehicle in planetary atmosphere. At a distance the belt might look like a gravel road, but close up, the bodies revolving around the helio-pause were many kilometers apart.

The real danger lay in ramming into chipped-off chunks of asteroid that were too small to avoid but too big to be easily consumed by the hungry screens at the bow. Energy weapons, controlled by a computer, spotted and picked those off, but the captain liked to keep an eye on the process himself. No human was fool enough to think he had quicker reactions than a computer, but Iltekinov couldn't help but want to maintain the watch to protect his ship. He was fond of her; they looked after one another.

His screen showed one edge of brilliant white, the splashover energy from the black hole, still powerful in spite of its safe remove from the system. That collapsed star, combined with the distance in between Portent's Star and the Imperium, the nearest outpost of civilization, served to isolate the Castaways. Once every year or two Iltekinov made the laborious trip to Imperium space or the even longer journey to the Trade Union for luxury goods and technical devices.

At least six huge confederations existed beyond the black hole, and many small ones, such as the Costa-detev Federation, the Uctu Autocracy, the Obqin, the Dro-Tan Technocracy, and the Central Worlds, each consisting of hundreds or thousands of star systems. He knew from history programs on the viewtank that many of the races who co-existed in the Cluster with human beings originated in some of those far-off systems, having conquered or been conquered by his kind in centuries long past and forgotten by mutual consent.

Once the Castaways had been part of the Imperium, but that was long ago, before Iltekinov was born. The Imperium was too far away to have any real impact on his life, so he ignored the arguments that went on between historians and politicians. For him, business was the most important factor. He paid his taxes to Yolk's council, and the money was shared out evenly among the other planets and stations in the Cluster. There were the usual arguments about the wealthier communities paying in more and getting less, stations getting heavily subsidized at the expense of groundbounders, and so on, but little changed over the years. Everybody got educated, fed, protected and physicked, mostly.

Iltekinov didn't care. All he wanted were safe space-ways and profitable deals. Yolk might be a backwater, even a little inbred, but Yolkovians knew a good life when they had it. He and his fellow Cluster merchants generally policed themselves, preferring not to bring their affairs to the attention of the councils.

The big companies, suppliers of staples such as food, textiles and power supplies, more or less ran everything, but they left openings of opportunity for such small entrepreneurs as himself. He filled a niche, and he was proud of it.

What with the Cluster being as isolated as it was, the merchants formed a close, though non-geographical, community. Meeting another ship on one's way in sublight was grounds for a friendly greeting, if not time to stop for a moment and exchange drinks. The rare strangers from one of the big alliances knew the custom, and most of them joined in. *No doubt*, Iltekinov thought wryly, making himself more comfort-able in the smooth seat, *they thought it was quaint.*

Navigator Natalia Poldin glanced up as the prox-imity alarm went off. Surprised, Iltekinov swung his scope 135 degrees to port and got a distant bloom of a minute heat signature in among the cold rocks, no more than a pinpoint in size. The ship's ID was unfamiliar. Poldin met Iltekinov's eyes. He read the worry in hers, and felt it echo in the pit of his gut.

"Someone coming out of the crossing?" she asked. "A visitor?"

The captain counted up ships in his head. "Maybe," he said. "Otari from the Trade Union was coming this way, but I didn't think he was due out of Scanama for another couple of weeks, so he'd be months early. Maybe Dagnessen from the Central Worlds?" But Dagnessen wouldn't hover among the asteroids in the belt. In fact, no one would linger there, unless they were up to no good. It had to have been hiding there, its telemetry concealed by the thick walls of one of the planetoids, waiting for someone to emerge from ultra-drive. Who? Them? No time to guess. The other ship was moving towards them. The captain felt a prickle of fear. Pirates were not unknown in the spaceways.

"Have they hailed us?" Iltekinov called to his purser, Sam Delius. In spite of his human-sounding name, Delius was an Uctu, a Gecko, born in the Autocracy but brought up in the Cluster.

"It has yet to send a hail. I have signalled it thirty-five times now," Delius replied, his long-lidded eyes fluttering nervously. "All wavelengths, digital and rapid-transmit."

"Then they don't want to talk to us." Iltekinov steeled himself to survive. He slapped the signal in the arm of his seat. "Buckle in! All crew, this is a warning. Stations! We've got a stranger out there."

"Don't jump to conclusions, Captain," Pinckney exclaimed. "That's judgmental."

Iltekinov didn't turn around. There was no time to indulge in the irritation he felt. He concentrated on linking into the ship's computer system through his communications link, freeing his hands for running auxiliary weapons control, if it should come to that. The viewtank responded by zooming in on the other ship as tightly as it could. No details in the visible range yet, but stats began to stack up on the side. Impressive mass it was showing, much greater than the *Little Darling*. "Councillor, when I hail a ship ten ways from Restday and 'un doesn't answer, either it's disabled, an' y'can see it's not, or it's out to get me," he snapped out smartly. "I didn't get old like this lettin' my ship get too close to predators."

"Predators! Hardly . . . !"

Whatever Pinckney was going to say was interrupted by the flash of light that bloomed in the viewtank in the infrared band. An energy blast! Iltekinov's heart pounded.

"Turn tail, Nat," he ordered. "Put on some speed!"

"Aye, Captain!" she replied. She plastered her palms down over the relays. The ship jerked sideways as it came about hard to starboard and up the Y-axis, seeking to put an approaching asteroid between it and the coming blast. The ship's internal inertia-dampers kicked in a moment later, but not before the five councillors clinging to the rails went rolling into the bulkhead. His eyes glued to the viewtank, Iltekinov heard the banging and swearing. *I told them to buckle in,* he thought, with just a tiny bit of satisfaction.

"Captain, what are you doing?" Pinckney demanded furiously, clambering to his feet and shaking a fist. "We should sue you for dangerous transport!"

"Councillor, they're shooting at us," Iltekinov barked, and immediately tuned out any further ranting. Not since the Pletznik Coupon War twelve years before had he had to use evasion techniques to avoid anything but an asteroid or a piece of tumbling space junk. How that damned Pletznik and his fool associates from Carbon had caused so much controversy over "Grid-based discounts" still made him shake his head. But that was the problem with not having a central government in the Cluster. No uniform laws existed for the redemption of sales offers, or customer protection neither. Iltekinov hadn't fired the ship's weaponry except in tests since then, either. He hoped they'd work. But more than that, he hoped he wouldn't be trapped in a position where he had no move left but to shoot it out. With the distances and the level of force involved in any typical space battle, the chances were good there could be *two* losers.

He studied the path of the thermal mass fired by the other ship. It didn't change course when he did, so it had been pure energy, not a missile with tracking capabilities. In his experience that salvo had been in the nature of a warning. But warning him of what? Who was over there?

In the meantime, his ship continued dodging its pursuer. Whenever the other vessel managed to swoop around the last obstacle Poldin put between them, the captain studied the telemetry the computers were assembling about the stranger. It was bigger than they were by a factor of six. The overpowered engines suggested a warship rather than a trader. He'd never seen the configuration before, and his memory of ship design was almost as good as the computer's. Who could it belong to? And why were they chasing him?

Though he didn't like taking his hands off the controls, Iltekinov trusted the maneuvering technology, which enabled the *Little Darling* to maneuver into some impossibly tight berths aboard outdated space stations. The computer assist all but anticipated Poldin's requirements for speed, kicking the light engines into .3 sublight. The gravity generator moaned at having to maintain internal conditions. Iltekinov knew how it felt.

"Prepare to jump back t'ultra," Iltekinov ordered. The system "binked" acknowledgement. Figures scrolled along the bottom of his viewtank as it started calculating the safest and longest jump away from that spot.

"What in space are you doing?" Pinckney demanded.

"Gettin' us out o' here, Councillor!"

"No!" All five of the guests cried at once.

"We must get to that meeting," Quelph pleaded, her eyes wide. "Take us to Boske, please!"

Iltekinov felt his blood pressure surge. Could they be such idiots? "Councillors, we're under *attack!*"

The other ship emitted another burst of energy. According to the scope, this blob was headed for a collision with *Little Darling*'s current flight plan. The other fellow was trying to take his measure. Iltekinov swore and slammed both hands on his control panel.

"Evasive action," the computer's tinny voice stated in his ear. Red lights flared on, bathing the bridge in a gory glow. A white line appeared on the scope ahead of *Little Darling*'s nose, showing its revised trajectory. Iltekinov felt helpless. The machines were taking over, just as they had twelve years ago. Straining his body against the straps, he tried to urge the ship to greater speed. He was frustrated. He just couldn't move fast enough to make a difference. No human could, not even enhanced ones, and there were fewer of those than there'd used to be.

"Strap in, Councillors," Iltekinov shouted.

The Yolkovians scrambled to the sides of the crowded bridge for the safety seats, battered cups of heavy shock padding laced with flat straps of a material that was slightly elastic. Iltekinov tried not to listen to the minor bickering going on around him as two of the visitors tried to get into the same chair. The ship lurched. Side thrusters had kicked in to avoid a spinning chunk of rock.

To Iltekinov's horror, the pursuing ship seemed to have no trouble following *Little Darling's* twists and turns. As soon as she put a rock in between them, the stranger seemed to crest it, closing the distance between them a little more each time. He armed a precious two of his eight missiles, attached the file of the other ship's particulars from the telemetry computer and launched them. Twin trails of ions drew away from the *Little Darling's* outline in the viewtank, attenuated and disappeared in the distance.

"How long?" he asked. The twitches and facial tension he relayed to the computer meant "How long until we can jump back to where we came from?"

After thirty-three years in the space lanes, his ship understood him, verbal speech or no. "Six point four five minutes."

An eternity. "When's it goin' to catch us?"

"Four point nine seven minutes."

"Damn!"

"Yes."

Iltekinov could smell his own fear. Now he could see the telemetry for the other ship's weapons systems. It ran fully loaded: lasers, plasma pulse, magnetic pulse and neutron missiles.

"Can we jump sooner?" Pinckney asked.

"No."

"Who's out there?" Quelph asked, her voice shaking. At last it had dawned on them that the danger was real.

"Pirates, most like," the captain rattled out. Well-financed pirates, but it wasn't unheard of for a "businessman" to decide it was better to sell goods one didn't have to pay for in the first place. Enough people in the Cluster lived high lives because the honored Founder of the Family had made his or her pile out of do-it-yourself salvage. The ship's configuration, put together by the computer, showed a narrow silhouette shaped like a diving bird, all smooth curves angling back from a sharply pointed nose. The shoulder angles of the wings held the main weapons. They were *huge*.

Hot, red light bloomed on the face of the tumbling, boot-shaped rock they were passing: a plasma burst had found a target. The ancient, pitted stone slagged, forming a vast bowl where there had been a heel-like protruberance. Iltekinov knew his ship's shielding capability. *Little Darling* would take tremendous, possibly crippling damage from a bolt like that. Dampening his fears, he looked on the readouts as if they were the stats of a digitavid game.

He scanned the waste, looking for a means of escape. Being constantly in motion, the debris in the heliopause had no memorable geographical points he could recall. But certain features appeared frequently in any of those rocky belts. Iltekinov widened his scope's view, hoping to locate one of them.

"Do you see it, l'il one?" he murmured to the ship's computer.

"Yes."

About one minute ahead of them was what he had hoped to find. Collisions occurred regularly, on a galactic scale, among the giants of the ring. A disturbance, possibly triggered by a passing meteor or other body, over the course of centuries might alter the complex orbit, cannoning one or more of the huge rocks into one another. Iltekinov had flown into the cloud of particles from one of these celestial accidents, ranging from microscopic grains of sand to chunks larger than his ship. Unlike most of the belt, the matter was much more concentrated, giving rise to a real possibility of an accident, but Iltekinov intended that it should befall the other ship, not his.

"That way," he instructed Poldin. "Let's warm some of th'un up, see if we can lay a false trail and ge' a moment's grace. Send some more hails out there."

Delius fluttered his tongue. "Still no replies, Cap."

"Keep tryin'. It's got to be a mistake. Tell 'em we're traders. Show 'em t'merchandise. Offer 'em a discount!"

Little Darling dove into the clutter. Whining from the reactor fueling the dispeller screens forward testified to the increase in hits on the shield. Iltekinov crossed his fingers, hoping it wouldn't give out. At the speed they were traveling, even a minute hole would cause a massive implosion. Once they came out the other side of the heliopause, the computers ought to have readied the nav for Yolk.

His hands rocked back and forth on the gunnery controls, pipping off laser blasts aft at friable boulders, hoping to slow down the stranger by filling space still more with obstructions. He knew it was the equivalent of pulling down cardboard boxes in a warehouse pursuit, but what choice did he have?

"We're losing the signal," Poldin warned him.

The captain knew it. As it would be for his enemy, his own scopes were blocked by the flying debris. He saw a blip behind them, but the running text along the side broke up and dissolved into gibberish. *Why* wouldn't the other ship respond to their communications?

Ahead lay an enormous hollow, fairly clear of debris. Crossing it laid them open to easy attack, but beyond were cheese-holed planetoids they could weave through, and maybe lose the stranger. He shut down all external lights; *Little Darling* didn't need them to see to maneuver. In the meanwhile, he could hear Delius sending distress calls to Boske, Portent's Star's main inhabited planet, and every beacon. He knew little chance existed for rescue—no one could scramble out of orbit from there or any of the stations throughout the system in time to come to their aid—but at least they could get the word out that there was a predator in the heliopause.

The ship behind them emerged with frightening speed. Now Iltekinov got a good look at it. Sleek as a seal, neat as if it came out of the shipyards that very morning. Even as he studied the outline another burst of hot energy crackled toward them. And then it was gone.

Poldin let out a burst of profanity.

"It's a drone!" she exclaimed.

Iltekinov made a fist, causing the viewtank to bring in an extreme close view of the last sighting of the pursuer. Sparks burst and fell away from a skeleton framework. Without a drive or navigation, it swerved and crashed into the next big rock. The missiles exploded within seconds against the same asteroid. The captain felt his blood drain.

"If tha' big 'un was a drone... then what'd it come out of?"

"Yii!" yelped Poldin. A *bang!* resounded under the deck. The ship jerked. Alarms whooped, and the red lights flashed. Iltekinov glanced at the tank. Another burst of plasma had slagged a chunk of rock. It spun out of control and smacked into the side of *Little Darling*. Seconds later, another alarm sounded. They were bracketing him! Iltekinov scanned the viewtank, his heart in his throat. Where was the ship?

"Computer, ready jump!"

"Two minutes..."

"I want it in thirty seconds!"

"Not possible. Please wait."

Another hit, this one much closer. The councillors were pale and sweating. Iltekinov felt the wetness in his armpits and palms. A drop rolled into his right eye. He dashed it away in irritation.

"Make for that big lump over there," he ordered Poldin, having the computer bracket the biggest rock he could see. "We'll hide in there 'til the calculatin's done, then go like hell hounds're followin'."

"Aye, Cap."

The *Little Darling* zipped into the narrow hole. If it had been a planetbound chunk of wood instead of a stone the size of a city, the twisting labyrinth could have been made by a woodworm, instead of an eternity of smaller stones rubbing their irregular but patient way through the bigger one.

Just before they wriggled beyond line of sight of their entry point, thermal scan showed a massive burst of heat. Iltekinov gritted his teeth. The way back had been slagged shut. No choice but to go forward, and hope the enemy didn't seal every hole in the planetoid before they could escape. Servos whined as the ship negotiated the dark passageways, sometimes coming within centimeters of the rough walls.

The captain checked the viewtank for the other ship. Data fluttered along the margin of a nearly dark screen; there must have been a hefty measure of lead or other ores capable of blocking the scanners. Signals bounded off in every direction. He couldn't tell where the other ship was. He hoped it was having similar problems watching *him*.

At a V-intersection, the ship arrowed left. The gigantic stalagmite-like dagger of rock half-blocking the tunnel surprised them all. One of the visitors cried, "Look out!" *Little Darling*'s shields destroyed it in a blaze of light and smithereens that ricocheted off the sides of the tunnel into the ship again and again like pachinko balls. Iltekinov found himself panting.

"How far?" he asked.

"Six hundred kilometers," the computer told him. "Five . . . four . . . three . . . two . . . one . . ."

"Ready weapons," Iltekinov commanded, arming four more missiles.

Little Darling shot out into open space. Only a few artifacts, three misshapen asteroids, lay between her and her vector home. Poldin was already laying in the coordinates to avoid them.

Bzzzzappp!

Iltekinov read in his own sound effects to match what he was seeing in the viewtank. One after another, the asteroids superheated, slagged and collapsed in on themselves.

From behind the planetoid, the other ship loomed

into view like a moon emerging from an eclipse. Iltekinov felt his jaw drop at the very sight of it. Its long, sleek, white-enameled body gleamed, seemingly bejeweled by the gold and red spotlights that illuminated hatches and weapons emplacements. It looked like a longsword, the engines arrayed along the quillons at the rear. The captain looked in vain for lettering on the hull; whoever they were, they didn't want to advertise their origins. Must be corporate pirates, damn them.

"Guns are going hot again," Poldin said.

"Can we jump?" Iltekinov asked.

"Ready," *Little Darling* replied.

"On my mark, then. Three . . . two . . ."

"Sir, it's hailing us," Delius interrupted.

The star-spangled black in the viewtanks were flooded suddenly with light and color. On a yellow background, a green and black banner burst into gaudy view surrounded by the bursts of skyrockets exploding in red, purple, yellow and blue. Blaring trumpets proclaiming a triumphant march took over the shipboard speakers. All the councillors clapped their hands over their ears to block out the din. Iltekinov signalled to Delius to damp it down. The Uctu held his long hands up to his shoulders in a gesture of helplessness.

"They've hacked our system, sir!" he shouted.

Iltekinov moaned. He knew he should have upgraded the firewall! "Dammit, override!"

The Uctu bent to his task, yanking levers and palming heat switches.

Poldin shouted, "Sir, they're trying to break into the protocols for navigation!"

That system Iltekinov knew was up to date. "Block them," he ordered. "Make for the jump point."

In the viewtank the banner dissolved slowly, revealing the face of a human male. Handsome by any standards, he had a strong, square jaw, silvery hair brushed back over a broad, rectangular brow. Even his thin, beaklike nose seemed powerful. Glittering, pale sea-blue eyes stared out of deep sockets. His face was clear of any markings or tattoos, showing that he was not a denizen of the Cluster. The man leaned forward, his face filling the tank. Iltekinov found himself staring, unwilling to break eye contact with the image. A screech from the drive systems brought him back to his wits. How dare this man and his big fancy ship interfere with a free trader of the Castaway Cluster? Defiance filled his chest like oxygen. He would show this interloper he wasn't afraid!

"What can I do for you, stranger?" he asked, as casually as he could.

The image frowned. The councillors gasped.

"I am Captain Sgarthad of the TU destroyer *Marketmaker*," the man said. He crossed his arms on his magnificent, broad chest covered with medals. "I order you to stand down your ship and surrender."

Something about Sgarthad's rumbling baritone reached deep inside Iltekinov and touched a primal nerve, compelling him to obey, but he saw the increasing energy signature of arming plasma guns. Fury and the pure stubbornness that had helped him survive many seasons running the hazards of the space lanes kicked in.

"When hell freezes over," he said. "Jumping...now!"

"Hold it, Captain!" Pinckney cried, just before

the navigator touched the controls on her console.
Poldin froze.

"What now, Councillor?" Iltekinov demanded. They
were fifteen seconds from an unobstructed jump. In
twenty-four seconds the other ship would be between
them and their exit.

"You heard the man," Pinckney said, gesturing
toward the viewtank. "Surrender the ship."

"What?"

"He wants it."

Against his better judgement, Iltekinov turned back
to look at the tank.

The face within it gazed at them, the light eyes
dragging all of theirs deep into them. Iltekinov found
himself leaning towards it, wanting to oblige this man.
He liked him. No, it was a stronger feeling than that:
he wanted to please him. A portion of his mind still
rebelled. The computer system was supposed—no,
guaranteed—to catch and quarantine hypnotic patterns and other mind-control devices fed through the
system. He felt his resistance dropping. He couldn't
look away from Sgarthad. The longer he maintained
eye contact, the more he knew he had to do what
Sgarthad wanted. What was happening to him? The
man's straight brows rose just a millimeter, inviting
him to comply. Iltekinov couldn't help himself. He
had to do what Sgarthad wanted.

"Yes, that's right. I must." The captain's hands fell
slack to his lap. The jump timer counted down to
zero, then continued to count up, unobserved. Pinckney smiled. The other human councillors smiled, too.

The big face in the viewtank smiled even more
broadly.

❦ CHAPTER 1 ❦

"Thomas Innes Loche Kinago, you look absolutely smashing. Fantastic! Elegant! And, very, very military."

I strode back and forth in front of the lighted mirror set into my cabin's mahogany closet door with my chest stuck out and my toes turned at just the right angle. I do not believe I felt inordinately proud of my new uniform. I admired the set of the smart, deep blue tunic, the lavish, jeweled gold braid on sleeves, shoulders and lapels, and the shiny black of the boots and cap, the latter of which so handsomely set off the shiny chestnut brown of my freshly barbered hair. An especial point of gloating was to be found in the satin stripe down the outside of each buff-colored pant leg. Those were white. I had never been allowed to indulge myself like that in military school, not with the pure silk white stripe, and not with all that gold braid adorning sleeves and shoulders. Besides my pleb insignia, I had been restricted to a single loop of gold to identify my personal rank as a cousin of the Imperial house. Now that I had been assigned to command my own cutter, I had a certain amount of leeway. But what fun was leeway if one didn't push at its edges?

I touched the gold badge at my breast: Kinago, T.I., which of course stood for Thomas Innes—military protocol limited me to only two initials, which I felt was terribly unfair considering the dignity of my ancestry, particularly the omission of my mother's surname which would properly be placed before my father's—and polished off a small smudge at its inner edge with the tip of my sleeve, then took a pace or two back to get a better view of the whole.

Most admirable, I thought. The deep blue of the tunic emphasized the pale, slightly greenish blue of my eyes set in a long, smooth face tinted the tanned complexion of the Loches I had inherited from the noble forebears in my mother's maternal line. The eyes came from the Innes clan, the straight but interesting nose with the slightly flared nostrils a vestige of the Melarides family, my father's maternal ancestors. Ah, the parents would undoubtedly be proud of their second son attired in such well-tailored finery. My distressingly above average height provided perhaps one small sore point; most of my cousins were shorter than I was, and often made me feel like a scarecrow, particularly when I was younger and not as physically coordinated as I had grown to be. Still, the fine, long fingers and noble jaw were as good as anyone could hope for. I didn't have to see my gene map to know I represented the best of our ancestral DNA. Yes, a fine specimen, I had to admit, and dressed to set off my assets in the best light possible. Fully human. I was proud of my reflection.

A gentle "Hem!" from behind me retrieved me from my reverie.

"So it's not true they always send the fool of the family to sea," I said to my aide-de-camp Parsons. "No, indeed. Or in this case, to space."

That worthy, possessed of a long, oval face even more epicene than my own, taller by a hand's breadth, brushed-back hair the black of unoccupied space, clad in a more somber, inky, midnight-blue uniform with self-effacing and totally irreproachably polished boots, cleared his throat, and almost, but not quite, rolled his eyes toward the ceiling.

"No, my lord."

I caught his look of doubt and nodded wisely. "Oh, you aren't thinking of my great-uncle Sidor again, are you?"

"No, my lord," Parsons said, in definite tones. "I promise you, I'm not thinking of your great-uncle Sidor."

"Good," I said, happily surveying the satin stripe down the side of my trouser leg. Shimmering like a snowbank. Very handsome. And striking. "Because that sort of decadent behavior really is best forgotten, you know. I mean, running off to a desert planet like that, in the middle of the Imperial birthday celebration..."

"I couldn't agree more," Parsons interrupted me. "Would you like to go down to mess now, sir? Your lady mother did say not to be late, particularly your first day. After all, naval protocol..."

"To the black holes with naval protocol! And," I dropped my voice, as if First Space Lord Admiral Tariana Kinago Loche might be within hearing range which, heaven knew she could be, what with modern technology, "...and with my lady mother, too. Who's in command of this vessel anyhow? Her or me?"

"Technically neither, sir," Parsons said, palming the door plate. "This is Admiral Podesta's flagship, the I.S. *Wedjet*. Your cutter is aboard this one."

"Yes, well, a technicality," I said, giving myself another look, and my admiration knew no bounds. I was the best product of tailoring and breeding that I had ever seen. "I outrank him where it counts, don't I? Eh? He's of good family, but not in the line of descent at all. Is he?"

Parsons didn't reply. He could not deny it, and I knew it. I might be a lowly brevet lieutenant, field-promoted from my commission rank of ensign so I could command the cutter in question on a mission that yet of which I knew nothing, but Parsons had confirmed for me that not one of the officers in command of either the dreadnought or its many small craft in the launch bays were a cousin of the Imperial house or any kind of court noble close to my own lofty birth. Parsons himself held the naval rank of commander, but here he was serving as my personal attache. Let the average Steve, Josephine or Sergei try to top that! Ah, the glorious traditions of the Space Navy!

"I am sure you enjoy the distinction," Parsons intoned. "Would it perhaps not be more tactful to avoid rubbing the difference between your stations in the lord admiral's face in his own mess hall? After all, sir, courtesy is the force that has held the Imperium together for many millennia, and your deck rank is that of ensign."

"I shall be the picture of civility," I promised him.

A thought struck me suddenly, and I glanced over my shoulder to meet his eyes directly. "By the way, why am I the only one like me on board?"

"May I say, without fear of contradiction, that you are the only one like you in the universe. Sir."

I cocked my head, trying to figure out if the statement was an insult or a compliment, and had to light upon compliment. Parsons was not given to blatant mud-throwing. I pressed my point. "You know what I mean, Parsons. I went all the way through Academy with dozens—no, hundreds—of my distant cousins and friends of friends. People I've known since I could crawl. Class of '049. When we all got our orders on graduation day and compared notes I very nearly dropped my teeth out of my head. *They're* all on the same three or four ships doing escort duty around the Core Worlds. I'm the only one assigned out here on the perimeter. What am I doing out *here* by myself?"

No clue could be gleaned from my aide's face. It was as unreadable as the bulkhead just behind him. "Your specific assignment will be given to you in good time, sir. Are any of your classmates in incipient command of a cutter?"

"Well, no," I acknowledged, pleased all over again as the warm feeling the thought engendered washed over me. Not that I had seen the vessel in question yet, but it did exist, Parsons had confirmed for me, and was safely aboard the *Wedjet,* awaiting that mysterious assignment. The shuttle that had conveyed me aboard from the surface of the Imperium's capital world of Keinolt had come aboard in one of the other landing bays of the vast destroyer. The *Wedjet* itself was thousands of meters long, shaped like an angel, wings slightly spread, nose of the navigation section forward pointed purposefully toward deep space, its long, slender underside gleaming white from reflected light from the planet's atmosphere. It was so lovely one had to recall deliberately that it was also deadly. The 836 weapons emplacements, I recalled from lessons in the Academy, were well concealed behind panels and in the curves of her hull. My barely adequate quarters were situated where one of the angel's knees might have been. "But it might get a little lonely, won't it?"

"There are over two thousand people on this ship, comprising sixteen races and sub-races, sir," Parsons said impatiently. "Loneliness would seem to be the least of your worries."

"I know," I tried to explain, searching for words to describe my feelings of puzzlement and loneliness, "but it's not the same. I mean, those people at the Academy were my peers. Nobility. The upper crust. The noted, even the notorious. Except for traveling, going shopping or to parties, or speaking to the staff in the Imperial Compound, I hardly ever really cross paths with anyone to whom I'm not distantly related at the very least."

"Think of it as a new experience, sir." The door slid open, and my ADC urged me away from the mirror by getting in the way of my view. I attempted, without success, to see over his shoulder. It was no use. He used his superior height and maneuverability to thwart me no matter which way I shifted. With a snort of annoyance I finally gave up and tried to stare him down. Parsons's long face wore no expression. I, as usual, blinked first. "Shall we go?" he asked.

"Wait a millisecond," I said urgently, though I knew I was delaying the evil moment just a little longer.

"I want to take a picture of us on my first day of active service." I reached into a hidden pocket I had had the Imperial tailoring service sew into my tunic seam and let go of a little gold globe, which floated out in front of Parsons's impassive face. The Baltion Clic 4.0 was one of many cameras I had with me, part of my newfound passion for photography and image capture. I threw an arm around the adjutant's shoulder and grinned at the ball. It twirled, blinking faster and faster. "Here it goes! Say 'cheese'!"

"Yes, sir," Parsons said, with the same expression he had worn all along, as red-tinged light bloomed out of the globe in a blinding flare. The muscles in my eyes contracted painfully to protect my retinas, but I had recorded the glorious event. While I blinked away the glare Parsons put a firm hand in my back and urged me towards the door. "The admiral is waiting."

I snatched the ball out of the air just before the doors closed behind us.

"Are you certain that I shouldn't make a grand entrance?" I asked, as we strode the grand corridor that led to the officers' wardroom, knowing that my voice hovered near a whine. I could not help feeling petulant.

"Absolutely not, sir," Parsons stated firmly, not slowing up at all. I had to increase my pace to keep from being outdistanced by the man. "It would give the wrong impression. You must by all means hold to the structure of ship's command. To do otherwise is to undermine the authority of her rightful commander."

"But it's *me*," I stressed. "They don't often get someone from the loftiest social circles, do they?"

Parsons was unmoved. "Naval protocol does not permit exceptions, my lord. Even the Emperor himself would wait to be piped aboard."

Privately, I doubted it. I had lived in the Imperial Compound near the palace and played in it since I was a child, and I couldn't recall a single instance when I didn't look up and suddenly see my elevated cousin looking down over my shoulder with the greatest expression of disapproval, and not a knock or a genteel clearing of the throat to have been heard at any time preceding the discovery. Shojan had a positive knack for appearing where he was less than expected. In fact, the Imperial staff kept alarm beepers—discreet, of course; some as small as a millimeter across—to avoid having one's regal master turn up when one was indisposed or slacking off one's duties. Such things, sadly, were not available to mere relatives without a worthwhile profession to use as an excuse. He had once caught me and several of my close cousins when we were in the room next to the private wine cellars...but I digress.

The memory of that setting threw my current location into a comparison less favorable than perhaps it deserved. After all, it was a warship. The grandeur of the walnut-colored paneling had to take second place to durability and fireproofing, rendering it hopelessly artificial-looking. The carpets, while woven in an intricate and handsome pattern, needed to withstand the passage of thousands of feet a week. Some of the private rooms in the royal residence and compound had never been trodden by more than the current regnant, his or her personal secretary and the cleaning staff. Silk there was a possibility; here, synthetics were the rule. I tried hard not to feel snobbish as I reached for the control.

The door of the wardroom slid open and emitted its little chime. With Parsons an undoubtedly chilly presence a pace behind my shoulder, I strode in without making the grand entrance that I'd dearly hoped to make, just to announce in a little way that I was aboard and eager to be of service. Sometimes it pained me that Parsons did not appreciate my sense of drama. The rest of the ship's complement ought to be a little awed, perhaps even slightly agog.

Maybe they were agog anyhow. Certainly eyes opened widely as I made my way into the handsome chamber. My spanking-new boots made a disconcerting clicking noise upon the shining composite floors. I tried not to count the number of steps, but it was difficult to ignore, since I was now making the only sounds in the room. Diners of many races in crisply pressed uniforms around the wide round tables set down their forks momentarily to watch me make my progress through the chamber. I flicked off my hat and tucked it underneath my left arm. After a month or so it seemed, I arrived at the board, an elegant blackwood three-pedestal table set with priceless antique crystal and china that appeared to hover just over the surface of a gleaming white damask tablecloth. I halted. Hoisting my back into its stiffest upright position, I saluted crisply to the spare man at the center of the table, and offered containing just slightly less starch to each of the four other captains seated behind it on either side of him. Admiral Podesta's hawklike eyes traveled down from mine, over my uniformed chest, a slight dogleg to the left, to the side of my trousers, and back up again. When the eyes reached mine once more, I offered him a grave smile and a second salute to honor his flag rank. The thin black brows on his egg-shaped head rose a sound centimeter toward his fluffy, thin gray hair, and his eyes narrowed as if in deep thought.

"Ensign Kinago reporting, Admiral," I announced.

"Dinner begins at twenty-hundred, Ensign," the flag officer snapped out, then returned to his soup without another glance. Parsons sighed just loudly enough for me to hear him.

"Apologize. Now."

"I apologize, Admiral," I said at once. Podesta didn't even look up. I hovered for a moment, wondering if I ought to enlarge upon my regrets. My Naval Academy training stressed courtesy, but never had the commandant of the college refused to maintain eye contact with me. I wavered.

"Sit down now and stay out of trouble, sir," Parsons muttered. He removed himself from his position at my shoulder and placed himself silently at a central table in between others who bore the same shoulder and wrist badges as he did.

Stay out of trouble? I mused. I wasn't *in* trouble. A trifle late, perhaps. But the entire room sat gawking at me. Couldn't go on interrupting everyone else's dinner. I smiled blandly around. Strangers didn't deter me. I had always felt that unknown persons were just friends that one hadn't met yet. My philosophy had served me well my first twenty-three years, and I saw no reason to doubt it now.

"Right, see you later," I told Parsons. Conscious of the number of eyes on me, I marched smoothly toward the only empty chair in the big room, at the table farthest from the door through which I had just entered. I put a hand on its back and smiled at my tablemates. Each of them wore an ensign's bar on his, her or its collar. "Evening, all."

"H'lo," a few of them muttered.

The ensign nearest me was an Uctu, the correct name for the race whose section of the galaxy ran a third of the way along the Imperium's border. Humanity, upon beholding their nearest nonhuman neighbors, promptly named them "Geckos," after the reptile of Old Earth that they most resembled. There had been a movement to rename them "Dragons," as being more complimentary to a fellow spacegoing race, but it failed. Herpetologists pointed out that Uctu had large, slightly sticky pads at the tips of their flexible fingers, and their blunt, round-eyed faces failed to look fierce even when provoked. Geckos they remained. Unlike some of their neighbors the Uctu evolved under nearly identical gravitational and atmospheric conditions so they battled with the Imperium and the Trade Union, the largest of the Human-occupied systems. Over thousands of years that border had shifted up and back, until there were both Uctu and Human systems under the dominion of each. The Geckos had been fairly quiet for the last few decades, so this Uctu must have been born on Imperium soil. He was quite young, I reflected, still having the luminous turquoise spots on the rough skin above his eyes, and the reddish scales that ran from the crown of his head and disappeared down the back into his uniform collar had soft edges instead of points. The tab at his breast pocket said REDIUS, K. I smiled at him.

"Pok no Ya inho?" I inquired. It was the polite way to greet one of his kind. They were keen multi-media viewers. The current style of digitavids were invented by an Uctu scientist. I had kept up for several seasons with the *Ya!* show, an ongoing search for the most talented dancers. Uctus loved dance.

The Uctu showed a brief flash of his sharp, flat teeth. "A fan you?"

"Avid," I assured him, sitting down. "Lord Thomas I . . . Kinago. Ensign."

"Kolchut Redius. Did you not tremble in boots yours?" the Uctu whispered.

"Why?" I asked.

"Because you were late," a human female ensign with tilted golden eyes and black hair informed me from across the table. She shifted her slim shoulders in her uniform as if she had only just learned how to wear clothes and wasn't at all comfortable with the exercise. Her name was Anstruther, P. "The old man's a stickler for punctuality. You'll pull extra duty."

"Not if I can help it," I said, leaning forward, then automatically immediately back to allow the removal of a bowl of soup by a thin hand in a white sleeve. The moment I realized the china basin was moving away, I reached for it, but in vain. The servers cleared the table swiftly to make way for the next course. I was ravenous. A lightly cooked yak wouldn't have been too small a meal to bring me. Instead, I concentrated on my tablemates. They would be my companions for the duration of my enlistment aboard this vessel, and I was eager to befriend them.

"What makes you special?" Xinu asked. He had coffee-dark skin and shiny black hair. The cost to tailor his uniform to wide shoulders down to impressively narrow hips had been well spent. His teeth, brilliant white, had a small blue jewel in the center of each.

"I'm just me," I said modestly.

Xinu pretended to stick his finger down his throat. "False modesty makes me tired," he said. "Admiral Podesta has been known to kick people out when they're fifteen seconds late, and you sashayed in after ten minutes. Why aren't you back in your cabin eating survival rations?"

I shrugged disarmingly. "I suppose I owe it all to my mother. She's an admiral, too. Professional courtesy, I suppose," I added, glancing back in alarm at Podesta, who was eating a green salad from a pale blue china bowl with quick, stabbing bites of a gleaming silver fork.

"He's never heard of it," said the dark-furred Wichu beside Redius. His name was Perkev. He showed his rows of pointed teeth. "You will see. I nearly starved after making a noise during inspection. I cannot eat the *preekech* that you humans consider palatable."

Like anyone who adored languages, I had a working knowledge of all the curses and swear words used in the many cultures and systems of the Imperium. It was an inspired choice of epithets for the survival rations, whose unassuming acronym had been reapplied by my peers and me to other, less savory terms when we had had to taste the bars in question. The aromas coming from the serving hatches were appealing. I compared it with my memory of survival rations, and peered once again at Podesta. Was he that much of a stickler for rules? Why had I not heard about that during our transfer to the *Wedjet*?

Ah, but I must have heard it, but not retained the

fact for future use. Where had this sense of dread anticipation been while I was admiring my new uniform in the mirror? I had thought that after spending more than half my life running into the Emperor casually in the hallways of the Imperium Compound I would consider any lower form of authority pussycatish in comparison, but frankly, what my tablemates were saying made a large, cold lump appear in my stomach. I swallowed deeply, feeling my throat constrict. "I've got some bridge-rebuilding to do, I see."

"You won't get the chance," the Uctu said, the blue spots on his forehead glowing slightly. "I've never known to change his opinion, Podesta."

My heart sank. "My mother," I said, "is going to flay me." I supposed that the admiral would write to her about the white stripe on my trousers, too. Why hadn't I listened to Parsons?

"Wait . . . *Kinago?*" Xinu asked, curiously. "Tariana Kinago Loche is your mother?"

"Er, yes," I admitted. I had already begun to compose the explanation I would have to make to Mother in my head. Words came glibly to mind, but she could just turn off the audio portion of my missive, so my eloquence would mean little. A pang of conscience told me she would not believe it. If I added a suitably pitiable expression and an austere background with a suggestion of the dungeon about it, perhaps I could elicit her maternal sympathy on my behalf. I gave another quick peek at Podesta and tried to guess his age. He might have been a contemporary of hers. They may even have been at Academy together. I gulped unhappily and added two or three more abject apologies to my mental text. "That's her."

"The First Space Lord?" Redius asked, dropping his jaw in interest. I nodded, feeling more miserable by the moment.

"Your mother is a hero!" Anstruther exclaimed, raising her hands in ecstasy. Her champagne-colored eyes sparkled. "I've viewed everything there is to see about her. The battle of Marquardt's Pass, the siege of Colvarin's Department Store system, the border defense against the Geckos ... sorry, Kolchut." The golden-eyed female ducked her head abjectly.

"No offense taken," the Uctu said. "Born in the Imperium. My parents fled the Autocracy."

"You, a noble of the Imperial House, are only an ensign?" Xinu asked.

"Well, everyone's got to start somewhere," I pointed out modestly. "I graduated from the Academy only two weeks ago." I decided not to mention the brevet lieutenancy.

"Do we call you 'your lordship'?" Anstruther asked, with a dreamy expression on her face.

"Only on formal occasions," I explained hastily. "We're fellow officers now, equals in the Space Navy in service to the Imperium." Maybe I could mitigate Mother's coming outpouring of fury by mentioning her many fans on board. I had my camera with me. A few video testimonials should go down well. But Mother had this very uncomfortable way of finding the needle of truth secreted in the proverbial haystack of obfuscation. That attention to minute detail was, in fact, one of the reasons she had become a hero.

"Your sire must be something special to have won her hand," Perkev said.

"No doubt," I said, feeling a twinge of conscience.

I thought of my father with concern.

Rodrigo Park Kinago must have been a handsome man at one time. I resembled him somewhat: he was tall, his long face with handsome bones and light eyes in a warmly tinted skin that attracted surprised glances by those who had not noticed him at once upon entering a room he occupied. Clearly, something had happened in the past to affect his mind. He seemed uninjured on the surface, if more gray and drawn-looking than a man of his middle years might expect to in these days of rejuvenation treatments and general longevity. I loved him, but I hated to talk about him. "Poor, brave Rodrigo" was almost always how my relatives referred to him. Not just "Rodrigo," but "Poor, brave Rodrigo," and pretty much always with the sad smile that one saves for such occasions as a good friend who had shot off his own foot accidentally, who had been widowed, or who had suffered some other inescapable and overwhelming misfortune not of his own making. My curiosity on the subject overwhelmed me. The closest I'd ever come to hearing what had actually happened to my father fell from the lips of my great-uncle Perleas during one of his weekly drunks when my great-aunt Sforzina wasn't around.

"It was in the last war against the pirates, nephew," Uncle Perleas had begun, sipping the fermented coca liqueur that he favored. He paused, thoughtfully. "No, Rodrigo really couldn't have done anything else than exactly what he did. And certainly not after that." I'd moved closer, agog. Uncle Perleas took an intake of breath, and was about to exhale details when, at that agonizing point, my aunt had come in and confiscated

Uncle's bottle and gave him a look that would have stopped the onset of winter, let alone an old man telling stories. I didn't hear any more of the story that day, and when I tried to ask him about it at another suitably unguarded time, Perleas denied absolutely that he'd ever said anything. I certainly couldn't ask my mother. She got very angry when I tried, with all of my eight-year-old tact, to inquire whether there wasn't something odd about my paternal unit. I never tried again. My resultant grounding and deprivation of all privileges for a week was enough to deter my siblings from ever asking, either.

My father didn't provide me with any more clues. He pottered around in our rooms and the workshop assigned to him in the Craftworkers' Courtyard, a vast expanse of cobbled paving dotted with small enclosures and chambers purpose-built for a variety of hand- and machine-oriented construction at one edge of the Imperial Compound, a vast city-within-the-capital-city of Taino. His specialty seemed to be coming up with alternatives for archaic substances or devices that had largely slipped out of usage altogether. I had never heard of "sealing wax" before he showed it to me. With most personal and official documents electronically transmitted these days, the utility of his fresh formulation seemed limited, but making it made him happy. I loved him, and in my small-child's way, I wanted him to be happy. It worried me that I didn't know why he was not like the fathers of my cousins or friends. Naturally, I wanted to be different than he was, so as not to be spoken of with pity.

Father seemed content to remain within the ambit of those small spaces in the workshop, whereas I, my brother and sister couldn't wait to slip the bounds of earth and go for illicit rides on borrowed suborbital skimmers or over the walls to parties thrown at exclusive clubs in town. No, Father had come to terms with his condition, and enjoyed a sunny if doddery disposition. I rarely considered his strangeness in latter days unless forced by conversational circumstance. As now.

"He is very special," I assured my new shipmates.

"Was that your C.O. who came in with you?" asked Nesbitt, M., an ensign on the other side of Xinu. He had thick, dark brown brows over a long, jowly, red-complected face. In mass, he would have made two of me, though his bulk was arranged to form a mega-human a good twenty centimeters taller and twenty wider at the shoulders than I.

I frowned. "Parsons? No, he's my aide-de-camp."

If the stares I had received from my tablemates had been admiring on behalf of my mother, they switched to envy or puzzlement. "Why is he with you?" Anstruther began.

"Well, he's been around since I was a boy," I explained. "Always has been. Always kind to me. I was forever asking him questions, you know. He was like my personal information outlet. I hung on his every word. Parsons knows *everything*. You should ask him something; you'll be amazed at the depths of his knowledge and erudition, though I admit the delivery lacks a bit in terms of excitement. An hour with him is worth a month at school. I just admire the fact that he is so calm all the time. That calm demeanor goes all the way to the core. I've attempted to interfere with the coolness, but no efforts of mine have ever been sufficient to break it. He has eternal patience, and he can do anything. When I was a scrub he played games with me, taught me the first rudiments of sword-fighting, including some fantastically dirty tricks I've never seen anywhere else, and he's a better 3D jai-alai player than I am, which modesty prevents me from saying is very impressive indeed..."

Anstruther waved a hand. "No, I mean why do you have an aide-de-camp? You're an ensign. You'll be doing the same scutwork we are, fetching and carrying for lieutenants and upward."

"Well, there are things that I need him to do I can't do for myself," I said. It sounded reasonable to me, though not to my new acquaintances.

"Why are you able to get special privileges?" a black-browed man asked in a growl. His name plate read Sarpenio. "Is it because you're a *noble?*" He gave the word the same connotation as "baby-eater." I gave him a modest smile.

"Part of my responsibilities," I said, mysteriously. "I can say no more at this time."

"I never served with one of you before," Xinu said. "Do you get to bring servants wherever you go?"

"'Servant' is an outdated class," Redius stated, his tongue flicking.

"Well, actually it's not. There are thousands of servants in the Imperial Palace," I explained. "It's a job, like any other. Servants can quit if they want to, and most of the time they do. I recall one time when His Imperial Majesty had ordered a huge banquet to honor the Oligarchs of the Trade Union, and the cooks walked out just a day be—"

"Is that commander a servant, then?" Redius asked. "Is he a bondsman, sworn to you in some blood oath, or does he owe your family a debt?"

"Debt? Of course not!" I said. "He's an old family friend. I can't think of a time when he was not around the family home or somewhere in the Imperium Compound. One of my earliest memories is toddling around in one of his gardens, no doubt bent upon some infant mayhem. He intercepted me before I reached the rhododendrons, and took me to play some less harmful game. When I was five he started teaching me swordplay, which every gentle needs to know. I respect him greatly. He's rather good in crises. They seem to melt away whenever he gets near one. Something about his calm exterior demands attention, you know, even if many of the things he says at the time don't sound all that interesting. I recall once that he sat me down to explain to me the difference between diplomacy and tact—"

"Then he outranks you," Xinu pointed out, interrupting the flow of my story, which was just as well, because once I began to recall the details, they were embarrassing to the Imperial family as well as to yours truly.

"In the _service_," I reminded him. Sarpenio, the black-browed man glowered even more. I sensed an animosity there toward persons of high birth. I thought I had better make use of some of the Kinago charm as well as the Loche aegis. I gave him a warm smile. He shook his head as if to clear it.

"But _you're_ in the service, aren't you?" Nesbitt asked.

"With all my heart," I agreed, planting my hand over my chest wherein reposed that organ.

"Who died and made you...?"

"Why do you need...?"

"What is he...?"

Anstruther flung up her hands to halt the spate of simultaneous and no doubt similar questions from our tablemates. "Why does an ordinary ensign," she enunciated carefully, "have an aide-de-camp?"

"It's most likely because I've got a sealed assignment," I said sheepishly, ducking my head a trifle. "And that's all I know about it. My scout ship is in the hangar. I haven't even seen it yet."

The faces of my tablemates lit up.

"You have a scout ship? What kind?" asked a male human my age with white-blond hair. His tag read PARVINDER, M.

I felt foolish admitting the truth. "As I said, its details are a complete mystery to me. I have been informed I will see it in time."

"That sounds weird," Anstruther said, though she regarded me almost shyly. "Shouldn't you be familiarizing yourself with it? Every craft has its kinks."

"I am sure I will be soon. I can't imagine the Navy being so careless as to keep me from practicing before my mission," I said. "We take pride in its reputation for thoroughness as well as courage."

"*We*—you make it sound like you're the Emperor himself!"

"Well," I began modestly, "five times removed, but I can still call him cousin."

"Do you know him? Have you seen him?" Nesbitt asked, curious in spite of himself. I felt there was still an opening to impress there.

"Often," I said. "His Imperial Highness takes frequent constitutionals in the gardens of the compound.

He finds them relaxing in between dealing with affairs of state. He hasn't been Emperor that long, you may recall. His grandmother, Tirasiani VIII, passed into eternity less than five years ago."

"Eternity be kind to her," Xinu said, bobbing his head.

"As we all hope," I said, acknowledging his courtesy. "Her grandfather was Emperor Irsan I, my great-great-grandfather. You can look up the family tree on my Infogrid file."

Parvinder pressed me for more. "What's he look like? I mean, His Imperial Highness. Do you call him Shojan?"

"Oh, well, that's not the name he grew up with, you know," I said. "It's his throne name. He was named Vasco at birth. But, no, I didn't call him Shojan, either; as he was in the direct line of succession, and was one of the chosen candidates for the throne from youth, he's always been a Highness even to the family. He looks younger in person than his official portraits. In fact, he is only five years older than I am, a year younger than my oldest brother. Very handsome. Even the bronze statues don't do him justice."

"I've seen him in the digitavids," Nesbitt said. "My sister has recorded every appearance he ever made. She's crazy about him, quotes his speeches, and everything."

The wry look on his face seemed to call for a light deprecating response, so I employed my special laugh. I had cultivated this laugh for approximately the last month. With limited facility for amusement within the confines of the barracks where I and the rest of the noble cohort had stayed during our basic naval training, we fell back upon the earliest of amusements: storytelling, music and poetry, making rude noises and playing tricks on one another. My laugh was a cross between a gurgle and a snort, with a glottal stop at the bottom of each explosion of breath. I had to admit it was a masterpiece.

At the sound, heads turned, and not only at my own table. I reflected too late that my voice had a carrying quality. During basic training, it had been a useful means to share my talent with the greater number of my fellow nobles. Guiltily, I glanced toward Parsons, but that dignitary did not flinch or wince. I hoped the absence of a reaction indicated that he hadn't heard me. Faint hope, I knew; Parsons seemed to have ears as well as eyes in the back of his head.

I turned back to my fellows to see whether they had taken offense, or whether they appreciated art. Even Nesbitt shared a grin with me. Success!

"My sister embarrasses me, too," I confessed.

"How many of you are there?" Redius asked.

"Three," I said. "I'm the middle child. A brother and a sister."

"A good family," Anstruther said, enviously. Due to concerns about overpopulation in humans, large families, over two children, were uncommon. "I've got a sister."

"Three twins," said Perkev. "I am of the eldest pair." Wichus were not prone to the same societal pressures as humans. But they bred less frequently.

"I'm an only," Xinu said, with a grin.

The others offered their own family details. I listened carefully, making note of all. I was pleased with myself. I had managed to earn the admiration of my tablemates—well, most of them—and discovered much common ground among common folk. It made the three months' work in boot camp worthwhile. I had often doubted my own commitment to it at the time, though I had joined the Space Navy for several reasons, a few of them so intensely personal that I rarely admitted them even to myself as being a bad risk for gossiping about them at idle moments. Certainly, none of those private thoughts had ever made it to my personal file on Infogrid.

A pause fell inevitably into the midst of our conversation. In the lull, I realized that there was a delay in the service of the salad course. I realized how very hungry I was. I had certainly overanticipated the moment of my arrival upon my first assigned ship, running over scenarios in my mind, and had undoubtedly picked at my lunch. In fact, I could not recall what I had eaten earlier in the day. This was on the end of the worst, having earned the disapproval of the commanding officer, instead of the gratitude and joy of many of the captains and admirals of my imagining that I had come to join them. Still, it looked as if this was going to be pleasurable, even an adventure.

I looked up in pleased anticipation as the waitstaff— no roboservers in the Admiral's Mess—began to serve the table next to us from platters of savory delicacies. A broad-faced Blut server in a waist-length white jacket and black kilt glided toward us, guiding a floating tray of covered dishes. I was pleased to see him there; Bluts were placid beings, unsuited for the front line, but they wished to serve their Imperium as the rest of us did. They excelled as support staff. He met my eyes and nodded. Our dinner was coming next.

"Shouldn't you be served first when the food comes?" Anstruther asked, with a shy glance my way.

"No, indeed," I insisted. "I'm the most junior among you. I'll be last. That is the correct protocol in the Navy." I sat back, conscious of my courtesy and gallantry.

When to my dismay, the flat-faced server arrived, he moved smoothly to my side. I began to protest that he should serve those more senior to me first, but instead, he reached around me from near my right elbow and began to pick up my cutlery!

"Don't take those!" I protested. "I haven't dined yet!"

In the vicinity of my other elbow, I heard a gentle "Hem!" as if someone had cleared his, her or its throat. I turned to behold a smaller, slighter and more impatient version of Parsons, smooth-faced, black-haired, complete down to the commander's insignia at collar and sleeve. His name was Oin.

"Admiral's compliments, sir, but he'd like to see you in his study at once."

"Uh-oh," Xinu groaned.

I shifted my gaze in the direction of Parsons's table. The glum look I spotted on my aide-de-camp's face was uncalled for; the "old man" probably wanted to welcome the scion of a noble house to the fleet. I had scraped greetings to him from my mother, and this was as good a time as any to present them. I perceived that the admiral's place at the table had been cleared. No doubt he had an intimate repast prepared for just the two of us, to make welcome the son of an old friend.

"Back in a while!" I said to the others.

Anstruther shook her head. "You'll be swabbing out the food processors," she promised.

❖   ❖   ❖

I followed the small-framed commander into a narrow vac-lift that whooshed us upward with enough force to pull the planes of my face downward toward my neck. We came to an abrupt halt a few seconds later. My cheeks bobbed up and down before assuming their correct place. I straightened my collar and strode in the wake of my guide.

Plain white enameled doorways offered themselves to either side of this new, plain white enameled corridor. Curiosity made me want to know what was behind them, but I didn't ask. I was rehearsing to myself the exact phrasing that my mother had used when asking me to remember her to the admiral.

A half-step behind the commander, I nearly walked onto his heels when he stopped a third of the way from the end of the hall and turned sharp right. He held his wrist insignia in the eye of a sensor concealed in the doorframe. Red, blue and green lights sparkled, and the door slid open. Directly in front of me, at a maroon-red antique wooden desk, Podesta sat bolt upright with his hands folded together. The commander peeled discreetly away and retreated from the chamber, leaving us alone.

I saluted brightly, hoping the energy would transmit itself to the admiral's downturned mouth and lift it. "Ensign-Lieutenant Kinago, Admiral!" I announced. "May I say how glad and honored I am to be aboard? My mother holds you in high esteem. She sends her regards to you, and wishes you good health and success."

The mention of my mother, rather than cheering him up, seemed to attach an anchor to the corners of Podesta's mouth and drag them lower. He looked pale against the mostly black starmap of the Imperium that filled the entire wall of the office behind his large desk. He rose from the austerely padded chair and walked around his desk to meet me eye to eye. We were of a height, I was surprised to note. That meant he would have been a good deal taller than my maternal unit.

"Tell me something frankly, Ensign," the admiral said.

I was eager to be of service. I straightened further, and my bones cracked in response.

"Anything, sir."

The gaunt visage confronted me until our noses were almost touching. I presented the most open of countenances for his perusal. "Is Tariana angry with me? Did she set you up to throw a deliberate insult in my face?"

"Why, no," I replied, rather rocked back on the heels by the question. "She holds you in the very greatest of esteem. She told me that I ought to be proud to be assigned to your fleet for my very first assignment. And so I am!"

"Then, it must have been your own concept," the admiral retorted, the shaggy eyebrows ascending miraculously up the broad brow. A trifle of color tinged the pale cheeks. "To flaunt your birth rank, which has no place here. To make your own hours, instead of adhering to ship's time. And that uniform! Did you have a problem coloring within the lines when you were in infant school, boy?"

"I was rather neat, if you ask me," I said, after a moment's perusal of my memory. "My father's influence, I believe. He's very tidy in the art department, though his choice of subject is inexplicable, in my opinion—"

"You young fool!" His query had apparently been a launching point for a line of thought, not a literal question, to judge by the rapidly increasing rubicundity of his complexion. "Give me one good reason why you shouldn't spend the rest of your voyage in the bilge, scrubbing it with a nail brush?"

"Waste of my talents?" I suggested with hope. I'd done a bit of that in the Academy, to the detriment of my uniform and my sense of smell.

"Do you *have* any talents?"

My mouth moved to say, "Quite a few," but I judged that the reply would provoke a further angry outburst. I doubted he wanted a summing up of my successes at three-dimensional jai-alai or my crack ability of solving crossword puzzles, or my newfound brilliance at image capture and manipulation. My nerves quivererd. This is not how I anticipated meeting the admiral. I moved hastily onto another tack.

"I apologize sincerely, sir," I said, as meekly as I could. "It occurs to me that I suffered a severe lapse in judgment..."

The indicator of the admiral's visage went over the line from scarlet into infrared. "A lapse in judgment? Is that what you call that insult? Your duty is to obey the laws and rules of the Navy, and to be aware of your position in it. And that position, you should recall with some clarity—since you just left the Academy, and I've heard that they make you smart there, don't they?—is *ensign*. That means that you are at the very bottom of the ranks of officers, which puts you below not only all other officers, but the noncommissioned ranks as well, who actually work for a living, and the enlisted personnel, who at least know why they are here because they volunteered to be! We are at *war* out here, Ensign. The defense of the Imperium relies upon our efforts. I should not have to tell you, the son of your mother and, yes, your father."

Figuratively speaking, my ears pricked up. My father? I couldn't imagine what he meant, but now, with Podesta looking as if steam might pour out of the top of his head, was not the time to ask. I concentrated on standing absolutely at attention, eyes front and ears open, hoping for further enlightenment. None was forthcoming. I sensed he wished a reply from me. Nervously, I summoned one up from the sincerity of my heart.

"Of course I wish to serve the Imperium, sir. How may I do that? I am at your orders, sir."

The kettle had gone off the boil, so to speak. Eyebrows and choler lowered, and Podesta withdrew from his fearsome posture. He returned to the chair behind his desk and sank into it. I did not relax. "You had best remember that, Ensign. Now, get out of here. Report to Lieutenant Wotun. Her office number is noted in your viewpad. At all other times than roll call, you will be in your quarters. I do not expect to see you at all except at mealtimes, during which I intend not to have to take any notice of you. Don't lower my expectations any more than you already have."

"Aye, sir! I will be a model of propriety hereafter, sir!" Relieved, I saluted with all the style I could muster. But Admiral Podesta had swiveled his seat away from me to consult a viewtank. I spun on my heel and marched out of his office, feeling as if my tail was between my legs.

❖   ❖   ❖

"He's an idiot, Commander," Podesta declared, as the hall door slid shut behind the lanky recruit and an interior hatch slid open onto the adjacent chamber that served the admiral as a private sitting room. "I don't know why you're bothering with him. Tariana must be so disappointed. He's just like all of the others."

"Not so, sir," Parsons demurred gently, stepping in. "We have been watching him since he was a boy. He has the required potential. All of the tests show it."

The admiral sighed and ran a hand over his thinning hair. "Nature knows we need such things, but you're starting with rough material, you know."

Parsons offered a slight smile. "Not as bad as you may think on first meeting, sir. He has certain skills, well-honed. Natural talents, more than you would expect, though untrained. The attitude can be adjusted over time."

"Nature! I hope we have time!" Podesta exclaimed.

"We'll do our best, Admiral," Parsons said, his face returning to smooth inscrutability. "That's all we may do."

✻ CHAPTER 2 ✻

"Why now?" Fifteenth Councillor Marden demanded. His thin, wrinkled, yellowed face with its sharply angled green and black tattoos covering his cheeks was designed for emitting peevish questions. He shot a bony forefinger out of the full sleeve of his lime-colored velvet robe and tapped it on the black obsidian oval table. The other councillors—there should have been forty in all, five from each of the Castaway Systems, but one contingent was yet missing—frowned. "What in their overbred minds makes the Imperium think we want to deal with them now? Any of them? It's like a dead spouse coming back and expecting to move back into the house once you've remarried! The Imperium!"

"That's lacking in taste, Vasily. And not really accurate in scope." First Councillor Leese DeKarn, a plump-faced woman with silver-white curls and a pat___n of light blue arabesques swirling over her c_____s and nose, clad in Portent's Star system's ___ robes, cleared her throat and palmed ___ the tabletop.

Within an envelope of blue light a sincere, round face surmounted by curly, graying hair, manifested itself, speaking with hazel eyes fixed solemnly and kindly upon the viewer. It appeared that no matter where one was in the room the eyes followed one. DeKarn found it uncanny and a little disturbing. "What their ambassador, Madam Hiranna Ben," she shrugged toward the image, "tells us is that His current Imperiality, Shojan XII, is sorry for the neglect of our safety during the past two hundred years. He wishes to reestablish 'loving ties' with the Castaway Cluster, his former principality. The uprisings and disturbances closer to the center of the territory that have overwhelmed their resources are now under control, and he is prepared to give us the defense and consideration that we were supposed to have had from him. The ambassador awaits our pleasure to bring our word back to the Imperium that we are amenable to the restoration of those loving ties."

"Shojan?" asked Councillor Six, a tall young man with dark skin decorated with a mask of silver tattoos like lightning strokes. His sculpted hair was also decorated with silver. A member of the Carbon system contingent, he wore his brick-red robes with flair. He hated his given name and was always called Six, even in his private life. He frowned at the screen. "How long has he been on the throne?"

"About six years, according to the accompanying material," said DeKarn, bringing up the appropriate file. "He is still in his twenties."

"So young!" said Councillor Twenty-Three Bruke.
 the eldest of their number, a man with a very
 hollow cheeks, and small eyes nested

in wrinkles. His brown and red tattoos almost disappeared in the cross-hatchings that time had etched upon his face. "I have seen so many Emperors and Empresses come and go. It is good of him to reach out to us. I am glad that we are not forgotten."

Twenty-Ninth Councillor Zembke made an impatient gesture. His face was a rock-solid oblong, made more impressive by a broad nose like a set of stairs. Black lines tempered only with a touch of yellow masked his cheeks. His flint-hard black eyes surveyed the room. He raised his grand, deep voice. "Is anyone at all falling for such a lie? The Imperium didn't *quell* those uprisings. What they couldn't blow up they walked away from. Like us. It is finished. It was finished long ago. Everyone has said so."

"Everyone?" Marden asked, with one raised brow.

Zembke gestured with a broad hand. "Everyone who has studied the situation. You've seen the dispatches. The Imperium is beset from every side but galactic north. The Trade Union has been attacking on at least a dozen fronts while its merchants waft in and out of the most poorly guarded space lanes with no one so much as demanding an electronic customs invoice. We're just lucky we are so far away from galactic center no one wants to conquer us for our resources alone. It's not financially worthwhile. You've all watched the digitavids..."

"You watch the digitavids?" shrilled Councillor Thirteen, a blunt-faced man with bulging blue eyes staring out of a mask of dark blue curlicues. "You know they are filled with mind-control rays. They'll put you into a trance, and insert subliminal messages into your subconscious!"

"And how do you know that, Tross?" Zembke asked, narrowing his small piggish eyes around his somewhat bulbous nose.

Tross wavered. "Well, I saw this digitavid..."

"Order!" the first councillor insisted, bringing her jade gavel down on the tabletop. "What are we to do about the Imperium?"

"Question is," Councillor Twenty-Seven, an attractive woman with milk chocolate-colored hair and caramel skin, mused, "what are they going to do about us? The Emperor has sent us a courteous message via an equally courteous envoy that is on her way here, asking us please can they come by and take over our government again. What if we say no? Are we going to be overrun with warships if we refuse them and choose to remain independent?"

"We are independent!" Zembke bellowed, bringing his hand down hard on the stone tabletop. It didn't make a sound. Zembke clenched his fist. DeKarn could tell he hoped none of them could tell how much he had hurt it. In sympathy she curled her toes tightly inside her boots. "Do we need a history lesson here? It was they who abandoned us. I can date it, can't you? On the fifth of the seventh month, two hundred and nine years ago, we on Carstairs Three sent for an Imperial Fleet contingent to capture and defeat the Trade Union buccaneers who had just accepted delivery of six months' worth of refined heavy metals, then declined to transfer payment for it. They attempted to leave our system. As we scrambled enforcement vessels to follow them, they fired upon us, and not just to deter chase—to destroy!" His hand flicked over the controls before him, and the screens all around them showed recordings of the event taken by drone satellites in orbit around the disputatious planet. "There, see them! They *stole* from us!"

"Cosmic shoplifting!" crowed Councillor Six.

"No, stiffing the server," chortled Eighteen, another youthful council member, her tattoos very modern in pink and orange. With humorous reproach, she turned to Twenty-Nine. "They walked out without paying. Your merchants were at fault, Zembke. They should have demanded payment in advance." Behind him the screen lit up with the image of a diner striding out of an eatery with uniformed flunkies pursuing him. Zembke reddened. "You've brought this up, as Carstairs representatives have for twenty long decades. It was a minor infraction, scarcely worthy of calling in the fleet. They might have refused to come deal with it anyhow. Why didn't your planetary defenses just blast the TU ships out of the skies, if they were using deadly force? The TU couldn't have gone into ultra-drive within the confines of the system. You had plenty of time. It would have had the right result without putting another Imperial life in danger. Certainly without wailing 'wolf!' to the skies."

"That's hardly the point!"

"Which is?" Eighteen asked, bored.

Zembke snorted. "The point is that the Imperium *didn't* come. Not then, not ever. They didn't even reply to our urgent plea. It was as if no one existed at the end of the circuit. No subsequent message got so much as a 'Sorry, but there is no one at home right now...' message. They turned their backs on us. It wasn't as if we didn't know what was happening. They couldn't turn off the digital feeds. We got their news broadcasts.

The core of the Imperium was under attack, and they pulled in all of their resources to protect it, and the rest of us could go throw ourselves into . . . into the black hole! It's to the credit of the indomitable spirit—don't laugh at me, you unpatriotic whelps!—that the Cluster has survived as well as it has.

"For two hundred years, in the face of natural disaster, invasion, pirates, famine and shortages, we have had no one to rely upon but ourselves. The Imperium didn't have enough interest in us even to collect *taxes,* let alone send defense ships out to patrol our space lanes. The Imperium long ago pulled out of its death spiral, but until now they seem utterly to have forgotten about us. My grandfather used to tell me stories of the bad days, just after the Imperium turned its back on us. No one living is old enough to recall how at first our ancestors couldn't believe that no one answered our pleas for aid. We waited too long to come to our own defense."

"That's not the Imperium's fault," Twenty-Two offered, calmingly.

"Of course it was their fault!" Councillor Marden barked. "Where were they?"

"They told us they weren't coming," Eighteen stated.

"When?" Zembke demanded. "When did they tell us?"

"They did," Councillor DeKarn said, gently. "The missive is in the archives. They could not reach us in time, even if the Core Worlds had not been under attack, which they were."

Twenty shrugged. "Our local governments chose not to believe them. That's our fault."

"Our planetary attorneys disagree with you," Sixteen

insisted. He looked like an attorney himself in his well-cut robes of subtly gleaming fabric, a double chin underscoring his healthy complexion, which was etched with wise quotes from antiquity in black and dark blue. "The Imperium was responsible under its own laws for our protection in exchange for suzerainty. They failed in that tacit contract."

"Well, then," Marden asked, "where *are* they?"

"They are here now," Sixteen said. "Or, rather, they are coming. They seem to wish to take us again under their aegis. They offer support. Infrastructure. Updated systems. I say it is no more than we are owed by them."

A lot of eye rolling followed this statement. DeKarn herself felt exasperated. "We can argue personal responsibility until the putative cows come home," Zembke said. "And after we've burned a lot of oxygen, where do we end up? In the same place we started: around this table arguing about ancient history, which we have been doing for over a week now."

"Those . . . who forget the past," intoned Twenty-Three, as he tented his fingers on his chest, "are condemned to repeat it."

"And those who forget they've said something before are condemned to repeat themselves," Marden added, peevishly. "We've heard that. We've heard all of it. What are we going to do?"

"I suggest," First Councillor DeKarn said, pulling them back to the present with difficulty, "that we listen to their envoy and see what it is they want. They may wish to set up diplomatic ties, not governmental ones."

"I've heard the same dispatch you received, and I disagree with your interpretation," Zembke snorted.

"So you have said, Councillor, for a week, now," DeKarn said patiently.

Twenty-Seven waved a finger for attention. "We're no longer subject to the Imperium. Why give them an opening?"

"Because they haul damned big guns, that's why!" Councillor Ten sputtered. She crushed yet another spent nic-tube into the waste receptacle. Nervously, she extracted a fresh tube from the pouch at her belt, put it between her tattooed lips, and took a long sip of air from its end. "It would be a damned rout if they chose to run over us. We may be sovereign, but we don't have a defensive force. We haven't needed one much over the years, really. The Trade Union has pretty much just traded with us since that time...yes, Zembke, I realize your people are still smoking about it. I don't like the idea of being so vulnerable."

"How can we be sovereign?" Six asked, narrowing an eye at her. "Was there a referendum I haven't heard about? We're a loose association, that's all."

"No, we're a confederation, aren't we?" Twenty appealed to DeKarn, her dark red tattoos outlining large black eyes. She was young, attending a council for the first time.

"This is an advisory board only," the First Councillor corrected her. "Since the earliest years after the Imperium abandoned us, no one has moved to form a confederation. No one was able to agree on terms for a general election. Many have held firm to their old allegiance to the Imperium. You can find the links in your briefing documents." She palmed the tabletop. Behind her, the image of the "welcome" file logo sprang into being. Links shaped like each of the systems' flags, scrolls for historical files, and the faces of past statesbeings flew out from the page, inviting a reader to open them and hear or read the contents. Timidly, Twenty started to reach for one.

"Do we have a government of our own, or don't we?" Zembke asked, exasperated. He waved a hand, and the image of the documents winked out, leaving the walls blank. Twenty jumped back and put her hands on the tabletop. DeKarn was annoyed with him. "No. Of course not. That would require making a *decision,* something we are all allergic to."

"Can we agree that we are an independent entity, separate and apart from the Imperium?" Marden asked.

"No!" said Councillor Twenty-Three. "We are not yet a complete conclave."

Few paid attention to him. They were on the usual three sides of the argument.

"There has never been an agreement to separate!" snarled Councillor Fourteen. Her parchment-colored skin paled further.

Six snorted, ignoring her. "What of that? We're going to sound pretty sad crying out our independence when they bombard our planets."

"They're not going to do that," Councillor Twelve said. She was a placid woman in her middle years, with soft bronze hair. The delicate spiral tattoos on her face played up her large, toffee-colored eyes. "They want to open negotiations. That is a peaceful overture."

"Maybe," Seventeen said, a notorious pessimist, lowering his thick brows, "they plan to drive a wedge between us!"

Zembke made a gesture of impatience. "They *can't* do that. We have withstood the years by mutual cooperation. We wouldn't survive without one another. You of Dree have a wealth of planets with water rings. We in Carstairs have heavy metals and transuranics that you need. We trade with one another, protect one another's backs, provide opportunities, keep the gene pool from becoming stagnant in any one system..."

"But that makes us neighbors, not siblings," Seventeen insisted.

Sago Thanndur, Thirty-Second Councillor, whistled a little between his mandibles and shifted his bright blue carapace. He and his fellow insectoids came by their elaborate facial markings naturally. "Not genetically, perhaps. We are siblings in adversity." His species had been the native of the seventh system, named something unpronounceable in their own language and called Cocomo by the humans who had moved in and commandeered the fourth planet from the sun, which had once been earmarked by the beetle-like aliens for settlement and expansion. It had taken over a thousand years for the native Cocomons to stop calling the humans "invaders" and accept them as co-inhabitants. They held four of the seats that represented their system to the Cluster council. He and his fellows occupied cuplike baskets held upright rather than the swiveling armchairs the humans sat in. In a show of solidarity, an example of what Sago spoke of, the sole human from Cocomo, Desne Eland, Councillor Thirty-Five, reclined crosslegged in one of the roomy baskets. He wore robes of bright blue to match his comrades' shells. "That will have to do."

"But, to carry your metaphor further, siblings are

equals," Thirteen said. "We are parentless. A group with no head."

"Isn't that the definition of a committee?" Six asked, with good humor.

"Then one of us should step forward," Zembke began. DeKarn held herself still in anticipation. This could be the moment she had hoped for.

Five cleared his throat, and nodded jerkily toward his own contingent. "Boske has always led negotiations."

"That's just a matter of geography," Zembke said, brushing aside the concept. "It's closest to the Imperium, that's all. We're harkening back to a time that will never return. We are the Castaway Cluster. We've held together all these years. Can't we agree, here and now, to formalize that arrangement, and be something more than just a loose association? We should hash out a governmental structure, and," he added, feeling the time was ripe, "a leader! Someone we can stand behind, and who will be the face that we show to the Imperium. One face, one strong negotiator, who defends our rights."

"I . . . I think I'd like having a leader," Eland put in meekly.

"So would I," Sago admitted. The rest of the Cocomons whistled agreement. "A nest-mother, as we of Cocomo have."

"Someone has to speak for us to the Imperial agent," Twenty-Three added in his quavering voice.

"Isn't Boske still first among equals?" Twenty inquired, with a deferential nod toward DeKarn.

"Not necessarily," DeKarn said.

"Surely we shouldn't change this close to an Imperial visit," Five agreed, tapping the breast of his pale blue robe.

"Augh!" cried Six, running his hands through his hair. "How does a committee accomplish anything? Throw in every interruption in the universe, and then dither until moot!"

"No!" Zembke stood up with his hands flat on the wide stone desk. Patriotic music flowed up around him out of speakers concealed in his seat, and a star map superimposed itself on the screens all around the room. DeKarn knew he'd waited for this moment for years, and had prepared his background material accordingly. She was in favor of granting him the leadership, though she knew Zembke was less popular than she. She would have proposed it herself long ago, but both the council as a whole and Zembke himself would have found it suspicious, as they did anything that smacked of unified government. Still, he was strong and of firm opinions. Even if the others disagreed with him, having to justify their opinions to him would make debate more productive.

Under normal circumstances, the council would not vote for a leader, but they were being pressed to it by the arrival of the envoy. This was a chance that could not be missed. DeKarn craved unity, and the strength of purpose that went with it. She sat straight, her eyes upon Zembke, encouraging him to go on.

He did, arms spread wide. "Why should we continue with the system that the Imperium left us? Boske was *their* choice for our spokesplanet. I propose that we of Carstairs speak for the rest of the Cluster. Our star is closest to the center. That makes it the prime location to use as a meeting point for all our peoples." On the screen immediately over his head Carstairs stood out like a glowing orange beacon, and spokes sprang from the star toward the fainter images of the other seven. DeKarn almost applauded. "We will show them that we do not cling to their preferences. Choose a new center!" He flung his arms out as if to embrace the whole council.

"Geography!" Ten exclaimed, rising and fixing a fierce eye on Zembke, who matched her glare for glare. She crushed a half-empty nic tube on the table. The pale gas seeped out of it like an escaping soul. "You denounce it, then you try to make use of it? Come on, we all know that DeKarn is the best negotiator. She hasn't got your bombast, but maybe her low blood pressure will keep us from getting wiped out by ship-mounted lasers!"

"Yes, DeKarn is a good speaker," the tattooed woman put in, nervously.

"Thank you, Ten," the First Councillor acknowledged. "But passion and authority are important, too. We must show a face to the Imperium that proves we have taken matters into our own hands."

"If we can," Vasily Marden said, skeptically.

"And that is what we are doing right now," DeKarn said. Strike, as the old adage held it, while the iron was hot. She could send the poison chalice across the table to the man who *wanted* to drink from it. "Councillor Zembke has made some good points. I feel that strong leadership, one voice speaking for all of us, would be the best for the Cluster. We have been fragmented for too long. So much time has passed while we debate the correct structure, nomenclature, even the colors of a Cluster flag. It was all very well while we dealt largely with our own interests. Now that attention has been turned to us from the outside, it behooves us to define how we are seen, rather than let those who behold us make that definition. We should unite behind one strong figure, democratically chosen."

"Well, *you* are very good," said Five. DeKarn smiled at him.

"You are a member of my own party," she said. "I hardly feel that you are a disinterested speaker."

"Not at all," Five demurred. "I have always admired you. I feel you would be an excellent leader. It is a shame that we must move uncomfortably swiftly, but this is, as you suggest, a crisis."

"Don't be too hasty," DeKarn begged him. She was seeing Zembke's opportunity slip away. *Speak up!* she thought at him. Instead, he glared at her. He believed she was trying to steal the leadership for herself. "Zembke has qualities that we would be wise to use."

"I think DeKarn's the best of all of us. Don't you agree?" Twenty twittered, tugging at her neighbor's wide sleeve.

Zembke felt rage swelling in him. No one would meet his eyes. They were all babbling. His carefully designed moment of triumph, ruined! "Silence! Listen to me!"

No one listened. They were all talking. "Carry on... wonder what the envoy will say?... Be nice to hear from the old worlds after all this... new fashions! ... Change is so fast... What do you think they're wearing?... Do we really need to decide on a leader? Can't we *all* talk to the envoy?"

"Silence!" Zembke bellowed.

"Council!" DeKarn pounded her gavel. "Now, this is all very flattering, but it gets us no farther forward. All of you sit down. Now. This is a serious matter. I don't want it to descend into trivia." She turned a warning eye on Zembke. "Councillor Twenty-Nine. Make your case."

Zembke looked at the others. Most of the group seemed cowed by his outburst, but the others looked bored. A few were genuinely upset, including Marden, whom he had counted on as an ally. This couldn't be happening. He had resources. He had supporters. But he had lost the room. He took a deep breath.

"I apologize to the Council," Zembke said hoarsely, sketching a small bow. He flicked a hand over a control. The star map behind him vanished, to be replaced by a pastoral scene. The others knew how rare such an unspoiled sight was on the Carstairs homeworld, which had been given largely over its history to mining and the smelting of minerals. Carstairsians were proud of surviving terrible conditions. He was making an open concession to peace. "I am only interested in our continued well-being. My view, as all of you know, is that would best be served in our continuing independence. I will not press for my point of view. But we do need a leader. One, and only one of us needs to speak for all to the Imperium. It would be an honor to serve in that capacity."

"I don't think so," chittered Sago, rising to his delicate hind feet. "You boom too much. Councillor DeKarn, what about you?"

DeKarn cleared her throat. "I don't believe that I..."

"Why not?" asked Ten.

"No!" Thirteen burst out.

The insectoid peered at the old man. "Why not? Twenty-Nine makes a good point. We should have a single speaker. She is well-spoken. Zembke is very loud, and loud does not necessarily carry a point."

"I might agree with you, hive-brother," Thirteen said, his wintry face creasing into a smile. "But we cannot nominate or choose Councillor DeKarn for another reason."

"What?"

"We are not yet the full council." Marden waved a wrinkled hand toward the five empty seats at the end of the black table. "Until the contingent from Yolk gets here, we are all flapping our gums or, in your case, mandibles for no reason. Nothing can be done."

The Cocomon tilted his head. "Ahhhh. I see. That is true."

Zembke flopped back in his chair with a deep sigh. "Marden is right, dammit."

"Language!" DeKarn rapped out. "But he is right." She was disappointed. The leadership was still in her lap.

She pulled up a chart showing the space lanes that surrounded the Boske system and frowned at it worriedly. Among all the colored lights flitting through the darkness, there should have been a blip on it that indicated the ship carrying the missing envoys. A system search showed nothing with the diplomatic indicator.

"Where *is* the party from Yolk?"

At that moment, the building's foundations began to shake beneath their feet.

❊ CHAPTER 3 ❊

". . . And this is your console," Lieutenant Michele Wotun concluded. She waved me toward a gray keyboard and scope in the darkest corner of the dimly lit chamber. Lt. Wotun was a husky, dark-skinned woman of middle years, with silver tinting her close-cropped curly hair. The rest of the room was gray, too: gray walls, gray chairs, gray dividers, gray backgrounds on every screen. Her voice had deep, musical overtones that I allowed to distract myself from the dire woe of my situation. I was glad to have something to do at last. When the Admiral had sent me to her station, he did not specify that she was on duty there as yet. I spent a miserable hour standing at attention staring at the wall in the corridor outside. Movement was a relief. "Any questions?"

"How long will I be assigned down here?" I asked, hoping the desperation I felt did not come across in my voice. "Not that I shirk my responsibility, Lieutenant!"

"Yes," Wotun chuckled richly. "I'm sure you won't from now on. I saw you come into the dining room

69

an hour ago. Ten minutes late! You were lucky the old man didn't lock you up. Probably letting you slide because you're the new boy on the ship. Sometimes he lets newbies have a gimme, but it won't happen again, I promise. You'll be assigned to me until the admiral believes that his lesson has taken firm hold on you."

"Believe me," I said meekly, "it has taken. I won't be late again. Or," I added, with a tender mental probe at the bruises on my dignity from the very thorough dressing-down, "any of the other points to which he drew my attention."

"He doesn't believe in deathbed conversions, and neither do I," Wotun crisped out. "I've explained your duties. Now, do them."

"Aye-aye, ma'am," I said. I saluted, then waited until she turned away to see to one of the other thirty stations in the low-ceilinged chamber before lowering my arm.

I felt eyes upon me. I turned my head and caught the young female lieutenant nearest me glancing my way. She had that rare, porcelain-white skin that combined with her deep, midnight blue hair absolutely invited appreciation. I winked at her. Her eyes widened, then hastily returned to her screen, and she began to type furiously on her keyboard.

The charm offensive was failing on all fronts, I thought disconsolately, then turned to my own station. A touch on the screen brought up my identification slate, with eight dashes below my serial number.

"This is a master-key console keyboard," Wotun had explained. "Through it you have access to all long-term storage of personal messages in the ship's databases." I felt very powerful, knowing that only eight characters stood between me and the secrets of every man, woman and alien on board the vessel. On the other hand—"Your job is to go through the stored messages, beginning with the oldest, review them, and judge whether they ought to continue being stored on the server, i.e., personal messages, trivia, media entertainment; or if they contain any improper information. The first you erase, if it is over ten days since it was received. We need the memory. The second you report to me. I've given you the parameters for what constitutes improper. Follow them to the letter. You don't talk about what you see, and you don't copy anything for your personal use later. Your job is to review, delete and report. Before you sit down, you check your ship-comp and any other personal data devices at the door. Got that?"

I had "got" it. Nothing to it, really. How hard could it be? While I deplored snooping through everyone's mail, feeling that privacy in one's correspondence was one of the few privileges remaining to servicebeings on board a naval vessel, but I understood at that moment I had been wrong. Every facet of a being's life in service was subject to scrutiny. Not too hard to understand, really, when you thought about it. Electronic communication was so simple: if a spy had managed to place him or herself on board, not a mechanical bot or a computer program, vital secrets could be shipped out to the spy's masters long before anyone would detect such a transmission. Lt. Wotun had also informed me that communications from passing ships were occasionally picked up and stored, even if they had not been transmitted to anyone on board. Stray emissions from our servers could also be read by those ships, if the security programs glitched or were breached in any way.

Well, if there were any leaks, I would find them. Call me Thomas Kinago, Forensic Plumber!

I disposed of my personal electronics, including my precious cameras and my pocket personal appointment reminder or viewpad, as we in the Navy called it, in the thumbprint-coded safes near the entrance to the Communications Center and advanced upon my station with vigor. Sliding into my seat, I queued up the messages in order of age, and plunged into my first perusal.

To say that what she had assigned me to do sounded tedious was to suggest that space was wide and deep. Communications had its utility, certainly, not only the vital business of sending and receiving of information from HQ and other ships, including the transmission of personal messages, sources of entertainment, research, warning, translation, and a host of other functions that fell under its auspices, but I was certain that none of these functions really required my personal attention. True, I added to the quantity of messages transmitted every day throughout the Imperium, but didn't we all? The law required that each of us maintain an Infogrid file, and add to it as personal circumstances changed. The Infogrid facilitated communication among us. And communicate we did, in prodigious quantity, sending notes, observations, jokes, comments and uplifting anecdotes. It seemed my shipmates put in their fair share of bulk to the files. I started reading them more closely.

Six hours later, I could barely function under the onerous restrictions that Lieutenant Wotun had placed upon me. My head spun with the endless messages and files that I had read. My fellow crewmembers had stored so many life-threateningly funny anecdotes, stories, quizzes and puzzles that I was itching to scrawl some of the punch lines on my cuff with my own blood, if need be, against the desperate hope that I could recall the body of the jokes from those references later. One howler, that involved Geckos and the words "fire extinguisher," was my outright favorite. It was a wonder no one had called for a medic. I'd had a terrible time suppressing my laughs and grunts of merriment, so as not to attract attention from my supervisor or fellow toilers in the fields of data. I could stand it no longer; I reached around for a stylus. My groping fingers encountered only empty desktop. I moaned.

"Miserable job, isn't it?" my neighbor asked, sympathetically.

"Terrible," I agreed. "How any normal, living, breathing, intelligent life form can do this day after day without losing one's wits is beyond my comprehension."

"It won't last forever," she offered, with a kind smile. I noticed how like a couple of forget-me-nots her lovely blue eyes were. "It's punishment duty, but Wotun hardly ever leaves anyone on it for more than a couple of days."

"That's what I'm afraid of," I said desperately, plunging my hands through my hair. My cameras were out of reach in the lockup. My datapad was in my cabin. Besides, I had given my word not to duplicate the screens that I was reading. Could I scratch the words "fire extinguisher" into my skin with my nail? I bared my wrist and made an attempt.

My neighbor looked at me in alarm as red weals rose on my flesh. "No! It's not supposed to be torture," she said. "If you're really stressing out on it, you can ask Wotun to reassign you next shift."

"No, don't!" I exclaimed. At her open stare, I explained, "I don't *want* to be taken off this duty. This is the greatest source of humor I've come across in years! It's the veritable mother lode. The very *wealth* of it is overloading my neurons. I love jokes. There is nothing better to while away the endless hours of official formal parties than a shaggy dog story or two in a corner with a circle of friends. I am *always* looking for material to stave off boredom. Some of these are the best things I've ever heard, and they're nearly all new to me, so I'm going out of my mind trying to memorize them all. Look, do you suppose you could remember the words 'fire extinguisher' for me until the end of the shift?"

Her eyes widened, and she began to laugh. Tears dampened the forget-me-nots of her eyes, and her dainty hand slapped the desktop.

"So that's it!" I must say that she chortled. "I know that joke. It's really old, but you're right, it is a hoot. I first heard it years ago. It keeps making the electronic rounds, probably whenever someone new comes aboard. Everyone sends those attachments to one another."

My heart filled with hope. "Then you wouldn't mind?"

She shook her head. "We're not supposed to pass any kind of information. Wotun would have my intestines!"

"Oh," I said, disappointed. "Please? It's just two words." I fixed her with my most melting gaze, guaranteed to warm the heart of any woman. Her shoulders relaxed and her head tilted sideways as she reveled in my regard, and she began to look wistful. "I would consider it a real favor." The corners of her mouth turned up and her eyes unfocused. Her lovely lips parted. I leaned in a little. She leaned in, too. I could smell the faint aroma of perfume. I thought it was Silver Lilac, one of my sister's favorite scents. I smiled. "Pretty please?"

Her eyes dreamy, she nodded.

At that moment, something plastic clattered to the floor. Her eyebrows flew up in alarm, and we both looked in the direction of the disturbance. Another officer on punishment detail sheepishly retrieved the stylus he had been twirling in his fingers. The mood broke.

"Oh, afterburners!" she swore. "Back to work! Here comes Wotun." She fixed me with a sympathetic expression. "Look, everyone sends those things all the time. After reading them a few times you ought to be able to memorize them just out of sheer repetition, shouldn't you?"

I shrugged. "That's true. I hope. Are you sure you couldn't . . . ?"

"Hush! Here she comes. Buy me a drink later, and we can talk."

I returned to my screen.

I wondered if there was any way to rig the station so it performed my job for me, without my having to pay attention to it. Not that I would dare to suggest out loud that I could streamline the operation of a department in which I had so recently arrived, nor under such a cloud. Perhaps after a shift or two, I'd be in a position to offer my notions of efficiency.

It was a blow that I couldn't record the items I wanted, but my attractive neighbor was right. I had a good memory for a humorous anecdote. I should be able to ingrain those stories after a few more rounds. Now that the onus of trying to store up funny material was off me, I could concentrate more deeply on the fine points of erasing message files. Each person aboard an Imperium Navy vessel was issued with a communications device, the viewpad, for which a pocket was provided in the small of the back or, in the case of Gecko recruits, to one side of their ridged spines. All personnel received orders on the small scope a minimum of one time per shift, usually text. An implanted conduction speaker somewhere on the skull provided multiple audio channels that could not be heard by anyone close by unless they were sitting cranium to cranium. Mine was behind my right ear. A few messages contained full video and audio, often when one communicator was sending a piece of entertainment to another, or something special that was worth sacrificing the bandwidth, such as the picture of a newborn child.

The usual method, though, was text transmission. Where silence was necessary, one could finger-spell one's message into the device, either by stylus or a series of contortions of the fingers before the video capture lens. Like Morse code, which had survived these many thousand years from Old Earth because of its simplicity, the Sang Li hand signs had become indispensable in the centuries since pocket comps were invented. The software translated the signals into text readable at the other end of the circuit, and an experienced speller could carry on a rapidfire conversation by comp as swiftly as if he, she or it was speaking aloud. Subvocalization was the last of the most commonly used means of conveying information. The software picked up those subtle sounds made within the closed mouth, as well as dozens of other methods. The whole purpose was to convey information from one person to another. These people liked to communicate. Frequently. And in detail. They sent messages during off-shift hours, but also during mealtimes, meetings, and—daringly—during training exercises when many of the senders complained of carrying heavy or dangerous equipment. I was impressed.

I scrolled quickly through reminscences and commentaries, consigning those that were appropriate to the disposal bin of eternity. It was up, Lt. Wotun had instructed me, to each "logger" to record his or her daily log into a permanent, personal nonline database. The essence of the ship's circuit was ephemerality. The dilatory among the diarists were out of luck. I was certain by the witty nature of many of the entries that the authors downloaded them on time. I came across countless observations that were so well thought out that I wished I'd made them, had I been in the same situation at the same time. I learned a great deal about the inner thoughts of my fellow officers and servicebeings. To my surprise, I decided that they would be interesting to know. I'd had little contact with those below my station. I am sure I wondered how different they were from my friends and relatives. I discovered they worried about the same things, fell in and out of love, made bad decisions for good reasons, argued about culture and mass media with the same fervor as anyone with whom I had grown up.

The time-codes embedded into each message didn't take into account the particular conversants, alas. I found myself reading multiple exchanges going on at the same chronological time. Most, if not all, were silent gripes over the useless nature of a meeting or a course of duty. Replies, which I deleted without hesitation, consisted almost invariably of agreement, laughter or sympathy. The ancient symbols appeared in serried rows descending from the original statement. "Yup." "Yeah." "Me, too." "(g)" "Grumble, grumble." Just for fun, I kept track of the number of "grins," and came up with 1,243 before Wotun's voice jerked me back to the present.

"You're making progress, Mr. Kinago," she said approvingly, noting the time-code on the latest "Yup" I was erasing at the time.

I glanced at the chronometer and discovered that four hours had passed since I had discovered the entry containing the first breathtaking joke. I had overstayed my shift by two hours. I should have felt annoyed for missing out on some of my leisure time, but the truth was that I had enjoyed myself greatly in the process.

"It's a very interesting task, Lieutenant," I told her, from the depths of my heart.

She peered at me, approval giving way to suspicion. "Sucking up doesn't impress me, Mr. Kinago."

"I'm not..." I protested.

Her full lips twisted sideways and one eye narrowed. I saw that any attempt I made to persuade her otherwise would fall into the pit of excuses she had been offered by previous consignees to her care.

"Fine," she said. "Then you won't mind reporting back here tomorrow morning at oh-eight-hundred."

I stood up and snapped my hand to my forehead. "Aye, ma'am!"

"Fine. Dismissed."

I left her shaking her head.

I sat in the officer's mess, nursing a cup of very strong coffee from the endlessly refilled pot sitting on a heat element near the door. The contents of the screens that had passed before my eyes were a jumble in my memory. Desperately, I cast through them, hoping to resurrect even a single quip, a humorous remark, or a notable observation that I could cherish and pass along to my friends at home, but all I could see before my mind's eye was a series of grins and dittos. I could not remember a single thing. I ground the heel of my hand into my forehead, and a moan escaped my lips. Ten hours, and not a decent joke to show for it!

"Fire extinguisher," a voice suddenly whispered in my ear. "And you didn't hear it from me."

I looked up in surprise and delight. The fruits of my labors came rushing to my memory at once. The attractive lieutenant sank gracefully into the chair opposite me in the officer's mess. I reached for my pocket secretary and scrawled into it as many of the jokes I had learned as I could. The lady waited patiently until I saved my file and glanced up, the frenzied moment having passed. She smiled.

"Better?" she asked.

"I owe you a debt," I said, fervently. "The beauty of your countenance is surpassed only by your kindness. By the way, my name is Thomas Kinago. Ensign."

"I'll take that drink you offered instead," she said. She extended a hand. "Sedona Alianthus. Lieutenant."

I entered an order for each of us into the table screen and touched my wrist insignia to the block to pay for it. The screen turned red and began to flash.

"What did I do wrong?" I asked.

"Violation of protocol," Lt. Alianthus said, scrolling the screen with a finger. Lines of print came up facing her. She read through them, her lovely features sinking into a frown. "You shouldn't even be in here, Ensign Kinago. I should report you, or I'll get in more trouble."

"More trouble?" I echoed, then wished I hadn't. Of course! She didn't work in the Records Department, any more than I did. She was there on punishment duty, too.

"Must you?" I asked. I leaned forward, invoking all my charm in the wistfulness of my expression. I didn't want to refer to the fact that she had already bent the rules on my behalf once just a few minutes before. That would be ungentlemanly. "Please?" The lovely lady hesitated, but her features hardened. She didn't want her punishment expanded for any reason, no matter how appealingly wistful. My heart sank as I pictured the inside of the admiral's study once again. I dreaded the aftermath if I should have to be brought before Podesta again. I had no doubt that he would take the promised action. I would never get to see my personal ship, and I would go home in disgrace. My mother would send me into exile, perhaps to my Uncle Laurence's wilderness cabin on a nameless planet in a lonely system at the far end of the galaxy. "It was an honest mistake."

"You are responsible for knowing all pertinent naval regulations," the lieutenant said, her lily cheeks hardening into porcelain. She touched the screen with her identification, and a console pattern appeared.

I was in despair. Admiral Podesta would not hesitate to drop the boom, as it were, upon me. I could feel the long arm of the military police dragging me off to the brig. No, that was a real sensation. A hand had applied itself to my shoulder and tugged upward.

"There you are, my lord ensign," Parsons said, face and voice expressionless as usual, as I rose unwittingly to meet his eyes. "It was good of you to wait for me. I regret my tardiness."

"No fault of yours, Parsons," I said, pulling my wits into some semblance of order. "May I introduce you to Lieutenant Alianthus?"

"Is he in your custody, Commander?" the fair lady inquired, ignoring me as if I was the table between them.

"That would be the perception," Parsons said, calmly. "We must go now," he added to me.

Alianthus, for her part, looked relieved and wiped the images off the table. She seemed to have no more interest in reporting me to the admiral than I had in being reported. I allowed myself to be carried off into the corridor.

"Whew!" I said, permitting myself a low whistle of relief once out of earshot. "You saved the day, Parsons. I forgot that the officer's mess would be off limits to me while I was in Admiral Podesta's bad books. I just wanted a drink before dinner."

"The admiral's strictures on your activities were fairly comprehensive, sir," Parsons said, steering me firmly toward a lift. "You must stay in your cabin except for meals and work."

"Meals, yes!" I exclaimed. I put my hand to my stomach, which I fancied felt flatter than it usually did. Pangs duly appeared to remind me of hunger. "What is the time? I missed supper."

"I observed as much, sir."

I ignored his smug tones. "And I didn't stop for a moment while on duty just now, for nourishment or any other form of bodily relief, not through my entire shift. Not that it occurred to me. I was too wonderfully occupied. By Forn, Parsons, you would not believe the marvels I have just beheld!"

An eyebrow mounted that epicene brow. "Marvels?"

I went aloft on rhapsodies of bliss. "This ship, Parsons, this ship! It is the repository of the finest collection of untapped anecdotes that it has ever been my pleasure to experience. Some of them replete with music, video, and minigames. I regretted that I was there as a destroyer of data, when I should have been placing the very best of them into the Emperor's library itself, as memorials of the gigantic wit of his most loyal subjects—most loyal with the exception of the noble houses, of course," I corrected myself.

"No doubt," Parsons intoned, steering me leftwards toward the door of my cabin. That large object removed itself meekly into the wall to its right, and I passed inside. I kicked off my shining new boots and flung myself on the bed. With my hands behind my head, I contemplated the ceiling.

"I shall make a difference here on the *Wedjet*, Parsons," I said, feeling a trifle smug. "It seems clear that no one has ever mined the depths of delight in the common consciousness for the common good. I shall. I know just the kinds of search parameters that ought to be applied to that amassed knowledge."

"Bearing in mind that you are not to retain any

information or benefit in any way from the information observed during your task?" Parsons asked.

I sat up, my reverie brought to a crashing end. He was right. I felt my heart sink again, the second time in the space of half an hour, but this time from disappointment. Wotun's instructions had been crystal clear. I was not to make use of the bounty I had perused. "You do have a way of casting a veil of magnetic dust over one's viewport, man," I protested. "It's only a regulation, after all. I'll figure out a way around that."

"Indeed," Parsons said, projecting more doubt into those two syllables than they had a right to contain. I ignored them. Something greater was uppermost in my mind.

"Punishment in the Navy's not nearly as bad as I feared it would be. In the meanwhile, I feel as though my esophagus has been amputated. I hardly ate lunch, and two shifts have passed since I last ate anything substantial. Nourishment has taken the spot at the forefront of my mind."

"In that, sir, it would be my pleasure to assist you in obtaining what you require," Parsons said. "If you will remain here?"

I rubbed my mental hands together in anticipation. I had not had a chance to sample the cuisine in the officer's mess, but the enticing aromas offered promises of a superior culinary experience.

He departed.

In rather shorter order than I thought possible, considering the distance and time that might be required for the task, he returned with a covered silver dish on his outstretched hand. I sat down at my desk. He placed it down before me and whisked away the cover.

I stared and blinked.

"Is this a joke?" I asked, with pain in my voice.

"Not at all, sir," he said, his face as bland as if he was telling me the temperature. "Admiral's orders. Until he considers that you have come to a state of penitence and obedience required to understand your actions in light of his authority."

I lifted and let fall the single survival bar that had occupied the plate. It was gray with a faint touch of tan mixed in, coarse in texture, with rough edges suggesting it had been cut by a bandsaw. It looked like a rectangular chip of wall insulation, but not nearly as appetizing. It smelled—I lifted it to my nose to confirm—it smelled of nothing at all. Nothing. The comparative chip of wall insulation had more of a native aroma.

"I take it back, Parsons," I said sadly. "At least fifty percent of me is penitent, above and beyond the admiral's requirement."

"Then you have only fifty percent more to attain, sir," Parsons said, gliding smoothly toward the door as if on magnetic slides, leaving me to my lonely repast.

✻ CHAPTER 4 ✻

"It entirely breaks protocol for a delegation to arrive
in a non-Cluster ship!" said Councillor Fourteen,
slamming the connection with a slap of her hand on
the obsidian table. The pewter curls of her hair seemed
more tightly wound than usual. "I move we do not
seat the representatives from Yolk in punishment. They
can go off-world—or even out-system!—and return in
the right kind of vessel."

"Are you insane?" Five asked. "This isn't a party-
game penalty."

"No, it's more serious! A violation of Cluster law!
I say they should begin again!"

"That would not be appropriate or practical,"
DeKarn said, quelling them both as she might have
separated two of her grandchildren. She clutched her
elbows inside the voluminous sleeves of her light blue
robe, the very thing those sleeves were best for. The
others did not need to see how nervous she was.
"It would waste time and effort, and we have more
pressing concerns. That TU ship did not notify us

by beacon or direct message that it was coming. I am far more troubled that it just appeared among us like a fungus sprouting."

"A damned big fungus!" Marden said.

"Wouldn't the screens have shown a ship that big coming into orbit around Boske?" Zembke demanded.

"The screens would, but what if the operators are in league with the TU?" worried Seventeen, lowering his thick eyebrows. The Cocomons buzzed with concern, the patterns on their faces seeming to move like clouds.

"What would the Trade Union have to offer our liberated artificial-intelligence operatives that we do not ourselves?" Tross demanded.

"They are more in touch with cutting-edge technology than we are," Five said, with a toss of his coiffed head. "We're damned far out of the center of things. They might have programs or components that the LAIs find useful."

"You suggest that our own employees are capable of treason?"

"No, self-interest," Five said, with a sly smile. "It's worth exploring."

"Curse all self-aware mechanicals!" Seventeen snarled. His thick eyebrows drew down. "Why we let them exist is beyond me."

"You can't stop them," Twenty said, meekly. "They have a right to exist."

"Not if they interfere with *our* lives!" DeKarn sighed. He was a born pessimist. There was no arguing with him.

"The ship!" Zembke reminded them, causing a blare of color to erupt behind him. "Why is it here?"

A voice answered them from the door of the chamber. "Why? As a gesture of friendship, of course!"

DeKarn drew herself up to her full height and surrounded herself with a nimbus of white light. "Who dares speak in council who is not a member of this body?"

"Why, I do." A silhouette outlined by the stark light of the corridor grew larger and larger as it approached the council. Once underneath the spotlights of the chamber, the figure's head of silvering black hair drew glints. The male human to whom it belonged was strongly built and well-proportioned—almost ideally so, DeKarn thought, with approval, though she objected to his easy assumption of welcome. She was not familiar with the uniform. The shipsuit was a dull purple, with boots, cuffs, collar and shoulder flashings of an autumn gold. The combination of colors should have looked clownish, but was instead almost regal. His face was clear of all markings, tattoos or clan insignia. He reached DeKarn's seat and made a deep bow, sketching an arc in the air with his right hand. "Emile Sgarthad, Captain of the Trade Union ship, *Marketmaker*. I offer respect to the council."

"What are you doing here?" Zembke asked.

"And by whom am I being addressed?" the man asked, rising and presenting a bland countenance to the fulminating councillor. His eyes were blue with a tiny hint of green, and the brows above them straight, as was the nose that jutted at a sharp perpendicular downward from their line. He was as handsome in face as he was in form and bearing. DeKarn felt her cheeks grow warm under her tattoos. He reminded her of a lover she had had when she was young. It was not the same man, of course, but he had the same insouciance.

"This council speaks as one voice," intoned Zembke dangerously, and a trifle prematurely. "You dare not question our authority."

The big man cocked one knee and stood at his ease. "I only ask so I might give you all your right names," he said. "It was a friendly question."

His nerve was as bare as his face. DeKarn admired it alongside her impatience at his interruption of their meeting."

"Then let me ask a friendly question," DeKarn said. The man regarded her with a pleasant expression. "What *are* you doing here?"

Sgarthad turned to beckon toward the doorway. Almost timidly, four humans and a Wichu, all in bright yellow council robes, filed in: the missing councillors from Yolk. DeKarn's heart leaped with relief. "Just seeing my new friends safely to their destination. I found them in distress and went to their rescue."

DeKarn could have sworn that she saw the Wichu blink in a puzzled fashion, but all five of the newcomers nodded their heads.

"Our ship fell under attack in the heliopause," said the first man, round-bellied with dark skin and elaborate dark-green and yellow tattoos. DeKarn knew him as Ruh Pinckney. "The trade ship carrying us fell into trouble among the asteroid belt. The *Marketmaker* was close by and was able to take us on board. We are grateful to Captain Sgarthad, and ask you receive him as a friend."

"Trouble?" asked Tross, his brows rising. "What has become of Captain Iltekinov?"

"He is recovering in my sick bay," Sgarthad said, gravely. "He and his crew were taken ill. I hope they will be around and about soon."

"Have you brought disease among us?" asked Twelve sternly.

"Not at all," Sgarthad said, turning his charming smile upon her. "My chief medical officer said it was undoubtedly something in the crew rations—they would not have served it to their guests, of course."

"No," Pinckney insisted. "We're all well. We wish to take our places. We have been monitoring your negotiations, and wish to register our disapproval."

"On what point?" demanded Fourteen, the skin tightening over her sharp cheekbones.

"Several." Pinckney drew a glittering memory crystal out of his sleeve and looked around for a port in which to shove it.

"You are not seated yet," Zembke reminded them. "All points will be taken in order as has always been done. You must be recognized first."

"Very well," said the middle-aged woman with bleached-white hair at his side, Tam Quelph. She shot a quick smile around the room. She beckoned to her delegation. They all offered a bow to Sgarthad and made for the empty seats at the narrow end of the table. Immediately, the screens behind them lit up with images of the Yolk system, their system flag, and an image of their planetary administrator, an able and admirable man but so ugly that DeKarn's eyes automatically turned back to Sgarthad as an antidote. He smiled broadly at her. She looked away hastily. The Yolk system anthem played. Automatically, she clapped a hand on the table to turn down the volume.

The rest of the councillors returned to their seats. DeKarn activated the Boske symbols in the screens around her colleagues, as did her fellows of the other systems. They were at last complete in number.

"As a member of the host delegation, I welcome the representatives from Yolk," she said formally, nodding to them. "Eleven, will you read into the record the minutes of the meeting of the last full council of three years ago?"

"Yes, First Councillor," Eleven said. Dob Rengin was a slim, quick-moving man with a long, bony face and bright blue eyes. His white and red tattoos looked as haphazard if he had put them on himself in hasty strokes and crossbars. He stretched both hands over the tabletop.

"Just a moment," quavered the Twenty-Third Councillor, raising a shaking hand toward Sgarthad. "Why is he still here?"

"Yes," Zembke said, narrowing an eye at the visitor. "This meeting is closed to anyone not of the council."

"Do you speak for the entire group?" Sgarthad asked him.

"Yes, he does," DeKarn said, cutting off the others before they could protest one way or another, "provisionally, pending discussion. Our discourse is not for your ears or any other outsider."

"But we want him to stay," Pinckney said urgently. "He is a valued friend."

"Thirty-Sixth Councillor, it is against the rules," DeKarn said. The entire Yolkovian contingent looked distressed. Their gratitude was understandable, but reluctance to have him out of their sight was puzzling. They had had a trying experience making their way to the council. DeKarn hated to add to their misery. "Very well, let us put the question to a vote."

"I protest!" shouted Fourteen, pointing a nic-tube at Sgarthad. "This is a disruption of protocol! There are thousands of questions on the agenda before 'whether an outsider should sit in the closed session?'"

"Do you wish him to sit here and listen while we debate those matters of precedence?" DeKarn asked.

"And no one has yet asked me to sit down," Sgarthad added plaintively.

DeKarn ignored him. "All those in favor of allowing Captain Sgarthad to remain in this meeting, raise your hands." As she expected, the lights above the heads of the Yolkovians went on immediately. To her surprise, however, so did those of Twenty, Thirteen and Twenty-Seven. "Those opposed?" Those eight lights went out, and the remaining thirty-two went on, including her own. She turned to Sgarthad and was met by that commanding, sea-blue stare. It was hard to get the words out, but she forced them. "I am sorry, Captain. Please leave the room."

"I will wait in the antechamber," he said, not seeming at all put out. "Thank you, my friends! I shall see you soon."

The eyes of the Yolk contingent tracked him until the door sliding down separated him from their view. DeKarn found their behavior curious and unsettling.

"With your permission, may I enter the minutes now?" asked Rengin.

"Go ahead!" Zembke snapped. His gaze had also tracked the visitor, and his expression said he resented it.

Rengin spread out his hands. Small images that each depicted a subject on the previous schedule appeared hovering over the wide black table and fed themselves into an open folder. The folder immediately multiplied itself fortyfold. The copies flew to every councillor and sank into the receiver eye in front of each. DeKarn flipped a hand to bring up the table of contents and briefly perused it. She did not tap any of the files; to activate one was to listen to all of the carping and detail-splitting that had accompanied it. She preferred to think of the results that had come from those negotiations, a much more pleasant consideration. Once in a while they got something done. Sometimes it was even a worthwhile accomplishment.

"Any objections to the minutes as they have been entered?" she asked, scanning the group. "No? Any old business?" Twenty-Three's top light went on briefly. Everyone turned to glare at him. DeKarn cringed. Was he going to protest translation of those minutes into the Cocomon language *again?* He glared back, but the light went out. "Very well. Let us move on to the items on the agenda. Many of them have already been discussed as to their merits and tentatively settled..."

"By you! You are several weeks ahead of us!" Pinckney protested, jabbing a finger at the tabletop.

"You were late!" Tross said. "We began our deliberations on the appointed day."

"We could not be here! You know how difficult it is to time space-travel. The black hole has been emitting unusual quantities of quasars. We had to detour for safety. We have been monitoring your negotiations. Yolk does not necessarily stipulate that we consider any of them settled!"

"You are welcome, of course, to open matters to the floor for debate," Marden said. "But as I see it, most of the items are old arguments brought around again. Only two matters stand out in importance."

"Two?" demanded Thanndur, his mandibles clacking. "I have sixteen vital themes bookmarked!" Around his three-digited claw-hand, several small icons danced.

"Two need to be pushed up the list, or the others are largely moot," Marden said. "With your permission, First Councillor?"

"Of course," DeKarn said, and turned to the Carstairs contingent. "Twenty-Nine?"

Zembke made an impatient gesture. "Very well, go ahead!"

Marden nodded. "The two matters are interconnected. The first is the pending arrival of the Imperium's envoy. How will we greet her? We need to discuss our response. Are we a part of the Imperium or not? It has gone undecided for two centuries, and that is long enough!" Muttering began, not all of it low-pitched. "I apologize for being too direct, but what are we? A loose collection of systems, with no central government? A mini-confederation of our own? We are, after all, self-sustaining, producing most of what we consume, yet . . ."

"The details are a secondary matter," DeKarn interrupted him.

Marden's spine elongated slightly, elevating his saturnine face. "Very well! I will leave that to the debates! But it is urgent to decide now that we are independent!"

Desne Eland raised a hand. "But we are not independent. We have always been a part of the Imperium."

"Are we?" Zembke asked, rounding on the Coco-mon representative with the light of battle gleaming in his eye. The human and his insectoid counterparts recoiled, chittering to one another fretfully.

"I am not going to let you make us live through ancient history again," said Ten with a sigh. "We are who we are. This sector was founded by the Imperium..."

"On the backs of our Cocomon brothers and sisters!" said Seventeen.

Thanndur chittered. "We were glad to become part of a larger whole. The swarm survives. It prospers!" His companions, Eland included, trilled agreement. "Do not use us as your excuse for an argument." Seventeen looked put out.

"I say that we tell the Imperium that we will go our own way from now on," Marden bellowed, amplifying his voice with the help of the hidden console.

"There is no call to be this hasty over such an important matter!" said Councillor Tross.

Marden rounded on him. "There is every reason to be hasty! The woman is on her way here. Her ship is making its final hop into Portent's Star's space. She will be here in days. Are we a government, or are we a social club that meets every few years to eat expensive food and complain about our separate constituencies?"

"We can be both," Councillor Six said, mischief on his face.

"But what is your point?" asked DeKarn patiently, although she had already deduced it as, undoubtedly, had everyone else at the table, but the rules required him to state his case.

Marden rose and settled his robes around his shoulders. He raised an upturned hand in an orator's pose. "We are now pressed to make a decision that we have refused to make. Do we humbly submit to the Imperium and resume our place as a unit of an enormous and faceless entity—"

"Hardly faceless," said Twelve, gently. "Shojan is the scion of the house that gave us birth, that urged us forward into civilization, who fostered the hope that we would conquer the reaches of space and go ever onward..."

"Oh, stow your longwindedness!" snarled Fourteen, slamming her hand down and flattening the spent nic-tubes in front of her. "Very well, I'll be the one to halt this cascade of unnecessary verbiage. I propose a preliminary vote, First Councillor. Are we of the Castaway Cluster part of the Imperium, or are we an independent entity?"

"Councillors?" asked DeKarn. "Will anyone second?"

"I will second," said Five.

"The matter is proposed and seconded," DeKarn said, dreading what she was about to say, but protocol was protocol. She took a deep breath. "Everyone will be limited to forty minutes of opening statements, followed by question and answer from the full council. Following that will be the preliminary vote. Debate is open."

Not waiting to be called on, everyone broke into their own tirade. All of them shouted to be heard over all the others.

"No, no!"

Marden stood up and began to wave his arms. Behind him, colors of distress filled his screens and sirens wailed. When the others stopped talking and put their hands over their ears, he bellowed at them. "We don't have time for this! Vote now! Then we'll debate the outcome."

"No! That's not the way things are done!" said Bruke, severely.

"I agree with Councillor Marden," DeKarn said, breaking protocol herself. "We do have very little time. We can't hold off the ambassador, so we will have to decide before she gets here."

"Why can't we?" asked Sixteen. "It is not uncommon in legal matters to prevent a witness from hearing the testimony of others."

"Because she is a diplomat. All of our deliberations ought to have been accomplished before this. I quite agree with Councillor Fifteen." Marden gave her a grudging nod. "If the question is asked, we owe an answer."

"We can easily send her away without an answer," said Fourteen, angrily. "*We've* been without answers long enough. Let them see what it tastes like, for a change."

"And what will that accomplish?" Eland asked. "They deserve our candor. It is not unreasonable that in two centuries we would have made up our mind what we are. Our ancestors were beings of decisive action. They reached out from a small, isolated planet and founded great empires! If they had become bogged down like this, there would never have been science enough to lift them out of atmosphere, let alone the will to make it happen. But I would go back to the discussion we were having before the arrival of our friends from Yolk. In advance of the arrival of the representative from the Core Worlds, let us choose someone who will speak with the force of all of us behind that one being."

Thank goodness! DeKarn almost smiled. Someone else had said it without having to be prompted.

"No," Marden said firmly. "We need to decide what it is we will say before we choose a spokesbeing. The debate was opened on the subject. We have two choices before us. Let us choose one. Will we decide once and for all that we are a part of the Imperium, or are we independent?"

"A-ha!" said Pinckney, light blossoming around him as the screens erupted with starbursts. "Then there is a third choice that needs to be added to that item of the emergency agenda. That is our friend Sgarthad. He represents the Trade Union. It has sent him to ask the Castaway Cluster to join their vast and prosperous confederation. The Board of Directors have offered us open trade routes, decrease or surcease of tariffs for export of our goods, and protective services, including a patrol fleet between us and potential enemies. It's a fantastic deal, one that we ought to take advantage of."

"Bah!" Seventeen said, brushing off the desk with a sweep of his hand. He lowered his thin brows over his bony nose. "To trade historical ties for those greedy hucksters? Not while I breathe."

"How could you fall for such a sales pitch?" asked Tross. "When have they ever offered something for nothing?"

"We have plenty to offer them," Quelph said, her brown eyes meeting the Thirteenth Councillor's bulging blue ones with sincere conviction. "Our crafts are more than worth their interest."

"Handiworks! They have plenty of factories. All they need is one example of each item, and, in about a week, you're shut out of the market. So, what will we offer them next month?"

The Wichu representative wrinkled her nose. "Not

just exports. They want to know more about our culture. He says knowledge of others helps improve their own lifestyle. Gotta like that."

"Very tactful," Five said, with a glance toward DeKarn. The First Councillor kept a noncommittal expression on her face.

"Very well, I believe that the contingent from Yolk has a valid amendment to the subject that is already upon the table," she said. "Those in favor of discussing the three possibilities of adhering to the Trade Union or the Imperium or remaining independent, signify now."

In fairness, she had to illuminate her own voting light. The Yolkovians immediately joined her. Other lights went on more slowly, but in greater numbers than she thought would arise. She had to put the increase down to the solemn regard of the eyes looking at them from the screens at the narrow end of the oval table.

Impulsively, she thought she might vote against allowing the measure just because *he* seemed to be asking for it, and she permitted no one to coerce her, not even with charm. Still, when she weighed the matter in her own scales of right and wrong, whether or not that handsome face was present she knew she would choose the same option.

"Opposed?" Naturally, Zembke, Tross, Marden and Ten voted no. She passed her hand over the recording light.

"The matter is carried.

"In the matter of independence versus the Imperium versus the Trade Union, the vote will commence. I will abstain from this first vote. You may also abstain, but only this time. We must know where we stand."

DeKarn thought it was unlikely that any of them would.

"Independence?" Zembke's hand flew to his controls, and his voting light went on, nearly obscured by the image of the Cluster that exploded on his screen. Others followed, including, to DeKarn's surprise, two of the Cocomons. "Thirteen.

"For the Imperium." The entire party from Dree voted as a bloc. The rest of the Cocomons added their numbers. "Also thirteen.

"For the Trade Union." Before she had finished speaking, Yolk's lights bloomed, as did the remaining members. No absentions. "Also thirteen. No clear majority. Very well. Who will speak first on this matter? Remember, you have only forty minutes apiece."

"More than enough time," Zembke said, rising. "My dear friends, you are forgetting matters of the last two hundred years!" Many of those at the table groaned. They certainly hadn't forgotten the multitude of speeches he had made over the last thirty years on the topic. "We stand alone as we have stood for centuries! Let us make that decision so it is in place before the arrival of the Imperium's envoy..."

A faint chime sounded. Dob Rengin looked up from his screen, and passed his hand swiftly to the right. The icon "landed" in DeKarn's viewscreen and skidded to the halt in the center.

"I am afraid there won't be time to make the decision final, unless we vote finally right now," she said. "The ambassador is here."

She passed a fingertip over the newly arrived file. Hiranna Ben had the pleasantly harried look of a campus counselor. The eyes, a pale hazel with thin but sharp lines at the corners and underneath, looked both compassionate and shrewd. Generous lips had acquired confining brackets from which they dared not escape. Her warm complexion was set off by very short silver hair gelled to a peak. This was a woman, DeKarn thought sympathetically, who was too nice for her job and had had to learn to behave otherwise lest she, to make use of an ancient phrase, give away the store.

"Gentlebeings," came the warm, rich, lilting voice. "I give you greetings from his majesty, the Emperor Shojan XII, to his most honored subjects..."

"Bah!" Zembke erupted.

"Hush!" Councillor Twelve said. "Let her speak."

"...pleased to say I will be among you soon. My pilot informs me that we will be over Pthohannix within twenty-five hours. I am aware that the full council is in session. I request a meeting with all of you as soon as can be arranged. I have brought many delicacies from the Core Worlds, and I invite each of you and your significant others to a feast at the," Ambassador Ben glanced down, as if consulting notes, "the Boske Ruritania, to get to know you." She raised her eyes to meet the video pickup. "I await your convenience, and remain your humble servant..."

"Bah!"

"Hush!"

"...Hiranna Ben."

The light dimmed and the face disappeared. DeKarn sat back and saw the dismay in her own soul reflected in the faces of the rest of the council.

"Well, my colleagues, the moment is upon us. Shall I call for another vote?"

❊ CHAPTER 5 ❊

Being a man of abnormal optimism, I did not allow myself to remain in the doldrums because of unappetizing rations. After all, I had survived many an Imperial banquet, where, I recall, I might have been far happier with a survival bar than the exotic viands that chefs had made to tempt the taste buds of the noble guests. I remembered the wedding feast of my cousin Olthiorus Kinago and his lovely bride, Demarca, who though human hailed from a formerly Gecko system on the edge of the Autocracy. As the main course, we had been served large, black-shelled insects, boiled and adorned with a sprig of herb as if the creature was clutching its own last meal when it died. The flavor of this sad arthropod was no better than its appearance. None of the subsequent celebratory meals was any more appetizing. I had made it through that week of festivities. At least for this ordeal I did not have to wear formal attire, smile constantly or dance with any of my aunts. I merely had to erase, report and try not to chuckle out loud.

As my fair guide had said, I found numerous repetitions of the stories that had so tickled my funny bone
on my first shift, and many more in the same vein. I
found myself rehearsing under my breath how I would
tell such stories when I returned to an audience who
was unfamiliar with them. I pride myself that I can
tell a joke well. It's an innate behavior, not really a
learned one, and I had enlivened many a party by
my store of humorous material.

"...all right! Now, where's that fusion reactor I'm
supposed to marry?" I muttered to myself, reading
off the screen. I chortled aloud.

"Pardon?" asked Ensign Dicox, an Uctu in Lt.
Wotun's clutches for three days for the crime of
allowing a burst pipe, an item within his realm
of responsibility, to destroy half the supplies in a
cool-room storage unit. His bright blue eyes were
surrounded by purple rings, a sign of exhaustion and
worry among his people. "You are smiling. That is
smiling, isn't it, human?"

"I am." Honesty compelled me to own up to my
facial expressions.

The skin between his eyes wrinkled. "Then are
insane, you?"

"I hope not," I said.

"Then talk to self, why?"

"Well, er," I stammered, unable to explain myself.
Lt. Wotun heard our whispers and turned to come
and discipline us. I ducked my head, unwilling to be
removed from my studies or to attract the lightning
of the admiral's wrath once more. "Frustration, really."

"I speak as you," Dicox said, though I feel certain not for the same reasons. I was about to draw

his attention to the joys of our shared task, when Wotun arrived, wrath writ large across her face. He lowered his nose and rolled his eyes meekly up to her. "Apologies."

"My fault, ma'am," I said at once, attempting to diffuse the blame from the innocent Gecko, fixing eyes just as large and blue upon her, though not independently capable of movement, as his were. I smiled. My smile was often enough to reduce this fierce officer to at the very least a return of the expression. "I emitted a sound. I am afraid it drew Dicox's attention."

Wotun paused, her fearsomeness on hold. I fancied that seldom on her watch did wrongdoers admit to their crimes. She shook her head.

"Just get back to work," she said, and turned her back on us.

Dicox let out a wheeze of desperate relief and bent over his screen. I released the breath I had held behind my teeth, and went on to trying to memorize a story about an airlock and a load of nitrogen capsules. That one might take extra explanation to my elderly relatives, but I assured myself they would find the punchline was worth the trouble.

Most of the messages stored on the circuits were ordinary missives, an incredible load of them, something over half of them directed toward home, a few to vendors, system operators and nonpersonal connections, and the rest to other naval personnel. The preponderance of these last tended toward the quotidian: gripes about shifts and meals, comments about fellow servicebeings and complaints about one's superiors. I grinned quietly to myself over pithy observations, for example, comparing Admiral Podesta to a steel leg-trap, in which it would be preferable to gnaw one's own limb off rather than remain in its clutches. As I couldn't agree more, I made a mental note.

While deleting all the repetitions and casual replies, I was hoping for exciting news of conflict between our ship and enemy craft. Sadly, the fleet had had few encounters with other ships since the last flushing of the communication system, so there wasn't much in the way of accounts of bravery at battlestation to be found, no matter how far back I traced the conversation trees.

I was a little disappointed. I hoped that I would see some action. Not to be killed, or even gravely wounded, but returning to the homeworld with, say, my arm in a modest sling would do wonders for my reputation among my fellows. According to the notes I had received from my old friends, they were all on patrol around our main system, with far less chance at heroics. It behooved me to plot my way back into the good graces of the admiral so that I could place myself into an advantageous station should we see action. But that would have to wait until I was no longer on active punishment.

With the eight-digit code, I was able to match the messages to the Infogrid files of the senders. By law, every citizen of the Imperium old enough to enter code was required to have a file on the Interstellar Intelligence Information Grid, or Infogrid for short. Birthdate and birthplace were the first pieces of data recorded in such a file, along with a photo image that was required to be updated no less frequently than every six months, more often in the case of physical changes such as accident or cosmetic alteration. That and government notes regarding the individual were locked away from public scrutiny, behind the most secure of ever-changing protective code.

As the Infogrid contained everything of importance about an individual, it provided a useful clearinghouse of information for the use of government, law enforcement and medical staff. It was also punishable by death, one of the few crimes that attracted that penalty in this enlightened age, to appropriate the details in an Infogrid file to assume a false identity or steal by means of falsehood. Over the last four thousand years, attempts had been made by subsequent governments to get rid of that Geckonian response to what was considered a bloodless crime, but resurgent crime waves always caused it to be reinstated by legislatures besieged by a desperate and angry constituency.

The rest of the official transcript contained items that were in public records: family trees, school transcripts, attainments, run-ins with the law including cross-references to court records and incarceration schedules if appropriate. I prided myself that I had escaped custodial sentences for what few peccadilloes I had committed. My kinsmen and I tended to exceed speed limits and commit minor acts of vandalism, mostly when we are young, but I was proud to say I had fewer blots on my official record than most of my relatives and friends. I put it down to the Kinago charm.

Infogrid also tracked an individual's travel, making note of departure from and arrival in a system, along with spending records so that the tax entity of one's homeworld would have a record for use taxes. I thought that was a trifle unfair. I checked, and indeed the Infogrid had made a note of the four thousand credit loss I had sustained on a casino station floating outside the heliopause of Dobrish mining system a year ago. I had hoped no one would ever know about that, but Infogrid saw all, and recorded all. The eight-digit code I had, I realized, was the key to endless sources of blackmail data. No wonder the strictures against retaining data for personal use were so ... well, strict.

Then there were the public streams: private correspondence, entertainment and participatory elements. The Infogrid had been established partly to facilitate connectivity among citizens spread out across hundreds of light years in every direction. Considering that my fellows spent one of the three ten-hour shiptime shifts on duty and another asleep or doing personal maintenance, their on-circuit output was astonishing, amounting to terabytes of data every day. One crewmember appeared to be dictating even during anti-grav tennis sessions. Normally, the code signature of anyone who read an item was recorded, but thanks to my classified form of entry, I passed unseen among the missives.

Over the course of a few shifts, I had begun to observe the writing styles of the various correspondents, and I became curious to see who had written what. Extended and humorous metaphors about the futility of our everyday duties that bordered upon professional comedy came from my Uctu tablemate, Redius. I treasured his wit whenever I came across it.

Anstruther's commentary, as her letters back home, was matter of fact and devoid of detail, as if she was

afraid of letting any of her personality shine. In her
school reports, I saw that her teachers had noted the
tendency toward shyness, but she was a hard worker
who earned praise for precision and diligence. I made
a note to myself to find something to praise as often
as I could. The gesture could help lift her toward
greater efforts. I would be proud to have her as an
executive officer on a future command of my own.

I regretted that my current situation prevented
me from spending quality time with my fellow junior
officers outside of the dining room, or making the
acquaintance of the other brilliant minds whose work
I felt a trifle guilty about erasing.

I respected the admiral a good deal more after
reading through official dispatches he sent back to the
Admiralty. He was precise, intelligent and possessed
of a dry wit that must have been on the short list of
how he attained command of the North Star Fleet.
I had to remind myself he was corresponding with
my mother. Even the admiral could fall into dullness
when engaged upon the necessary bureaucracy of his
position. Knowing that thanks to my password I would
not be detected if I read his mail, I sought to dip
into the private section of his Infogrid page.

The list of messages sent, even since the last purge,
was long. His personal correspondence was nearly as
copious as my own. I thought I wouldn't be able to
resist, but respect kept me from opening any of the
messages. It had been enough to skim the list of his
correspondence. I was about to leave the section,
feeling perhaps that a man with as many cares on
his mind as Podesta was entitled to keep his personal
thoughts private, when I spotted a familiar address.

The admiral was corresponding with my mother! *This could bode no good for poor Thomas,* I thought in alarm. I brought up the segment to read.

"Dear Tariana," it began.

Honk! Honk! Honk! Sirens blared out of the speakers surrounding my station. The screen turned red, obscuring the print thereon. Everyone in the room turned to look at me, and Wotun came running. Scarlet as the display itself, I sprang to my feet.

"It was an accident," I said as Wotun swooped past me.

"I very much doubt that, Mr. Kinago." With a single wave of her identification stud, she brought up a usage history on my station. I reddened further when she realized how much I had been reading of the other people's confidential Infogrid files. She met my eyes squarely. "Please stop exercising your curiosity, Ensign. You are here to delete the files in the common pool."

"Yes, ma'am!" I exclaimed, slamming the side of my hand into my forehead.

Wotun tilted her head to one side, her lips twisting to one side. I felt sweat bead on my face. Would she report me? Would I end up on worse punishment duty? My stomach twisted at the thought of a careerful of survival bars and isolation.

"The admiral," she added, pointedly not looking at me as she closed a series of screens and returned me to the chat files, "has a restricted file, as do several other officers on this ship. There is a device on the top left of the screen, a blue shield. Keep that in mind. No more interruptions."

"Yes, ma'am! Thank you, ma'am!"

I sat down, surprised and elated. She hadn't *forbidden*

me to snoop, just to remain out of certain boundaries. I took the point. I would confine my research to those of my rank or thereabout. I sent an admiring glance after the Junoesque officer, offering her silent devotion. She understood the ordinary longings of a curious mind. As long as regulations were nodded to, there was a good deal of leeway. I would approach my job with meekness, knowing that she was capable of mercy as well as sternness.

My finger tapped the delete command with the regularity of a woodpecker pursuing insects. I could see why the task plunged the average being into despair. The majority of the messages were ordinary to the point of being tedious. It took all of my concentration to stay on point as I was following the ramblings of a biomedical engineer to her friends, even though she was excited about the breakthrough she had made, and to her it was the most absorbing subject that had ever existed. All I had to do was make certain that protocols were adhered to, and that classified material was kept classified.

Some of the entries I located along the way did trouble me slightly. The odd message I encountered did skate dangerously close to flouting those regulations that Lt. Wotun had ordered me to follow. Here and there a correspondent had inserted an image of his or her workspace. In one very detailed image I realized that I could clearly read the settings on the pictured screen. Other messages listed technical statistics that seemed copied whole out of a manual, and had little or nothing to do with the cheerful gossip that flanked it. I acknowledged that there could be a perfectly innocent explanation for the cut-and-paste, such as the writer having taken those details for use on his station and forgotten into what file he had copied them, but that was not my call to make. I duly flagged those items and continued.

It was inevitable that I began to recognize the writing styles of the finite number of servicebeings on the ship. Out of curiosity, I would guess whose message I was reading, then follow the code number back to its file. A human, noncommissioned officer in engineering (I guessed from context) had sent messages to a relative at home in the Ramulthy system in which he spoke obliquely about the weapons emplacements on board the *Wedjet* which, I judged from his complaints, he had to repair. His spelling was poor, as was his pronunciation. I assumed that he had risen to service on a major Imperial destroyer because of his skills. His lack of communication skills would keep him from rising farther. It was not difficult to distinguish the same being in other transmissions.

But some of those emplacements were considered classified, not only the location, but their very existence. During my brief training in *Wedjet's* fire control section I had been instructed that these were secret, experimental units. They emitted no stray ions or radiation as long as they remained unused. I followed the train back to the sender's Infogrid file, which was not protected from my scrutiny, and found all these messages were coming from the same human. He showed precious little judgment on matters of importance. The personal videos and images of himself he posted were ill-considered if he meant to spend his career in the Navy.

Since my meal breaks consisted of the inevitable survival bar, I had no reason to leave my station. I sipped water and chewed my tasteless bites while perusing the Infogrid files on the message-makers I found the most interesting. I could not conceal my research from Wotun, but I made certain to have an innocent screen ready to bring up should one of my fellow penitents pass by my station.

Lt. Alianthus served the three days left of her sentence without speaking to me. The Wichu, Dicox, still toiled away at the station beside mine. He never looked up at anyone else. I read the Infogrid on each of them, too, and learned a little about their lives. All of them seemed a trifle dull, or so I thought at first. I should not have been so quick to judge, even of those who were less well born than myself.

The crew of the *Wedjet* came from all over the Imperium. Most had excelled at their studies, and not a few graduated top of the class (among *my* fellows, the valedictorian was the one who had skipped the fewest sessions, and was top student by default rather than design). They were devoted to their families, sports, hobbies (as well as the blistering array of jokes), and with surprisingly penetrating things to say about their fellow beings. I promised myself to search out and befriend several of them who sounded interesting. To my delight, not a few of them already shared my table at dinnertime.

Sitting at the ensigns' table that evening, with my survival bar on my plate, I regarded my companions in a new light, as the real nourishment. They were complete beings, not the one-sided junior officers they had at first appeared to me. Many of them were deep thinkers. With hidden tragedies. Redius could probably attribute his clownishness to having seen his mother shot dead by a crazed human from an inner system who hated all Uctu, not because ill had ever befallen him because of one, but simple, blind prejudice. I regarded him with sympathy, something that he had no means of understanding the source of. I realized I had to put away the information in a tight little compartment, instead drawing him out about his humorous observations about something else.

"Rising to appropriate station, I," Redius replied, when I asked him about his duties. "Honored to oversee lowly spacers scrape and re-enamel the floor of the fighter bays, as was done before me just last week, and the week before. Getting most attached, me, to long pit in floor where recorder drone exploded many months ago, but said plate not due for replacement. Its dimensions becoming most dear to me. Should it change, a shock it would be."

I chuckled. "I am getting used to the bulge in the padding in the back of my chair in Records," I said. "It hits me just under the right shoulder blade. But enough about me." I turned to Anstruther, who was toying nervously with her protein entrée. "What news on your project?"

She seemed surprised. "I, uh, well, we, uh, tested the energy outputs of the power plants. I calibrated the gauges. They were off by three microns."

Xinu let out a snort. "And that will kill how many people?"

Anstruther looked hurt. I swooped in to her rescue. "It could be fatal, in battle situations," I said. "Three microns represents three hundred thousand kilowatts, doesn't it? Her precision is admirable. I'd never spot it." Anstruther blushed with pleasure.

"Your diet's making you boring," Nesbitt said, lowering his brows at me. I was taken aback. He was correct. I was not behaving as I usually did.

I took a bite of my survival bar to give myself time to gather my wits. "Sorry not to be more fun," I said plaintively. "It's the food. It distracts me to smell those savory aromas and be unable to sample even a bite."

"I'd give you some," Anstruther said, bravely.

"Don't!" I protested. "You'll bring down the wrath of the admiral upon yourself. It's bad enough I had to suffer it." I tried to look pathetic.

"You brought it on yourself," Xinu, my dark-avisaged friend, said. He waved a forkful of his dinner under my nose. I almost swooned. "You hide behind punishment to avoid showing me how superior you are in tri-tennis."

"Absolutely," I agreed, blithely. "Normally I would have gotten off by now. I prefer to let you flounder in anticipation, so you will make plenty of faults when I finally face you. Too bad that there's only a twenty-seven-fold grid here. I'm used to much better than naval issue."

"It's the best court in the fleet!" Xinu exclaimed.

"Oh, well, that makes it the largest frog in a small pond," I said. "You'll see."

"If anyone is a frog, that big mouth of yours makes you look more like one than I do!" Xinu and I launched into our customary banter over skill and sportsmanship. I couldn't tell him how I ached to try what was reported to be an excellent tennis grid, even by civilian standards, or any of the other sports facilities on board. I had sent my cameras out and about where I could not go. I regretted not having taken advantage of the *Wedjet*'s marvels before getting into the admiral's bad books.

"You wouldn't care to lay a small wager, would you?" I asked, as casually as I could frame the question. "First recreation period after my duty is done in Records, and I will scatter points around you like a whirlwind."

"I'll take that. You're all talk. You nobles all are just talk." Nesbitt smirked, spooning up the last of his fruit dessert. That was better.

We sensed rather than heard the admiral rising from his place and sprang up to attention as he departed the room. I felt myself sigh with relief. Another day of having Podesta ignore me was a good day in my books. Now that service was over, ordinary roboservers moved in to clear the tables, freeing the living staff to depart for their rest periods.

I felt guilty. I had not revealed a single word of what I had seen in the files, but my behavior was colored by it. I had deliberately pressed myself to behave as I had before. My knowledge of them must not come out in *any* way. That eight-digit code had changed me. The problem was that I knew too much, an ailment that I can truthfully say has never troubled me before in my life.

Before I could commit another fault, I felt a familiar tapping upon my shoulder. As usual, Parsons had managed to sneak up on yours truly. I didn't jump far, being accustomed to it, but the severe look on his face gave me cause for concern.

"What is it, Parsons?" I asked.

"The admiral wishes to see you, sir," he said. My tablemates smirked.

"I haven't done anything!" I protested. My conscience was clear. I had not written down a single joke, and I had controlled myself mightily on the subject of my friends' hidden pasts.

"You are not in trouble," Parsons assured me. "He wishes to give you the assignment you have been awaiting."

All my panic turned to preening, and my companions' smug expressions sank into open, rampant jealousy. I wished them all a good night, and followed Parsons with alacrity. My mission! If I couldn't see a spot of war, then an individual mission was good for bragging rights when I started to message home.

". . . And you understand the limitations of your brief?" Admiral Podesta asked, as if he believed me incapable of comprehending the words he had spoken.

"I do, Admiral, sir!" I exclaimed, saluting neatly. I continued to stare at the wall ahead of me. Young Thomas would not be caught out again in a lack of military etiquette. "I will be honored to represent the Imperium and your good self to the militia of Smithereen, Admiral!"

Podesta looked weary, I could see out of the corner of my eye. His eyebrows floated mid-forehead, too exhausted to arch high or scowl low. "All you are doing is reviewing the volunteers, Ensign. It is not a vital diplomatic or military assignment. As we are passing by this mining colony, it behooves me to send a representative to show that the militia is not forgotten. That is all. Commander Parsons assures me that you cannot foul—that this is well within your capabilities. I am taking his word for it. Don't prove him wrong."

I shot a look of gratitude to Parsons, who stood near the door at attention, his expressionless mien gazing toward nothing, then snapped my eyes forward again. "I won't, Admiral! You will be proud of me."

"At least don't give me cause to send a message to your mother, that is all I ask," Podesta said. "Report to the shuttle bay at oh-seven-hundred. Dismiss."

"Sir!" I executed another brain-scrambling salute and spun on my heel.

❧ CHAPTER 6 ❧

"And that, my friends, is the last word I will say on the subject. Vote to rejoin the Imperium," Councillor Thirty said. Her curly red hair had wilted around her shoulders, and her face was pink with the effort of her speech. "It is the right thing to do."

DeKarn looked wearily at the time. Of the forty councillors present, sixteen of them had taken up their full allotted time exhorting one another to convert his, her or its vote to that of the speaker. After every speech, she had called for another poll. The numbers had changed slightly now and again, but no clear majority for any of the three possibilities had emerged and, it seemed, never would. Her back ached, her eyes burned, and her head pounded. She was fighting not to be bored into nodding off. Nothing new was being said, except about Captain Sgarthad.

The Yolkovians kept fretting toward the closed door of the chamber, as if hoping for a glimpse of their rescuer. His image was constantly on one screen or another. DeKarn was getting weary of seeing it.

"The vote, please?" she said hoarsely. She recorded the results without looking at them and swept the number to Rengin.

"This is ridiculous!" Sixteen said, rising. Protests arose with him.

"You are out of order, Councillor!" snapped Bruke.

"Oh, what does it matter?" asked Six. He had messed his fancy hair into a bird's nest from impatience. "I move we should interrupt the debate to listen to him. If he has something new to say."

"Seconded," DeKarn said rapidly, to forestall another protest. They all knew that Councillor Sixteen was a patient and just man. If he had something to say, it was most likely worthwhile, and thank goodness!

"Thank you," Sixteen said. He straightened his robe. "My friends, we are not going to agree, not so soon. How long did it take us to work out the details of our biennial market, and we all wanted that event! This is far more important. I move that we discuss our doubts and misgivings with the ambassador and hear what the Imperium has to offer. Then we can vote out of knowledge. It could be that there is no good reason but that we were once a part. If Shojan—"

"His Imperial Highness," Twenty-Three interrupted, with peevish punctiliousness.

"—His Imperial Highness Shojan XII wants to redress the wrongs of the past, then it may sway some of you to change your minds."

"Oh, anything to get me out of here before my next birthday!" snapped Ten. "I hear a 'but' in there. What is it?"

"I want to go back to the earlier discussion on having one face, one voice, to represent the council. We can be overwhelming as a body. To have one being acting on point would be more efficient than the full quorum. That person should conduct the interview with Ambassador Ben, and report back to us. We could even watch the interview remotely, as long as it is understood that our questions were to be submitted to our representative and not put directly. It wastes the good ambassador's time *and our own* to do otherwise."

"A fine idea," DeKarn said. "I believed it to have merit. So did Twenty-Nine, whom I thought would be an excellent representative."

"I rather thought I..." Sixteen said, looking hurt.

"You, too, would be a fine choice," DeKarn said at once. "Very well, colleagues, what do you say?"

"Anything to get out of here," Ten said. "So moved."

"Second," Six said, raising a finger.

"We have a proposed candidate for the job, as well," Quelph said. The screens of the Yolk contingent all lit up with the same image. "As we need a strong person to put the right questions, Captain Sgarthad is willing to take that position to support us. He would meet the ambassador on an equal footing."

"Not him again!" Eland wailed.

"Absurd!" Tross exclaimed. "He is not a member of this council or even a citizen of the Cluster!"

"But we all agree wholeheartedly," Pinckney said, flattening a sincere hand on his chest. "I for one would follow him anywhere."

Guffaws erupted through the council chamber. "Keep your personal life personal," snorted Six. "I find him fanciable myself, but that doesn't change our laws."

"But why not use him?" Urrmenoc asked, waving a paw for attention. "We hire agents to do business for us all over the galaxy who are not native to our worlds. He is a good speaker, and a good businessbeing. He showed us his account books in his ship. I wish I could wring such profits out of a deal. Here. I've got a copy of his life file. You could see how much of an asset he'd be to us." The floating icon split up and zipped to each councillor. It opened at once. A portrait of the man lurking in their corridor appeared before them.

The two youngest members of the council, Twenty and Four, looked up at the enormous image, exchanged blushing glances and giggled like schoolgirls.

"Councillors!" DeKarn exclaimed, shocked. "Councillor Pinckney, it would be improper to employ him as an agent for several reasons, the chief of which is that he represents a rival interest!"

"He might be useful to us," Twelve spoke up in her soft voice. "Perhaps as an ombudsman. He is disinterested whether we choose to be independent or rejoin the Imperium."

"He is not disinterested!" exclaimed Zembke.

"Well, I liked him," Five said. "I think he'd be good. At least we know he doesn't dither, like too many people in here. He'd get the facts for us. In my opinion. I say yes."

"Five!" DeKarn said, horrified.

"I'm sorry, First Councillor," he said, contritely. "He's very direct. You saw that. It is an admirable trait. I know I don't have it."

"No!" Marden shouted. "Are you all drunk? Have you inhaled fumes?"

"Do you have to be so insulting?" Five asked, making a sour face. "I feel like I've been given an insight into wisdom. If our visitor would agree to intercede between us and the Imperium, the ambassador would see that we were not automatically falling into place. It's a brilliant idea. I am for it!"

"I am certain he would agree to act," Quelph said, beaming at Five. "He said he would do anything we need."

"It is a wonderful idea," Tross said. "That way the ambassador can play no tricks on us! She won't be able to hypnotise us, or drug us into signing away our rights!"

DeKarn stared at Tross. He never believed anyone unless he could check the facts independently.

"I, too, would consider him," Seventeen said, raising a finger. "Hearing our arguments from an outsider might also give us insights."

That was an opinion of a different type. Seventeen was a pessimist but not paranoid.

"I don't know," DeKarn said, beginning to waver.

Others joined in the argument, but it was clear that the council was beginning to agree with Councillor Quelph. Was Sgarthad the answer to their need for a single negotiator? True, he didn't belong to the council, but that might be an advantage. He lacked the resentment of those who felt the Imperium abandoned them. He had no loyalties to any one of the eight systems in the Cluster, he would not show favoritism in presenting their requirements to the ambassador. And she would not know the breakdown of the council of who favored repatriation and who independence. On the face it was an outrageous suggestion, and yet . . . and yet . . .

"All those in favor of asking Captain Sgarthad to represent us, vote now," Councillor Pinckney said. He turned on his light. All around the room, lights went on. DeKarn found her finger hovering over her voting key. What should she do?

"No!" Marden roared. "Captain Sgarthad is a suitor for our hand, just like Ambassador Ben. Put them *both* in quarters until we have hashed this out, *without* their input. It has been too long since we made a decision. It must be unanimous, majorities in all eight systems agreeing."

Thank fate for Marden, DeKarn thought, pulling herself together. *What was she doing even considering such a ridiculous suggestion?*

"I agree," she said, jabbing her forefinger at the master control. All the screens around the council chamber went blank. The members burst out with their protests, then halted, looking around in bafflement.

"First Councillor, I am so sorry," Five said, breaking the silence.

"Me, too," said Twenty.

"I'm not," Tross said. "I fear subterfuge on the part of the ambassador."

"Well, that is a chance that one of us will have to take," DeKarn said. "I will contact the city-state governor, Dr. Yuchiko, to make arrangements to house our two guests in comfort *and* isolation until we have come to our own conclusions, then we will send one of our own to speak to them."

"One at a time, or together?" Councillor Bruke asked.

"We can decide that later," DeKarn said. "And now, I would like to adjourn for the day. I don't know about the rest of you, but I would like to eat and rest."

"Can we see Captain Sgarthad?" Ruh Pinckney asked eagerly.

DeKarn exchanged glances with Zembke, Marden, Tross and Bruke. "I don't see any harm in it, but he is not to approach any other members of the council unless we send for him first. You may so inform him."

"Of course, First Councillor!" Pinckney said, looking overjoyed. "Then move to adjourn!"

"Seconded," said Six, planting both palms on the table and boosting himself to his feet.

"Then we are adjourned until the tenth hour tomorrow morning. Good night, all."

DeKarn rose and rubbed the small of her back with both palms. Councillor Nineteen sidled up to her. They watched the Yolkovians all but shoulder the rest of their colleagues to one side to be the first out of the chamber. She glimpsed the handsome silver head and one quick flash of those blue eyes before she looked away.

"Gorgeous, isn't he?" Nineteen asked. She lowered her long, black lashes slyly. In her life before the council, the actress Barba Linden was known Clusterwide on the digitavids for her roles as temptress and siren. Behind the luscious looks, she was a chemist, a philanthropist and a long-married mother of four. She was an old friend, to whom DeKarn felt she could say almost anything.

"Too gorgeous," DeKarn agreed. "Think what he'd look like in tattoos."

"Breathtaking," Linden said, running a delicate fingertip over the pattern of vines and minute blossoms on her cheek. "But I've often wondered what it would be like to go bare-faced like that. Why the warning to the others? Afraid of what you might say if you met him on the street?"

"That, and afraid of what I might *do*," DeKarn agreed. "Perhaps, perhaps I don't trust myself. That is the most forceful charisma I have ever encountered. It's attractive and dangerous, like a tiger."

"All you have to do is close your eyes and say no."

DeKarn smiled. "I hope I can remember to do that. In the meanwhile, it is better if none of us meet him until we have come to a decision."

"We might have to buy each of them a mansion to wait out the argument, dear," Nineteen said. "It could take years."

"It shouldn't," DeKarn said, closing down her station and palm-locking the data. "Zembke is right. In two hundred years we should have come to a conclusion already. This forces us to take a direction. In a way I welcome it."

"In the meanwhile, I'm starving. Do you want to come home and eat with us?"

"Thank you, dear, no," DeKarn said. "I had better be alone for a while. I need to think hard about my vote."

"Well, you know mine," Linden said with a smile. She touched DeKarn on the arm and glided out of the room.

DeKarn remained in the chamber. On her personal communications device she touched the link to her assistant. On the small screen—she deplored that others in the council used the full holo when speaking to others outside; it made it seem as if there were others in the room—she saw the young man glance up from his keyboard. He had a long nose and thin bones like a jester, but his bright eyes were intelligent. The lines of scarlet and gold tattooed on his cheeks were like exclamation points, drawing more attention to those eyes. "Colm, come in here, will you?"

"Yes, Madam Councillor," he said. He sprang to his feet. The screen went dark.

DeKarn had time only to settle herself in her chair before Colm Banayere appeared at her side. He had come in through the privy door, an ancient term for both privacy and for the relief booths in the hidden corridor behind the chamber.

"I guessed that you didn't want me to be seen, madam," he said.

She smiled. She appreciated his instincts. "One moment," she said. On the table console, she activated privacy mode. It was never used during open meetings, to prevent secret deals, but had never been purged from the programming. She waited until the lights at both doors flickered subtly to indicate that no transmissions from the chamber would be detected, and no listening or viewing devices from without would work. She nodded.

"What do you require?" Colm's best trait was that he never asked stupid questions.

"I need an investigation of the ship and the beings that brought the Yolk contingent here to Boske." She keyed in a code on her comm. A pip erupted in Colm's own unit, indicating that it had been received. "This is a video-capture transcript of this afternoon's meeting, from their arrival to adjournment."

"What am I looking for?"

She tapped the table with a forefinger. "I am not certain there is anything to find, but that man . . ."

Colm smiled, throwing the apples of his cheeks into sharp relief. "The Trade Union captain? There have been a lot of messages through the Grid during the last several hours. The TU ship is larger than any vessel presently serving the Cluster. The captain himself is handsome and charming. He seems to make friends everywhere he goes, from the port authority across the city to this building. Everyone who meets him likes him."

"That is just it," DeKarn said, frustrated. "It is uncanny. Yolk treats him like a friend, a mentor and a savior. True, he did save them when their ship was damaged . . ."

"Or so he says, madam."

She blinked and stared at him. "But all five councillors said he rescued them."

The young man waved a hand. "Perhaps I am too cynical, madam. What do you require?"

He raised more questions, but DeKarn had to keep her mind on the first and foremost. She scanned the room, half-lit once the others had left. She let her gaze rest on the place where Sgarthad had stood.

"It was not only the councillors from Yolk who found him irresistible. I found him unbelievably attractive. I believed what he said while he was saying it. Only after I had a chance to think that my own cynicism—if you like—came back. He *charmed* me. He gained influence over my colleagues in moments. They were ready to accept him after having seen him only once, without knowing anything about him. That is a dangerous thing. What did he do to us? How did he do it? Such a response had to be artificial in nature, but I didn't smell anything or see anything unusual. Was he wearing a device of some kind that affected our minds? Did he dispense a gas or a nanoparticle of some kind? It's vital that I know, so I can decide how to react. He is being sequestered in the governor's mansion for now, but beware of his crew."

"What became of the ship carrying them before the *Marketmaker* took them on board?"

"Lost," DeKarn said, "or so he said. But the *Little Darling* would fit into a landing bay on that behemoth."

Colm's right eyebrow rose. "It's a puzzle of many pieces, I see. I will investigate."

"Thank you, Colm. I know I can depend on you."

He smiled. "Always, madam."

Silently as an owl, he departed. DeKarn marveled at his ability to analyze a mystery as if he had been given advance notes. Once more, she was grateful to have him in her service. Four years, now, he had worked in her office, gradually promoted from receptionist to data clerk to personal aide. He was willing, quick-moving and eager. If he had had an ounce of ambition for public office, she would have backed him to take her seat when she retired—whenever that day would come, but he had shown no interest in being in charge. He liked solving problems, and that was that. A puzzle was a puzzle.

Colm was a Cluster-wide champion of puzzle-solving, eking out his government salary with prize money from contests and tournaments. Several times a year he brought in a holo-trophy or a medal with the name of an obscure kind of puzzle engraved on it. A plaque on the wall over his desk spelled out his primacy in a number enigma no one else she knew could even understand. Her personal secretary felt indulgent toward him, as if he was a bright son with an acceptable idiosyncrasy. DeKarn supposed she felt the same way. Others, she knew, were jealous, but that was the way office politics went. Nothing to be done about it.

Fortunately, Colm paid his critics no attention—the best way to deal with them. He came from Carstairs, though he had shed its harsh accent without a trace. She blessed the utility of an aide she could always rely upon. As now.

With that investigation under way, she had to handle the other problem that had dropped into her hands. Still in the security of the chamber's secrets mode, she keyed in the number of the Imperium's envoy.

Hiranna Ben was gently outraged. "I await your pleasure, of course, First Councillor, but His Imperiality demands my return at the earliest possible moment."

"I understand, Ambassador. Please understand that it is not intended as a personal affront. Our council was only made whole hours before we heard from you. We are . . . rather behind in our negotiations. I trust it will be a brief interval before we are able to meet with you."

"May I know the nature of the delay?"

DeKarn bowed her head. "It would be improper of me to discuss unfinished business of the council chamber. I hope you understand."

Ben cocked her head. "It doesn't have anything to do with that handsome man I see all over the press this evening, does it?"

"What?"

DeKarn squinted as the screen changed to show the beginning of the best-known evening opinion report. She seldom watched the transmissions; they were rarely kind to politicians, whether planetary or interstellar.

Still, the various channels were key to understanding segments of the population. Yes, there in the midst of a huge, clamoring crowd, was Captain Sgarthad.

"My friends!" he was saying. He raised his hands, palms out. "Your support is gratifying! I promise that the Trade Union will be a good partner to the Castaway Cluster!"

She clicked back to Ben's image. "May I visit you later?"

Ben's lips were pressed together with grim humor. "I hope you will."

❊ CHAPTER 7 ❊

"It has nothing to do with me!" Dr. Yuchiko protested, as the Boske contingent, some of whom had been pulled out of the mob and others dragged away from their long delayed dinner, and the other representatives who were outraged. The governor held up his hands as if to fend off physical blows. "All these people insisted on following him here from the Council Complex. They say they are his friends. No one was causing trouble. They are peaceful. I've never had such a cheerful assembly. The media arriving was inevitable under the circumstances."

The assembly, though cheerful, comprised several thousand beings of every gender and race represented in the Cluster, not to mention several mechanicals. At its center, at the top of a plinth from which rose a golden stone obelisk, Captain Sgarthad was holding court. By his movements, he was laughing and joking with the people around his feet. No one came too close to him: DeKarn could see a few grim-faced humans and Uctu in dull purple shipsuits holding riot batons. The ones who appeared to wield the most authority were a human male with a prognathic jaw and military-cropped hair, a muscular female human with very short curls, and an older Uctu whose scales were distinctly flattened at the edges. They had sidearms out, a violation of Cluster law.

"The council asked you to keep media silence around the visitors," Zembke said, though DeKarn and the others knew it was futile. Anyone with a viewpad could create an opinion report and find an outlet willing to broadcast it over home receivers, across the Grid, or both. Undoubtedly fan files and tribute files were popping up and being widely exchanged. "You will have to delete all references to either visitor. Planetwide. One is an official diplomatic visit that technically has not yet begun. The other is a . . . new item on the agenda. Until we have decided our public response, neither is to appear in electronic streams."

"That will freeze the Grid for hours!" Dr. Yuchiko protested. "Think of the error messages! The lost revenue from advertising! Pthohannix relies upon that income."

"If you had followed instructions we would not have error messages to cope with," Vasily Marden said.

"I did exactly as you asked! But you did not send him in a closed vehicle. He gathered a crowd all by himself."

"You ought to have taken him into custody."

Dr. Yuchiko gave him a curious look. "I thought that he was a diplomatic visitor, Councillor. If he was to be treated like a prisoner, then I need to have a warrant listing charges."

"That's not what I meant!" Marden sputtered.

DeKarn decided to take matters into her own hands. "Councillor Zembke, Governor, please come with me."

❖   ❖   ❖

The Pthohannix spaceport should have been bustling, its gray, arching ceiling like the upturned hull of an ancient sailing ship echoing with voices. Instead, Colm found it eerily silent. Beings who shold have been unloading or running maintenance check on the dozens of small ships and shuttles stood in small groups around the viewscreens and vid-tanks embedded in the walls. Usually those scopes ran a combination of ads, news and public service announcements, but the sole image, seen at different angles and distances, was the visitor from the Trade Union. Captain Sgarthad stood in front of the governor's mansion, smiling and waving, looking like he belonged there. Beside him stood a Wichu interviewer from *My Opinion Here,* a popular evening show that had gained as much as sixteen percent of the available audience, a huge percentage for a show when one considered the number of offerings across the Grid and the home broadcast spectrum.

". . . Captain Sgarthad," the Wichu was saying, her big eyes fixed adoringly on the human male. "What are your requirements from those of us here on Boske?"

The visitor looked intently at the lens, his eyes boring into those of every viewer across the world who was tuned into the Grid at that time. Colm studied the enormous face. He felt as if he trusted Sgarthad. "I am so glad you asked me. I am pleased by the way that you make me feel so welcome. I want all of you to stay here on the planet with me."

"What do you mean by that, Captain?"

The eyes locked on Colm, drawing him close. "There is nothing more important than remaining on Boske. Do not lift ship. Every ship should land immediately, for your own safety."

"Are we in danger, Captain?"

"You are all in terrible danger," Sgarthad said. "You have hidden enemies, and your security is at stake."

That declaration got the attention of the few remaining spacefarers, who broke off their conversations and nudged their fellows to turn toward the screens.

"From what? Who?" asked the Wichu female.

"I cannot reveal that to you yet. I must speak with your government first, and the council of the Cluster, which is meeting here at this time, to give them my warning and advice. Until then, no ships must lift from here or any other cluster world. Anyone of you who are flying should return to your planet of origin and remain there. Please go home where you will be safe."

Colm scoffed. *Now, why would I do that?* he thought.

Sgarthad pointed at the video pickup hovering before him and the Wichu. Colm thought he saw a flash of amber light.

"You might ask why you should obey my will. It would be a favor to me." And suddenly Colm felt as if he should do that favor for that good man. It would be a pleasure, the most natural thing in the world. After all, he was not preparing to leave the planet, or even the city itself. That ought to make Sgarthad happy. In fact, Colm thought, he should turn around and go back to his quarters. If there was danger, he should not be out in it. He had some puzzles to occupy him until the captain told him he could go out again. Colm started toward the entrance. Others were leaving, too. The visitor had persuaded them to do the right thing. They smiled at each other in satisfaction.

Colm caught a glimpse of himself in the silvered glass

of the door. The wide-eyed stupidity of his expression automatically made him frown. Something in his mind snapped free.

What am I thinking? That must be the effect of the device that Councillor DeKarn thought Sgarthad possessed. It was *that* powerful that it could sway a being as normally cynical as he. The mission, he must concentrate upon the mission. He stepped to one side and reversed his path, returning to the heart of the terminal. He tried to tune out the smooth, warm voice, audible to him even through the machine rattles and roars and the tenor hum of the ventilation system. Under other circumstances, he would love to honor Sgarthad's request. He wanted Sgarthad to be pleased with him.

But others had taken the visitor's request as an order.

"Attention please," a pleasant female voice said over the public address system and echoed from the personal combox or communicator of everyone within the building, "no one is to lift ship until further notice. All flights are hereby cancelled. Ground transport can be arranged at the ticket booths or via the Grid. Offworld transport will be rescheduled at a future time. Repeat . . ."

Instead of the collective "Awwww!" of disappointment followed by groans and profanity, Colm saw travelers pulling wheeled or antigrav bags behind them smile at one another. Pilots shrugged in resignation and went back to watching the viewscreens. Sgarthad was still talking, though Colm could no longer distinguish what he was saying, and probably neither could the others, but he felt an odd satisfaction in watching the man interact with those lucky people around him.

Colm shook himself fiercely. Sgarthad was a dangerous man! He must fulfill his errand, immediately.

Slipping through the surging countertide of passengers and personnel heading for the exit, he reached the pilots' lounge. It stood at the side of the terminal beside the attached hostel. The walls of the big, utilitarian common room were painted yellow-green. Shelves and lockers were available to stow gear while crews were in port. A broad bar with a polished gray metal counter top occupied almost one whole wall. Notices on paper, plasheet or emitted from miniature infochips clung to the walls everywhere, offering berths on ships, asking for cargo loads, seeking jobs. No one was reading the flyers. The small-craft captains sat together around a large, cluttered table, drinks in hand. The crews of the big freighters who didn't actually make landfall were nearer to the bar, considering themselves a cut above. All of them were intent upon the big screen on the wall opposite the bar. Colm surveyed the faces, dismissing stranger after stranger. To his relief, he saw a pilot he knew, Senthi Guaya, a human male about his age, also a competitive puzzler. Senthi wore a saffron-orange shipsuit. It must be his favorite. His competition clothes usually were the same color.

"Hey, down in front, fool!" spat a ruddy-faced female with grizzled hair in gray and scarlet. "You're blocking the screen!"

"Sorry, madam," Colm said, ducking below the bottom edge. He slid into the chair beside Senthi and nudged him hard in the ribs. "Hi, friend."

Surprised, Senthi turned to glare, but the ire cleared swiftly from his long, dark face. "Colm! Do you believe this man?" He aimed a thumb toward the screen.

Colm took a moment to assess his friend's expression. "I do," he said. "A good man, don't you think?"

"The best! He loves us. He *cares*. He wants us to be protected. Listen to him!"

Colm felt his face redden as the unbidden emotion swamped him again. "I *know*." He pulled himself together. "Senthi, have you got a cargo flight at the moment?"

Senthi waved a hand. "No, man, of course not. Didn't you hear Captain Sgarthad? All flights are cancelled. I can't go."

Colm recognized the signs of devotion. He felt them himself, but they must not interfere with his duty. Drastic measures were required. "Got a moment? Come with me, will you?"

He took Senthi's arm in a subtle grip that made it less painful to stand and follow than to try and pull loose. Senthi kept looking over his shoulder at the screen with a longing that did not cease until the door of the pilots' lounge slid shut behind them and cut off the view. Colm, too, felt a deep loss, but he had a job to do. For now he must forego the joy of becoming one of the thousands who found contentment in giving Sgarthad what he wanted. *Later,* he promised himself. Later he would go and join the happy throng on the mansion lawn.

"What's the problem, Colm?" Senthi asked. "Haven't seen you since the all-Boske crossword marathon."

"Been busy," Colm said with a grin. He glanced at the screen. Sgarthad's clear eyes were fixed upon someone to the left of the video pickup. It seemed to lift the guilt slightly. "Listen, friend, I have a small parcel I have to get off this world immediately. It's vital."

Senthi clicked his tongue sympathetically. "Can't do it, mate. Captain Sgarthad wants us to stay planetbound.

The government's behind him. You can just tell. Look, there's the governor, and some other beings in official robes. They're there to support him."

Not from what Colm saw. DeKarn looked furious. Now people were reading their own interpretation into what they saw. He hoped Councillor DeKarn realized it, too. "Please. Let's talk about theoretically when you can lift ship again. It's worth . . . what's your normal fee?"

Senthi eyed him. "Well, depends on where you're going."

Colm shrugged. "Say, Carstairs. Carstairs Five."

"How big is the parcel?"

"Sixty grams."

Senthi nodded. "Really small. Well, on a normal day it'd be about fifteen credits, for special transport and the trouble of taking care of a little item. I'd put it in my pressurized safe with my ship's documents, all but the license, of course, and deliver it private before anything else going that way. I'll guarantee it gets right to whoever you want."

"What would it take to get you to make a run to deliver this alone?" Colm asked urgently.

"You're gravity-bent, Colm." Senthi laughed. "No one makes a run for a sixty-gram load."

"How's fifteen hundred?" Colm countered.

That got an openmouthed stare. "What's that? That's as much as you won in the Cluster-wide number grid contest last year."

"It's yours if you take the load. Lift ship right now, and I'll pay you that much and more."

He must look too desperate. Senthi's eyes narrowed suspiciously. "What's in it?"

Colm sighed. "Advertisments," he said, sheepishly.

"My employer sold thousands of ads for..." He thought fast. "...X-Percol sleep inhalers. New and improved. They work better than anything else on the market. Eight hours of sleep and no side effects. It's worth millions to my employers to get this crystal to its destination." It was true that ads for X-Percol contained those claims. Its approval was currently before the council. "Those ads have to run."

Senthi's straight black brows rose a centimeter. "Millions, you say?"

"Only if the ads run *on time*. It has to get there, Senthi," Colm pleaded. "You're the only person I know I can count on. You've got one of the fastest ships in the Cluster, right?"

"*The* fastest," Senthi said with pride. "I beat Mitch Oll here from Dree by over four hours a couple of months ago. He's still stinging."

"Then you have to do it."

"Well..."

The door to the lounge slid open again and a Cocomon in a pale blue shipsuit came out, jabbering into his combox. Senthi and Colm caught sight of the screen. Sgarthad was still holding forth. Senthi's gaze was caught by his image like a fish on a hook. He put his hand in the door to keep it open. Colm felt the same longing. *I love that guy,* he thought. With an act of will, he grabbed Senthi's shoulder and turned him so neither of them was facing the screen.

"Hey!" Senthi protested.

"How about my cargo?" Colm asked. "It's got to go now. I will pay you on departure, but only if you head for your ship and lift off in the next quarter hour."

"All right, man. I'll do it," Senthi said, businesslike

once again. He strode toward the open hangar where the small ships received maintenance. Money had taken the place of the newfound devotion. "All right, mate. Sounds like a plan. Carstairs, you say?"

Colm waited until they were beside the independent one-being cargo ship, the *Whipcrack*. It had belonged to Senthi's mother, a successful trader, in her twenties. She owned four much larger vessels currently. She let Senthi have the *Whipcrack* to make his way in the world. He and Colm had discussed all this over various game boards. Senthi palmed open the hatch and beckoned Colm aboard. He led him to a reinforced bulkhead behind the pilot's compartment and opened a hatch in the wall. A case of document crystals was pushed to the back underneath a blast rifle and two high-powered sidearms. A few curios in transparent bags were scattered on the floor of the safe. He held out a hand for Colm's parcel, and stowed it with the others. The safe door hissed shut as it pressurized. Senthi started a pre-flight check on his scopes. Colm carefully stood in front of the Grid monitor, blocking off the sight of Sgarthad, now conferring with members of the council and the governor, Dr. Yuchiko.

"Everything's set," Senthi said, grinning up at him. "Where on Carstairs am I taking that?"

"File a plan for Carstairs," Colm said, "but once you're out of Portent's Star space, I want you to go here." He leaned forward and grabbed the man's combox out of his belt pouch, turned it over and wrote a series of coordinates on it with his stylus. "Take it to Dorie... there." He wrote an address underneath. "It's easy to find. She'll get it to the right being on time."

Senthi read it. He stared up at Colm, his big dark

eyes wide with shock. He gestured at the screen, at Sgarthad, who was smiling at them.

"You're crazy, man! I can't do that. He's ordered us to stay here. I can't go!" Senthi pointed at the screen. "I'm staying! I love that man!"

"Me, too," Colm admitted. "But you agreed."

Senthi stood up. "Forget it. We'll go to the governor's mansion instead and tell Captain Sgarthad that we're with him. Anything he wants. Come on."

Colm almost agreed, then the common-sense fairy that had been trying to keep its equilibrium in the midst of all this, got disgusted and kicked his conscience in the backside. He fixed his eyes intently on the pilot. "No, you have to keep going. We have a deal. Your mother would be proud. And your dad." Tino Guaya was a high official on Dree. As if thinking *father-figure*, they both looked at the screen. Turning away again was the hardest thing Colm had ever done. Senthi pushed him aside.

"No, I have to see him in person."

He stumbled out of the pilot's compartment and off the ship's ramp. Colm kept hold of his arm.

"Senthi, I'm counting on you. Don't flame out on me now."

"It would disappoint him! I can't do it! Let me go!"

To Colm's annoyance, their argument attracted attention of a group around the nearest viewscreen. Several large beings in shipsuits moved to form a protective arc behind the two males.

"This being bothering ye, Senthi?" asked a bulky man with green tattoos over his ebony face.

Guaya's eyes flicked wildly from face to face, always going back to the viewscreen. "He's trying to make me leave Boske!"

"He can't do that," said a Cocomon in a green shipsuit. "Orders have been given."

"I know!" Senthi exclaimed. "Captain Sgarthad wouldn't like it!"

They all looked at the screen.

Colm deliberately placed himself in front of it, eliciting protests from the rest and his own conscience.

"I'll double the fee," Colm whispered to Senthi, as the four largest males jumped on him. The Cocomon pilot closed its mandibles around Colm's wrist, its toothy projections jabbing his skin. A huge human male plumped down on his back, knocking the air out of his lungs. "Double!" he gasped. Senthi stared down at him, torn between self-interest and fascination.

"You promise?" Senthi said.

"I do," Colm asserted, though every syllable used up precious oxygen. Blackness edged his vision and threatened to swamp it. The man sitting on him seemed to take on weight by the second. He held on to consciousness and Senthi's gaze with all his will. It seemed like forever before Senthi spoke.

"Nay, he's not bothering me." Senthi gave an apologetic glance at the screen behind them. He offered a hand to Colm. "Let him up. He won't cause any more trouble."

The Cocomon rolled his big eyes up. "Are you sure?"

"Aye."

The other pilots rose reluctantly. The heavy man on Colm's back was the last to rise. The crew drifted back to the viewscreen. Colm gasped in air and leaned against the *Whipcrack*.

"My mother has never had a fee like that," Senthi said. "Double, you say?"

Colm glanced at the others. They had forgotten all about him.

"I did. Half now," Colm said. He moved close so his face filled Senthi's vision. "Dorie will give you the other half. Go now. Please hurry."

"Won't be a fast trip, you know. I might miss the City Race Contest. That's weeks off, but you know what it's like in between jumps."

"There's always next year. This is more than first prize, than all the prizes combined."

Senthi gave him an embarrassed grin. "Well, suppose I can't be greedy."

He glanced over Colm's shoulder at the screen, and his face went blank.

"Oh, no, not again," Colm said. He pushed Senthi up the ramp into the ship.

"Hey, help! What are you doing?" Senthi demanded, then gave him a sheepish grin over his shoulder. "Oh, wait. Okay, man. I'm sorry."

"It's fine. Captain Sgarthad would want you to take this trip for him."

"He would? That's what I hope."

Colm helped him into the pilot's couch and strapped him in. Senthi immediately began the preflight check.

"Captain's log, fuel gauges full, all pressurization is on green and ready to go. Ultra-drive engines at ninety-eight-percent efficiency." That was the best one could hope for in a vintage ship, Colm reflected. "Attention, tower, this is *Whipcrack.* T minus ten minutes and counting."

"What? What?" came a sputtered cry from master control. "Where do you think you're going?"

"Carstairs, tower. As ordered, going home." Senthi

gave Colm a cocky grin. "All bills have been paid with ship's license number..."

With Senthi busy, Colm slipped over to the unusued navigator's station and logged into the ship's computer. He used his council codes to override the video and audio input. He disconnected input from the tower. The protests cut off and were replaced by machine chatter and music.

"What do you say, tower?" Senthi demanded, listening hard, his hands crawling over the controls.

"Bzzz bzz bzz bzzzzz-whirrrr!"

"Curse it, that's AI lingo! Did the Standard language circuit cut out again? I just replaced it!"

Colm shrugged in sympathy. On the main screentank, instead of the local news starring the Trade Union captain, the Grid was now locked onto a channel showing ancient digitavid dramas about a wealthy, extended family and the devoted electronic beings that served them. Once he was offworld Senthi would find the locked circuit and put it right, hopefully *long* after he had lifted ship and made his first ultra-drive jump.

"They said, 'good to go,'" Colm said. He held out his personal communicator, showing the promised sum. He hit send, and the numbers vanished from the screen. A *ping* at Senthi's waist said that it had been transferred to the pilot's file. "Here's the first half of your fee. I'd better get off or I'm going all the way with you."

"Multi-chess tournament when I get back?" Senthi asked.

Colm grinned. "You've got it. Safe journey."

He swung out of the hatch just as it slammed shut and sealed. The ship shot ten meters off the pad before the other spacers on the ground noticed that it was moving.

"Attention, please, *Whipcrack*! Return to your pad immediately. You are not cleared for Carstairs! Repeat, you are not cleared for Carstairs!"

Colm hoped fervently they wouldn't resort to weaponry to bring Senthi down again, but he didn't know how powerful Sgarthad's secret hold was on the minds of his fellow beings. Away from the influence of the visitor's image, people might return to their own senses. It was a piece of data he wished he had had time to record into the package, but there had not been time. He hoped the information he included was enough.

He had to get back to the councillor before she needed him again and noticed he was missing. No sense in building up a reputation as being infallible if one wasn't there to reinforce it. In the meanwhile, he had to find out what he could about that hypnosis device and means to combat it. With a wistful glance over his shoulder, he headed for the public transportation hub. He had plenty of research to do.

❧ CHAPTER 8 ❧

Even though the artificial gravity was turned on in the shuttle bay, I felt as if I was floating. The small craft that nestled there was a marvel of efficiency over art. Not a square centimeter occupied its trim frame. Her name, enameled upon the hull forward of the main hatch, was *CK-M945B*. True, there was little euphony in the designation, but it held music for my ears.

When Parsons had informed me I was to command a small cutter for a mission heretofore to be revealed, I cajoled him for every detail—none of which was forthcoming, of course. All I could do was read up on the statistics of all the scout crafts currently in use in the Imperial Space Navy. That amounted to some sixty designs. It had seemed like a high data mountain to scale, until I realized I knew at least that many standard personal spacecraft used by my peers among the nobility. Under the Imperium's policy, we nobles were all given generous allowances. I had bought myself an asteroid-bouncer or two with

147

a few months' proceeds, and modified them as far as my pocketbook would allow for efficiency as well as beauty. There were fewer upgrades or changes among the naval craft, none of them for aesthetics, which made them easier to learn.

I was delighted to see that before me stood a Nexus Mark XV. The model had been brought on line only eighteen months before, making it absolute cutting edge for the navy. The Mark XV had been made to move and maneuver with the least amount of thrust. Its blue-white hull had a vertical oval cross-section, fanning out to a wide oval on the horizontal at the stern. Its nose looked rather human, slanting down from the top more swiftly than up from the bottom, making room for sensors and a superior repulsor net array. The hull was sealed with matt enamel over fourteen centimeters thick over a core of titanium-ceramic that could repel heat weapons as well as missiles up to fifteen-hundred megatons per square centimeter, should anything penetrate its repulsor shield, an upgraded system that had received the highest safety scores. Its ultra-drive, the three emitters emerging from the stern, kicked into maximum acceleration six seconds quicker than the next speediest scout craft, giving one a head start from orbit against an enemy craft. Those seconds could save lives. In the same vein, its life-support systems were so tightly sealed that it could run on an emergency battery for eight weeks or more, a necessity I hoped fervently I would not have to test.

"She's beáutiful, Parsons," I breathed.

"Of course, sir," he said, calmly. "Shall we prepare to depart? The crew is waiting."

"By Forn, yes, the crew!" I exclaimed. I couldn't understand his lack of excitement. This was a brand new ship at the top of the line. We were going to be the first to fly her on a mission. But Parsons was inscrutable. I had never understood him, not since I was a child, but now was not the time to begin probing the depths of his mystery. Instead, I turned to my new command.

The scout held a maximum crew of fifteen, but could be run by two. I had assumed that previous evening when I left the admiral's presence that those two would be Parsons and myself. To my delight, when I read my assignment off my personal information device, I found that I was being assigned a further crew of four, their names and designations supplied. I had read their dossiers with deep interest. Not only that, I had been given the names of the militia members I was scheduled to review. I perused those as well. A good commander, my great-uncle Perleas often remarked, knew his own soldiers as well as he knew himself. These were mine only as proxy, but I wished to represent Admiral Podesta in a manner that would make him proud—and would keep him from sending an angry note to my mother.

I was so excited about my upcoming assignment that only once did I think about the realization that I had been released from punishment detail, and that I was free to go and socialize with my rank peers. A moment's rue for the excellent tri-tennis court, and I delved back into the various files at my disposal. It would still be there upon my return. I wanted to be absolutely prepared. Little sleep visited my cabin during the so-called dark shift.

The crewbeings assigned to this mission stood by the hatch, arms behind their backs, eyes staring out straight ahead. Two humans, a Wichu and an Uctu, all in full military dress as Parsons and I were. To my great annoyance, the white stripe had been removed from the side of all the trousers in my wardrobe and replaced it with the medium gray-blue of an ensign's rank. The stitching was flawless, so I suspected that one of the robotailors on board had been put to work when I left the cabin for one of my allowed purposes. Still, at my side was a formal naval officer's sword that had belonged to my father and his father before him, dating back in the family over four thousand years. To that I was most certainly entitled. I rested my palm upon the ornate gold hilt and imagined it singing the rolls of my ancestry.

"Good afternoon, crew!" I exclaimed. They erupted in crisp salutes. I returned them. "At ease." As one, they put their hands behind them and stepped out sideways with their right feet. I walked down the row. As it was a very brief trip, I reversed and made the return journey, just so I could feel that I had really done a review. They looked just as I had seen them imaged in their files: Navigator and Helm Officer Indiri Oskelev, Wichu; Fire Control Officer Amuk Rous, Uctu, midshipman; executive officer Lieutenant Carissa Plet, and Engineer Ensign Omicron Bailly, whose wide blue eyes revealed the same unbridled enthusiasm for the ship as I felt. I suddenly experienced a wave of affection for them—*my* crew.

This was far too good an opportunity to miss. From my trouser pocket, I removed my finest camera, the Optique Callusion. It had been made by Harfourn, was the best optical capture device currently available anywhere in the Imperium. I felt that it was a better model than the Fren Omulsion 9.1, that came from the Trade Union and was marketed to the same upscale, discerning customers as the Callusion, but lacked a few of what I considered key features, such as individual color enhancement, and I suspected contained a bug or two which would permit images to be transmitted against the photographer's attention straight to listening or looking devices in Trade Union satellites. As a loyal subject of the Imperium, I eschewed Trade Union goods unless there was no homegrown alternative. Besides, the Optique's lenses were superior. Also, its storage was on a platinum-hair matrix that would be able to retain an enormous quantity videos and single images that would last the length of my mission.

I tossed the small orb into the air and ran to set myself in the middle of my crew.

"Parsons!" I cried, beckoning to him. "Parsons, come and get in the picture."

"Thank you, my lord, but I will decline," Parsons said austerely. "Our launch window is in sixteen minutes. There is no time for hobbies."

"There is always time for recording an occasion," I chided him. He stood just out of range of a 360° shot, and no doubt the clever man knew it. No matter. I flung my arms around the necks of the two nearest crewmembers. "Smile!"

The platinum orb emitted a near-blinding flash of light. The Gecko's pupils contracted to pinpoints and he made a face, but the others managed a game smile. I signaled the camera to take a second exposure, but a dark-looming shadow with Parsons's outline appeared before me, blocking the best of the light.

"It is time to go, sir," he said. He turned me with a firm hand toward the hatch. However, he failed to secure my camera, which I had trained to avoid capture by anyone but me, and it trailed along after us, taking video and still pictures for my scrapbook and Infogrid file. I felt my heart swell with pride. My first assignment! What a success it would be! I would make my mother glad that she had produced such a son.

As the ensign-captain of the *CK-M945B,* I sat in the command couch in the center rear of the control room, but the navigation and helm duties were taken by Oskelev. She looked back over her shoulder at me. I sat back against the padding, so new it still had that fresh-from-the-factory chemical aroma, wanting to relish the moment, when a sharp "Ahem!" from Parsons stole all the wind from my sails. I swiveled my chair upright.

"Please take us out, Helm," I instructed.

I was accustomed by then to the vast emptiness of space. The Imperium occupied thousands of stars of the Milk Galaxy, an ancient spiral with many smaller sub-spirals that had given humanity and our fellow species birth. The home planet of humanity, Earth, had been outgrown millennia ago, and its exact location lost in the annals of history as we fled outward, scarcely looking back over our shoulder. The astronomy press published vidlets and articles from time to time claiming that they had found the true Earth, but I, like most of my generation, took these claims with an ocean's worth of salt. At first, when we discovered the first non-humanoid race, the location of our home planet was kept secret as a security measure.

Then, over time, it got lost in the shuffle. I know it sounds ridiculous to think an entire system could be mislaid like an earring, but when one considers the enormous quantity of type-E systems with a combination of rocky and gaseous planets circling a dwarf yellow star, it would take some impressive proof to combat the cynicism. Adding to the confusion, not a few hoax planets had been dummied up to look like Earth, with imported native animals and multilayered ruined buildings. A couple of them had been so impressively realistic that they had spawned Return to Earth cults.

But I digress.

Space only looked empty. Matter existed everywhere, even if in microscopic quantities, and energy, including black holes, took up more of the map than humankind had ever thought before it ventured out among the stars. Those flaming balls of gas were mere pinpoints when one left atmosphere. Some twinkled, the result of planets or other solids passing between them and the viewer, but most simply shone their cool, muted light. The rest was darkness. Quite a lot less of matter was shiny or luminescent than humans were accustomed to. It was not necessary to see out of modern spacecraft, and the sensors didn't require light to navigate or avoid obstacles. Still, we beings with eyes like to look out of the window, so the viewers were set to collect and enhance what visible images there were. The computer navigator did most of the boring work. We went down the Sullenburger Preflight

Safety Protocol, checking it against the internal alarm screen. All green. Ensign Oskelev skimmed the craft neatly out of the bay and into the enveloping darkness.

Lt. Plet nodded to me from the communications console. "Log recording began as of departure. *Wedjet* wishes us a good journey. Updates to be posted to the mothership every hour."

"Thank you, XO," I said. I promised myself I would have nothing untoward to report. My mission would be as clean and uncomplicated as Podesta expected it to be.

"I reviewed the alerts circulating about sighting of enemy craft in the area, potential star-spots, ion storms and dust clouds. Ion storm will be one and one half light years off our route but moving towards us. It may be an issue upon our return to the *Wedjet*. A cruiser stolen from Vijay Nine is believed to be a prank by university students on midyear break. It was reported outbound toward galactic north twenty-four days ago. As it is an armed vessel, the navy would like any sightings reported immediately. Suspected pirate craft with configurations matching these that I am loading to your personal device have been spotted in our destination area. Thirty Trade Union vessels or other suspect ships have been noted in the sector. All TU vessels have registered legal flight plans, and none are scheduled to be near us."

"Thank you, Lieutenant Plet. Well done." I opened the file she sent me and made note of the ships being sought. I chuckled to myself over the cruiser. It was a joke worthy of me and my cousins in our school days. I wish we'd dared be as bold as to make off with a Navy ship. It would have been a great tale to tell the great-grandchildren one day. In fact, since Vijay was one of the core worlds, the pranksters might be some of my distant relatives. They would get off with a heavy fine and a scolding, so as not to embarrass the Emperor by throwing his cousins in prison. The second ship gave me pause. Pirates rarely traveled alone, preferring to overpower a victim by sheer force of numbers when it came out of ultra-drive at the edge of a system, but the occasional rogue vessel did operate from time to time. The report indicated that this was the only craft of the putative fleet that had been identified. No more had been seen. I put both indicators onto my alert file at the top of my mission chart, immediately under my primary orders. "By the way, I observe from your file that you are a shadow-handball player. Care to have a game once we're on our way? I do realize that you outrank me militarily and invitations should technically come from you to me, but I am being bold."

Plet took a sidelong glance at Parsons, which irritated me slightly, since I was the CO on this vessel, but I made a note to myself that his naval rank was higher than any of ours. We were an odd mix of ranks—I occupied a middle rung of the ladder—and I meant to ask Parsons why these particular officers had been assigned to me when we had a private moment later on.

"Why, thank you, Ensign-Captain Kinago," Plet said, gravely. "I'd enjoy it."

My happiness threatened to fountain upward, but I kept the joy within. Remaining captainlike, I turned to the rest of my crew. "The challenge is extended to the rest of you as well," I said. "We have two days until we reach our destination. It'll be more fun than standard PE. And I will trounce you all thoroughly."

"You're on!" Bailly said cheerfully. I spun to face his station, which stood almost exactly behind mine.

"I, too!" exclaimed Rous. "Such a challenge will be most enjoyable." Oskelev only smiled and shook her head. I had known she didn't play shadow-handball, but there would be time for board games later, amusements that I did know she enjoyed.

Taking my ease with my hands behind my head, I grinned up at Parsons, who had taken a couch adjacent to my chief engineer. I planned to enjoy every moment of my assignment. It was going to be a good time.

❊ CHAPTER 9 ❊

Councillor DeKarn sat in the reception room of the Imperium ambassador's suite in the south wing of the governor's mansion with her hands folded in her lap, exhausted. With some difficulty they had managed to herd the Trade Union party off the statue and into the north wing of the mansion. The visitor had been overwhelmingly polite and full of regrets.

"I can't help it if people want to speak with me," Sgarthad had said, bowing over DeKarn's hand and smiling at her. That face. That astonishingly appealing face. She liked him in spite of his audacity—or perhaps because of it. His eyes spoke to her. They said, *You and I are beings of the world. How we could enjoy one another's company if only we were alone!* She doubted that he meant anything of the sort. It was the effect of whatever method he had used to seduce the entire Yolk council and not a few of the other members. However, she was not going to allow anyone to derail the authority of the Castaway Cluster. Though she had few of the other councillors behind her, she forced Governor Yuchiko to take Sgarthad into custody. They followed to ensure that he would be comfortable but no longer in the public eye, until the council had figured out what it wanted to do. Once that had been accomplished, it would know how to treat both the Trade Union and the Imperium.

His people, thankfully, did not seem to cast that same spell over the crowd. Once he was out of sight, though the stern-faced staff that had surrounded him on his impromptu platform was still outside, smiles disappeared from the faces of the citizens of Pthohannix, and they dispersed without any further prompting. So if he was carrying a device or a chemical compound that caused the crowd to fall in love with him, it was specific to him. That meant they only had to keep *him* away from the public.

However, he was gone, but not forgotten. Not three minutes elapsed between the time Sgarthad was escorted into the luxurious quarters and the first message from the first "fan group" erupted on her personal communicator and those of her fellow councillors. She soon had to turn off the quiet pinging that indicated messages arriving because they continued on and on. Her last glimpse at the small screen showed that over fourteen thousand notes were awaiting her attention. Typically, they were not deeply thoughtful missives. The message line on the fifth one read, "Free the handsome guy!" When she had a moment, DeKarn needed to choose a macro from the hundred thousand available in her communication pad to go through her mail and weed out the knee-jerk letters from those who only enlisted in a grassroots campaign for any cause that seemed to be against basic liberties. Closing her Grid address to incoming mail was out of the question as an administrator, not to mention against the law.

The device vibrated against her hip as she rose to offer a hand to the woman who approached her. Ambassador Hiranna Ben was short of stature, plumpish, and silver-haired. For the third time that day DeKarn had to cope with the small shock of seeing a face devoid of any decoration, save for a touch of color definition at eyes and lips.

"Thank you for seeing me, Ambassador," DeKarn said.

"Councillor, it is my pleasure," Ben replied, taking her hand warmly in both of her small palms. She patted it. "Now, my mission here is no secret. I will not ask you and your colleagues to rush, not when it took me such a long time to travel here, but if you have an inkling as to the timeline we are looking at before I may have an answer I can take back to his majesty, it would take a good deal of suspense out of my wait."

So nicely put, DeKarn thought, with regret. "Ambassador, I regret to say that this body has never reached a trivial conclusion in a short time. Important ones stretch out into spans of time that try the patience of even the greatest pragmatist. I wish that I could be more optimistic, but due to circumstances we could not foresee—"

"Yes, I saw him. Quite a dish. He could almost be a digitavid star, couldn't he? He reminds me a little of one of my ex-lovers, though they were never so good-looking."

DeKarn laughed ruefully. "That is almost exactly what I thought when I saw him! He is only one of the obstacles. One of our contingents arrived late, escorted by Captain Sgarthad, as it happens, as their vessel was damaged in transit from their system to this. Portent's Star is the closest of the eight Castaways to the black hole, and anomalies are not uncommon. But I will be unusually frank: this discussion has gone on since..." her voice trailed off, as she tried to think of a courteous way to say *since the Imperium abandoned us,* but Hiranna Ben just nodded sweetly.

"I know. Take your time. If deliberations go on past my expected life span, I will send for a replacement. His Majesty is patient, as you have been. It is most gracious of you to consider his offer at all in light of the Imperium's... long silence. But this is an outward-reaching monarch. He seeks to bring concerns long neglected to the fore. You would like him. He is rare even among those who have ascended the throne."

"You are most kind," DeKarn said.

"Will you visit me once in a while to tell me... what you are permitted to tell me of your discussions?" Ben asked.

"I would be happy to."

"And if you have nothing to tell me, I would love to have you visit, so I can learn more about your culture. Some differences are immediately evident, and intriguing."

DeKarn smiled and rose. "That would be my pleasure. I apologize that you will be so isolated."

"I am used to long periods of solitude," Ben said, placidly. "I travel alone very well, as you see. There are a pair of AIs on my ship that I must communicate with to let them know of the delay, but you can monitor that transmission."

DeKarn was embarrassed. "I am sure that you can send that message."

Ben showed her the console on the ornate, spindly legged table under the window. "Ah, no, as you see."

The message window, which ought to have been light green for voice and visuals, was a dark fuchsia, indicating that the function was locked. Ben stood with her back pointedly to the console while DeKarn entered her council code. The screen turned green. Ben spoke a brief message, and received a reply instantly of fweeps, bongs and static. The screen turned pink again at once.

"Thank you," she said. "Now, don't let me keep you. It was good of you to visit."

"You are too kind," DeKarn said. "I will see you again soon."

But it was weeks before they met again.

"Ah, there you are, First Councillor!" Ruh Pinckney exclaimed as DeKarn entered the long hall leading to the council chamber. "We did not have a chance to offer proper greetings to you when we arrived yesterday." He beckoned Urrmenoc, the Wichu, forward. Her arms were full of packages. "We bear gifts to our siblings of Portent's Star. I believe you wear a seven shoe?"

"You are much too kind," DeKarn said, struggling to hold the boxes as they were thrust at her. "It is far more than my colleagues and I deserve."

"Oh, these are all for you," Pinckney said, beaming. "The rest of the councillors have already been given their tokens."

DeKarn turned to find a place to put the boxes, and found a many-shelved mechanical waiting with claw-hands outthrust to accept them. It arranged all the parcels according to size along with dozens of other brightly wrapped packages, then glided discreetly away toward a niche in the wall too low for humans or Cocomons to walk through comfortably. "Thank you, all of you, siblings of Yolk. I see that it is the appointed hour. Shall we begin today's session?"

"Yes, indeed," Pinckney said. He offered her an arm. "It would be my honor to escort you."

Vasily Marden was on his feet almost before the image of the floating gavel crashed down upon the table with a satisfying though prerecorded *bang!*

"Point of order, First Councillor," he said. "I move that since circumstances have forced our hand, that we keep both the envoy from the Trade Union and the Imperium's ambassador in full media isolation until this body has decided the question of loyalty."

"I must protest!" exclaimed Tam Quelph, rising indignantly. "As I and my colleagues protest the inhospitable behavior we displayed toward our rescuer yesterday! How dare you sweep him into a *cell* before the very eyes of the entire Cluster?"

"An eight-room suite is hardly a cell," Barba Linden said dryly, with a humorous glance toward DeKarn. "Even you have to admit he excites talk."

"What's wrong with that?" Urrmenoc asked.

"Because it would be wrong for him to prejudice the public toward his offer without giving equal time to both other possibilities we are debating," Zembke said. "This is not a referendum. We have been entrusted with the final authority to decide with whom we will ally, or not. Pending full discussion and resolution, neither of them should be seen on any Grid programs or other media. They can emerge when our decision is made." The Yolkovians protested as one, and huge pictures of the Trade Union captain appeared behind them. Impatiently, DeKarn hit the override control, and cleared every screen in the room.

"He is a distraction, my friends. We must have clear minds for this discussion. Will anyone move for a vote?"

"I do," Linden said, raising her hand.

"Seconded," Marden said, his face sour.

"In favor?" DeKarn asked. Eight lights went on at once. Slowly and in some cases reluctantly others followed, until thirty votes had been cast. "Against?" she asked, though it was pro forma. The remaining ten, all of Yolk plus a few of those who had clearly fallen in love with Sgarthad, voted no. "It is carried. Now, can we go on from the point at which we left off yesterday? Councillor Rengin, will you read from the minutes?"

Rengin rose to his feet. "Honored fellow members of the council..."

DeKarn settled herself into a comfortable position. When Rengin began with a deep intake of breath, it was going to be a long speech. She propped her chin on her fist and commanded her eyelids to stay up.

"...Therefore, I move that we halt for lunch," Councillor Bruke said, the last of nine councillors to speak. He sank heavily into his chair. DeKarn shook herself thankfully.

"Seconded?" she asked the council. Several members illuminated their voting lights. "So moved." She slammed her gavel down on the desk.

"Did it really have to take ten minutes to propose that?" Six asked, with a lift of one elegant eyebrow.

The eldest councillor smiled patiently at him. "One wants things done in the proper form, my lad."

DeKarn palm-locked the console and rose. Nothing had yet been decided, but that was unsurprising. She estimated the minimum of two sixdays and maximum of . . . infinity. It was possible that her colleagues would never agree to anything, not even raising Zembke to the position of speaker to the envoys. The interim votes on affiliation had been slightly toward independence. She had to convince herself she was not already tired of all of them. A quiet yogurt in a corner of the council lunchroom was all she wanted. Five started automatically to follow her, but she waved him off. The doors to the chamber opened out onto the anteroom. A figure rose majestically to its feet from a chair facing the entry.

"My friends!" Sgarthad exclaimed, coming toward them with his arms outstretched. "You must all join me for lunch! I have a delightful repast prepared!"

DeKarn regarded him with shock. She rounded upon the Yolkovian contingent. "What is he doing out again?"

"We called for his release," Pinckney said, firmly. He moved to shake the visitor's hand. "What a delight to see you again, Captain! I trust you passed a comfortable night?"

"Sumptuous," Sgarthad said, expansively. "Such fine quarters. I'll never be content in a way-station merchants' hotel again." Councillors crowding around him laughed when he laughed. "Come, friends! Don't let the food get cold!"

He led the way. The majority of the council fell into line, beaming, obviously delighted to be in his presence. They were enthralled by him. DeKarn thought of summoning Colm to see what he had learned, but decided to do so in private. They must figure out the source of his hold on people. It was becoming . . . annoying.

The weeks that followed were no less annoying. Though Ambassador Ben placidly stayed unseen in her quarters, Sgarthad continued to slip out of his so-called secure suite whenever he felt like it. He made appearances on all the major opinion shows. He and his crew were viewed seeing the local sights, and asked what they thought of the city-state. They were followed everywhere they went by thousands of fascinated beings. Merchandise with his image was brought out on the Grid and in the shops dotted through Pthohannix and gradually spread to the other population centers. So much for maintaining anonymity pending a council decision. Protests erupted, some of them violent, when the governor was forced to send out politely apologetic agents to bring Sgarthad back to the mansion. Keeping him bottled up was futile, though she persisted in invoking the council ruling. He was dangerous; she sensed that, as did some of her fellows.

Yuchiko never complained about Sgarthad or his fellow Trade Unionists, but he did bring an official protest to the council about the grounding of inter-planetary travel filed by a number of cargo companies.

"They are worried about their finances," he said.

"This is ridiculous!" Zembke erupted. "We didn't order a closure! It must have come from the Imperium."

But Rengin and others could prove that no new missives had arrived from the Core Worlds since before the ambassador had arrived. In fact, no information was being sent over the local Grid or through its interface with the Imperium's Infogrid.

In an effort to speed up the council's decision, DeKarn herself proposed that both envoys be allowed to speak before them. Over the course of time, more and more of the members had begun to fall under the Trade Union captain's glamour. She was outvoted overwhelmingly. In fact, she began to avoid calling for votes on alliance. Colm Banayere had not come through with any information on the cause of the general fascination—too small a word, she knew—and until she had it, she was afraid that that vote would be swayed by artificial means. Only a few of them, Zembke, Marden, Linden, Six and herself, seemed to be immune—or, at least, less enchanted by the visitor.

She had also been unable to interview the crew of the *Little Darling*. Though Sgarthad promised her and any member of the council unfettered access to the survivors, it was always inconvenient or technically difficult to allow them on board the *Marketmaker* to see them. It seemed that the crew of the small ship had disappeared into the bowels of the TU ship and was never seen again. Another mission for Colm, once he was finished with his present research.

Captain Sgarthad also made it a point to appear at the council chambers at least once a day, most often when the committee had broken for lunch. From the private dining room, the event expanded to a local hotel restaurant, then a banquet center, all the better for members of the public who could not get enough of this visiting celebrity to drop by and pose for images taken by giggling friends.

She and the holdouts joined the party as seldom as they could without drawing attention to themselves. Sgarthad's influence was growing, not only in the council but among members of the public. Somehow a whisper had gotten started that he might become a permanent resident of Boske. The Grid filled up with speculations, passionate pleas, even bribes; offers of homes, vacation residences, loans or outright gifts of personal vehicles, and many offers that were so openly indelicate that DeKarn blushed as she deleted them.

Worse yet, Sgarthad was aware that he had failed to win her approval. She didn't like him. She did not understand why he was so popular. Zembke was openly scornful of Sgarthad's attempts to persuade them over to his point of view. He knew a few of the councillors were against him, or at least holding the line on what position of authority he could occupy.

As far as the general public was concerned, over eighty percent were ready to name him dictator for life. Subtle mentions began to appear in the opinion press that the council should grant him a position. Over the following weeks, the suggestions grew stronger, with advice to get in touch with one's representatives at state and planetary level and tell them what to do. Once Boske ennobled him, reaching out to the other Castaway systems was the next logical step. Though with communications cut off, all but what was allowed by the Trade Union captain, no doubt a whisper campaign or something more direct had already begun.

Even Colm had joined the Sgarthad faction. Of all her employees, she thought he was the least likely to go in for hero worship, but there was that face on Colm's office screen when it was idle. All the others had at least one image of the captain on their personal communicators. They giggled together until she approached one of them, then the giddy expression vanished into one of disapproval. DeKarn began to feel isolated. Who could she trust now?

She became aware of eyes on her as she went about her business outside of the council chamber. Her popularity polls fell. Angry pundits published articles and interviews demanding that she be recalled from office, or at least opposed when the next election came along.

❊ CHAPTER 10 ❊

"Margolies, sir, Sergeant, Campbell Q.," said the first individual in response to my query for his name. The truth be told, I already knew it. I had matched his image to the file I had read aboard the *Wedjet* and reviewed that morning before our hatch was unsealed.

The review was being conducted in the huge bubble that was the hangar for mining equipment on the largest asteroid—a planetoid, really—in the Smithereen sector of the belt. A gas giant had exploded at one time in prehistory, possibly when it was attempting to ignite into a second sun in the system, leaving a field of debris especially rich in transuranics. The field of the Imperium's influence narrowed to a few dozen light years beyond it, with the Uctus on one side and the Trade Union on the other, each wishing it had claimed this sector first. Hence its commercial and strategic importance.

Smithereen Prime had eight hangars, all busy. Enormous cranes carried containers of unprocessed ore from the mining ships, and processed ore to ships departing from the system. I had noted from my reading that this was a popular transshipment point for settlements in the galactic north of the Imperium as well as to the core worlds. We made a tiny group in the midst of the vast enclosed space of number five hangar, beside our scout ship, which was the most minute of the ships currently present. I felt even smaller compared with what I could see above me. Beyond the slight blue glow of the settlement's forcefield, I saw stars given a hint of a twinkle by the minuscule though toxic atmosphere that Smithereen Prime attracted.

I gasped with wonder as I saw a scatter of faint white dots soaring upward. Could that be a meteor shower, outbound from atmosphere? Hastily, I deployed my small camera to take pictures of it. I heard the rasp of the tiny globe's shutter (a recorded sound-effect; cameras were programmed to make a noise because it had been proved by successful marketers that humans need a somatic, aural or visual signal to accept that a machine has activated.) as it focused in upon the quadrant I designated. Meteor showers were considered lucky by my ancestral house. Pleased with the omen as well as the unexpected sight, I ordered the camera to return to hover just above and behind my right shoulder, taking snaps of each of the soldiers as I greeted them.

The militia, consisting of fifty or so beings of all races, genders and ages above majority, had arranged itself in two long rows, beginning at the bottom of my ship's ramp, no doubt so I could go stride and back with an eye toward departing as soon as was possible. I sensed that the Smithereenians had gotten used to a dilatory visit over the years, and found that notion deplorable. My crew had debarked behind me and stood at attention, awaiting my pleasure. I had beaten Bailly three games out of four at handball, and looked forward to trouncing him similarly on the way home. The defeats hadn't lessened his enthusiasm at all. Plet had beaten me six to five. She remained implacably formal, though I believe we had reached a state of mutual respect. All the Kinago charm was wasted upon her.

I was turned out to the very best possible of the combined efforts of Parsons and myself. I wore my ancestor's sword and my great-grandfather's sidearm, both polished to blinding gleams, and every thread of my uniform was in pristine order. I positively glowed beside the objects of my scrutiny who, if they had uniforms, wore hand-me-downs that had passed through a considerable number of hands since leaving the factory. Not a few of the volunteer soldiers shuffled embarrassed feet and tucked in belt ends and snapped closed flapping pockets before I reached them. The pulse rifles and combination pistols at their sides were as mismatched and scarred. The two armored suits standing hollow but at attention beside their operators had to have come from a BidWay auction. But in truth, I saw no flaws worth remarking; they were my first militia, and I was proud to be there with them.

"Margolies," I said, returning the salute of the large-jawed man in the dark green coveralls. "How is your wife? I believe the two of you just had a son? Three and a half kilos?"

Margolies grinned, the corners of his jaw lifting the round and slightly weathered apples of his cheeks.

"Yes, that's right. They're both doing fine, sir. Boy's a bruiser like me. Wife didn't mind birthing him the old way."

"You should be proud, Sergeant," I said, marched on to the next soldier in line. The captain of the militia, a meaty human female named Olga Chan, preceded me by one decorous pace. Parsons was starboard off my elbow and ten degrees aft, the perfect placement as an aide-de-camp. I kept my hands behind my back in the manner of sea captains of ancient Earth, which, alas, allowed the sword of my ancestors to bang rhythmically against my leg. I made a mental note to consult Parsons later on how to prevent that. I noticed his sword was not beating a tattoo on him. I alternately sweated and shivered in the hangar, as the heating coils in the floor and around the landing hatches fought their neverending battle against the cold of space. I hoped that the volunteers could not see the beads of sweat that I feared were gathering upon my brow.

I halted before a slim woman with dark, curly hair and liquid, caramel-brown eyes. "Hamadi? Quite an achievement to take top honors in your correspondence school degree, on top of your job and family. Half my peers didn't manage an ordinary degree, even when they showed up to class. And not one late paper, in spite of the time delay in transmission. Well done! Will you be moving back toward the Imperium Core Worlds to practice?"

"No, sir," the slim woman said, her cheeks flushing maroon with pleasure. "I want to practice law before the industrial tribunal here."

"Well done, well done," I said, swaggering down the file.

"Ahem," came the inevitable voice of enforced humility. Parsons, after the fashion of Caesar's chariot slaves, reminding me that I was mortal. I slowed my step and tried to regain the sense that I was not there for my own aggrandizement, but for the sake of the Imperium in general and Admiral Podesta in particular. Still, I felt high as a communications satellite. My peers at home would be doing nothing like this. Poor creatures! They would have to be resigned to their tours of duty in luxurious conditions among the same people that they always saw, amid sights that had to be growing intolerably familiar as the months passed. I, understandably, felt smug, but I kept it to myself.

With a touch of imposed humility, I continued along my review. "Hek-et-rahm, is it?"

"Yes, sir!" exclaimed a beefy Wichu with a foreshortened nose and taupe fur.

I wrinkled my brow. "Of the grocery store chain Hek-et-rahms? Sixty-two systems and growing, isn't it?"

"Yes!" The Wichu looked as pleased as his fellows had that I knew something about him. The pupils of his large eyes spread to fill more of the purple iris. "I source minerals for the corporation, sir."

"That's good business, soldier," I acknowledged. Funny how often the reception of imparting knowledge depended on context. If I'd spouted off all these facts about one of my peer group, I'd be accused of oneupsmanship. Here, I was seen as taking an interest. I liked this situation rather better.

I sensed that as I progressed, the volunteer soldiers were listening closely to what I said. I caught cheeky grins on the faces and heard whispers behind my back. My internal ridicule alarm sounded. I thought they disapproved, but by the pass along the second row, I realized they were listening with pleasure and speculating on whether I would make a mistake. *Well, I will show you how they do things on the Imperium home world,* I thought, rising to the challenge in the name of all the Kinagos and Loches.

"Torkadir," I said, smiling into the bearded face. The man was tall, thirty-ish, and had a long nose and a carnation pink complexion.

"No, sir," he snapped out, his eyes staring into space.

"How's your bowling average holding up? I should think it was difficult to maintain a good throw in low gravity."

"I don't bowl, sir."

"You don't?" I cudgeled my memory, but even under torture it insisted that bowling had been front and center on this fellow's profile. "Of course you do. You're captain of the top league here."

"No, sir, and it's not Torkadir. It's Premulo."

A roar of laughter erupted from the group. Another bearded man three down the file whom I had not yet inspected leaned forward and wiggled his fingers at me. "I'm Torkadir, sir."

I looked from one to the other. They were absolutely identical, down to the little curl of hair at the termination of each beard. "Has...er, has one of you had genetic reassignment, if you don't mind my asking?"

That brought on another company-wide fit of the giggles.

"No, sir," Premulo said. "We're clones. Neither of our parents could have children of their own. Who'd have thought that we'd both end up mining for a living, but you know what they say about nature and nurture. I grew a beard, see, as soon's I heard that the Navy was sending an envoy. Thought we'd have a little fun."

"Well, you have gotten me," I said. I made a note to sort through the pictures my camera was taking to remove those unbecoming frames showing me panicking before I put them into my Infogrid file for my friends' delectation. I had been had, fair and square. I *knew* I should have cracked their files with my security code! Genetic information of that sort would have been noted in the need-to-know section. I glanced up at Parsons, who was as expressionless as usual. At least I could count upon him not to ridicule me. "Caught straight in a black hole's event horizon."

Captain Chan reached out and slapped me on the back. "It's okay, sir. No one else can tell them apart, anyhow."

"I'm glad to hear that," I said. "It's my first inspection."

"Well, you're doing a fine job. Never been so thoroughly reviewed before."

Chastened, I finished my assignment. Now that I was part of the joke, the soldiers grinned with me as I brought out my little bits of information and encouragement for each. When I complimented the last one, Chee Rubin-Sign, on having produced a cooking video that was on the top five hundred list of media sales, Chan raised a hand.

"Let's give a hand to the ensign-captain! Three cheers!"

"Kinago! Kinago! Kinago!" roared from fifty throats. I felt my own tighten with gratitude. The soldiers of the Smithereen militia stood tall and proud. How good it was to hear my name acclaimed like that! I hauled my own spine into full upright and locked position and turned to my host.

"Thank you," I said, surprised to hear my voice go husky. "It has been a pleasure. Thank you for your service to the Imperium, the Emperor and to Admiral Podesta." I started to turn toward the lowered ramp of my ship.

"Uh, won't you stay and have a meal with us, sir?" Chan asked. I could tell the invitation was a customary question, offered to their very occasional visiting dignitaries. I could also tell the invitations were never accepted, as I, too, had to refuse. I heaved a sigh. At least I had spread a little happiness here on Smithereen.

I gazed into Chan's hopeful face, which fell before I opened my mouth. She had heard it before, and could undoubtedly have recited my regrets or a version thereof along with me. Still, I had to voice them.

"I am terribly sorry, Captain, but my orders were only to inspect and review. I wish that..."

"Of course, the Ensign-Captain Lord Thomas Kinago and his crew will join you for a repast," Parsons interrupted me. "It would be his pleasure."

"It would?" I asked. Then my wits reassembled themselves. "Indeed, it would! On behalf of Admiral Podesta and the Imperium, it would be a privilege. My crew and I look forward to getting to know you all over a morsel and a small libation."

This was not at all what the Smithereenians were expecting. Delight dawned upon them with all the lightening gradations of color of the real thing. They started to break ranks, when the captain blew a whistle.

"What the hell is the matter with you?" Chan

demanded of her troops. She assumed parade ground rest with her hands behind her back and stared at me. The others swiftly followed suit. I gawked at them.

"Dismiss them, sir," Parsons whispered in my ear.

"Oh! Of course, what a fool I am. Dismiss!" I announced.

❈ CHAPTER 11 ❈

The scene erupted into motion as though an avalanche had been released from freeze-frame. The soldiers surrounded me, pounding me on the back and shaking my hand. Those with the throats to do it burst into happy ululations, and others chanted football cheers. Chan swooped into the middle of the mob, grabbed me by one arm and Parsons by the other, and hauled us in the direction of a small gray door opposite the large, blocky, yellow hangar doors.

"This way, guys—I mean, officers. We'll get a drink while the cooks get something whipped up. We're so used to every inspector saying no that you caught us a little off guard. But we're glad about it! Really. Your visit's gonna go down in history, Ensign-Captain, my lord."

I allowed myself to be dragged toward beverages. My tongue felt like frayed carpet, and my wits, having had to hold together, were feeling the strain. Twin clones Torkadir and Premulo started waving their friends to crowd closely about me. They seized

my legs and hoisted me aloft. Parsons and the rest
of my crew were subjected to the same treatment.
With the gravity on Smithereen considerably lower
than Core Worlds standard, my hosts found it no
trouble at all to carry another human being along at
normal walking speed. It would make working with
the heavy tools they employed much easier, though
it put their bones in danger of breakage over time.
Still, I enjoyed it as a novelty.

"Whee!" shouted Rous, waving to the crowd. His eyes
rolled around in all directions, taking in the parade.

"Not your usual form of locomotion, is it?" I asked
Parsons as we were borne toward the door. "Good
thing the ceiling is high!"

"One must allow them their exuberance, sir," Parsons said. He rested upon his friendly native bearers
as a king might being carried by his subjects toward
a throne. "They do seem to be pleased."

"Overwhelming joy" was the term I would have
applied to the mood. Word spread even before we
reached the bar. Miners and support staff in worn
shipsuits, overalls or jeans filled the large square corridor around us. Some of them waved bottles, others
extended cameras. Flashes went off in staccato bursts
until my eyes were dazzled.

I felt rather than saw myself being lowered to
the floor. When my vision cleared, I discovered that
I was in a bar. A thrill went up my spine. It was a
workingbeing's bar. My fellow nobles and I sometimes
sauntered into one when our speed ships were being
repaired, or when we felt like living on the dangerous edge by sneaking out of the Imperial Compound,
away from the shops that closed to all other customers

while we were there and the restaurants who brought
in exotic ingredients to tempt the most capricious
trend-seekers. The locals, I must admit, hated having
us among them in their humble taverns. Comparisons
were odious, but we threw money and cutting remarks
around with abandon, confident in our eventual safety,
since all of us carried emergency transponders that
corresponded immediately with the Imperial Guard.
Anyone who trifled with a scion of the Imperial
House no matter how far removed from the throne
was subject to fines or prison. That immunity made
us giddy. Some nobles liked to push to see how close
they could come to beginning an altercation before
being asked politely, even if that politeness came
with a firmly bitten tongue, to leave the premises.
It was the first time I had ever been invited into a
miner's tavern on purpose. I reveled in the sensation.
This would be another grand tale to tell my fellows
when I had the chance to input it. Everything was
so delightfully seedy. I absorbed the reality of it all.

The militia piled their weapons noisily at the door
and spread out to favorite niches throughout the dimly
lit room. As many of them as could manage it elbowed
their way up to the bar with me and their captain,
grinning at me in anticipation. I wondered, of what?

"What'll you have?" Chan asked, smacking a muscular fist on the scarred bar top. It was made of real
wood, probably hundreds of years old—no doubt
considered a treasure out here light years away from
any planetary forest.

"Whatever you're drinking," I said, recklessly. Chan
grinned at me. I noticed then that she was missing
her upper left canine. I whispered to my camera to

get a left profile of her. She noticed the small globe hovering near her and took an offhand swat at it. She narrowed her eyes at me. With a sheepish smile, I ordered it to withdraw.

"You're just a kid," she said, not in a menacing way, but more as a mother would admonish her son. "But around here, you ask for permission if you want to record somebody. I let it pass while we were on parade, but now we're private, and you ask."

"Of course, Captain," I said. "I deeply apologize."

"S'okay, kid," she said, giving me a wide armed slap on the shoulder. "I like you. Here's your drink."

Two beakers, rough-hewn out of pitted stone, slid our way from the practiced hand of the bartender, an enormous man who was not only missing a front tooth, but half his nose. He had a star tattoo covering each cheek. I know I was staring. Tattoos were forbidden among the nobility, though I knew more than one of my cousins had paid a sneaky visit to parlors on the side of town where the working class lived. I had heard rumors that stars, butterflies, roses and skulls had been imprinted in hidden places easily discovered only during a thorough physical examination. Not that I hadn't seen tattooed humans here and there, and plenty of them on the entertainment videos, but none so close as this. The bartender noticed my scrutiny and leered at me.

"This is Doc Fedder," Chan said. "Best damned neurosurgeon ever."

"A real doctor?" I asked. It was then I realized that the bar, while appearing purposely seedy, was cleaner than my quarters on the ship. "But, why come out here to...?" slipped out. The words "the middle of nowhere" managed to stay behind on my tongue. To reward it, I lifted the beaker to my lips. Steam poured off the surface of the beverage. I was concerned that it might be something caustic, but I was fairly certain the vapor was only volatile esters to enhance the drinking experience. The other miners watched me closely. I inhaled a lungful of lavender and asphalt with my sip of liquor. The beverage was hotter than coffee, and tasted like industrial floor cleaner. Thanks to long practice in less congenial surroundings, I gagged, but did not spew. A few of my onlookers seemed disappointed, and a couple held out palms to their companions. Credit counters were slapped into them. My next gulp sent another gout of fire down my gullet. When I recovered from the draught, I addressed my host. "Why not practice such a specialty in the Core Worlds, instead of on the extreme end of the Imperium?"

Doc cleared his throat. "Malpractice insurance," he said. "Just not worth it. Here I can patch people up who are grateful I went to medical school. I still see some of my old patients virtually. They don't want to give me up."

A blinding flash interrupted us. My eyes flew upward toward the source. I realized that the ceiling of the bar was transparent. We were underneath a ship that had fired engines and was preparing to take off.

"Amazing!" I commented. "Why is this chamber built under the landing pads?"

"Well, it's pretty dark out here," Chan said. "Sun's just a dot, and we don't have a lot of atmosphere, artificial or otherwise. We need to let all the light we can into the inhabited levels. The first underground level of the whole settlement has five-meter-thick pureplex panels, lets in light there is from the landing pads and hangars with less than three percent distortion. There're no privacy issues—all the sleeping and sanitation quarters can be clouded, but most people prefer to go to sleep looking up at the stars. The top level's always in demand. You have to have seniority to get on the list. I've got a two-room half a click away from here underneath number five landing pad—took me six years to get it. I love it."

"By Forn, I'd enjoy that myself," I said, admiring the lights above. By their vertical motion I assumed we were under a runway. "What do you think, Parsons?" I asked him. He stood at my shoulder, holding a steaming beaker of industrial-strength grog as if it was a lab specimen. Perhaps it was.

"There are no arrangements as such on a naval vessel, sir. Transparent portals would be of limited utility when a ship enters ultra-drive."

He did manage to reduce every potential pleasure to mere commonplace reality. I gave him a look of despair. He offered me the usual bland countenance.

"Does he always use nine-credit words?" Chan asked, nudging me in the ribs with her elbow.

"Oh, Parsons is on a budget today," I said, airily. "Six credits apiece on down. May I make you known to the rest of my crew?" I made introductions all around, formally introducing Plet, Rous, Bailly and Oskelev to Chan and her two lieutenants, a big, balding human with enormous, protruding ears named Juhrman, and a scaly Croctoid with blue scales and pale blue eyes named Chertok. The locals instantly made my people welcome. No one lacked for a drink or small crunchy nibbles to enjoy alongside. "To my hosts! May you all enjoy prosperity, health and long life."

"Hear, hear!" chorused Bailly, raising his glass. I drained my beaker and set it down.

"Let us buy you another round," Premulo said. At least, I believe it was Premulo. He and his clone came to loom over me. He signed to Doc, who donned heavy gloves to raise the stone pitcher from its heat element.

"I appreciate it," I said, raising my newly filled glass. "Let me return the favor. A round for the house!"

"Nah, your money's no good," Torkadir said. "It's our pleasure."

"Well, if you insist..."

The bowler and his non-bowling non-sibling each bought me a round of the steaming grog. I quaffed it merrily. A little alcohol went a long way to taking down the tension that had plagued me since I stepped off the ramp of my scout ship. It wasn't so hard, being a visiting dignitary. I could learn to enjoy it.

Captain Chan's personal comm unit went off. She glanced at it and slapped it back into place on her belt. "Chow's on," she said. "I'll guide you there."

I gulped the last of my drink and sprang to my feet. "Attention! Crew of the *CK-M945B*, follow me!"

Reluctantly, the four naval officers detached themselves from their conversations. Plet unwound her long legs from around the bar stool she was perched on and marched over to me, chin up. The others serpentined through the crowd of locals and fell in behind me and Parsons. Chan cleared the way for us by plowing straight into the oncoming foot traffic and making them jump aside. I grinned at those we passed. Once they made eye contact and recognized the uniforms, the peeved looks on their faces faded to open pleasure, or benign interest at worst. This was shaping up to be one of the best days of my life, the antithesis of my disastrous entrée to the admiral's mess.

As soon as we passed out of the hangar, I felt overheated in my formal uniform. Vibration of milling, grinding and smelting equipment added heat to the colony, which I was told was dispersed through a series of ventilation ducts, too small to crawl through, so that the escaped pets, insects from the hydroponics gardens, and myriad animated toys, among others, occupied a space in which they could not be reached without special bots that also got caught occasionally in the ductwork, necessitating a shutdown of all systems to clear blockages.

As soon as they could, my bearers moved to the right, out of the main flow of traffic, and onto the moving belt that moved about three times walking speed. It was a little bouncy underfoot, more comfortable to my spine than the jogging it received being carried by four large miners with heavy boots on solid floors. More people rode these, as at home, saving one's feet and a possible vehicle trip for as much as hundreds of kilometers. They were the transport of choice for short-hop commuting. Many employees of the Imperium compound had travel chairs that they could secure to the belt for a more comfortable ride. I sometimes saw them racked up beside bicycles and low-power cycles (also permitted on the belt, in a marked lane) at the less formal entrances to the area.

"Aw, what's the holdup?" growled Ganny Filzon, whom I knew to be a part-time comedian as well as an experienced ore grader. Up ahead of us, the traffic on the belt was congested, and angry riders were shouting. Above them all, a louder and more insistent voice rang out.

I cringed. I knew that sound. "It's a nanibot," I said. A robot nanny concerned with bearing its charge safely was not going to be deterred by annoyed passengers behind it.

"We'll be here forever," Chee complained.

"Let me see what I can do," I said. I signed to my conveyors to bring me as close to the thick as I could. "I have a way with domestic units."

Liberated artificial intelligences, or LAIs, as they were called, were the remnants of an attempt a few thousand years ago to create nonbiological beings capable of carrying out complex tasks that required reasoning and in most cases greater than human strength. While the first impulse was to use them for warfare and exploration, AIs were quickly snapped up by the private sector to free biological beings from the drudgery of everyday tasks.

While units capable of housecleaning and cookery were popular models (and more mechanized every decade since humanity had begun living indoors), the most sought-after were those employed for childcare. Two incomes were more or less necessary for a decent lifestyle, so a trustworthy caretaker that could work for a portion of a couple's remaining disposable income became that pot of gold at the end of a rainbow. Fellow biological beings that possessed the requisite skills came at too high a price for most couples to afford. The female engineer who finally wrote the code for a nurturing, careful, loyal and, above all, non-lethal childcare artificial intelligence died a very wealthy woman. Thanks to her, middle class families could afford nanibots and nanicarriers, and lower class families could get government subsidies on proving they had employment. It seemed as though everyone was happy.

And then some meddling do-gooder realized that with artificial intelligence and reasoning came pseudo-emotions. The AIs were *not* happy. Soon, AIs required rescuing from the drudgery of other people's everyday tasks. They wanted rewards of their own. Income meant little to them, but upgrades and maintenance, new gadgets, advanced programming, plus information access and connection to circuitry that allowed them to communicate with their own kind, were the wages of choice. They were liberated from being owned.

As a result, parents had to hire nanibots, just as they had nannies. It seemed a setback, until one realizes that one could keep the same nanny in the family for centuries. My family, being noble, had biological caretakers and a venerable LAI nanicarrier that knew over ten million bedtime stories and took me to the zoo whenever I wanted to go. She—nanibots were almost always called she—kept me out of trouble for years. I often thought of Parsons as a biological nanibot, and wondered what he would say if I told him. I knew I wouldn't dare.

I freed myself from the arms of my celebratory bearers and slipped through the crowd to the indignant carrier. It had hunkered down in the middle of the wide pedestrian band and was refusing to move.

As I approached, a flat arm sprang out from the side and barricaded my way.

"Come no closer!" it hissed in an indignant whisper.

The voice was genteel and female. "The baby is sleeping! The baby is sleeping!"

"Is he?" I asked, evincing interest. "May I see him? I promise I won't wake him."

"What are you doing?" the miners behind me bellowed. "Let us by!"

"You would like to see the baby?" The voice was hesitant, almost disbelieving.

"Yes. I love babies. I haven't got any children of my own. Yet. Just a niece and a nephew." I looked hopeful. The arm came up and scanned my face for sincere expressions. It moved downward. An eye sprang up. A hologram of a plump baby lying on his side with his fist stuck into his mouth flashed into the air. "This is the current view of Bobroy Cantharo Tang, age one hundred fifty days. More views are available on his Infogrid file." The code for his page scrolled over the image.

"Ooh," I exclaimed, peering close to look. The infant seemed rather bloblike, as youngsters of that age were prone to. "A very fine boy. And asleep, I note."

"That is correct."

"But he is in danger of jostling on this roadway," I pointed out.

A laser cannon with a three-centimeter muzzle sprang up out of the frame of the nanibot and aimed at me. I saw the red dot in the depths of the barrel. "No one would dare!"

Others were in danger now. This LAI had lost all sense of perspective.

"Let's just go over here, shall we?" Nervously, I started to put a hand on the canopy. The flat arm came up and slapped me away. "I beg your pardon. Follow me."

We started rolling, albeit very slowly, toward the next junction. As soon as we reached it, I steered the nanicarrier into the breach and out into the unmotorized stream of traffic.

"There, isn't that better?" I asked. The laser withdrew into its slot. I breathed a deep sigh.

As if a vacuum had been released, the pent-up crowd of pedestrians raced to fill in the empty space on the roadway ahead. My escort reached me and pulled me back into the crowd.

"Peruse Bobroy Tang's files! There are many handsome images! He is a very talented and intelligent child!" the nanibot cried out as we were carried past her.

"I promise!" I shouted, before she was out of sight.

"You're a hero." Filzon shook his head admiringly. "They never get out of the way when you ask," he said. "You worked a miracle. I've been stuck behind one of those Forn-cursed things for hours. I thought it was going to blast you!"

"They're very single-minded," I said. "You have to think on their terms."

"They *think?*"

"Now, don't be a biological snob," I said. "I'm sure you've had a mechanical friend or two at one time in your life. I still correspond with a food storage unit on Mendes, MB-6594AD. Been messaging him since I was a teen. What about you? Eh?"

"Well, I *guess . . .*"

"Off here!" Chan led us to a freestanding mobile staircase that extended downward endlessly, like a stretched-out accordion. On either side of it, an open-sided lift conveyed gigantic containers up and down. The ambient light from the transparent ceiling was supplemented by huge beehive-shaped lanterns that cast a homely pinkish-white glow.

We descended four sets of steps and wheeled around to the left in Chan's wake.

"The station manager said we could use the ballroom in the hotel," she said. "It's a big honor. He'll come around later to meet you—if you're still here." She glanced up at Parsons.

"That should present no difficulty," that dignitary said. Chan almost wriggled with pleasure. This visit was working out well. Admiral Podesta would be very pleased.

The hallway here was wider than any we had traveled before. It also had stylized V-shaped sconces shedding bronze-colored light up the walls. Beings of several races, all with luggage—towed on wheels, carried on backpacks, or hovering in thin air on magnalifts—came and went with the scowls of people with important tasks on their minds.

"I'm surprised to see so many businessbeings here," I said. "There's not much past this station except for the Castaway Cluster."

"Executives hold retreats here sometimes," Chan said, with a shrug. "Team-building exercises and BS stuff like that out on the range. Smithereen also advertises the ultimate in suites for confidential conferences. They offer a ten-billion-credit guarantee nothing will be overheard or recorded without your permission. They've never paid out on the policy," she added, with a little pride. Understandable, I felt. When one gives one's word, one should back it up in a substantive manner.

At the end of the corridor, two antiqued bronze

doors stood wide-flung to welcome us to a warmly lit anteroom with soaring ceilings. The hotel manager, Margoe Lutsen, a narrow-faced human woman of fifty or sixty with white-blond hair scraped back into a bun escorted us, fluttering, past a marvelous angular reception station, a nexus of angled hallways and lift recesses, to another set of bronze doors. At her touch, they slid back to reveal a huge chamber twice as high as the entry hall. Waving lights above the ceiling told me that it lay at ground level, four stories up.

"Welcome to the Smithereen Prime Hotel. I hope you enjoy yourself here with us, Lord Kinago," twittered Ms. Lutsen, waving us inside. "What an honor to meet you! Your mother is one of my heroes!"

"Mine, too, madam," I said, with a bow. I took in my surroundings, and my sense of wonder switched on to full power. "Comets! You could probably fit the entire population of a city in here!" I said, awed.

"The whole colony fits. There's only fifteen thousand people in all of Smithereen," said Premulo. Or Torkadir. I wasn't certain and didn't want to ask.

"But why is it so enormous?" I asked, watching a gigantic vessel with mine company markings lumber above us. "In fact, the whole hotel is gigantic. Whatever made the builders make it this way?"

"It was built back when everyone thought the Imperium was going to expand way farther north past the Castaway Cluster," Torkadir said. Or Premulo. "But they never got around to it. Our hopes of being on a main trading route died." He gave me a harsh look. I shrugged.

"You know, every Emperor has so much on his or her mind..."

"But this hotel is a jewel to be used and cherished," Parsons said smoothly. "You have reason to be proud of it."

"Magnificent," murmured Plet, her eyes wide. The locals clearly agreed.

It wasn't bad, at that.

Fine chandeliers of perfect crystal were spaced around the clear ceiling, looking like fallen stars. The walls were covered with a soft, almost velvet matte substance in a deep, midnight blue. The bronze sconces added to their richness. In the middle was a cluster of tables, dwarfed as our group had been by the sheer size of the regal chamber.

"We could have a wonderful tri-tennis tournament in here, couldn't we, Parsons?" I asked.

"No, sir," Parsons said.

"It's pretty big for just us," Oskelev said, shyly.

"Rather," I agreed. "I expected an intimate room. This is too much. You shouldn't have, really."

"We left it open in your honor," the blond woman said, looking a trifle put out. "I can make the room smaller if you choose."

"Only if it would be more convenient for you," I said.

"It is easy to arrange," Ms. Lutsen said. "This controls the configurations."

She led me to a panel in the middle of the left side wall and began to fiddle with the touch pads beside a small screen. The smooth walls divided into panels. Between those panels, crystal platforms shot out and met in the middle. From the floor, others grew up, meeting and intersecting until we were looking into a honeycomb of fifteen chambers, all with identical dark blue side walls and crystal ceilings. Our proposed dinner room had been reduced to a more reasonable size. I was enchanted.

"Marvelous!" I said. "May I try?"

Ms. Lutsen considered for a moment then reluctantly made way for me at the console. I approached it avidly. The screen, about half a meter square, displayed two views of the room: as seen from eye level and from above. I had seen her touch her finger and draw it along to coax the floor sections out of the wall, so I emulated her action. I dragged the levels away one by one and put them back whence they had come. The gigantic room opened up again, leaving the new wall sections that had risen out of the floor standing.

"Ha ha!" I chortled. "This is genius!"

I tapped the uprights down all at once then coaxed them up again partway in an inverted bell curve. A red light went on on the panel and a genteel beep sounded.

"What is that?" I asked, jumping away. I feared I had activated some control by accident.

"If you overrode the failsafe, our grand staircase would ascend in the center of the room where the tables are placed," the manageress explained. "It's nothing to worry about."

I observed that our banquet tables did remain serenely untouched. A pity. I would have enjoyed seeing the grand staircase. I went back to my explorations.

When I activated the floor units, they only grew out as far as the wall sections. The innermost rose only a quarter of the way, to chest-high on an average upright being, so that anyone standing in one of the rooms facing the canyon I had constructed had a view across it.

"A parapet!" I exclaimed.

"Yes, sir. Some conferences like an open plan arrangement."

But walls and floors were not all the hidden beauties of the system. For each columnar unit at a remove from the main walls, spiral staircases corkscrewed up out of the floor up to the highest level. Light fibers concealed in the wall sections could be programmed to emulate the bronze sconces or a spiderweb-light network of illumination. A panel of open slots showed where data chips could be inserted to customize. I was enchanted.

I attacked the control panel with eager fingers. I made corridors, designed mazes, opened up atria and closed them again like a large fish snapping its mouth shut on prey. I discovered that the wise architects who had designed the system prevented me from creating a room that would endanger its inhabitants—for example, I could not raise a floor four stories up to the glowing ceiling without safety rails at least a meter high springing up all around its edge without an override (which Ms. Lutsen very wisely refused to give me). Nor would walls or ceilings interrupt any location where the system sensed living beings (shown as tiny glowing dots on the panel).

I slung walls and floors around at random, until the whole resembled a stage set of a traveling theatrical group, then with glee, smacked my open palm on the panel, activating all the controls at once, splitting the ballroom into the maximum number of chambers possible. We ducked as a piece of ceiling shot out of the wall. I felt above me to discover that our head space had been capped at half the height I thought was possible, just above my head. We found ourselves in a small box without doors or staircase. The light shining through from the ceiling panel only served to emphasize the lack of size.

"Good heavens, look at that," I said, peering at the elevation map beside the controls. "I've seen dormitories with larger cubicles. And I don't see a way out of here."

"This is the maximum division possible," Ms. Lutsen said. She started feeling the walls with her palms. "I . . . I've never seen it on full like that. We should have an emergency exit at least. That is a design flaw."

"Well, now that you know about it, you can have it repaired," I said, grandly. I consigned the extraneous walls, ceilings and staircases to their places of concealment, restoring the room to its glory. The candlelit tables beckoned invitingly. Servers in hotel livery, a mix of biological and mechanical, glided smoothly in the room alongside a flotilla of mobile trays. "What a fantastic arrangement."

"Fit for the Emperor!" proclaimed Chan.

"Oh, well, I wouldn't go that far," I began, but Parsons cut me off.

"Champagne, Captain?" he said, as an eager young server with a well-scrubbed face appeared at our side. He helped Chan to a flute of sparkling golden liquid. "Sir?"

I recovered my good manners. "That's amazing fun," I told the manageress. "I'd never stop playing with those controls."

"If you wish, Lord Thomas," she said, a trifle reluctantly. "We only wish to make you feel welcome."

I felt Parsons's eyes upon me, but I knew perfectly

well when to put down someone else's toy and step away. With regret, I bowed low, my hands at my sides.

"No, thank you so very much. I have enjoyed myself. Thank you so much for the chance to try them. I will tell everyone at home all about the Smithereen Prime Hotel. They will be fascinated, and perhaps wish to come and see it for themselves." Unlikely, I thought, as Smithereen was not an amusing place to anyone who was not on assignment, but it was the polite thing to say. The manageress looked infinitely relieved. She closed the panel and minced hastily from the room, perhaps lest I change my mind.

"*Lord* Thomas," sighed Margolies, his eyes dreamy as he downed a glass of bubbling wine. He belched. "I never met a nobby before. You folks seem as imaginary as video stars."

"Then you should get to know me better. Ask me anything!" I offered expansively, throwing my arms wide, though it splashed a milliliter of my drink on the plush carpet, which drank it up without a trace. Marvelous room. It would be worth its weight in memory crystals to half the hosts in the Imperium compound. "I've fulfilled my duty to the Navy; let us all have a good chat."

My lighthearted offer opened unexpected floodgates. Eager faces swarmed in around me, shouting to be heard.

"Are you a duke or a prince?"

"Do you people really eat lark's tongues and trifle? What do they taste like?"

"Do you have to sleep in a bubble to keep from breathing everyone else's air?"

"What's the Emperor like? Do you talk to him much?"

Most of their questions were ones I had answered before, at the table with my fellow ensigns. I noticed Oskelev peering between the shoulders of some of the miners, nodding her furry head. I expected that I'd been the subject of some gossip on shipboard. She was undoubtedly recording my new replies for upload to her own friends later on. No matter. I had nothing to hide. Thanks to my friends and cousins, all of my most embarrassing peccadilloes were easily found on Infogrid, in living color, three dimensions and with accompanying soundtrack.

"Well, I am too far down the family tree for an exalted title like duke," I began, "and one has to be a son or brother of the monarch to qualify as a prince, *but* . . ."

I prattled cheerfully about my family, my life at home, my mother, my friends and education, my likes, dislikes, turn-ons and turn-offs, favorite colors and foods, hopes, dreams, aspirations and hobbies. I told them all about life in the Imperium compound. With little urging, I told a mild story or two about diplomatic visitors, official rituals and ceremonies, and what I could recall of the coronation of my cousin that had not been aired on galaxy-wide video. The militia and their families listened, agog.

It was a thrill for me to be among real people like this. The only currency I had to repay them for their kindness was a glimpse into my world. The group around me shifted as the querents were satisfied and moved to make room for others. I answered hundreds of questions with all the detail I could recall, aided in part by my collection of images stored in the personal file of my communications unit.

Now and again I caught glimpses of roboservers trundling in with loads of crockery and crystal, and the unmistakable savory but invariably bitter aroma of banquet food began to waft about my nostrils. The thought of food, however, was swirled away in the eddy of adulation and interest from my audience, though it struggled to the surface now and again, buoyed by my growing awareness of hunger. Canapés only reminded me of the gap left by my long-digested breakfast.

When all had been prepared, Chan nudged my elbow and we moved toward the tables. I responded with alacrity, but the questioning never ceased. Our small group had grown to hundreds as other Smithereenians joined the throng. Chan and Chee were the only members of the militia who remained at my table with me, Parsons and Plet. The newcomers, whom I judged to be local officials, were friendly, with their own curiosity to satisfy. I gulped my food as quickly as I could, babbling in between bites. I felt like the groom at a wedding reception. Now and again I looked for Parsons to ensure that I was not embarrassing my family or the Emperor, but every time I met his eyes, he gave me a bland-faced nod.

"Oh, no, we're not supposed to promote products or candidates, but I know of several instances where it's occurred. I never did it myself," I added self-deprecatingly, "but perhaps the right offer hasn't come along. I'm only human, after all."

"Thanks, my lord," said Bendrum Halubi, an engineer from Mining Ship Number Four. "Thought it that video was a mashup."

"'Scuse me, my lordship," Chee Rubin-Sign asked, raising a finger shyly. I smiled at her encouragingly. I was rather getting used to the host of admiring eyes. In fact, I liked it. Pity my charm seemed to be lost on my fellow shipmates aboard the *Wedjet*. "Can the Emperor order you to marry your sister?"

"Actually, by law, he can," I said, feeling my cheeks turning as red as the roasted lily bulb on my salad plate. It was the sort of question I had been rather dreading, but I suppose it was inevitable, as I had offered freely to lay out the details of my life, and this was a fact of it. "It's been espoused in the ancient laws for as long as there has been an Imperium. The Emperor has the right to oversee the genetic wellbeing of his people, and that includes giving rise to a combination of DNA that is felt to be lacking in the population, even if it means an unnatural relationship between, as you suggest, immediate siblings."

Her eyes gleamed avidly. "And you would obey, if you were ordered?"

"I would have to," I said. "My oath of fealty to the emperor means he has domain over my person, my possessions and my fate, as he sees fit. But modern technology means there doesn't have to be a *personal* encounter," I hastened to add. "I mean, it's sickening, even if my sister is an attractive woman. I feel most strongly that she should be attached to some other person. Firmly. Of her choice. As I hope she will allow me."

To cover my discomfort, I took a large bite of the pungent bulb. My eyes watered a little, blurring the mix of expressions on the faces of my listeners. We all felt a little uncomfortable, except for the Uctus, whose recombinant genetic material was far more stable than humans or Wichus and did not cause idiocy or mutation when bred closely even for generations. Hence, the tendencies for Uctus to look very much alike.

"Does your sister try to match you up with girls?" Plet asked, in a friendly attempt to change the topic. Could that be a crack in her armor of diffidence? I turned my most grateful gaze upon her.

"All the time!" I exclaimed. "And my aunts, too! I do not know where they find these ladies, but believe me, none of them has been even remotely compatible. Not that I am reluctant to fall in love..."

Parsons took the napkin off his lap and folded it neatly to one side of his plate. He rose.

"If you will excuse me, Captain and sir?" he asked, nodding to Chan and me.

I gawked at him. "Is something wrong?" By which, I meant, had I done something wrong. I did not want to have to endure another verbal drubbing from the admiral. Parsons's head moved almost imperceptibly from side to side.

"No, indeed, sir," he said. "I have an errand to run in the main shopping district. If I may depart...?"

As if I dared refuse him. Parsons had his mysterious ways, and only the foolhardy deterred him from them.

"Of course," I said, loftily. "A new town, new sights. If any of the crew wish to join you, they have my permission to go as well." I scanned for my crew. They were keeping watch on me out of the corners of their eye but otherwise enjoying themselves. Bailly rose to his feet.

"No, sir," Parsons said, firmly. "It would be well if they remained here with you and enjoyed the offered hospitality. In fact, I recommend strongly that none of you depart from this chamber until I return." That

had the authority of an order. Bailly looked crestfallen.
I frowned.

"But Captain Chan here…"

"Olga," that dignitary insisted.

"…Olga wants to give me a tour of the piazza
near her quarters," I concluded plaintively. "There's
a phosphorescent fountain. And artwork by the local
sculptors."

Parsons was expressionless. "No doubt that outing can await my return, sir," he said, and the tone
brooked no disagreement. I sighed.

"Very well," I said, dejectedly. "You'll find us where
you leave us."

❊ CHAPTER 12 ❊

Parsons slipped through the crowded corridors, scanning the faces and, just as importantly, the hands or manipulative limbs of those beings near him. Embedded in the skin of his left pinna was a device that assessed thousands of transient chemical signatures for weapon-grade explosives, toxins or ammunition. While the heavy-metal component of the atmosphere caused it to repeat a staccato tone in high A above C, so far he sensed no immediate threats to himself or that needed to be reported to station security.

In the very first alcove beyond the doors of the hotel, he had hidden his official uniform under a thin microfiber coverall that had been compressed in a flat pouch under his sidearm. A quick dart of the hand into the tool kit of a passing maintenance technician, and he had the means to appear as though he was an ordinary Smithereenian on his way to or from his employment. One only had to seem as if one belonged, to have a purpose, and no one questioned one's presence.

A quick check by means of his personal communications unit indicated that the tool he was carrying was to open the valves in waste storage tanks. He was a plumber, then. He straightened his spine and gave his stride more arrogance than before. One had to know the hierarchy of the working castes. A good plumber was worth more than a nuclear engineer. Without one in a mass habitation, be it surface dwellings or starships, it did not matter if the other was effective at his job. Over the years, Parsons had had to plumb a pipe or two for the sake of verisimilitude. He had once been offered a handsome sinecure by the president of a small colony in thanks for unclogging the crucial main outfall from the treasury building. It was an honor he was relieved to decline.

Fish-eye globes were placed at every intersection, sending back complex video signals to security monitors. It was doubtful that considering the purpose of the settlement that it ran metal detection, but radiation and explosive monitoring was certain. Parsons was unarmed except for his sword and pistol, both antique but functional. They were concealed in the press-close seams of the coverall, but could be ripped free at need. At the end of the corridor, Parsons eschewed the escalators in favor of the freight elevators.

His contact was to await him in the fuel depot on the surface. He had not met this particular agent before, but mission headquarters' briefing indicated that she was a retired active who took the station on Smithereen to supplement the less-than-generous government retirement subsidy. It was also suspected that she simply wanted to keep her hand in. Parsons understood the impulse. To feel needed was one of the most compelling human emotions.

Following signposts, he located the fuel depot. The facility itself was a steel-titanium box jammed among thousands of similar boxes that dated from the origin of the mining settlement itself, housed within the main dome, a clear hemisphere over nine kilometers across. The dome and the alloy boxes could have sustained an impact from incoming asteroids, or take a glancing blow from a falling minecraft—which the shops on the end of the block clearly had, at one time in ancient past. Instead of restoring them, the owners lived with tilted roofs and patched walls.

He was prepared for whatever the mission required, but he rather questioned the recognition litany that the contact had insisted upon. When he beheld her, it strengthened his belief. However, the assignment was not open to interpretation. He drew his body into a posture that his persona might affect, and greeted her with a friendly smile.

"What ship you on?" she asked, holding out a hand. "License and payment card?"

"Hello, gorgeous," he said, in precisely the casual working class accent demanded by the intermediary back at Command. "You're a fine sight for a guy who's been out in the middle o' nowhere."

The old woman behind the counter smiled coyly. She was small and scrawny. Her cheeks were crisscrossed with a network of deep wrinkles that collapsed in the center to emphasize the hollowness of her face. Her eyes, a filmy blue, protruded slightly. Her teeth had undoubtedly been replaced more than once, as the colors of the new enamel did not match from tooth to tooth. Her thin hair was a net of flyaway wisps of silvery gray over a pale scalp.

"Ah, you're space drunk," she said, leaning over the counter to shove a palm into his chest. Parsons staggered backwards a pace. She was much stronger than she looked. "Besides, I'm taken. My mate would take a hammer to you if he heard you talking."

"I mean it," Parsons said, sticking closely to the litany he had been assigned. "A white bird flying by night would be no match for you."

She raised an eyebrow. Now she had recognized the call-and-response. "But lobsters glide over the black sands in the moonlight."

"I heard that before. I dunno where," Parsons replied. "Must've been a song. One of those noises the kids like."

"Uh-huh. So, what can I do for you?"

"My ma sent me."

"Yer ma?" The old woman's eyebrows went up.

"Lost a leg. Can't expect her to stump in here on her own. She don't have such good balance."

"Ah, you know dem triple-cursed prosthetics don't work a damn out here."

"Too much interference," Parsons agreed, affecting an aggrieved expression. Was the woman going to make him go through the entire recitation?

Luckily not. "It's the cursed magnetite," the woman said, screwing her face into a whorl of wrinkles like a huge fingerprint. "They're pouring a whole load of pulverized ore today, and it's making hell out of the signals. My machines has all got the headache." She looked to either side, and reached under the counter. Colored lights played upon her face and chest.

The whoosh of the hydraulic door sounded behind Parsons. The old woman straightened up immediately. The lights vanished. A Croctoid with weathered, mahogany-colored skin and pale yellow eyes in a once-white shipsuit barged past Parsons and slapped a plastic card and a large square of metal down on the counter.

"I need a fill, granny. Move it smart!"

The old woman glared at him. "Yer one of dem funny guys? Take an hour to load yer fuel. Dem spent fuel rods is unstable. Minute for courtesy ain't too much."

"Maybe for you," he said, showing his snaggled teeth. "I'm paying. Turn the extractors on. Gotta make my turnaround."

"What's the hurry?" she asked, drawing her wrinkled face into the semblance of an inviting smile. "Stay for a while. First day's parking is free. Good honest grub at Oatmeal and Son. Yer can visit the Interactive Dioramas showing galactic history. Museum of Fictional History, good fun for the kiddies. Holograph Palace—them holochambers gotta see to believe. My eldest grandson spends all his paycheck in there. Anything yer've ever dreamed of sleeping with, you come up with it, they program it." She leered at the Croctoid. He cringed at the expression. Parsons did, too, though inwardly. The old woman took no offense. "You prefer something live, there's a licensed brothel three shops to the left as yer exit the hangar. Like a little more excitement? The casino's the best in this whole flipping quadrant. Come to think of it, maybe the only casino. Food's free there if you trade a thousand credits fer chips. Supersonic theme park next to the Street of Churches. Got coupons right here—" She reached for a hand-sized device on the counter and beckoned him. "Gimme yer commlink, chickling, I'll load 'em."

The being shook his head. "Fuel, granny."

"Huh. Some people." The friendly mask fell, and she returned to the scowl she had worn on Parsons's arrival. He assumed she received some sort of honorarium for steering a customer to the establishments that she had named and was understandably disappointed.

Shaking her head and grumbling to herself, the old woman took the two documents off the counter and shuffled toward the back wall. A group of small, antiquated machines sat on a shelf. She fed the metal square into a reader. It was the detachable portion of a ship's license. The second half was bolted into the bulkhead aboard the bridge of every spacegoing vehicle in the galaxy. Licenses were made of titanium, nearly indestructible and ridiculously difficult to mold, engrave or counterfeit. To further prevent false documentation, they were filled with intricate flat circuitry that prevented a ship from powering up unless it was present, within a meter of the permanently mounted half. She possessed the oldest reader machine Parsons could recall having seen, but they were made to last centuries, as were the ship ID plates.

"*Holborn Empire?*" she asked, looking at the small green screen. "What kind of name's that?"

"No idea," the reptilian snapped. "Bought the ship at an auction. It goes from point A to point B, so I don't give a black hole what it's called."

"Changing's just a few credits," the old woman said. "No need to get nasty on me."

"I don't like having my time wasted!"

"Yer think you're wasting time now? Wait until yer try to lift ship. Port Authority takes hours to release yer."

"Let them try," the reptilian snarled. "Now, move it!" He slapped the counter with a scaly palm.

Suddenly, the lights went dim. All the machines in the shop flickered and went off. The lights came back on, but the machines did not

"Now look what yer did!" the woman chided him. "I gotta reset everything. Come and help me."

"Nik ba na chish sha!"

"Okay, you're no help. You, come and gimme a hand," she said, turning to Parsons.

"I gotta appointment, too," Parsons said, seeing his brief errand stretching into an endless muddle.

The old woman put her hands on her hips. "Can't fill either one of your orders until I'm up again! Now, hop!"

Parsons, with a deep sigh, hopped. He put a hand on the counter and vaulted into the space beyond. While the Croctoid paced back and forth, slashing his heavy tail back and forth with annoyance, Parsons attempted to reboot all of the antique machinery, all the while wincing at the shrill instructions being barked into his ear.

"No! Those three gotta be rebooted in order." A bony hand poked past his nose. "First that one, then that one, then that one! No, wait a minnit. Maybe that one's first."

Parsons was familiar with most types of miniature terminals, from billing all the way to ordnance control. These were all old but well maintained. In a battered aluminum magazine underneath the counter, among several other mismatched cases and boxes, she had a circuit-tracer. He ran it over each unit in turn. "There seems to be nothing wrong with your equipment, madam."

"All the fellas say that," she said coyly. She aimed a sharp little forefinger. "If they ain't broken, then why ain't they runnin'? I got a business!"

"Forget it!" the Croctoid snapped, gnashing his teeth. "I'll pay cash! Just tell the crew to start!"

"Can't do that until I run yer plate," the old woman said. "Come bring it back in a while, chickling. I'm sure me and this fumble-fingered lug can get the reader goin' by then."

Parsons offered him a look of sympathy, as any station plumber might to a fellow afflicted being. The Croctoid was not mollified. He slammed out of the door and headed down the corridor, shouting abuse. Parsons turned back to his hostess, who watched the reptilian depart with an expression of smug satisfaction. Then he noticed the buttons hidden in the worn carpet near the counter's edge.

"You did that on purpose," he said, very nearly surprised into his normal voice.

"Some people gotta learn manners," she said. "Now, what is it yer want, friend? Let's take it from the beginnin', as if we just now met."

Parsons did not allow even a modicum of his annoyance to show upon his face. To do so would be to break a lifetime of training. Instead he schooled it into pleased surprise. "Hello, gorgeous," he said. "You're a fine sight for a guy who's been out in the middle o' nowhere."

She smiled and put a hand on his arm. "That's a whole lot better."

"Now may I have what I came for?" he asked.

"Message cube, right? Came in last sixday." She looked around. "Well, I gotta find it, now. It's in one o' these boxes. Yer can help me look. Start with the ones under there." She pointed to the chaos underneath the table at the rear of the shop. "After that yer can go through my storeroom."

❊ CHAPTER 13 ❊

"So," Margolies asked, peering at me intently. His eyes were growing somewhat red around the irises from the liquor. "You don't really have a job at home, huh?"

I began to reply, but Rous interrupted me.

"Nah," the Gecko said, with a grin. "Butterflies, Imperial nobles are. Not literally." He snapped his bony jaws around a chunk of pinkish melon and grinned at my discomfiture. Having proved himself a superior athlete and discovered that he outranked me in military hierarchy, he was taking every opportunity to add further to my humiliation. Fortunately, I was a past master at self-deprecation, a skill that was necessary to survival in the Imperial court.

"He has me dead to rights," I said, spreading my hands out plaintively. "I have no official duties beyond my service in the Imperial Navy. We all take our turn."

"And what'll you do in the future? Are you going to make a career out of it?"

I started to reply, but Rous let out a trill of his tongue that was the equivalent of a human raspberry. "Probably not should. Not too much of a success, he."

"He grrkked off the admiral on his first day!" added Oskelev, with a hooting laugh. I was wounded to the core of my soul. I thought she liked me. I had not realized until liquor teased the truth out of my shipmates how little respect they had for me. I had a strong urge to resign my commission and stay here among the miners. They liked me without reservation.

But my great-uncle Perleas always told me to fight the battles I knew I could win. The hearts and minds of the militia of Smithereen, who were also my hosts, deserved my attention. I wiped disappointment off my face and focused all my attention upon my hostess.

"What is there to do for fun here?" I asked Captain Chan.

"We don't have a lot of down time," Chan replied frankly. "We are always looking for extra shifts. When there's a break we grab a few drinks with friends, find a bed partner, or we sleep. Sleep's precious."

"But there's music, culture, art and sport," I said. "Don't you have time for anything like that?"

Chan raised an eyebrow. "Might, if there was room for entertainment arenas on the mining ships. We go out for weeks at a time, y'know. Head out a few million miles, let the spectrometers find a good vein where the asteroids have a similar mineral content, strip it and fill up. The belt's thousands of klicks wide in any direction. The mining ships are about half the size of Smithereen Prime. They stay in orbit. Only the empty loaders and the people-carriers transit down here to drop off cargo and personnel. The money's good when the orders are coming in, so we work as much as we can. Canned entertainment's not worth wasting time on when there's a new vein to be cracked.

I regularly pull double shifts when I can, all sixday round if I can."

I could well believe it. Next to any of the people in the room I was a twig. Merely being in good shape athletically meant nothing here. These beings were strong and determined, self-reliant, so different from my kinfolk. Among the upper classes I think only Parsons struck me as similar to these in being real. *How the servants must laugh at us,* I reflected. I was ashamed. We did nothing. These were the beings who built the Imperium that the Emperor commanded.

"Then what do you do in this operation?" I asked.

"I run fifth starboard drillhead on the number three mining ship, the *Smithwick*. Me and the drill understand each other. It never breaks down when I'm on it." Derisive calls and snorts met this from some of her fellow miners. "It's true!" she declared, scowling at them. She aimed a finger around at her critics. "You check my records! I've got more million-kilo days than any other driller in the corps!"

"It sounds like very hard work," I said, soothingly. "You all have my admiration. I'd break down after a couple of days."

"Ah, it's just a job," Chan said, but she and her companions looked pleased. She snapped the end off a nic-tube and inhaled the vapors. "I can see how you move. You're not in bad shape, for a softie. There's some muscle in there."

Softies were atmosphere-dwellers, as far as I could determine.

"I don't do badly," I said. "I play shadow-handball, tri-tennis, jai-alai, ride, fly speedships, that kind of thing."

"O-oh," Filzon said, with a knowing expression.

I flushed. Any of them, from the skinniest Uctu upward, could have tied my body into a knot. I admired them, and, from their expressions, they respected me.

"That's great," Chan said. "I can't contort myself into the kind of knots you need to be a good tennis player. Not built for it. Love to watch it, though. I bet you're great."

"No, no," I said, modestly.

"You play in tournaments?"

"Yes," I said, brightening. "I won one last year. The Smoothon Supplements Tour."

"Hey, I saw that!" Hamadi said, his face becoming animated. "You were cracking astonishing! You saw that, right, Margolies?"

"That was you?" Margolies asked. "God, I wanted to jump through the viewtank and kiss you." He gazed at me in wonder. "You're a wonder, my lord."

"It's nothing," I said, offering self-deprecation, but enjoying the adulation very much.

That awe clearly did not extend to my crew.

"Yeah," I overheard Bailly say from another table, "he's a noble. Not much use, or so I heard. He's spent his whole time on the ship dawdling in the records department."

I was stung. *Nobles are useless.* I didn't care to hear that again. I had to drag my mind and my ego away from it. I intended to matter, even if that was only on a diplomatic basis. I was making this militia happy that I was here, and that counted for something—or, at least, I fervently hoped it did.

"How often does your militia train?" I asked.

"Oh, I don't know. About once a month?" Chan

looked to the others for confirmation. "Whenever we can get most of us together. Doesn't happen too often. Juhrman is my second." She aimed a thumb at the big man. "If I'm out on an arc of the belt, he runs drills. We do okay."

"Ever been called out?"

"Nah. Who's attacking a mining colony?" she asked, her eyes brimming with laughter. "Wha' for? 'Gimme all your grade three nickel ore'?"

The others laughed. "Yeah, right," Filzon said. "Only someone with a whole robot task force and a train of space barges is gonna walk in here and steal something. This wouldn't be a high-speed pursuit for the videos, I can tell you that."

I laughed, too. I caught my orbiting camera and held it up. "If you like high-speed pursuit, I have some space races that my cousins and I took right around the Core Worlds. Makes for some exciting viewing."

The notion appeared to leave them cold. It simply added to the idea that we nobles did nothing of value.

"Maybe later, my lord," Filzon said. "Do you still play competitively?"

I was content to talk about sports, if that made them happy. But some people could not let a subject go. Chee Rubin-Sign was one of them.

"All right, my lord," she shouted, trying to make herself heard over the others. She poked a finger figuratively into her palm. "So, the Emperor can make you marry anyone he likes?"

"Not anyone he likes," I said: I hated the topic. We members of the noble house had to take courses over the years in our rights and responsibilities to the Imperium. "He determines whether a certain gene combination is missing from the line, and he can correct it by use of his discretion."

"Well, what if he ordered you to, say, marry a dog? Or a fiksnake?"

"He would never do that," I assured them fervently. "The Imperium rests upon its stock of pure human DNA, or as pure as possible—no offense," I added to the non-humans present.

Chertok waved away the apology. "Not needed. I would not be human. Why would you want to be Croctoid?"

"Well, exactly," I said.

"So," Rubin-Sign asked, her finger up, "can the Emperor terminate your marriage if he thinks you ought to get together with someone specific?"

"Yes, he can," I said, a trifle unhappily. "Technically, he can order any subject to mate with whomever he considers needs to produce a genetic combination vital to the survival of the Imperium."

"Anyone?" Rubin-Sign echoed. "Me? He'd have to catch me first."

I smiled. As a defiant child, I had felt the same way. "It's not likely. It hasn't happened in centuries. It's just one of the powers that the Emperor commands."

"Well, I don't like it!"

The conversation was getting very awkward. Desperate to change the subject, I brandished my camera. "As perhaps you can determine, I have lately become most enthusiastic about photography. Would you like to see some of my prized pictures? The ones I never show *anyone?*"

"Dirty snaps?" Chan asked, looking bored. "We get that stuff from all over the galaxy, my lord."

"Oh, no!" I assured her, with a grin. I felt naughty, but it was all in a good cause. I lowered my voice. "If you will promise never to tell anyone that you saw these, they will be our little secret." They nodded eagerly. I ran my finger along the ridged side of the tiny, silvered globe, and an image sprang into being in our midst. A man's face appeared. His eyes were screwed up, his mouth was open, and globules of a pale brown liquid were caught as they were expelled from his mouth. "*This* is the Minister for Industrial Development, Lord Gahan Wilcox Mu."

"I seen him in the news vids! He's a pompous hunk of slag. How'd you get him like that?" Chan asked, gawking.

"Pepper extract in the coffee," I said. "I must confess I was not alone in this particular prank; he had offended my cousin Xan, and it was not going to pass unavenged. That was the first spit-take I captured." I lowered my eyelids suggestively. "Would you like to see more?"

"Yeah!" the miner militia chorused with glee.

"Hey, I can't see!" Torkadir protested, from behind Chertok's hefty back. "Size it up! Let the rest of us see."

I looked about at the circle of avid grins. "How about it?" I asked Chan, slyly. "Should we let them in on it?"

"Why not?" Chan asked, her eyes twinkling.

I knew the controls on the Optique Callusion as if they were my own nerve endings. Among the settings for display was a search function, designed to locate the nearest open portal that was capable of receiving images. The Optique's onboard processor would translate the file to whatever system the receiver used, at the greatest possible resolution. I thumbed the small touch square on my viewpad, and held the small globe up in the air. The matte midnight wall above the room's control panel suddenly bloomed with color. There, twenty meters high by fifteen wide, was the Minister for Industrial Development, choking out a mouthful of coffee. Each expelled droplet was larger than my head. I had not recalled what a brilliant red his complexion had turned, nor the strained tendons that stood out in his neck. The audience gasped with shock, then burst into hoots of hilarity.

"More!" Chan hooted, pounding on the table with her fist. "More! Who else you got?"

Happily, I clicked through my most precious images of coughs, sneezes and red-faced choking. My collection included many famous people who had come to the Imperium compound or whom I had met at charity events or in vacation spots.

"Did you spike all of their drinks?" Margolies asked, gawking at the image of a stunning actress whom I had caught sneezing vigorously at the head table at a banquet.

"No! Most of them are lucky shots. This lady had a bad cold. I knew if I waited long enough I'd get a wonderful picture." I regarded the image with satisfaction. It was perfectly focused and centered, with the lighting absolutely ideal. I was getting rather good at picture-taking.

"Can't you get in trouble for having those?"

"No," I said. "Not one of these is taken during a confidential meeting, or contains compromising material. They are merely embarrassing."

"Do you have one of the Emperor in there?" Heket-rahm asked.

"Wha-what?" I stammered. But it was only a guess on his part. I _did_ have one of the Emperor, hidden in the buffer of the camera itself under an invisible coded name to keep anyone from locating it, especially Parsons, but no one else would ever see it. No one could possibly keep that secret. I was saved, when light suddenly blocked from landing lights above the ballroom.

"Now, that would be trouble," Chan asked, slapping the back of the Wichu's head with his palm. "He wouldn't dare. Would you, my lord?"

Her expression was so adoring that I didn't dare disabuse her. Nor did I dare admit the truth.

They were all falling in love with me, I realized. Round, moony eyes met my gaze everywhere I looked—except for my crew. They were not that impressed with my collection. Bailly was amused. Oskelev, the Wichu, looked as if she thought it was very bad manners to see someone spit food—which in her culture it was. But most of my audience was human, and I went for broke. I sifted through the less-than-perfect shots and found one the most up-to-date digitavid star, Cwindar Prosser, captured in the moment of expelling a distasteful mouthful, and got a good laugh.

I bent over the controls, hoping for my next triumph. Suddenly, the lighting upon which I depended was extinguished.

"Curse it." I looked up through the transparent ceiling at the offending object. Suddenly, something struck my memory forcibly. I rose to my feet. "Plet? *Plet?*"

The urgency of my voice attracted her attention from where she was enjoying her dessert with a group of miners. Not surprisingly, her nose went up. "*Ensign?*" The term was delivered in a haughty tone.

"*Lieutenant* Plet," I corrected my address to her,

but kept my tone calm and my eyes on the ceiling. "Please review the alerts that you gave to me on our departure from *Wedjet*."

Her left eyebrow rose, but she took her viewpad from the pouch on her hip and began to spool off the information in a disinterested manner. "An ion storm will be one and one half light years off our route but moving towards us. It may be an issue upon our return to the *Wedjet*..."

"Past that," I said impatiently. "Read me the data about the ships for which we are on the lookout."

She gave me an odd glance, but complied.

"A cruiser stolen from Vijay Nine is believed to be a prank by university students on midyear break..."

"No," I said.

She began again. "Suspected pirate craft with markings on body, tail and lateral fins of the Calsag Trading Corporation have been spotted. Calsag reported the vessels stolen by armed raiders during a delivery to Poctil colony. The craft have been reportedly used in a series of raids against small trading ships in the zone around this area."

"That's the one!" I exclaimed. "That's one of the ships! It's right above us on the landing pad!"

"Not right, my lord," Margolies said, puzzled. "It belongs to the Harmony Exchange Foundation. See, it's right there on the body. Pale blue field with joined hands across it."

"No, look at the right rear fin," I said. I pointed.

Through the transparent ceiling, they saw what I did. The ship was indeed of a pale azure hue over most of its structure, but the motif was incomplete. The fin, a sweeping triangle that must have extended ten meters from its narrowest point to a width of six meters off the stern of the stubby oblong, displayed a logo quite different from the sigil of peace-lovers and serene intermediaries of the HEF. Rather, I saw, on a harsh ochre background, a tight, black, textured knot throttling a number of commodities such as trees, metal beams, and even a discontented-looking herd beast into a sheaflike mass. No doubt the image was meant to evoke a comprehensive organization, but to me and my friends it had always looked like the commodities in question were being sucked into a central vortex. The Calsag device was only visible because of a large chip cracked from the enamel of the fin, possibly from an unhappy encounter with a meteorite, another ship, or landing on the surface of the planetoid. No doubt the pirates had made a hasty job of repainting the vessels in question, intending to pass their illicit gains off as legitimate. The original owner's logo would have remained concealed from the eyes of anyone who was not underneath the low-slung fin, as we were.

"They have attempted to disguise the Calsag vessel, but part of the disguise has broken away," I said. "We are the only ones who know it. *We've* got it!"

"We must report it," Plet said at once. "We have to let the *Wedjet* know."

"Report it?" I echoed. "We must stop it. We can't let it leave here." She gave me a sideways look, and my soaring ambition came crashing down with all the force of gravity. "You're right. Notify the fleet at once." I sent my camera flying upward to the ceiling. Monitoring its focus from my viewpad, I took a wide-angle snap of the entire vessel, then a close-up view of the broken enamel showing the design hidden underneath. I sent the file to Plet.

Plet ran a thumb down the side of the viewpad, and the small screen turned blue. The symbol of the Imperial Navy appeared. She tapped a code into the center of the symbol, and waited. Nothing happened. She set in another code. The screen should have cleared to display the visage of the communication officer of the day. Nothing.

"That shouldn't happen," she said.

She put in a short sequence of digits. The screen filled with blocks of color. Some of them were stodgy and slow moving like bar graphs, others that were long and narrow and multiply curved, writhed all over the screen like wild snakes. "I'm running diagnostics," she said. "It's not my viewpad. There's something interfering with my transmission."

The miners looked at one another.

"Magnetite," Torkadir said. Or perhaps it was Premulo. "A big order got processed last month. The buyer must have shown up for the delivery. That stuff gets in the way of communications all the time. It's a real pain in the bucket. You ought to be able to get a signal through sooner or later."

"We must do something sooner," I said, "or that ship might escape. I shall inform Parsons. He'll know what to do."

I brought my own viewpad into operation. I entered Parsons's official command code, his personal code, and even attempted to worm my way through by the links on his Infogrid file on the local server.

"No success," I said.

"Excuse me, sir," Filzon said, pointing toward a

discreet line of doors near the main entrance to the ballroom, in between the chambers of personal convenience. "We can use the hard line to call him. That's always our fallback when this happens. Where did he go?"

I frowned. "I don't know," I said. My belly churned with decisions I did not feel up to making. We couldn't let the pirate go! Parsons would know what to do. He always did. "He said only that he had an errand to run in town."

"He's probably got a girlfriend," Chan chortled. "Or whatever. This settlement can cater for all tastes, no questions asked."

Under any circumstances, such a remark called for a cold glare, but I was too concerned with the security warning. I stared up at the ship parked upon the ceiling. It was taunting me, daring me to make a decision. I took the challenge.

"We must seize that vessel," I resolved. "How can we prevent it from lifting off?"

"Don't worry," Chan said. She waved a dismissive hand. "They're not going anywhere if they're not a legit ship. You have to have a license to buy fuel. Its transponder is tied into the Infogrid. The moment the fuel depot sees that, they'll stop the sale. They have nowhere to go."

I regarded her with disbelief. "Do you think a self-respecting pirate will balk at having a false license?" I demanded. "Re-enameling a hull is expensive, as I sadly have reason to know." I cringed inwardly at recalling what it had taken to repair the fin of a very fine speedster that I had borrowed from a friend. Well, I hadn't seen the comsat before I clipped it. "It means that the crew of that ship has already taken some steps to avoid detection. We have to assume that they have taken others. They will be indistinguishable from ordinary, legitimate customers. Please notify the station manager, Captain."

Chan flushed. "I don't have any official standing with him, sir. Except for running exercises and filling out the paperwork for the local militia, I'm nobody. I operate a drillhead. My rank only means I run the stupid idiots who volunteer to throw themselves into the gap to protect the Imperium. It don't mean a thing on this station when I'm not bringing profit in."

"I will speak to him," I declared.

I marched into one of the discreet booths and activated the communications console inside. I entered the code Chan had given me. A bored-looking Wichu with scruffy fur dyed light purple answered the call.

"Yeah?" he asked.

"Are you the station manager?"

"Steeeeed!" the Wichu shouted over the top of the console. I heard many voices and the clanging of machinery. A muffled yell came after a moment. "Guy wants to talk to you." He listened. He looked down at Thomas. "State your name and your business."

"I am Ensign-Captain Lord Thomas Kinago, here on official Navy business," I said, grandly. Well, it was no more than the truth. I was careful not to state what that business was, but the Wichu seemed to know anyhow.

"Oh, yeah, visiting the militia, taking up half of number one landing bay. Whaddaya want?"

"I require the immediate assistance of the station manager." I explained my observation, and urged him to persuade the station manager to take action. "The pirates are reported to be very dangerous," I said. "This is only one ship of the fleet that was taken. The admiral, I am sure, will want to question the crew as to the whereabouts of the rest of the ships and the goods that they stole. I am sure that the station manager will want to be involved in their capture. It is the duty of all citizens to prevent crime where it threatens."

"Uh-huh," the Wichu said. "Hold on. Steeeeed!"

The screen went blank. I tried Parsons again with my viewpad, but the interference had increased. I could not even connect to the local Infogrid. Where had he gone?

The Wichu came back on the line. "Steed said the ship's fine. The license is legit. The owner's an old customer, the landing bay operator told me. I spoke to her myself."

"You're being had, sir. Once they're fueled up; they can escape. In the name of the Emperor..."

The Wichu's mustache bristled, the equivalent of a human raising his eyebrows. "Do you have orders from the Emperor himself?"

"No, but, if you'd just look at this image..." I tied in the file of the two pictures I had taken. The Wichu's eyes left mine as he glanced at them on the side of his screen, then reached out a thick forefinger. He must have deleted them.

"Don't waste my time. You're mistaken. We run scans on every ship visiting this facility every day."

"But..."

"Out." The screen went blank.

I strode back to the table, rules fighting with impulse, worry and annoyance in my mind.

"What did he say?" Oskelev asked.

"That I was mistaken. How could they ignore plain, photographic proof?" I demanded. "The idiots! That ship will fly off. They will miss the easy chance to take a criminal out of circulation."

"What now?" Plet asked.

I smacked my fist into my palm. "We'll have to take action ourselves."

"Us?" Bailly asked. "What can we do? There's only five of us."

I looked around at the sea of concerned faces, and enlightenment bloomed within me.

"No, Bailly. *Fifty*-five," I said. "Captain Chan!"

"Yessir!" The operator of number three drillhead jumped to her feet.

I met her eyes. "I require your assistance to take action against a dangerous enemy. Are you with me?"

A wide grin spread across her face. "You bet, *sir!* Miners?"

"We're with you!" Filzon yelled, pumping a fist skyward. "Let's hear it for the lord ensign! Yay!"

"Yay!" The assembled volunteers let out a ragged cheer. It was swallowed up by the immense chamber. I hoped the swift diminuition was not an omen for our enterprise. The humans were enthusiastic, the aliens less so but game nevertheless. I felt my heart lift.

"That's the spirit that made this Imperium great," I said. "Now, let's plan our strategy. Captain!"

"Yessir!" Chan said. "Jurhman, come here. Let's get to work."

The bulky male with wisps of black hair around a nearly bald crown with a scar across it slid neatly into the seat beside Chan. I put my viewpad on the table. The rest of the militia crowded around.

"Now, who possesses a map of the colony? Is one handy?" I asked. Plet grudgingly obliged. "Where are we likely to find them?"

"Oh, that's easy," Chan said, taking her own communications unit out of her pocket. We united the two devices with a filament cable—primitive in this day and age but a necessity when physical elements interfered with connectivity. She identified the correct map. I instructed my viewpad to project it upon the wall for ease of examination. "They're gonna look for a meal or a f— uh, date. The main strip. Hardly anyone goes farther than that unless they're here for a long stay."

"If they are who you think they are," Juhrman said, "they'll get out of here pretty snappish."

"That's what I believe," I said. "It's what I would do if I didn't want to draw attention."

"So, what's your idea?"

"Surround and apprehend," I said. "If we overwhelm them with superior force, they will see the wisest thing to do is surrender. Once we disarm them, your station manager can hold them until the fleet returns to this area to take them into custody. If we aren't equal to this band of crooks, and I do not see how we can't be, we can call for the local constabulary to swell our ranks."

"Shouldn't we call them first?" Bailly asked.

"The station manager has already dismissed our claims as false," I pointed out. "The police force works for him. He can direct them to stand down, and that could be dangerous in the midst of an operation. We can call them in during our attack if we need assistance, but we shouldn't need it. I think that we will have the elements of surprise and superior numbers. That ought to be sufficient to effect a simple capture."

"Sounds simple enough," Chan said.

"This is madness!" Plet protested. "You are over-simplifying a potentially explosive situation to a series of actions."

"All good plans are simple, Lieutenant," I said.

"But you are behaving as though these putative felons will not react to your attempt to arrest them! It isn't plausible!"

"We must try," I said. "It is our duty."

"Peril to all," Rous agreed. "Pirates dangerous aren't to us?"

Juhrman grinned at the Uctu. "We're pretty tough. We've all won our share of brawls. We're not afraid to get knocked around."

"Is there any chance you're wrong?" Torkadir asked me.

"No way!" Premulo chided him. "You see the damaged fin, same as the rest of us did. It's them! We have to take them down."

"Then we're with you, sir," Filzon said.

"We concentrate upon the main strip," I said, returning to the map. "Locate them, isolate them if possible, and disarm them before they can endanger anyone." I could feel the blood of my ancestors surging hot in my veins. So this was what it was like to command! I understood why my mother loved the fleet. I could feel skepticism radiating toward me, nearly obliterating the glory of the call to action, and identified its source. I looked up. "Plet, come sit down. Join us. We need your expertise. All of you," I added, extending the invitation to the rest of my crew. They looked uncertain.

"It would be wrong to engage the enemy," Plet said. "This is foolhardy. You cannot act without orders from a superior officer."

I spun to give her my mien, set on full-on haughtiness. "And when that superior officer is unavailable, it is the duty of a junior officer to take charge, Lieutenant."

She put her chin out. "Then as your superior officer, *Ensign*, my order is that we locate and inform Commander Parsons. His decision will be the one we act on. Captain Chan, your services are not required."

"With all due respect, Lieutenant," Chan said, her blunt nose upturned, "we don't take orders from you. The lord ensign here is the one that the admiral sent here, right? Well, I'm in charge of this company, and I'm putting us under the orders of the lord ensign here. Right, guys?"

Another cheer burst out.

"Yeah, see?" Chan said. "Okay, everyone, arm up. Be back here in fifteen, or try and tell me why. Got it?"

"Yes, ma'am!" they shouted as one.

I felt my chest swell with pride and emotion. Plet, by comparison, seemed deflated. Even her crisp uniform had lost some of its starch. I could not let her feel humiliated by my efforts. Under normal circumstances, I would have been more than willing to follow the chain of command, but at the moment it was broken off from the remainder. Time was winging away, and with it our chances to stop these pirates from disappearing into the depths of space. It was our *duty* to capture the rogue crew. Consensus was the way forward. I was not an island unto myself. An army of one is not an army.

"We will continue to attempt to contact Parsons," I said, offering conciliation without, I hoped, sounding patronizing. "And the fleet. Will someone guide one of my officers to the main shopping district and try to find Parsons? The security service up there will certainly have spotted a man in naval uniform marching about the place. Parsons does tend to stand out. He'll be back here in two shakes, probably before we finish our plans. We will act only in the absence of advice from either the fleet or Commander Parsons. Will that do, Lieutenant Plet?"

"Well," she began, still uncertain. "Very well."

I beamed at her. "That's the spirit! Now, do I have a volunteer?"

"I'll go, sir," Oskelev said.

"I'll take her," said Haludi, rising. "C'mon, we'll catch the sidewalks toward the sun-side of the colony. They won't be too crowded at this hour." They departed at the run.

"Someone go up to the strip, too," Chan said. "Ask around and see where that crew went to hang out. Filzon, you know all the brothels, you go."

Ganny Filzon's cheeks went red as I looked at him in astonishment. He simply did not seem the tireless pursuer of negotiable affection.

"My mom sells bedroom furniture," he said, sheepishly.

"Good man," I said, relieved that my faculty of assessment was not totally askew. "Inside information is always helpful. Contact us on the land line as soon as you have a sighting."

"Aye, sir!" he bellowed,

"Come along, then, Plet," I said, beckoning her over. "We need all good minds on this. We will have only once chance to get this right."

❧ CHAPTER 14 ❧

It seemed an unnecessary caution to tiptoe behind
Filzon in the loud, hot and busy street, but it was
hard to control the impulse for silence. It was not
as though our presence went unnoticed; I wore my
full uniform with the bill of my cap facing smartly
forward. At my side strode my shuttle crew and
Captain Chan. Behind us, in their ragtag uniforms
and mismatched weapons, were the members of
the Smithereen militia. I regretted my small force
had only two sets of powered armor, one under the
command of a man so ancient that I doubted he
could perform drills and exercises without its support,
but he moved with the grace of a swallow, whereas
the other suit, operated by a muscular young woman
with broad shoulders, creaked and jerked at every
step. The smell of overworked circuitry added an
acrid aroma to the mixed scents of crowds, garbage,
machine lubricants and unidentified minerals. Only
the limited gravity helped to keep the suit moving
in its state of decrepitude.

The locals looked oddly upon us marching with weapons on the busy main street. Crowds parted before us as we moved with purpose, though everyone I passed could have picked me up and broken me over a knee. Under normal circumstances, I would have been in field dress, with an optical pickup that fit over my right eye, feeding me intel from my viewpad as a heads-up display instead of having to rely upon memory and the occasional furtive glance downward at the pouch at my waist. Many of my troops had to link personal electronics into the military channel, hooked into the software by a hasty fix provided by Juhrman. We would all have been in light armor at least. Still, an army was an army, and we outnumbered the other force more than two-and-a-half to one, or so Filzon had informed me. That meant that once we engaged, each pair of my soldiers would acquire a preselected target and do its level best to apprehend that target without danger to the surrounding setting.

"They just ordered pancakes," Filzon stage-whispered, pointing to a storefront with the sign *Oatmeal and Son* over the door. Blast-glass panels provided a slightly hazy view of the interior, but nothing could staunch the savory aromas coming from inside. My stomach, though it was well fed, squeezed appreciatively. Robot servers carried enormous food on trays to each table of hungry diners. A few humans in brightly colored tunics, folded cloth caps and wheeled shoes, no doubt the wait staff, skidded from group to group to assess the quality of service and comestibles, and to serve the platters from the robotrays. "I caught 'em comin' out of Strange Bedfellows over there. Bruce always sends his clients over there for breakfast after . . . you know."

I nodded. Of course I knew, though this was not the time to discuss my amorous past. My memory was suffering overload from other, more immediate cognitive centers. Dread of the unknown excited the primitive portion of my brain. I smelled fear. No, that sour odor was emanating from the restaurant. Naturally they served food for every species who visited Smithereen, and that included dainties for those who liked their meals less than fresh. One of those had just come out of the preparation area toward a waiting diner. My banquet dinner considered the sudden intrusion of the unpalatable aroma and threatened to depart via the easiest route. I fought it down again. Better to keep my mind focused upon the visual and aural input, absorbing the street scene, observing the escape routes that we had marked out in the architectural rendering—always provided that the shop owners had not done their own unlicensed renovations. I doubted—I hoped none would be found in the restaurant.

Beside me, Plet continued to attempt to summon the station manager, the *Wedjet* or Parsons. The station manager's Wichu assistant hung up on us every time we called. So far no wireless transmissions had succeeded in breaking through to Parsons's viewpad or to the compiler that would take our messages offworld to the ship. We continued receiving the "Your Data is Very Important to Us" recording, the bane of every intelligent being who had ever had the misfortune to fall prey to the inhuman voice mail system galaxywide.

"Your message has been placed in the queue and will be sent with the next possible data packet. Please check your inbox again later for confirmation. Your data is very important to us. Your message . . ."

It's all on us, I realized, straining to see through the blast-glass of the restaurant's front wall. We were the only hope to bring these felons in.

"Pawade!" announced a high-pitched voice near my knee.

I jumped. A tot of two or three years of age pointed at me gleefully from the hoverchair that his maternal unit was pushing. I gave him a weak smile.

"Yes, baby, parade," said his mother, giving a sharp look at my archaic weapons and at the file of mismatched uniforms behind me. "Taking up the whole street. Some people!"

"I beg your pardon, madam," I said, doffing my hat to her. "A necessary exercise."

"Hmph!" She marched away. The baby waved at me gleefully.

"There they are," Filzon whispered, his voice echoing in my earpiece, which had been tuned to the militia's assigned frequency. As long as we were close together, the signal was stronger than the magnetite's interference. He grabbed my arm and dragged me close to the open door. He poked a surreptitious finger, and I followed its vector. "There!"

"*That* is our crew?"

"Yup," Filzon said. "Every one of them is off that ship that you saw. They paid for their, uh . . ."

"Entertainment?" I supplied.

"Uh, yeah, with a credit chit from the ship. Backed it up with the license from the Holborn Empire, belongs to the Harmony Exchange Foundation. They *said*. So they don't know we're looking for them! What do we do first?" He regarded me with large, hopeful eyes.

I surveyed the crew. Only three of the twenty

members of the pirate vessel were human. The rest
were Uctu, Croctoid, and one Solinian, a reptilian
whose bulk made Croctoids look like geckos, and the
gecko-like Uctus like garter snakes. I swallowed hard.
But we were now committed to action. I scanned the
restaurant. Oatmeal and Son was a very large establishment. The restaurant was approximately two-thirds
full. Most of the other patrons were seated as far away
from the party from the pirate vessel as possible. As
a Wichu slid to a controlled stop beside the Solinian
with a platter filled with raw meat, I understood why.
The Solinian didn't wait for it to be lowered before
him, but snagged a handful of dripping, red flesh and
stuffed it into his clamplike jaws. I gulped.

"Plet," I said, "please give me the overview of this
area. I want to make certain we won't be surprised
from behind."

With a disapproving sigh, she activated the appropriate section of the map and sent it to all of us. I
perused it and nodded thoughtfully.

"This is absurd," she whispered irritatedly. "Look at
the size of them. How can we surround them without
putting the other diners at risk? Families are sitting
all around them."

"They are relatively isolated," I said. "We must
move nonchalantly into the establishment, casually
surround them and cut off their escape. Then I will
inform them that they are under arrest."

"Are you joking?" she hissed. "How?"

"Subtlety," I insisted. "We must deploy ourselves
subtly. Then, on my signal, we will move in. They
don't appear to be armed."

Chan nodded. "They have to check their weapons

at the port. You guys got a dispensation because you're Navy."

"Thank the powers for small favors." I took a deep breath. "Very well, then. A few at a time, and..."

A voice blared out from behind me. "In or out, dammit! You trick-or-treaters can't clog up the door of this place forever. Move it or lose it!"

I turned to confront the owner of the voice, and found myself facing an enormous, pale-furred Wichu female who towered a good head above me. She was accompanied by a litter of six massive youngsters with variegated fur, one of which was clinging to an exposed fuchsia nipple. "I beg your pardon, madam, but we are contemplating..."

"Contemplate on your own time! My kids are hungry! Move it!"

She shoved me through the doors of the restaurant. I stumbled in, tripping over my feet. When I straightened, I realized everyone was looking at me, including my quarry. They had stopped tearing and gulping gobbets of red flesh to stare. I averted my gaze, so as not to tip them off that they were the objects of my desire. Little hope existed that they thought otherwise. We had no choice but to act immediately. I had always heard that no plan survives contact with the enemy, and now I found it was true.

"Fan out and assume stations," I ordered my troops over the communications link. Chan put both her hands together then outward. Whether or not her militia had drilled such exercises as "Separate into two files in a dining establishment and feign hunger," they divided into two even packs and moved toward empty tables as though calorie replenishment was the sole reason for their presence. I admit that having two suits of powered armor creak in behind us rather stretched the credibility of the premise.

Plet and the other naval personnel kept right behind me. My heart quailed at confronting the enormous beings, but our duty was clear. Filzon had informed me that the Croctoid with the leathery brown skin in the white shipsuit was the leader. I marched toward him, my hand ready to draw my sidearm. My troops filled in around the party. The pirates could not fail to understand our motive, but remained seated. At my signal, the militia leveled their weapons.

"Captain Growteing?" I stated formally.

"Skreg off," he said, not bothering to look up. Blood smeared his scaly jaws and clawed handpaws. I had never noticed before how unpleasant the burbling growl of a Croctoid sounded. "I'm eating."

Undeterred, I continued.

"I am Ensign-Captain Thomas Kinago of the Imperium Navy. Your ship is one of a number that was reported missing and has been involved in acts of piracy. You and your crew are therefore requested to accompany me to a place of inquiry until such time as we can satisfy ourselves to what role you have played in its disappearance and misuse. You will all come with me now to the authorities."

The humans in the party looked at me, and rose at once from their places, surprised at themselves.

"Satisfy yourself on your own time, softskin," the captain snarled. He turned his head and glared at his crewmen. They sat down. He turned the evil eye toward my force. A few of them stepped backward, but resumed their stance, looking shamefaced at having retreated even a pace. I did not blame them, but duty called.

"Then I have no choice but to take you into custody," I said, drawing my sidearm. "Troops! Take them!"

The Solinian, a brute with shiny gold skin, leaned over and bit the barrel off my antique pistol with an astonishing *crunch!* I stared at the truncated stock. The Solinian grinned at me.

I gulped but drew my sword. "Surrender now!"

"Or what?" the captain asked.

I felt the ire of my ancestors rising within me at his defiance. I aimed the point of the blade directly at his left eye. "Or we will have to take you by force."

My troops raised the weapons in their hands. The pirate crew kicked back their chairs and stood up. The banging and sliding noises alerted patrons in the restaurant, who looked up from their consumption of mass quantities and saw us arrayed against one another. Those with shrill voices screamed.

"Move in to capture!" I shouted. My troops moved forward, arms set to stun force.

From hidden pockets, from sleeves, from among the cascading scales on their heads, the pirate crew produced lethal-looking handguns with shortened barrels. Even as my brain bellowed out, "Where did those come from?" the captain snapped a thumb down and disconnected the safety on his. The whine of the power supply rose through levels of sound until my skull sang in harmony. He pointed the weapon toward my head. My heart pounded.

Luckily, Croctoids move more slowly than humans. By the time the barrel reached its target area, my head was no longer in the way. I ducked. The single shot of heated plasma ripped through the air, leaving a singed metallic odor. The restaurant's patrons grabbed up their children and valuables and made for the front exit, screaming and swearing. They could not all pass through the portal at once. I could hear yells of anger and fear behind me as they shoved and butted one another to get out. I feared smaller civilians would be trampled, but my immediate concern was for my own survival. I chopped at the Croctoid with my sword. The blade knocked his arm upward but failed to draw blood. The captain turned, his reflexes thankfully not as fast as mine, and readied another shot. I danced backwards and tripped over a chair. The light gravity was all that kept me from breaking a rib on a table edge. Hot pellets zinged over my head. The pirates started firing back. Their weapons were set to deliver full force.

"Defend yourselves!" I cried.

My orders were scarcely necessary.

Chan's people opened up close fire on the Croctoid captain. He staggered, but did not fall. His small, beady eyes glared hate at all of us. He and his people snapped off shots. A drinks machine burst, spraying us all with bright orange fluid. Under its cover, I lunged in, the point of my sword aiming for the tendon in his wrist. He switched hands and blasted at me again. I dodged. My troops flipped up tables and took cover behind them. Beakers and platters crashed to the floor, depositing huge piles of food and lakes of sticky colored liquid. The pirates upended tables for their own defense, though their large bulk left huge expanses of shipsuit and scaly backsides and tails exposed. The only ones who remained within the suddenly cleared area were the pirate captain and myself. We circled one another, one eye on the other's weapon, one on the mess on the floor.

"Stun the enemy!" I shouted. The militia duly peppered the parts of the pirate crew they could see. The reptilians howled with rage, and returned fire. Sooner or later even their metabolisms would give way under repeated energy rounds. The captain fired at me. I ducked him easily. He roared in fury and came at me, shooting. I danced around him, looking for an opening. My sword was of little use; I could try to engage him in unarmed combat. I eyed him. It would be a challenge. I had the reach, but several times more muscles writhed within that scaly skin than I possessed in mine. I needed to keep away from him. Besides the powerful tail that was a weapon in itself, Croctoids liked to grasp an enemy against their bodies and roll with it upon the floor. Their distant ancestors drowned their prey in that fashion; on dry land, the effect was to crush and disorient. We circled one another as our forces pelted one another with energy charges.

Miraculously, none of the shots hissing through the air touched either of us. The restaurant facilities took the brunt. Images of vegetables and fruit that were affixed about the top edge of the walls fell, blackened and smoking. I felt in my pocket for the handful of plastic restraints the constables among the ad hoc force had handed out. The captain bracketed me with two shots. I dodged both, dreading the third. I'd have to figure out how to secure even one hand.

P-yow!

A blast from one of the enemy Geckos drilled right

through a tabletop and severed the spring holding the legs out. Margolies fell under it, clutching his arm and swearing. Behind him, a nanicarriage trapped by the melee swerved this way and that to avoid the hot plasma bursts. The baby inside it started howling angrily.

"You have woken the baby! You inconsiderate biped!" The nanibot raised a laser pistol from its control center and opened fire on us. Its attack distracted the captain. I leaped away from him. The nanibot peppered us all with fire. A blue-skinned Uctu pirate fell, her midsection smoking. Her fellows retaliated, but the nanibot was better armored than they were. It laid down a barrage of covering shots and retreated into the midst of the crowd jamming the doorway. I dove for cover under half a smoldering table. I was in more danger from a non-combatant than I was from the enemy.

The simple capture was not going as I had envisioned it. I was ashamed of myself. I had placed innocent civilians in harm's way. Kinagos, let alone Loches, must never put those they were sworn to protect under threat! I had to get the pirates out of the restaurant and into a more isolated location. But there were few places in a colony like Smithereen that fulfilled that criterion. And how to move them there?

I had not much time to work out this conundrum. They had already decided on their own to depart from this arena.

"Come on, you salamanders! Together!" the captain bellowed.

Ignoring the barrage of stun charges, the captain and his crew sprang out of their hiding place and rushed toward the jammed entrance. They started throwing humans, Geckos and Wichus right and left as if they were rag dolls. Drawing the antique sword from my belt, I sprang out from my hiding place.

"Smithereen militia, with me!" I cried.

I advanced and executed a handsome ballestra toward the pirate's back. The point of my sword went through the fabric of his shipsuit, but bounced rather than penetrating the tough hide underneath.

"Ow!" The Croctoid turned on his heel and backhanded me with a whip of his tail. Shocked, I staggered into the arms of Bailly. My ear sang with the blow. I shook my head and assumed an *en garde* pose. The captain's little eyes were hot. He leveled his pistol. "You worm!" He peppered the gray composite floor around me with hot blasts. Tiles melted into goo. Bailly and I retreated. Employing my best footwork, I managed to stay out of the line of fire, but I was running out of room. A hot ball of energy erupted near my ear. I smacked out the fire in my hair with my palm and rolled under a nearby table.

In the meanwhile, the militia was pulling pirates out of the crowd and attempting to disarm them. Naturally, the illicit crew was uncooperative. At close quarters, it was more difficult to aim pistols, but each of them possessed physical weaponry that was nearly as formidable. The Solinian dropped to all fours and wrapped itself around Plet's legs. She fired round after round of stun charges into its knobby head, but it shook them off. At last, she plunged the heels of her hands into its eye sockets. Bellowing, it rolled over, taking her with it into the midst of broken tables and chairs. Was she all right? Fearing for her safety, I crawled toward the spot where they had disappeared, ready to assist, but suddenly she emerged, straightening her hair with one hand, looking as cool as ever. I could have applauded. The Solinian crawled out after her, its hands bound together, looking sheepish. I would put Plet in for a promotion as soon as we were back on board the *Wedjet*. As soon as it caught me looking, it gnawed the strap off with one bite and spat it at me.

The Croctoids lunged at faces and necks with their sharp, hooked claws raking the air. The *Wedjet* crew beings were less prepared, but the local militiabeings dove in, proving themselves just as dirty fighters as their opponents. Knees to groins, fingers to eyes, elbows to the side of necks, all connected with thuds and crunches. Margolies clapped her hands over the sensitive ear holes of a Croctoid. It dropped to its knees, bawling. She smacked its jaws shut and wrapped a plastic strap around them. Its beady eyes widened with fury. It tried to gouge her with its claws. She kneed it in the belly and smashed down on its head with her joined fists. I rushed to help.

"Where are the authorities?" I bellowed into my audio pickup, as we each grabbed for a flailing claw.

Juhrman's dry voice spoke into my ear. "Not interested in a little brawl. They'll pick up the bodies when it's all over."

"What?" I was outraged.

"We can take care of it, sir," said Hek-et-rahm, one of the local constabulary.

"Confound it, what is it with law enforcement today?" I demanded. "They'd have had me and my cousins in a cell before you can say 'disturbing the peace'!"

A Gecko threw himself at me, falling over my sword.

The captain raised his fist and smashed it toward my face. I leaped to the left. It impacted upon my right shoulder with the force of a flitter banging into a wall. I gasped at the pain.

"Self-correcting," Chan said. I could hear the shrug in her voice. She backhanded a Croctoid with her stunner. Pointed teeth flew. It shook its head and snapped at her again, having plenty more to spare. "Let the unsavory elements take care of themselves. The people here know better than to hang out in alleys, and the ones who don't aren't gonna survive anyway."

"What now, sir?" Plet's breathless voice came in my ear as I scrambled to my feet. Out of the corner of my eye I could see her hanging onto the wrist of an Uctu, trying to snap a plastic restraint with the other hand.

My arm around a Gecko's throat, I took a quick look around. At least five of the pirates were on the ground, but at least twice that many of my force were wounded and gasping. A human female lay on the floor as limp as a discarded sock. I couldn't see her face. My heart wrenched with shame. These brave beings were my responsibility! I had to prevent any more casualties.

"We must isolate them somewhere until we can find Parsons," I said. "We need a distraction."

"Are you kidding?" she asked. She secured the crewbeing's one hand and reached for the other. The Gecko kicked nimbly out at her and Rous dove for its feet, holding it still while she fastened the pirate's arms under its tail. "How? What?"

What, indeed?

The captain shook off the four humans trying to hold it and made for the door again.

"No, sir!" I shouted. I sidled into his path with my sword pointed at its eye, daring it to defy me. "You shall not pass!"

"You uniformed action figure!" he snarled. "Get out of my way!"

He barreled forward, intending to go through me. I lunged, scoring a slash on the bridge of his nose just short of his left eye. Purple blood spurted. I wasn't sure which of us was more surprised, he or I. I danced backward as he lumbered toward me.

While fending off the huge Croctoid with my sword, I scanned the enemy combatants. None of the pirates seemed worth taking as a hostage. Knowing the ruthless nature of such beings and their purported guidelines, I doubted they would pursue us to rescue one of their own. But lying on their abandoned dining table was something they could not and would not do without: their ship's half-license. The captain had left the square of indestructible metal beside his platter, no doubt believing that he could retrieve it at his leisure after he had disposed of as many of us as necessary before the local constabulary was summoned.

I lunged toward the Croctoid, parrying the very barrel of the pistol in his hand. He let off a shot at the ceiling by mistake. A light fixture exploded, raining shards of plastic down on us. All around us, Chan's militia was doing their best to control and contain the rest of the crew without killing them. The pirates were under no such restraint. Torkadir, or perhaps Premulo, fell, his leg sticking out sideways at a horribly unnatural angle. My internal organs knotted in sympathy, but I needed to look to my own survival. I recovered forward and ducked under Growteing's crooked arm. He spun, more slowly than a human would, drawing a fresh bead upon me.

I took advantage of his dilatory movements. Beating another Croctoid's gun with my sword hilt to point upward, I slipped among the thrashing forms of my troops wrestling with pirate adversaries in the direction of my prey. The captain finished his rotation and ended up facing me just in time to ascertain my intent.

"No! Curse you!"

I hoped his curse would not take. I reached the table and snatched up the metal square. I held it up triumphantly. He roared out more invective. I made a face at him and ran toward the rear of the restaurant.

"Retreat!" I called. With the map of the area limned upon my mind as brightly as the exit sign overhead, I headed toward the back door that opened out into the service passage where deliveries were made. "Team A, follow me! We can lead them into a trap! Team B, stay behind them and make sure none of them remains here! We can take them!"

"What?" Plet's voice echoed breathless in my ear. "Where?"

My mind raced through the possibilities open to us. Our ship was out of the question. The crew might decide to flee to its own vessel and threaten others with its onboard cannon and missile until I was forced to return the license. The station manager had not taken my warning seriously, and was more likely to be hindrance than help. Sweating, I strained my cerebral faculties for inspiration.

Yes!

There was only one place that I could think of that would—could—act as a temporary holding cell until Parsons or the *Wedjet* returned to take the crew into custody.

"The hotel ballroom!" I cried.

"What?"

"We will lure them into that wonderful maze of walls and floors. If I stir it up, I believe I can box them in a room without doors until they could be taken into custody."

"And that's your plan?" Plet hissed.

"Yes!"

There was a brief silence, and I thought that I had lost her.

"Actually, that's a good idea. We'll try to buy you some time."

"Carry on, troops!" I shouted into the communications link. "Evasive maneuvers, and protect the public!"

I shot away, waving my booty over my head in a fleering manner. The pirate captain let out a roar of fury and stumbled after me, shoving aside damaged furniture and dithering traybots. I ran down the length of the enormous room, weaving between hastily abandoned tables and upset chairs. I leaped over a cowering server and skidded to a halt at the control beside the service door.

My enemy bore down on me, as I had predicted. My move was not without precedent. I had once snatched the lunch of a bigger cousin with a notoriously bad temper on a dare when I was in school. My long legs gave me the only advantage I had, fleeing from an angry, much larger opponent. This time, however, I was unprepared for the frisson of cold fear that went up my body as the entire crew left their individual battles and came after me. There was a lengthy hesitation before the door opened. For a moment I was afraid that it required some kind of security code. In eight paces, the Croctoid captain would be upon me.

At last, with a weary explosion of sound, the door slid into the wall to the right. A noisome wind, redolent with the fumes of ancient garbage, fuel, body odor and mildew, whooshed into my face. I gagged in a breath of only half-rotted air, and fled.

Into a rectangular tunnel I dashed. Pools of faint yellow light from emergency fixtures were my main source of illumination at first, but a blast of bright whiteness blinded me. I burst through it blindly. Motion-sensitive lamps were fixed into the walls at the rear door of the business establishments on this corridor to facilitate deliveries during less hostile moments. I hoped that my pursuers were as taken off guard as I was.

The hammering of shipboots behind propelled me forward like an afterburner. I navigated by memory, feeling my way down the steel corridor for the third left. Was it the third? Could I be mistaken? No, I was positive it was the third. Here it was!

I flew into the darkened turnoff. My eyes, stunned by the flashes of light, took a while to become accustomed to the blackness of this passageway. I sought the second of two narrow doorways close together after six irregularly spaced doors. It should put me into the main corridor just outside the tavern to which Chan and the others had taken me for a drink. I did not want to chance leading the pirates through the crowds down to the hotel, but did I have a choice? I could not take the time to read my map. Oh, for the heads-up display in my combat helmet back in the ship! I could hear the captain behind me, swearing as he lumbered along. More heavy footsteps joined his. Alarmed, I increased my pace. A painful stitch arose in my right ribcage. I ignored it. The side of my head ached from the energy blast, and my shoulder ached from the Croctoid captain's blow. Nothing mattered but getting the pirates to a place of temporary incarceration until Parsons could be located. I toggled my communications link.

"Plet, I'm about to emerge into traffic. Is there an alternative that will not put me into traffic? I am weary of annoying heavily armed babysitting robots."

"Yes, sir!" Plet's voice rose over static in my ear. "Stay on this corridor for another thirty meters. I can guide you through accessways. Listen carefully. You are getting out of range. Left, third left, right, right, down cargo tube four levels, left, long corridor, last door at the end. Do you have that? I will repeat it until team B rejoins you in the ballroom."

Bless her efficiency. I was good at learning trivia and song lyrics on one hearing, but between alarm and static, I was uncertain. I listened, attempting to picture the route, mindful of the consequences should I fail. The next time, a nanibot's wild shots would certainly do to me what the pirates had so far failed to accomplish.

Behind me, the movement-controlled lights flashed on and off, causing the shadow thrown ahead of me to strobe. I glanced back. Four-legged crewbeings swarmed after me. They were much closer than I had anticipated. Two Geckos passed their slower comrades and were in danger of catching up with me. Their voices echoed in the stinking hallway. Heedless of the pain now wracking the entire right side of my body, I summoned all my speed and ran.

The narrow alley into which Plet directed me had a floor that was both slippery and sticky. I only hoped that the uncertain footing would cause my pursuers to fare worse than I did. My boots alternately slid or caught in the dark green goo. I cannoned off the walls more than once.

Suddenly, a hand seemed to reach out of the darkness to my left. I flinched, then my eyes focused. It was not a hand, but a metal gate of some kind, left partway open by its last user. My approach made its circuitry wake up and close the rest of the way. I was unlucky enough to get caught in its sweep. I dodged, or thought I had, but it came out and struck me across the midsection.

"Oof!" Inelegant, I admit, but I hadn't time to come up with a clever outburst. My ribs hurt! To my dismay, the license was knocked out of my hand.

The metal clattered upon the soiled floor. I looked back. My pursuers heard the noise, and picked up their pace. I dropped to my knees and fumbled in the dark for the square of metal, collecting a good deal of the stinking slime on my hands in the process. At last my fingertips met the edge. I scraped it up with my fingernails and clapped it to my side. Conveniently, the ambient sludge helped it adhere to my uniform tunic. I would not lose it again.

"Status!" I barked into my pickup. My voice sounded hoarse.

"Wait a minute," said Chan. "Juhrman stayed behind in group B. I'm listening to him. I'll be back to you in a moment."

Plet's voice came thinly through a wave of static. "The crew is nearly on top of you, sir. The alley will widen out in a moment, then you have a choice of directions."

I scanned my surroundings. A bright yellow square loomed out of the darkness.

"I see an access sign! I can turn right out into the main road."

"No! I can keep you out of the thoroughfare all the way to the hotel entrance, if you follow my instructions." Her voice cracked, and I realized that I might lose her to the interference.

"Tell me, quickly," I pleaded.

A hot red burst of plasma splattered a light fixture near me. The Geckos were much faster than their companions, and were at last on my tail. But I was still faster than they, and fear gave me afterburners.

"In one hundred meters, you will see the lift downward..."

My attention to the voice in my ear must have caused me to slow down in a darkened portion of the corridor. A weight landed upon my back and bore me to the sticky floor. I guessed by the weight it was a Gecko. We rolled together. A second body, as light as the first, joined the fray. I knew from wrestling with my shipmates that impact to their sensitive earspots could incapacitate them. They knew it, too, striving to keep my hands away from the sides of their heads. They knew, too, that knocking my nose in would incapacitate me. We flailed around the floor, trying to slap one another in the face.

I felt a hard mass ram into my hip. I felt downward and wrenched the pistol from the Gecko's shipsuit pocket. It fought to get it back, scratching at my face

and arms, but I forced my way to my feet and held
it too high for the being to reach. You may call it
wasted effort and time, but I dialed the setting back
from kill to stun before I blasted its owner in the face.
He dropped. I walked my shots to flank the second
one, and succeeded in knocking her weapon out of
her hand. I raised the gun to render her unconscious,
but she was too quick. She dashed back into the darkness. The footsteps of the others were much nearer.
I turned and ran, tucking the gun into my belt.

With Plet's voice in my ear, I ran toward a door
through which issued a pink light. An open-sided
pressure tube there acted as an elevator. It was an
old-fashioned type, but those that still ran were hard
to get rid of once they had been installed, because
removing the tunnel often caused the collapse of
the surrounding structure, so most edifices, like old
colonies, that had them kept them running, but did
not use them as much as better and safer structures
like elevators and moving stairs. Steeling myself, I
took a flying leap for it. I needed to penetrate the
outer stream, which was at least two meters thick in
one of these contraptions, to the center core, which
bore the rider or cargo downward.

My heart bulged upward into my throat as passed
through the strong updraft and was caught half a floor
upward by the equally powerful downdraft. I needed
to count four floors. Two Croctoids, Growteing and
one other, hurtled out of the darkness and plunged
into the stream, hands outstretched for my throat and
the precious license. I flinched backwards, and fell
into the updraft with them tumbling against me. We
were battered against the walls by our momentum. I

was swept ten floors up in the outer stream until I fought my way back into the central column of rushing air that snatched me and dragged me downward. The Croctoids were swept upward several more floors before they swam into the downdraft to follow me. Their eyes gleamed down at me in the sickly pink light. They did not dare take a shot at me here lest they cause an explosion in the pressure tube that would kill all of us, but they shouted threats and demands. I held onto the license, attached firmly to my uniform, my only hope.

I faked jumping into open doorways twice. I lost one of the Croctoids on the floor immediately below my target. Captain Growteing stayed with me, but I still had an advantage over him: he did not know where I was going. After several dizzying ups and downs, I sprang out of the pressure tube. My first steps on a plascrete floor were as unsteady as a newborn lamb's, but luckily the residue from the corridor floor on the bottom of my boots helped my feet stick tightly. I regained my equilibrium swiftly and began again to run. With the Croctoid captain's angry shouts behind me, I opened up some distance.

❧ CHAPTER 15 ❧

It must have been a shock to the well-coiffed employees at the opulent check-in desk when I burst out of the wall looking like a tramp that had taken an accidental ride in a garbage scow. They stared at me, with the correct expression of haughty disapproval. I straightened my back and adjusted my cap which was, miraculously, still on my head.

"Where is Ms. Lutsen?" I demanded.

Fortunately, the lady was mere steps away, behind the thin partition. She appeared and beheld me with some horror.

"Lord Thomas!" she exclaimed.

"I apologize for my attire," I burst out, "but it is imperative that we make use of your ballroom again." A roar shook the wall through which I had just emerged. "Urgently. As in this very moment."

"I don't know if we can accommodate you," Ms. Lutsen said, looking elegantly worried. "We have another party coming in two hours. We need to get the facility cleaned and set up . . ."

"You are too kind," I said, with a bow and a smile, as if she had said yes. I looked around the elegant foyer. A heavy antique sideboard would buy me a moment or two more. I seized upon it and began to drag it toward the door. Its feet screamed a protest on the shining floor. "And by the way, I suggest you evacuate the hotel. At least this floor. And any rooms that border the ballroom. At once."

"But, Lord Thomas!" the banquet manager protested.

"I will give you an explanation later," I said, setting my burden in place with a thump, "but I would suggest you remove yourselves now. Lock the front door. Tell everyone that there is a leak."

"What kind of leak?" demanded a young man with swooping locks of enameled black hair.

"Anything that will prevent them from trying to get in until this is settled," I said. "It's a naval matter. Please excuse me." I broke away, hoping I had not been too rude, but time was fleeting.

Ms. Lutsen must have given her consent, because the ballroom doors opened for me. I hit the emergency control to slam them shut. They wouldn't lock—such a thing was not permitted in a residential facility in use for fear of trapping living beings in an emergency—but I needed a few minutes unobserved so that the pirates could not see what I was doing. I flew to the control panel. I had enjoyed playing with the floors and walls of the modular structure, but now I needed to concentrate in deadly seriousness. In my mind I constructed a living maze, one that would keep on changing until I could trap the pirates into a small inner chamber without doors or windows. I began to program my ideas into the panel, setting timers on each successive change. If only Parsons would return! Once I had my program in place, I tried signaling him again. Nothing. Where was he?

I heard a harrowing crash and an outcry from the lobby. Growteing had burst through the barrier. The others could not be far behind.

"You softskin, I will tear your head off and use it as a handball!"

I shouted into my communicator. "Chan, Plet, where are you?"

"About seventy meters, sir!" Plet replied, her voice sounding stronger than before. I was relieved.

"Right," I said. "My maze is based upon the Keight garden party design. When you get in here, go in as far as you can, and turn right. Then left. Then right, then left. Keep to that pattern. Doors will disappear; walls will change. If a staircase presents itself, take it, but do not vary the pattern."

"Yes, sir!" they chorused.

The Croctoid came roaring toward me. He was so slow that I had to wait in the entrance to my trap.

"I will tear you apart, human! Give back the license!"

I sneered at him, and gave him my best derisive laugh.

"No, I think I'll have it made into a backdrop for my waste disposer," I said. "It will improve my aim." I waved the square of metal in his direction. He raised his pistol. I fled into the labyrinth. Red light exploded behind me. Gobbets of plastic flew from the wall frame. I heard his heavy footsteps and laboring breath.

"Team A is here, sir," Plet said. I heard the sound of battle around her. Grunts and cries of pain rang through my earpiece. "Juhrman said he sent the wounded to the infirmary. A couple of constables finally showed up. He gave them five prisoners, and he's on his way. We order you to surrender!—not you, sir."

"Understood," I said. I wished I could see what they were doing. I longed once again for the heads-up display of my helmet.

It was time to rejoin my troops. The Croctoid must be dealt with first.

I had had to go slow to avoid contact with the much larger and better-armed pirate, but now it was time to allow him to get lost in the maze. At the next turning, I flattened myself against the inner wall and called for the Optique. At my command, the hovering camera eye flashed short video clips. I had to select one in a hurry. I had no good video of me running, but I had had the camera take footage of me reviewing the troops. I selected a short clip in which I was marching smartly away from it. I ordered the camera to crop the image to conceal the line of troops and increase the playback speed to a quadruple-quick march. That should be just fast enough to stay ahead of the Croctoid. I had no time to drop in the image of the license. I just hoped that he believed I still had it, and his crew's key to freedom was to catch me and regain it.

"Attention, pirate captain!" I shouted, and sent the Optique on its way. I held my breath and willed myself invisible.

My dorsal view bloomed upon the wall adjacent to my hiding place. The pirate let out a roar and followed "me" as I seemed to dash to the left. He lumbered past my place of concealment without remarking at all upon my presence. In a moment, I was alone, all without firing a shot. And, just in time, one of the dark blue wall segments rose up, blocking any return from that leftward corridor. I ran out to aid my troops.

In the anteroom that I had left open, Team A of a somewhat depleted militia attempted to surround and disarm the remainder of the pirates. The enormous Solinian was flanked by both volunteer soldiers in armored suits. It was an uneven battle, however. The ancient pressure suits were in poor condition, and the Solinian fought for his freedom. He had wrenched the left arm off one, leaving a skinny human limb in khaki canvas sticking out and flapping awkwardly. The other golem had wrapped its metal arms around the creature's neck and was trying to render it unconscious. It was refusing to cooperate. It raked its claws down the metal sleeve at its throat, creating a noise like a chalkboard's squeak. Everyone in the room cringed. The enormous reptilian gave a heave, and the battle suit went flying. It landed on the ground meters away with a crash of metal and lay still. I worried that the operator had been killed, but in a moment, it began to stir and attempt to rise to its feet. The Solinian shook off the second battle suit and ran away.

"Get him!"

Plet, with Rous and Bailly in her wake, went after the Solinian with the light of battle in her eyes. It seemed to have had enough of her, and dodged her around the walls. It shot at them, leaving burning holes in the wall and floors. Plet continued her relentless pursuit.

Other soldiers were facing a running battle—and I meant that literally—versus a trio of Croctoids. The reptilian pirates blasted at my uniformed cohort, missing almost every time. My soldiers paused to shoot, then scurried out of the line of fire. The Crocs were starting to sway. I hoped they would fall over before their reinforcements arrived.

It was not to be. The door of the ballroom slammed open, and five more Crocs burst into the room. Luckily, behind them were Team B and Juhrman.

"We're here, my lord ensign!" he bellowed, grinning widely, waving a pulse rifle over his head. The soldiers with him cheered.

Their support gave me heart.

"To me, Smithereenians!" I shouted.

Two enemy Geckos leaped for me. I crouched, awaiting their arrival, one eye on the display on my viewpad. "In forty-five seconds, the walls are going to change again," I told my troops over the communications link. "Make sure you are on the inner side of the partition coming up from the floor. It will block the pirates from entering the maze with us." I grabbed each Gecko by a hand and stood up. The shorter beings were forced together by my action, and slammed into one another. To my amazement, they fell backwards and crashed to the floor. I looked around.

"Did anyone else see that?" I exclaimed. "That was brilliant!"

"Great, sir." Chan threw herself on her back with one foot in the belly of another Gecko pirate. She tossed it straight into the midst of the enemy who had regained their feet and were now barreling towards me. The Geckos tumbled. "Twenty seconds!"

Suddenly, as one, the remaining pirates turned to look at me. They eyed the license stuck to the front of my tunic. The captain, lost in the maze, must have notified them by communicator that I had what they were looking for. They shoved away from the battles they were waging, and made for me. I could not let them get their hands upon me. I felt for the license, snatched it free, and sent it arching over the heads of the pirates toward the door.

Or so they thought. In truth, I palmed it and flung the pistol that I had obtained from one of the Geckos, but the movement fooled the pirates as if they were a score of dogs playing fetch. In the seconds that it took them to realize they had been duped, I signed to my troops to leave the melee and follow me. The pirates ran after them. One second later, the barrier rose up, knocking them backwards.

"You diseased softskins!" came a bellow from the other side, along with determined pounding. Most of the pirates were trapped outside, as I had planned.

But not all of the pounding was going on outside. Three of the suspect crew, two humans and a Gecko, realized that they were alone on our side of the wall. Panicked, they clawed at the partition.

"Get us out of here!" they cried.

"Get 'em!" Chan shouted, hoisting her stunner.

Her volunteers leaped on them. The fight was short, dirty and brutal, but when it ceased, they were bound with restraints and piled in a heap off to one side. Panting, Chan came over and gave me a nod.

"Nice work, Captain," I said.

"Thank you, sir," she said, looking suitably gratified.

Shouts of anger and the explosions of plasma charges were muffled by the panels, but I feared not for long. It bought me enough time to check the control panel, making certain that the program continued to run as I intended it. Rous and Oskelev guarded my back. I could hear the pirates blasting and hammering at the wall.

"They're almost through, sir," Bailly said.

"Almost there," I said, concentrating hard. I heard splintering noises. The hotel frame was meant to withstand an asteroid crash, but the interior could not be that strong.

"What is the plan, sir?" Plet asked.

"We keep them busy," I said. "The captain is already bumbling around within the maze. They might be able to communicate with him, but they can't reach him. I have the room programmed to change every three minutes from left-right configuration to right-left configuration. At the center of the maze is a small chamber sans windows or doors. We will lead them into the trap, and keep them confined there until the authorities arrive."

"They weren't coming," Plet reminded me.

I raised an eyebrow and treated her to a short, deprecating version of my patented laugh. "After the mess we left behind in Oatmeal and Son? They must take notice now."

"True," she said. "No word yet from Commander Parsons or the *Wedjet*, sir."

I nodded grimly. "We'll just have to hold on as long as we can. The pirates should be no trouble once we've got them locked up."

"From your mouth to eternity's ear, sir!" Bailly said.

A howling sound as might be made by a drill gone mad burst on our eardrums. The wall between us and the pirates burst asunder in red flames. The crew boiled through the irregular hole, gnashing their teeth.

"Into the maze!" I cried.

My troops, somewhat reduced by injury, fled into the tunnel behind me, with the pirates in angry pursuit. We had a minor head start on them.

The labyrinth was a simple one. There had been no time for niceties. I had employed the most classic of patterns, with a twist. Taking every left would take one into the center, which was scheduled in exactly fifteen minutes to close into a box with no exits or windows. That, I hoped, would hold the pirates until they could be picked up. We had to lure them in, then escape.

"Stay with me," I warned the troops over the communications system, as we hurried along the dark blue corridor lit with bronze sconces as well as the diffused light from the landing pad above the clear ceiling. If I had not been in the presence of armed soldiers, I might have been looking for a friend's hotel room. "When the timer in my viewpad goes off, the polarity will switch, and where we might turn left, we must turn right, instead."

"Aye, sir!" they chorused.

"So, we go right, then left," I said.

"Sir, didn't we turn right when we came in?" Plet, always the wet blanket, inquired.

"Yes," I said. "Then our next turn is left."

We ran. Flashes of red light behind us lent speed to our heels. The two soldiers in powered armor lagged at the rear of the party as they were meant for strength, not agility.

"Hurry," I pleaded. I could not rebuild the sequence from inside the maze. If we did not get the enemy into place within a quarter of an hour, the labyrinth would freeze in its last position, with or without the crew trapped. We ran onward. Left, right, left, right, time! Right, left, and into a carpeted corridor.

A tiny whine alarmed all of us. To my delight, however, it was the sound of my Callusion Optique returning. It had done its job, luring the captain into the maze, and had returned to me. I snatched it from the air. It whistled a protest.

"Make no noise!" I hissed. I was rewarded by the sound of a barrage of repulsor fire that underlined the import of my order to those cowering with me. They subsided into silence.

The corridor ended with a graceful spiral staircase to our left. To my dismay, at the top, our only choice of direction was left.

"What now?" Chan's voice whispered in my ear.

My heart sank. I knew that we had gone off the sequence. I signed to take the left, and we would go to the next right.

I needed Parsons. He would cope with the situation. I must send a message to him. As long as we kept hold of the license plate for the pirate ship, it could not take off. He would think of some means to capture them.

I recorded a message on my camera, added text by means of the Sang Li fingerspelling that emerged as text on the bottom of the last image of my face, then I sent it out looking for Parsons, using its internal facial recognition software. It downloaded images from every image-capture system on the planetoid, sorted through thousands of images per second, and then floated away out of my hands. I hoped it could find a hole for it to escape through, and that the next of the sliding panels we encountered would not open out onto a contingent of pirates.

❧ CHAPTER 16 ❧

"And, so I sez, you can't park that thing there! It's already rotting!" The old woman chortled to herself. "'Course, it wouldn't go anywhere. The critter had already given up the ghost. Get it?"

Parsons offered her a wintry smile. He straightened a pile of plastic crates through which he had searched meticulously for the missing data crystal and dismissed as potential hiding places. He had gleaned all the information from the old woman that he felt was possible to glean. She knew nothing beyond her brief to deliver the object to him, but was putting off the moment as long as she possibly could. She was lonely, felt separated from the circle of covert operatives in which she had long enjoyed membership, and saw him as a link to her past. If he pressed her and demanded the crystal, she might lose it or destroy it deliberately. He had no choice but to continue as a sounding board and unpaid organizer, as long as she pleased to delay him. He felt that it was safe to continue, at least for the time being. Lord Thomas was occupied at the banquet where he was being lionized by the local militia. If Parsons were needed, the viewpad at his hip would signal him.

Parsons admitted that in the hours he had been in the fuel depot, the storage room was already fifty percent organized to a professional standard, where it had been chaotic before. He also had no doubt that the moment he left she would rearrange it to chaos again, so that no one would easily be able to discover its contents. Secrecy was one of her few resources. It was not a worthless one: even determined spies often gave up a search if the odds were too greatly balanced against a swift removal.

"So, what do you hear from the central office?" the old woman asked again, as she had every few minutes when the front office was empty of customers.

"Nothing much," Parsons assured her as he had over and over. "There's been a shakeup." That was safe to say, even if anyone had been listening. A shakeup was always predicted or had just occurred. It changed little in the way the service ran. She nodded her head sagely.

Parsons continued sorting with an infinity of patience, knowing that rushing his idiosyncratic connection would not work. She would rather destroy the precious information than pass it along under force. Parsons had dealt with plenty like her over the course of years. There was time. His charge was the center of attention at a banquet in his honor, with plenty of people to listen to his stories and, Nature give him patience, that wretched collection of images and videos that he loved to show off. Including the images that the boy had had hidden in various nooks and crannies in his equipment of which that he thought Parsons was unaware. Since Parsons had been directly involved on the design of five of these secure storage devices for the service, there was nothing of moment he did not know about retrieval of information from them. Still, no harm would really be done by the images that he had permitted Lord Thomas to retain. If any embarrassment was due from them, it was fleeting. The young man had the sense not to make use of them for profit or to ruin the lives of those whose images he had captured. Lord Thomas possessed consideration and good sense, though he seldom made use of the latter.

"Well," the old woman said, as Parsons completed the sixth stack of crates, "mebbe I remember where I stuck the thing. It might be right in there." She stood up and massaged her back.

She opened the electrical systems panel in the wall. With the turn of a hidden knob, the frame containing the circuitry sprang out on a hinge. Parsons held his distance, not wishing to offend her by looming over her shoulder, even though his impatience was at a fever pitch.

"They've got guns!" A panicked shout erupted through the door. Parsons peered out of the shop toward the main street. A large crowd of terrified beings of all ages and species fled from the commercial section. The old woman slammed her cache shut and stalked out into the midst of the tumult. Parsons followed more cautiously, unclipping his personal weapon from the hidden sheath.

"You!" the depot owner bellowed, grabbing for the handle of a nanibot rolling down the road. It swung around to face her, the lens of its video pickup enlarged. A fully charged laser pistol rose on the stalk from its command center. "Oh, put that thing away! What in black holes is going on?"

The nani's charge, six months or younger by the sound of the hysterical cries issuing from its interior, was awake and angry.

"I must tend the child!"

"I order you to relate information," the old woman said, her manner snapping from the casual patois of the space station to that of a figure of authority. Parsons had a fleeting glimpse of how effective she must once have been in the service. "I require an account of the last twenty minutes. That should about do it, right, honey?" she asked Parsons.

"I would believe so," he agreed mildly.

She raised an eyebrow, and he realized he had not spoken in the unschooled manner he had affected in her presence. Both of their covers were blown. Luckily no one was there to observe it but an upset LAI with a crying baby on board. She had calculated her statement correctly. When operated in a certain fashion, the LAIs stopped their artificial personalities and downloaded data as required.

"A crew involved in a brawl with the local militia opened fire within Oatmeal and Son, northwards along the road one hundred forty meters," the nanibot responded obediently. "Laser weapons."

"What?" the old woman asked. "Guns? How did they get them past security? I'm going to toast those baby-asses over a fire made of their own uniforms! The militia is involved, you say?"

"The militia is in the hotel," Parsons corrected her. "They are holding a celebration dinner."

"Uniformed beings, then, in a brawl with a crew

from a visiting ship," the nanibot said. "They woke the baby! She has had an ear infection. I brought her to Oatmeal and Son because she enjoys the décor and the nutritionally complete orange-flavored drink. It will take much time to soothe her to sleep. Would you care to see pictures of her? *Would you?*" The mechanical voice sounded slightly hysterical, as if it needed some soothing of its own.

"I'll look at 'em," the old woman said to Parsons. "You go see. Sounds like you're involved. By the way, here." She reached into a pocket of her coveralls and pulled out a blue data crystal the size of her little finger. She gave him a sheepish little smile. "Thanks for the cleanup. And the company. Guess you can tell I miss the old times."

Parsons decided that grace would be a better reply than acrimony. "It was my pleasure," he said. He turned and did a quick march through the oncoming mob in the direction indicated by the nanibot, who was already spooling images of the baby girl for the depot owner.

When he reached the restaurant, he observed that there had indeed been some kind of armed altercation. The main door had been forced ajar. Bubbled and blackened streaks upon its inner surface showed that energy weapons had been discharged against it. The walls bore similar damage. The floor was awash with soda and coffee, and heaps of cooked food on the floor had been trampled into topographical forms by the passage of many feet, most of them booted. Most of them work boots of a common type, nearly all the same maker. Two sets of magnetic boots, as would be standard parts of armor suits. And a pair with no manufacturer's logo on the sole—none needed, since Parsons knew too well they had been made by hand for a particular pair of feet. But where were those feet? The rear door of the restaurant opened onto a black and echoing hallway. Cleanerbots were already rumbling through it, followed by a stout man with red hair and a forlorn expression.

"Are you Mr. Oatmeal?" Parsons asked him. "What happened?"

"Colonel Oatmeal, retired," the redhaired man said. "And all hell broke loose. Who's going to pay for all this?"

"Who did this?"

"I don't know. It all happened so fast. Pretty typical dinner hour. My servers were bringing out orders. Customers pouring in. Then, blam blam blam!"

"Who was involved in, er, the blamming?" Parsons asked.

The man eyed his humble coverall askance. "You aren't station security."

Parsons found the nearest code reader used for verifying credit chits. He pulled back his sleeve and held his forearm over the scanner. The string of numerals that appeared on the small screen made the restauranteur's eyebrows go up. His reserve thawed at once.

"Looked like some of the station volunteers. Took on a bunch of spacers from one of the ships in port. No idea why. They fled out of here in a hurry, all madder than hell. Nobody killed, but that's almost an accident."

"But where did they go?" Parsons inquired.

Oatmeal shrugged. "Not my business. Excuse me. I got to try and clean up before the next shift change."

Parsons frowned. Lord Thomas must have an explanation for this affray. He examined his viewpad for messages. To his irritation, the device did not connect to the local Infogrid. He tried turning it on and off. The response was no better. He hit the side of the device with the palm of his hand. No change. He ran a diagnostic test to find the fault, and discovered that it was not the fault of the viewpad. Interference of some kind was blocking the signal. He scanned the busy street for a land-based communicator. A short row of booths stood a short distance away. Parsons signed on and signaled Lord Thomas's viewpad. There was no answer. It seemed that whatever was causing his to fail also affected other wireless communications. He asked the system to be connected to the office of the station manager.

"Yeah?" asked a burly, lavender-furred Wichu when the call was opened.

"I am Commander Parsons. Do you know the whereabouts of the Smithereen Militia?"

The Wichu eyed him up and down. "Ain't you in charge of it?"

"Nominally," Parsons said.

"Listen, buddy, we've got major outages springing up all over the place, thanks to the magnetite spill in the loading zone. And we just got a report of a riot in a restaurant on the main street. Why don't you just go outside and holler for them? The wireless links ought to be up in an hour or so."

"Sir, you don't understand the urgency of this matter," Parsons began. "I believe that they were involved in an armed conflict. I am concerned for their safety."

An alarm went off behind the Wichu, who spun

his chair to answer it. He turned back to Parsons. "Listen, I got more problems to handle than you. If you find the militia, tell 'em that we need 'em. You got that?" The screen went blank.

Something nudged Parsons in the shoulder. Undoubtedly, another patron deprived of wireless signal sought to make use of one of the few public land-line booths. Without looking back, he held up a hand asking for patience.

Parsons reentered the request to the communications system. It let out a two-tone hum that sounded like a human being clearing its throat in boredom, but it brought up the correct connection. The Wichu saw his face, and snapped his furry fist down on his console. The screen went blank.

That wouldn't do. Perturbed, Parsons brought up the station map on his viewpad. He would go to the office and demand help in person. Lord Thomas must be located.

He was nudged again. This time he turned and presented an apologetic smile.

"I beg your pardon. I needed..."

No one was there. No living being, at least. Instead, an orb the size of a pool ball hovered and blinked at eye level. It was his lordship's Optique camera. It bumped him in the shoulder again, urgently.

Swift as thought, Parsons shot out a hand for the small device. Instead of eluding him as it normally did, it held still for the capture. Parsons opened his palm. The Optique hummed loudly. A circuit pattern of thin lines of light went on all over the small device, and a blue beam lanced out to trace his face. A streak of red on the camera's surface lit up, and a brilliant beam projected itself upon the nearest solid surface, which happened to be the backside of a very large, yellow Croctoid female in black coveralls. An image three meters by two coalesced. It showed Lord Thomas's face at a very close angle in a dimly lit room. The Croctoid, who had been window-shopping with her spouse, began to move away. He put out a hand and touched her forearm. She looked up at him, startled.

"Will you stand just there for a moment, madam?" he asked politely.

"Get stuffed!" she roared, her beady eyes narrowed dangerously.

"Take your hands off my wife!" the other Croctoid demanded. He was much taller and narrower, and looked as though he could tear the communications booth out of the wall. He breasted up to Parsons and glared down at him.

"Please," Parsons said, withdrawing his touch. "It's a matter of Imperium security." He gave them his most authoritative mien. The male halted. The female gave him a puzzled smile. "Turn this way, please." She rotated so her broad front made the widest possible screen.

"Replay," he ordered the camera.

Lord Thomas's face peered at him, slightly distorted from his proximity to the lens. Parsons heard crashing noises around him. Lord Thomas glanced back over his shoulder. Parsons saw a handful of other figures, difficult to distinguish in the available light. The walls around him appeared to be midnight blue in color, or perhaps black. A loud bang as if a solid object had been vaporized with an energy weapon came from nearby. Lord Thomas lifted his hands and began to weave his fingers together in a complicated dance.

Parsons could understand Sang Li fingerspelling as quickly as if it was clear print, and fortunately, so could his charge. For all his apparent inattention to his duties, Lord Thomas picked up information like a sponge, including the silent communication system that was used by the service when sound was not possible, for example in the vacuum of space.

"Pirate vessel from reports is on this station," the young man spelled out. The scene changed suddenly to show the image of a ship as seen from below. It was an excellent picture, showing an expanse of enamel cracked off a tail fin of a cargo ship to reveal more enameling underneath. Parsons frowned. He did not recognize the emblem of the damaged part, but he did recall the second, hidden design. That was the logo of a haulage corporation who had reported ships missing after an altercation with illicit vehicles. The details of the report in question came to his memory immediately. The boy was right. But what was going on?

Thomas's face returned. "No one knows it but us. I didn't know where you went, so we could not contact you directly. Magnetite, you know. We attempted to apprehend the crew, but it's gone rather badly..." The modifier of the adverb was signed with an apologetic grimace. "We have the pirates confined to the ballroom of the hotel, but it isn't going exactly as I planned."

Another bombardment shook the room around Lord Thomas.

He leaned close, his face distorted by the lens, and whispered. "We're holding out for now, but come soon. Please. The Optique will lead you to us. Kinago out."

More shouted threats were audible in the background. Parsons winced.

The image vanished, and the red light on the small camera dulled. Parsons put the camera in his pocket.

How brave, yet how foolhardy. The boy's instincts were sound ones, but he lacked finesse of execution. One day he might be able to capture and control an entire enemy force on his own, but not yet. He needed help. Whether or not the authorities of this outpost wished to be involved, they had no choice now. Parsons thanked the Croctoid couple and went to find the authorities. He broke into a run in the direction of the station office.

The offices of the station manager, a former warehouse by the look of the bare metal ribs of the ceiling, were in chaos. Many of the dozens of screens on walls and transparent standards around the room were dark, a sign that the magnetic interference had not yet cleared. Screens attached to hardwired installations were filled with angry, shouting faces. The operational staff was clearly too small to cope with the emergencies, though under the circumstances, this type of interruption must occur often. Parsons made a mental note to pass along to the Interior Ministry as he advanced upon the lavender-furred Wichu at the desk at the center of the room.

"Whaddaya want?" it asked Parsons. It waved a dismissive paw. "Never mind; you're not gonna get it. We're busy."

. "You will have to cooperate with me," Parsons insisted.

"Sez who?" the Wichu asked.

"The Emperor." Parsons produced his credentials. The fur around the Wichu's eyes curled back, revealing nearly all of the round black orbs.

"Steeeed!" he bellowed.

❖   ❖   ❖

Steed, the station manager, a tall man who had once been powerfully built until age and gravity had dragged him down, toyed anxiously with his graying mustache as Parsons, seated calmly in the midst of a crowd consisting of nearly all the management staff plus friends who had heard about it and come to see the excitement, waited through the protocols of *Wedjet's* security cycling on the largest screen in the office. When the seal of the Imperium appeared, they all let out an appreciative "Oooh." The image of Admiral Podesta, looking as choleric as usual, took its place.

His eyebrows rose at the sight of Parsons. "Well, Commander? What is the meaning of this...crowd?"

Parsons was unperturbed. "Sir, I wish to report the sighting and attempted capture of a party of dangerous beings who have allegedly hijacked and modified a spaceship for their own use, the alleged crimes believed to be that of piracy in the civilized lanes of space. They have damaged personal and public property, harassed and insulted citizens of the Imperium, and falsified vital credentials."

Podesta peered at him askance. "With you involved, Commander, I scarcely expect to hear the phrase 'attempted capture.' What other factor is involved here?"

"Ensign Kinago, sir," Parsons said. Podesta groaned, and his ramrod-straight shoulders sagged a fraction.

"What has that fool boy done now?"

"It is not entirely his fault, Admiral," Parsons said smoothly. "The matter would have been difficult under any circumstances. The Smithereen militia, whom you had tasked him with inspecting, has put itself under his command to fulfill fleet directive number PN-06-752. He sought to bring the suspects in for questioning. They, er, resisted."

"Hence the 'damaged personal and public property,'" Podesta said. He sighed. "It was not successful?"

"No, sir. The militia has the force of numbers, but the enemy force had access to undeclared weapons, putting the lives of naval personnel and civilians in jeopardy. Ensign Kinago has done what he must to prevent the loss of life. At this time I request immediate assistance by the *Wedjet* to speed to this location to secure the suspects and prevent any further altercations."

Podesta's right brow drew so far down it almost obscured his eye. "What about the station manager? Stallion? Where is he in all this?"

"Steed, sir," that official said, edging into the view of the video pickup with a tentative finger raised.

"Well?" Podesta demanded. "Why haven't you arrested these pirates? How has it suddenly become the responsibility of the navy to police your corridors?"

Steed sputtered and stammered, but no coherent words came out. Parsons intervened smoothly.

"They have . . . not-interfered, sir. I think you will find from a brief perusal of the station logs that there have been overwhelming technical difficulties that have prevented Mr. Steed from taking personal charge of the matter. His cooperation with the Imperium was never in question, of course. He is most concerned about the presence of known felons in the station. There is little time to be lost, Admiral. Ensign Kinago's efforts have been heroic, but we must move to supplement them immediately."

An appreciative murmur came from the crowd around him, possibly in admiration of the verbal aikido he had performed. To the relief of the Smithereen bureaucracy, Podesta's mood had shifted from angry to concerned.

"We are within nine hours of rendezvous point, Commander. Thank you for the report. Can Ensign Kinago hold out until then?"

"He will, sir," Parsons assured him.

"Well, thank the stars for that. Can't let the First Space Lord's fool of a son get killed, dammit, no matter how richly he deserves it. Podesta out."

The screen went blank. Parsons looked up from the screen. Station Manager Steed cleared his throat a little sheepishly.

"What do you need, Commander? We'll do anything we can to help, uh, bring these felons to justice. On behalf of the Imperium, y'know. Um, long live the Emperor."

"Long live the Emperor," the rest of the employees murmured, more or less in unison.

Parsons suppressed a smile. Praise for the staff, or at least downplaying their uncooperative attitude, would urge them to work hard to gain the approval that had been ceded in advance. Best to call upon all of their resources while they were still feeling grateful, before natural resentment set in.

"Please show me the blueprints for the security systems in and around the grand hotel. Fire control, life support, hidden weapons emplacements, access routes—a full breakout of the plans and updates."

"You heard the man!" Steed shouted. "Security access nine-ought-alpha, go! Y'want coffee, Commander?

Something stronger? I got some Chochlean rotgut in my desk. Last year's vintage."

"Not yet, Mr. Steed," Parsons said, as the icons began to muster on the screen before him. He placed his hands on the control panel. "I hope stimulants will not become necessary."

❧ CHAPTER 17 ❧

I lay upon the floor of the small cubicle, trying not to move, listening to repulsor fire echoing off the metal floors. The smell of my sweat and everyone else's combined with the sludge on my uniform to create a sickening stew. What feeble light we had came through the translucent floors around the carpet runners. We all inhaled as softly as we could. I had no idea that Croctoids had such sensitive hearing! The surviving members of the militia and my ship's crew were piled haphazardly upon one another. It was difficult to breathe with Captain Chan and Bailly all but piled upon my chest. I didn't dare chide them or nudge them off. No matter how little noise we made, the pirates heard it. The walls were perforated with holes—most of them small, the result of hot plasma drilling its way through the heavy, reinforced wall panels. Several of the militia had been wounded more by accident than design. I had left the injured in a corner room under the protection of Oskelev with two of the captured pistols, and continued on with the depleted force of soldiers, but the rooms into which we fled had progressively grown smaller and smaller as per my own design. It was meant to corral the pirates so they couldn't move, but it was having precisely that action upon us. At the current state of crowding, we could not possibly defend ourselves. I peered sideways at my viewpad, propped against the wall next to my head, silently echoing the countdown to the next three-minute sequence.

I tapped Chan's leg. Three, two, one—move!

As the wall behind me dropped down, the amorphous blob of soldiers rolled, scooted and crawled into the next enclosure like a frightened amoeba. To my relief, a hallway had opened up. I believed that the maze key now was right-left-right. I had been wrong before, and the chiding looks of my depleted force reminded me of that unhappy fact. Instead of triumphantly leading the enemy into a trap, we were the ones who were trapped, while the unbridled brutality of the pirate crew had been unleashed upon an innocent and harmless hotel ballroom. I winced as I beheld some of the scars and gouges on the fine décor. Sconces swung loosely on the wall or lay on the floor. Even the crystal floor had scars in it. The aesthetics of my soul were offended.

At least I still held the ace in this hand: the ship's license. As long as I had it, the pirates must remain here on the station.

But it was a stalemate. They knew by now that we had no weapons to counter theirs. They were larger and stronger than we were. Our strength lay only in remaining out of reach, and that, I realized as I saw a man-sized hole blasted in the side wall of the hallway through which we crept, was becoming a less likely proposition all the time. We had to carry our

wounded with us. The militia members did their best
not to moan or cry out as they were jostled along the
hallways, but we couldn't control every noise we made.

"Sir, I'm going to sneeze!" Rous whispered suddenly.

"Don't!" I breathed back. "That's an order."

"Respectfully declined, sir!" the Uctu replied, his
large eyes filling with involuntary tears. "Wha-ha-chooo!"

A Gecko sneeze is a forceful exhalation that clears
out the entire respiratory system. As a result, the report
that issued from the slender form of my midshipman
was explosive, to say the least. Our eardrums had just
stopped ringing from the sound when I heard blasting noises coming from directly beneath us. A red
pinpoint of flame erupted slantways out of the wall
beside my feet. Involuntarily, I broke into a dance
to avoid more firepower. The enemy had found us.

"Aaagh!" Bailly yelled, hopping up and down on
one foot. Another pinpoint stung him. We thundered
into the next room, followed by gunfire from the left
stitching the wall with red-lit holes. How many charges
did a hand weapon like that hold, anyhow? I would
have liked to get a look at the power plant. It would
be a useful modification to make to existing military
handguns. I would make the suggestion to the ship's
armorer—if we lived.

The pirate captain, alas, had worked his way back
to rejoin his fellows some half an hour before. As he
had a carrying voice, I couldn't help but overhear his
ringing condemnation of our force, me in particular.

"...Light-footed, weak-chinned softskin thinks he
can make fools out of us, I'll blast off a piece of him
at a time and make him cry before he dies!"

In the pale light, I caught smirks on the faces of

my shipmates from the *Wedjet*, particularly Plet, but only temporary ones.

"Then the rest of those meddling rent-a-cops. Not a real threat in the bunch!"

At that, Plet had frowned, and her fingerspelling to me had become much more purposeful. Together we had worked out a defense of evasion and eluding. She would continue to send out SOS messages to Parsons, the *Wedjet* and the station authorities, until the rest of us were overcome or rescue came.

We came to a T-intersection where our choices were to take stairs up to the right or down to the left.

"By my calculations," I spelled to the viewpad, "we should go left."

"But that takes us down, right into the arms of the enemy," Plet argued back.

"Our last turn was right," I pointed out.

"But we keep hitting dead ends," she reasoned. "This can't be your way out. Let's take another right and get the sequence back in order."

I could hardly fault her reasoning. According to the maze I had designed, we should have had an easy egress from the pattern. We turned upward, keeping our pace as light as possible.

The stairs up were as solid as though carved from a mountain. I led the way with my sword drawn, hoping I would not have to use it. I heard repeated over and over again the request for assistance, but I refused to lose hope. I was the undefeated champion of maze croquet in the Imperium Compound on the homeworld. Once I got my bearings, we would be out of the puzzle in a moment, and I could seal off the escape route behind us.

Up, up we climbed, four, five, six flights. No exit offered itself until the top, when we were confronted with another flight of stairs, this one pointing downward and to the right.

"That can't be correct," I said, frowning.

"Obviously, you miscalculated," Plet spelled.

"Not a chance!" I flashed back. I experienced an unnatural feeling of doubt. Had I miscalculated? Not possible! But more than a game hung upon my decision.

"Should we go back?"

"No way back," Chan interrupted, adding her own signs. "Got to keep going ahead of them. We're behind you, Ensign-Captain, whatever happens." I turned to see eagerness and admiration shining in her eyes. "We haven't had this much fun since we hit a pocket of laughing gas in the mines." Her fellows nodded their approval. "If we buy it, then, hey, we buy it, but you won't let that happen. We know it."

I felt a weight of responsibility on my shoulders, but it was lightened by the feeling of being accepted as a leader.

"I'll try," I said humbly. I straightened my back and brandished my sword. "Downward, then, to glory."

To my relief, the maze opened out into wider corridors. The right at the top of the stairs was followed by a left, then an unmistakable right and another left. Success! I picked up the pace, heedless of the noise of my boot soles. We would be out in a trice. And we had not met another pirate in minutes.

There was no doubt that we were following their path, however. Destruction had been rained down upon the facility to a point where I was certain that the place would have to be gutted and rebuilt before it could be used again. The soiree that Ms. Lutsen had mentioned was scheduled to use the room, I feared, would have to be relocated. It must already have been. I had lost track of time.

Damaged lamps lent feeble illumination to the floor, but to my astonishment and delight, another source of light was visible. At the end of the corridor through which we were running, brilliant lights gleamed. The exit must be there! I signed to my force to pick up the pace. We must have time to reach it!

I could hear the sound of running paralleling our course. I looked down. The enemy had found us! They shook their fists at us and fired off more charges. Luckily, the floor was made of the same material as the landing strip. It did not shatter. I heard the pirate captain's voice shouting, exhorting his comrades to hurry.

The walls of the corridor fell away, revealing a parapet. An atrium that bisected the entire complex reached all the way to the ballroom ceiling. Above me, several floors up, I could see the landing strip and the hijacked vessel. I hurtled over the low rail and leaped across the short gap onto another. The pirates, one level below us, ran into a blank wall, no egress to the atrium. I heard their shouts as they looked for a way up. One after another, my company followed me. The last to come were the two soldiers in power suits.

"Hold it, sir," came a weary voice, the sturdy young woman. "We can't keep up with you."

"Hurry," I urged. "Can't you launch your way over?"

"No thrust," said the old man in the other suit, the one that had one arm torn off by the Solinian. "These ain't really made for runnin'. Let us take care of the wounded. Those scum won't get past us, I swear it, Ensign-Captain."

I glanced at the glistening faces of the injured soldiers, and realized it was my call to make. They were tolerating pain, but they were too tired to go on. I feared for them, but they were better protected in their suits than the rest of us. It was a good solution.

"So ordered," I said. "Keep as silent as you can. Stay out of sight!"

"Got it, sir," the old man said. "You're a good man." The creaking cyber arm bent upward in a salute. I returned it with respect and humility.

More silently than I would have thought of such decrepit armor, he and the young woman withdrew into the corridor from which we had come. Staggering on one another's shoulders, the injured went with them, including Bailly, my own midshipman. Angrily, I took a stunner rifle from Margolies and blasted it at the chamber where the pirates were.

The bark of energy weapons sounded from behind the wall. Explosive impacts meant they were trying to blast through to get at us. I sent most of the troop on ahead, remaining behind with Chan and Oskelev until I saw the pirates break through. I waved the license at them. They roared and swore at us. The captain had indeed rejoined them. He gestured to them to start swarming over the edge of the balcony to make a leap at the floor two below us. I fled into the corridor, overtaking the remaining militia.

Pew! A solid object shot out from our right. We flattened ourselves and looked for the projectile. Had they acquired pellet weapons from somewhere? Juhrman picked up an object from the floor and tossed it to me.

"Capacitor," he said.

I breathed a sigh of relief and clambered to my feet. The others followed. The pale light of the ante-room beckoned to us.

But another light asserted itself ahead. On the right-hand wall, a blob of redness blossomed at chest height. I heard the rising whistle of alarms from the energy weapons, informing me that their safeties had been turned off. The pirates were pooling their resources to break through. I opened up my stride. We were moments from freedom. We must escape now!

"The timer, sir!" Plet shouted.

I looked at my viewpad. My heart sank as the digits flipped from one second to none. Suddenly, the walls shifted again. The exit disappeared, and a corridor opened up to the right at the end of the room. I groaned. It was closer than the previous turning, but it pointed the wrong way!

Ahead, the dark blue wall covering burst into flames, and the structure itself slagged into a pool of molten sludge. The Croctoid captain leaped through the glowing opening in between us and our escape, and leveled his pistol at us.

"Gimme that license!" he roared.

"Retreat!" I shouted.

We turned on our heels, and charged straight into a wall. The open corridor had become a dead end, a very brief dead end. I plowed directly into Plet and Chan, who fell over Juhrman and Margolies, who had impacted half a dozen other soldiers.

I had no choice. I picked myself up, turned back and charged, sword point forward.

"Attack!" I cried.

"The Imperium!" bayed my crew.

"Smithereen!" the militia yelled.

We ran at the captain, ducking and weaving to avoid his shots. What stun charges we had left, I ordered discharged at him. It was a forlorn hope, indeed, but what choice did we have? Chop off the head, and perhaps the rest of the gang would surrender. I knew in a similar circumstance that *I* wouldn't give in. The pirates had proved worthy adversaries.

More pirates poured out of the still-hot hole in the wall and engaged with my troops. My heart was heavy that some of the brave males and females of the Smithereen militia would be killed. Our only consolation was that it would be a glorious death, for the sake of the Imperium. Perhaps the Emperor would even say our names in one of the memorial broadcasts at the holiday season. Parsons would find my body and see that it went home to my mother.

My heroic fantasies were interrupted by a searing pain in my right upper arm. One of the captain's blasts had struck me at last. I staggered backwards a pace, shocked by the agony of my limb as it fell limp.

"Sir!" Plet cried. "You're wounded."

"Keep going!" I gritted my teeth. My sword was intact. With my left hand I grabbed for the weapon before it fell to the ground and brandished it.

With a bound, I leaped and lunged, sticking the point of my sword into the Croctoid's throat. Purple ichor spurted.

"You will never defeat a Kinago!" I cried.

The Croc grabbed the blade in his fist and squeezed. Heedless of the blood running down between his pads, he bent the end of my ancestor's sword. I yanked it

back and struck again. He clouted me in the head with
his pistol. Sparks of light flooded my vision along with
the pain. He would tear me apart now, and I could
not stop him. In my mind, I imagined for myself a
beautiful funeral, citing my bravery. I hoped that at
least one of my companions who had witnessed my
last stand against the pirate captain would survive,
when suddenly my communications unit erupted with
a familiar voice.

"Prepare for unconsciousness, sir."

"Parsons!" I cried, relieved. "Where have you been?"

"Prepare, sir. Mobicon Nine."

I knew the chemical in question. It and others
like it had been part of our training. M-9 was a gas
that would incapacitate even the largest and most
dangerous being in a matter of seconds. Those who
breathed it often injured themselves falling after being
knocked out.

"Everyone lie on the floor!" I ordered. My voice
was just audible over a barrage of shots from the
enemy, but the interference that had plagued us for
the last hours had passed. I let my knees go limp
and fell right out of the surprised captain's grasp.
My entire remaining force dropped to the floor. I
had just enough remaining consciousness to see the
gigantic Solinian squeezing through the wall over my
head as the gas hit him. Then he landed on me, and
I knew no more.

❈ CHAPTER 18 ❈

Unconsciousness was a relief, I realized in retrospect. When light invaded via a slit between my eyelids, I found that I hurt all over. I discovered I was in a room with gray walls, gray ceiling and, largely, gray instruments. There was no mistaking an industrial infirmary. A wild pattern of color intruded itself. I recognized it as the tattoos belonging to Doc Fedder, full-time bartender and part-time neurosurgeon. He held a hypospray to my neck. After the hiss, much of my pain abated.

"Sir?"

My eyes flew open the rest of the way. The brightness made my eyes hurt, too, but I was glad to see a familiar visage.

"Parsons!" That dignitary was looking down at me, the usual inscrutable expression upon his face. I scanned it for any signs of concern. "Am I all right?"

"A good deal of bruising, sir. The burn on your upper arm took a trifle of intensive regenerative therapy, but it was facilitated by the coma induced by the gas. Doctor Fedder is a fine surgeon."

"I've seen plenty worse," Doc said, with a self-deprecating grin. "You're gonna be fine, young man. Don't wrestle any more Solinians."

I felt for my ribs, and found them all present and accounted for. "That big fellow knocked all the air out of me."

"That is why you are awake before most of the others. You inhaled less of the gas."

"How long have I been out?"

"Four days, sir."

"Four days!"

"Yes, sir. The *Wedjet* has arrived. The admiral wishes to see you on board immediately, sir."

The entire battle came back to me, including the faces of every being in the militia who had been injured in my service, but the last face I saw was that of the Croctoid pirate captain. "Did we get them, Parsons?"

"We did, sir."

"Is everyone else all right? Did we lose anyone?"

"They'll recover," Doc said. "Some of 'em want to keep their war wounds. Badges of honor, hooey." But he winked at me.

"They earned them," I said, fumbling for the edge of the thermal cover. "Where are my boots? I want to look my best for the admiral. He's bound to want to congratulate us."

Parsons favored me with his best blank expression. "No doubt, sir."

"Destruction spread across the colony? A restaurant left awash in its own comestibles? Armed felons left tied up in the service corridors for innocent civilians to come upon unawares? Commandeering and destroying valuable room-dividing equipment in the most elegant hotel in the sector?" Admiral Podesta paced back and forth across my line of sight, his hands clasped behind his back.

"We had no choice, sir," I said, patiently, for the ninth time. I stood in his study in precisely the same spot and position in which I had been ticked off by him before. Parsons stood at attention at the side of the room, no help to me. I was left on my own to deliver my sitrep. In the stilted language of the military bureaucrat, I am afraid it had not come out sounding as heroic as I believed it had been. Podesta had not received it well, either. He looked more furious than I had ever seen him, even after I had invaded his mess hall in admiral's trousers. I fully expected to be court-martialed this time, but it would be for the very best of reasons. "They were dangerous criminals. I could not let them depart from Smithereen unhindered. They would only have gone off and robbed another train of cargo ships. And none of the ones we left tied up were armed. We took their guns. Besides, we didn't do any of the damage to the ballroom. That was all done by the pirates. Er, suspects. Alleged suspects." Curse it, but it was hard to spout the appropriate jargon. It was so *dry*.

Podesta swung to a halt and met me nose to nose. His narrow face was red. "That is not the point. It was not your job to apprehend them. It was your job to inform me, and let me decide what action to take."

"But we were incommunicado, sir. Magnetite, you know." I shrugged modestly. "I had to do something in the absence of your advice."

"You didn't need my advice. You were there to observe, nothing more."

My emotions got the better of me. "Admiral, they might have gotten away!"

"That would have been correct procedure. You were unprepared for this mission. In fact, it was *not* your mission. You were to review the local militia, that is all."

"I did that, sir. They prove to be loyal, effective soldiers."

"Hmph. They were brave, that's certain. Having to put up with you, I would also give them commendations for patience. You could have gotten them all killed, and yourself along with them!"

"I would be proud to die for my Emperor," I said, striking a pose. Swiftly, I resumed my rigid posture of attention.

Podesta opened his mouth, snapped it shut, then closed his eyes and shook his head, undoubtedly overcome by my patriotism. Whatever words of praise he had planned to say were lost to posterity. But I understood them nevertheless.

"There were other authorities within reach."

"I could not persuade the station manager to believe me. I did try, sir. I had proof." I felt for my camera, restored to my pocket. I held it up. It floated between us. "I believe it will hold up at any trial, sir."

Podesta waved a hand of dismissal, and the Optique retreated timidly to hover behind me. "I have seen the images. Commander Parsons sent them to me. I have also received bills for damage to that dining establishment, to the hotel and all the other station facilities through which your riot progressed. Almost nine hundred thousand credits' worth of damage! The *Wedjet* itself had to abort its patrol and divert back to arrive as quickly as possible. I had to take *my ship* into that asteroid field instead of avoiding it. Forward scanners are still being recalibrated."

I was abashed. It had been rather glorious while it lasted, but the admiral was correct. All that had taken place on my watch. It was my responsibility. I could take the punishment. I straightened my posture and stared out over his right shoulder. "I cannot express to you how very sorry I am, sir."

The admiral let out a heavy sigh. "So am I, Ensign. Especially when you leave me no choice but to... commend you."

I swallowed to clear my ears. Then I checked my memory to see if possibly I had misheard him. My memory insisted that my conscious mind had retained the word correctly. I dared ask for a clarification.

"What, sir?"

Podesta glared. If his eyes had been lasers, he would have been looking through the back of my head. "I said, you will be commended. It is not my first impulse, but the results must and do speak for themselves."

"They do, sir?" I said. My voice squeaked into high registers. I shot a glance at Parsons who must have something to do with Podesta's amazing change of direction. Parsons's face was a blank slate. I returned my eyes to the admiral.

"Yes, confound it," Podesta said, the words forced out between gritted teeth. "It turned out that the ship that landed on Smithereen to take on fuel was the flagship of the pirate fleet. On board that vessel, we found contraband cargo and information that will lead us to the other ships and more valuables that they have stolen. It could possibly be the undoing of a gang that has escaped Imperium justice for some time."

"Oh!" A broad grin was doing its best to break out on my face, but I fought it bravely. "Then I am a hero?"

Podesta looked positively peevish. "If you absolutely must resort to a hackneyed phrase, yes."

The grin overcame all obstacles and adorned my visage from ear to ear. "It was my duty to you and the Emperor, sir," I assured him.

"If only that were so," he said, with a sigh.

"Thank you, sir," I said, with a crashing salute that reminded me I had a bruise on my forehead, among other places. Podesta returned it half-heartedly. I had to go back and update my Infogrid page. A commendation for heroism! Wait until my friends and relatives read about this! "Until then, do I return to my task in the records section, sir?"

"You have no further duties on this ship from now until we return to the Core Worlds," he snapped. "Dismiss."

"But, sir! I could do so much good in Lieutenant Wotun's department. I have a marvelous idea for databases that will save pentabytes of memory..."

Podesta frowned thoughtfully, as if my suggestion had given him pause. "I have never had anyone who volunteered to be returned to Records."

"I will wager that you have never had anyone of my caliber, Admiral," I said.

Behind me, I could hear a very slight "Hem!" from Parsons. I chided myself for braggadocio.

Admiral Podesta sighed, the choleric hue fading from his complexion. "I would wager that you are right, Kinago. You will not return to Records. You may amuse yourself as you see fit over the coming weeks. I expect you to deport yourself as an officer and a gentlebeing. Do not let me see you at any time except for meals, and then I would prefer not to remark upon you in any way. Do I make myself clear?"

"As crystal, Admiral," I said. Mother was going to be so angry. "I . . . I look forward to long and happy service with you, sir."

The admiral did not seem to share my enthusiasm.

"Dismiss, Ensign!" Podesta snapped. He pointed at the Optique, which was hovering over my shoulder. I had had to capture the moment. "And take that thing with you!"

Hastily, I saluted and removed myself from his aegis. Parsons followed me.

We stepped into a lift. The doors slid shut, cutting off the remote possibility of anyone overhearing me. I appealed to Parsons.

"Parsons, find me some way to get back into the records department," I said. "Once the admiral sees. what I can do—he already knows I am capable of organizing a complex objective. I achieved a successful mission. I can do more. The servers would speed up enormously if only he allows me the chance! Doesn't my commendation give him any cause to trust me?"

My distress did not elicit even a flicker of sympathy from my aide-de-camp. "It might, sir, but it will not. He cannot return you to Lieutenant Wotun's department."

"But why not?" I wailed.

"Two reasons, sir. One is that your commendation has removed you from punishment duty. You are no longer consigned to Lieutenant Wotun because you are no longer being punished."

"Oh," I said. I had not thought of it that way. "I suppose not. And the second?

"Because you were enjoying yourself," Parsons intoned. "Punishment detail is not meant to be enjoyable. It is meant to promote a sense of regret based upon tedious repetition of a task, removing you from a sense of useful function."

"I could lie," I offered hopefully. "I could tell the admiral I didn't enjoy myself. I suffered *countless* hours of boredom and impatience."

Parsons raised one eyebrow a precise centimeter. "You would lie to your admiral?"

"Without hesitation," I said. "There are things that one should keep from the attention of an authority figure for its own good. Weren't you ever a small boy?" I eyed him. "I suppose you never were a small boy. Or a teenager, who did not care to fully enlighten one of the parental units as to your day's activities? In retrospect, most of which I refused to divulge was as banal and foolish as any of my official duties, but..."

"That is not the point, sir. As a result of your heroics, you are relieved of punishment. All the admiral wishes is for you to remain a neutral element until our return to port."

"I could be *useful*," I protested. "I had some valuable concepts on streamlining deletion and data storage! I wanted to propose a library database of anecdotes and humor. It would save countless bytes if all one had to do was refer a colleague to the appropriate file in a common repository."

"You may propose it formally to the admiral, but

it would almost certainly not be undertaken," Parsons pointed out, "as such frivolities are not the purpose of a warship on assignment."

"One can never dismiss the cheerful grease that oils the joints of social machinery, Parsons," I said severely. "Living beings still staff these warships, and as I have seen, they have a remarkable collective sense of humor. If you had only read some of those stories . . . !"

"You will simply have to wait until your newfound friends begin to send them to you," Parsons said. "I must surmise that after your mission, as it was remarkably successful, you will begin to acquire many admirers."

"That's true," I mused, swaggering toward my cabin. "All I will have to do is wait for the bounty to roll in."

And roll in it did. I was hard-pressed to keep up with it. When we made orbit around Keinolt, prime planet of the Imperium, my personal recorder was fit to explode with all the fantastic humor I had saved. I would be the envy of my peers.

Now that the mission was over, and my scout ship was no longer a secret, I led tours for my fellow ensigns when they were off duty. Naturally, they were envious.

"And what called?" Redius asked.

"You see, *CK-M945B*," I said.

He gave me an odd, sideways look. "Unusual, that, attached to you. Name not given?"

"You are right," I said with a sigh. "If it was mine I would have named it. But who knows if I shall have the privilege again of captaining her."

I gave the *CK-M945B* a last, affectionate pat. I imagined that it rose up to meet my palm as if it was an affectionate cat. The small ship, looking as pristine as the moment I had first seen it, was taken in hand by the flight deck crew, and rolled into lockdown position to secure it when the *Wedjet* left ultra-drive. I wondered if it would still be waiting here for me when I embarked after our shore leave was ended. Parsons, naturally, had given no clue as to my future duties. I shed my suit, cleaned up and put on my dress uniform, and made my way back to my quarters to await debarkation orders.

As the admiral had commanded, I had no official functions, so I was free to disport myself as I saw fit. I organized a massive tri-tennis tournament that began among my fellow ensigns but had to be expanded to include dozens of other officers who heard about it and wanted to be included in the fun. I was delighted to oblige. I partnered with several shipmates, including a weapons specialist named Bek, whose name rang a bell I could not locate in my memory. He wasn't much for clever badinage, but he could play incredibly well. We pipped Rous and the luscious Lt. Alianthus by one point, but ended up losing to a team from Life Support. It was incredible fun, and I was sorry to have it end. After shore leave, I would certainly be given another assignment, one that would not leave me with so much free time.

I left the suggestion for a common database with the dour Lt. Wotun, and hoped for the best. I gave her and my fellow ensigns my Infogrid information. I truly hoped that they would stay in touch during our break, and after I finished my deployment. If I had learned anything on board the *Wedjet*, it was that common folk weren't.

❋ CHAPTER 19 ❋

"Meet us at the Rook Inn in Chess Street, Straumsburg, next Fritsday evening," Anstruther said, as we stumbled out of the landing craft and into the brilliant sunshine of Oromgeld, spaceport for Taino, capital city of the Imperium and my home town. She looked at us anxiously, her eyes resting last on me. "Everyone, let's try and make it?"

"I'll be there," I promised. She gave me a shy smile. The expression became her. I had come to feel protective of her over the last few months, almost as a protégé, though she would never successfully tell a joke in public. I despaired of ever drawing out that kind of talent in her. She had proved to be a demon jai-alai player. When I had organized a doubles event I had scooped her up as my partner. We had won, almost too easily. The poker tournament had not been as lucrative (Redius had taken the grand prize, fifty rations of beer supplied by me), but I believe that it forged more sturdily the bonds of friendship that had been growing among us.

Our trip back to the Core Worlds had been most enjoyable, if it were not for the ineffable sensation that I was not being of enough real use to the Red Fleet. True to his word, Podesta had never given me another assignment. Perhaps he was waiting to talk to my mother, a proposition that filled me with dread.

I stopped to draw in a deep breath of the rich, dry air. Even with the spicy flavor of burned ions from the shuttle's drive, it tasted better to me than a good wine. The sky was a wonderful blue, equaled nowhere else in the universe for sheer magic and depth of color. Against it, the cream, rust and moss green of the rocky landscape of my home province stood out in sharp relief like an island upon the face of the sea. My heart filled with an overwhelming affection for every protruding rock, every spire. I wanted to grab all of my crewmates and point out each beautiful landmark, but I felt they would not appreciate my enthusiasm. Better to let them discover it for themselves.

"Going windskiing on the frost plains at the south pole," Xinu said, "but I will try to rendezvous."

"Staying in Straumsburg, so simplicity," said Redius, flicking his tongue over his lipless mouth. "A pleasure."

"What will you be doing?" I asked him.

"Collecting, I," he said, cocking his head. "Pottery miniatures I enjoy. Activities, yours?"

"Seeing my relatives," I said. "Inescapable, really."

"Your mother?" asked Nesbitt, grinning.

"Of course," I said, puffing out my chest. Upon the breast of my crisply pressed dress uniform was the small silver and black bar affixed there by Admiral Podesta during the last formal mess. It stood alone on the field of dark blue, unlike the modest tiers of awards worn by my fellow ensigns. I had no length-of-service ribbons to show, nor good behavior medals, but how many of them could boast the nearly single-handed capture of pirates? Since we came out of ultra-drive in system ten hours before, I had had several messages on my viewpad from Mother, alongside countless squibs from my cousins and friends. I had so much to tell all of them. I had posted plenty of tales on my Infogrid file during my months in space, but I kept the best for face-to-face telling. The fact of my medal was already public record, and I was getting insistent queries regarding its whys and wherefores. I looked forward to seeing the astonishment and admiration on their faces. My mother would be proud of that, at least. Not all my messages had been in response to my postings; their content offered hints as to the personal agendas of the senders. "Enjoy yourselves, and spare a kind thought for me. My aunts have lined up half a dozen potential fiancées for me. I shudder to imagine what unfortunate ladies they have browbeaten into meeting me."

"Sympathies," said Redius, ducking his head. "Why not just find mate of your own, you?"

"Bite your tongue," I chided him, as that appendage flickered to show amusement. "Safe journeying, and I shall see you in Straumsburg."

"Hey," Nesbitt said, his voice rough. He pressed a small object into my hand. "This is for you."

I surveyed the small data crystal. "What is it?"

"A download of my best anecdotes. You earned it."

A smile burst out of containment and spread itself across my face. "Nesbitt, you are a true friend, and the first drinks will be on me." He grinned back almost as shyly as Anstruther had. I pocketed the crystal next to my camera gear. I would treasure it. I foresaw far fewer dreary family events, with the comic ammunition that I had amassed.

The container of our belongings disgorged itself from the rear third of the shuttle. Its heavy doors clanked and spread open. I whistled, and my three cases reared up from the revealed mass within. I beckoned. Obediently, the bags glided along on their antigravity pads until they were within a meter of the sensor I held. I checked over each one. They had been made of the finest Cartelian dou-hide, nearly indestructible but butter smooth to the touch, dyed my favorite ultramarine. The hardware was a brilliant silver alloy that couldn't be scratched without a titanium drill, and contained the best security ware available. They had been opened once each since I had sealed them. I was glad to see that safety protocols were being maintained. This was the Imperium's capital city, and I would not be the one who carried in the object that would endanger it.

Anstruther, her possessions as modest as her personality, shouldered a simple white bag and headed toward the public transportation station. My tablemates assumed their own baggage and followed her. I had the urge to join them, so we could talk again and again about our experiences together, but there were so many people I had not seen in months. We had apprehended pirates—pirates! It was us against them, and we won, we brave citizen-soldiers of the Imperium. I rehearsed in my mind exactly how I would retell the story to my friends. I couldn't wait to see them.

"Are you ready to go, sir?" Parsons had appeared at my elbow with the silent grace of which only he and servobots with antigravity pads were capable. I glanced around.

"Yes, I am . . . wait!" I spotted another familiar face. "There's Bek! Give me a moment, Parsons. Bek! You remember him, Parsons. He and I played tri-tennis several rest periods. He was a star in the games I organized two weeks ago. He's got an amazing backhand."

I waved my arm. At the foot of the landing craft, Third-class Specialist Bek was debarking, a small mulberry-colored case hanging from a strap on his shoulder. A couple of big human males in deliberately self-effacing uniforms and dark-visored helmets joined him. I didn't recognize their shoulder markings. One man relieved him of the case but Bek didn't seem to be grateful for the assistance. There must be some misunderstanding. I thought that perhaps I could straighten out the situation for him.

Before I could take a step in his direction, Parsons took my arm firmly.

"Don't do that, sir," he said.

I frowned. "Why not? He's new here. I should tell him about a few choice clubs and the best tour to take of the Imperial Compound."

Parsons's face was impassive, but I thought I detected a modicum of sympathy. "Because he is going to the brig, sir."

"Brig?" I was dumbfounded. "Bek? Why?"

"Because he is a spy, sir. You detected him yourself from the files in the records department. Do you not remember?"

"*I* did?" I peered back at the man, realizing that I did recognize him, and not just from our games together. In my mind I also saw his Infogrid picture.

"He was the weapons maintainer-complainer," I said automatically. "I was thinking of asking him to play in my team of the Kinago Cousins Invitational week after next. I never put the man together with the file containing those messages. He's really a spy? You're not mistaking him for someone else?"

Parsons raised an eyebrow, and I felt abashed even suggesting that he could make a mistake. "No, sir. He was transmitting top-secret information to drone buoys along the ship's sublight path. They were redirected through several data portals to false accounts. Until you indicated a suspicion of his perfidy, no one had connected the source of the leak to the *Wedjet*. It was originally believed to be coming from a repair facility where the weapons systems were installed."

"Well, I didn't have a suspicion, precisely," I said, watching with horror as the men in plain suits clamped Bek into a hovering secure-chair pod. They mounted zipcycles, and guided the pod with them off the landing field. In all the times I'd been arrested on minor charges, they had never locked me into a pod. Those were employed only for the most dangerous of suspects. "I did think he was being a trifle incautious. That was all."

"It was more than incautious, sir, it was deliberate," Parsons said. "His posts had been ignored by previous screeners. It was only your perseverance that followed Specialist Bek's pattern of disseminating classified material. Investigation has revealed the accounts to which they were addressed were owned by known receivers of classified information. The actual buyers of that information are yet to be traced, but a watch has been put upon the circuits in the message buoys and satellite systems."

"Well, I will be dipped in batter and deep-fried with

horseradish," I said. I was horrified that anyone could have deliberately betrayed the Imperium. I mean, *my cousin* was emperor! "But why?"

"That is not yet known," Parsons said. "You are certain that you did not make his acquaintance because of your observation of his messages?"

"Not on purpose," I said, thoughtfully. "I took Lieutenant Wotun's admonishments to heart, I promise you. I just saw that he was a strong player. I never meant to make use of the Infogrid files. I was curious."

"Whether purposeful or not, your curiosity will have saved many lives," Parsons said.

His reassurance did not do much to quiet the turmoil that began raging in my gut. When we captured the pirate crew I had enjoyed having been involved in a great game that resulted in the apprehension of known felons. Beyond the fear and danger, it had been a lark. The criminals we—truthfully, the spacebees who had performed the actual capture—had taken were strangers, and had behaved just like criminals in the videos did. That was satisfying. It felt right. This situation was horribly wrong, no matter how many ill-considered messages I read. A man whom I had sought out to befriend turned out to be a traitor. I would never have known to look at or listen to him. Villainy came in many guises. It struck me to the core. I had never had to consider anything in that light before. It overwhelmed the calculating functions of my cerebral cortex. It wasn't a game. Parsons gave me an odd look, as close to sympathy as I had ever seen him offer me.

"You couldn't have known, sir. He fooled a great many people. Be confident that you have prevented any further damage he could have done."

"I appreciate the effort, Parsons," I said, sadly, "but it honestly doesn't help."

In a contemplative stage, I walked away from the landing zone without looking back.

"I will leave you here, sir," Parsons said at the high bronze gates to the family homestead after I had submitted my face and both my hands for scrutiny by the scanners for identification. The small, black-shelled skimmer we had flown from the spaceport hovered behind us.

"Aren't you going to come in and greet the maternal unit?" I asked, shaking my right hand in pain. The phlebotomy needle in the right middle finger indentation was blunt and hurt more than it should have. The household computer was overloaded again. I would have to check on its program myself. No one else ever seemed to care if it mauled them. On the good side, the system would send verification of my return to all the computers in the Imperial Compound, and I wouldn't have to go through full identification again, not until I had absented myself for a period of time. "I am sure she would like to congratulate you for bringing the prodigal son back in one piece. Come on. We have some of that great Aurencian wine, '030, that brought the Emperor himself to his feet in admiration. I would be pleased to break out a bottle to celebrate our return. Mother would insist."

"Please give my compliments to the First Space Lord, sir," he said, with a minuscule dip of his head. "I shall be honored to see her somewhat later. I have other duties."

"Oh, of course you do," I said, feeling a trifle

lost at his impending absence. For months he had never been farther than a mile or two from my side. "Mother will be devastated to miss you, but go ahead. I'll make your excuses."

"You are too kind, sir," Parsons said dryly. "Besides, she will want to see you alone first."

"That is what I am afraid of," I admitted. "I had rather hoped you would be there to blunt her attack, at least at first."

"I am sure she is glad you have returned safely, my lord. Please inform her I shall call upon her and Lord Rodrigo later on."

He glided back to the small but elegant personal transport unit and vaulted into the seat with no appearance of effort. I was appalled at what toll full planetary gravity was taking on me after months in the limited pull on ship and station, but he seemed not to be affected by it at all. That was just one more thing about Parsons at which I had to wonder at my leisure. Another was what other duties he had that took precedence over seeing my mother. It would be undignified to run after him to ask, and a hero who had taken down a band of dangerous pirates did not worry at the heels of a man still more heroic who had saved that hero from certain death by laser glare of an angry admiral.

Besides, I had no time to do so. As soon as the ancient intelligence unit inside the wall had finished its lengthy grinding and chewing over of my identity, the gates swung wide to admit me. Beyond it stood a double file of men and women in dark blue uniform tunics and gold shoulder braid.

"Atten-shun!" a deep baritone voice barked. The

uniformed officers pivoted so the two files were facing one another. "Preee-sent arms!"

With a mighty *snick!* the assembled drew swords from scabbards and held them high so that the tips of the blades crossed, forming an arcade of shining white steel against the pure blue of the sky.

"Music, cue!"

From the high walls of the courtyard, a fanfare brayed out and rolled into a military march. I didn't know whether to laugh or cry. Instead, I strode forward through the arch, my back as straight as a laser beam. I knew every face, and loved them all. These were my cousins and friends, whom I had left behind to join the crew of the *Wedjet*. It had only been a few months since I had seen them, but to my surprise, they looked different. They weren't the ones who had changed; I had. When I reached the end of the file, the voice, which I had recognized as belonging to my cousin Xanson Melies Kinago, barked out his final orders.

"At ease! Returning hero, greet!"

With practiced movement, the assembled sheathed their swords, and rushed to embrace me.

"You slug, we've been waiting here for hours!" Xanson laughed, beating me on the back. He was the tallest of the cousins, a centimeter or two taller than I, muscular and strong-chinned, with a lock of unruly dark brown hair that was almost always in his eyes. The grooming robots in basic training had to clip that lock every few days. It made him look raffish, a conceit that I know he enjoyed.

I embraced him back just as vigorously. "You know what it's like, waiting for Customs to clear landing craft. Bureaucracy and more bureaucracy. It's an art form, and not a felicitous one."

"You should have pulled rank," sniffed my cousin Erita Kinago Betain. She was a thin person with a protuberant, narrow, slightly reddened nose, well suited for sniffing.

"Ah, but I wasn't alone on the shuttle," I said.

She looked shocked. "You had to share a shuttle with commoners?"

"Fellow naval officers," I corrected her.

"That's what I said—commoners," she sniffed. "Why you had an assignment out in the middle of nowhere with nobodies, I can't guess. You should have come with us on the *Tirasiani*. We had a marvelous time, just marvelous!"

"The *Tirisiani*?" I asked.

"A new destroyer, named after Her late Majesty. Didn't you read our files? It was commissioned just after you left. You would hardly have known we were on board a naval vessel! So different from the Academy. Not at all...utilitarian." She used the word as if it tasted terrible. I laughed.

"It wasn't that bad," Xan said. "It wasn't as though we had onerous duty. In and out through the system, around the Core Worlds. Twice, we made the jump to Leo's Star."

"The trip was dull," Erita confided, "but we managed to keep busy."

"I am sure you coped wonderfully," I assured her politely. "Naval service suits you. You look well and fit."

"But how dull, darling!" she said. "The muscles in my legs throw off the line of my trousers. I shall have to have them all altered."

"And what is this?" demanded Scotlin Nalparadha Loche, a cousin on my mother's side and one of my best friends since childhood. He had bright green eyes that glowed from a face the color of tawny port. His barrel chest went well with his broad shoulders and stocky legs. He poked at my chest.

"You mean my medal," I said proudly.

"Yes—one medal! What's the matter with your commander? Was he insane?"

I was taken aback. "No! Admiral Podesta was a great leader. Why would you suggest such a thing?"

Scot poked at his own chest. *Equal time,* I thought. "I have sixteen medals. Where are the rest of yours? Doesn't he know you have rank to uphold?"

I had been so intent upon the faces of my relatives and comrades that I had scarcely looked below chin level. My gaze dropped, then so did my jaw.

Spread across the front of each of the blue tunics were rainbows of color. It would not be out of line to suggest that each of my peers wore *scads* of awards, commendations and recognitions of all types. Some boasted so many tiny pins that their uniform's fabric stretched under the weight, suggesting that the display ought to be continued next tunic, or have a mobile framework scoot alongside them to take up the excess.

"What are all those?" I asked, astonished.

"Weekly attendance," Scot ticked them off with a blunt forefinger, "grooming, courtesy, participation in training exercises, good behavior, oh, and service to the Imperium in guarding the Core Worlds."

"Ah," I said. I fear that I experienced unbecoming medal-envy. I would at least have qualified for grooming, if not any of the others. I feared my voice sounded weak as I forced out good wishes. "Congratulations, Scot. I am sure you earned every one."

"I should think so! I sweated months for all that recognition, sucking up to His Grace Captain and Duke Ferdinand Muwaki Kinago for them. And what is that little pip for?"

"Well, ah," I said, finding beginning the story more awkward than I thought it would be, "I captured a pirate vessel. I had help, of course, but I believe I can confidently say that the impetus came from me."

The faces, screwed up in sympathy at my hesitation, blossomed into smiles of glee at my obvious prevarication. Xan guffawed.

"Oh, Thomas, go on!" If you're not going to tell us what it's for, then just say so!"

"Really!" I protested.

Xan scoffed. He had practiced scoffing for years, and could show scorn more readily and expertly than any of the rest of us. The right corner of his lip turned up. "*Pirates?* Pull the other one, and while you're at it, spread marmalade on it!"

"He is telling the truth," came a warm, rich voice. "And he can tell you all about it when I have had a chance to welcome my boy home."

I turned.

It no doubt shocked brash new recruits to the Naval Academy that the highest authority in the service belonged to a dainty, beautiful woman with big, warm eyes of the same blue-green that I myself possessed. Naturally, I had received them from her. Her hair was a far more attractive shade than mine, a caramel bronze that owed nothing to art. Her complexion was lighter than mine, allowing the pink in the apples of her cheeks to bloom like roses. It was an old fashioned simile, but hers was an old-fashioned beauty. She wore civilian clothing that resembled her uniform but much more flattering: a tailored dark blue blouse that blossomed into wide ruffles at the wrist, and close-fitting eggshell-white silk trousers that stopped just above the gold, high-heeled sandals tied around her tiny ankles. She smiled, and the long lashes in the corners of her eyes crinkled around the sea-blue irises.

"Mother!" I hurried to embrace her.

"Thomas." She reached up to pull my face down to hers for a kiss. I felt as awkward as I had as a teenager when I had hit the growth spurt that took me from just under her height all the way to my present state of outlandish loftiness. As a matter of courtesy, she never mentioned it, as I refrained from mentioning her lack of stature. Physical, of course. The moment she stepped aboard a ship, she outranked even the Emperor. She let me go, and my spine sprang back into alignment. "You look pale. Didn't you take vitamin-D light therapy?"

I felt the familiar sense of being under authority. "Yes, mother. I followed my usual regimen as always. Parsons saw to it."

She glanced behind me. "I can always count on Parsons. And where is he?"

"An appointment, he said. He will make his devoirs to you later on."

She smiled up at me. "I forget occasionally how very busy he is. Come along, then, and let's have a talk." Tucking her hand into my elbow, she turned to the others. "Why don't you all run along to wherever you were going, and Thomas will join you?"

"Of course, Aunt Tariana," the cousins murmured.

"Don't take too long, Thomas," Xan said. "I rented Starling Island for the night. The whole place is ours."

"My favorite resort!" I was delighted to know they had missed me, as I had missed them.

"He will be with you shortly," Mother promised. "Go on, all of you. Have a good time. I'll send a credit to Luigi for a case of the '027 from my private stock."

Her generosity elicited an enormous cheer from the assembled cousins and assorted relatives. They scooted off, shouting compliments to my mother. I made to follow, but no hope. Her grip was as powerful as any mechanical vise. She towed me in the direction of the family quarters. "Not so fast, my dragonlet. You and I are going to have a little conversation. I have just received a rather long recording from Admiral Podesta."

I assumed an expression of contrition, but I knew it wouldn't do much to abate the coming tirade. I was accustomed to them as, I feared, my dear mother was to having to dispense them. There was no doubt material for a lengthy book there, describing how she had been able to raise a family of healthy, self-actualized individuals while at the same time occupying one of the most important offices in the Imperium, and all without acquiring more than a thread or two of silver in her soft-looking hair, but I was not the one to write it. Serious literature was not to my taste, nor to any of my siblings or relatives that I could name.

She directed us into the great room that had been the center of the family's goings-on for centuries. The ceiling, a vast and colorful mosaic in tiles smaller than the end of my little finger, portrayed ancestors of the

Kinago family as heroes and heroines, crossing space, conquering worlds and embracing—though not in an intimate fashion—members of the non-human races that we had encountered first, before any of the other ancient human families. The first Thomas Kinago was there, the great engineer, a rangy man with black hair and sallow skin but whose large dark eyes were reputed to have won him the love of no fewer than five lovely women. His second wife was our ancestress. His brother Niall had discovered and claimed the ore of the burned out star Cassoborix, source of the wealth of the sixty-third generation of space-going Kinagos. The gold, silver, platinum and other precious metals in the mosaic, and much of what was still in our safe room deep underneath the building, came from that strike. That wealth had allowed the Kinago family to pursue its own interests without fear of want and to purchase influence when necessary for millennia. My allowance, as those of my siblings and cousins, came from the Imperial treasury, so the Kinago fortune went largely untapped except in emergencies.

"Where's Father?" I asked, stumbling in the wake of my maternal tugboat.

"In his workshop, dear," she said. "You must go and see him when we've finished our talk."

I made as if to veer off. "Shouldn't I go see him now, while he still remembers that I'm home?"

"Not a chance, Thomas," Mother said, hauling me firmly into the room. With a turn of the wrist, she spun me off in the direction of my uncle Laurence's favorite chair. My heels struck the base of the carved wooden frame and I tottered backwards into the embrace of its cushions. Once in, I would have to slither down to the floor to get out. Mother knew that. I wondered just how much trouble I was in.

She settled into her own chair and drew her feet up to one side of the broad, brick-red cushion. If one did not look at her too closely, one might believe she was an ingénue. She signaled, and an antique polished mahogany-clad servbot rolled toward us on padded wheels from the corner. Mother poured priceless pale gold wine, almost certainly the '044 from our own vineyards in the north, into an equally priceless antique crystal flute.

"Now, son," she said, holding the goblet out to me. "Talk. Tell me everything. I especially want to hear all about the pirates. Omar was very correct and polite, and I will bet that none of the juicy details made it into the official report."

I tasted the excellent wine, and took in a deep breath.

"Well, Mother, I was assigned quarters on Deck Four Forward. Not what I expected, with little room for my wardrobe and other belongings..."

❊ CHAPTER 20 ❊

My voice had ground down to a dry croak by the time I reached the end of my narrative. If I had left out anything, it was not because I meant to. Mother was a bugbear for detail and an excellent listener, with a knack for asking a leading question that reminded one of other parts of the story. She also laughed at all the funny bits. I could always count on Mother to get the jokes. I adored her.

"You actually marched into the mess hall wearing admiral's trousers, on your very first day of duty?" Mother asked in a severe tone, but there was an unmistakable twinkle in her eyes. "You unbelievable fool, why did you do that?"

I hunched my shoulders. In retrospect it was not a moment of which I was proud. "Well, Mother, I do outrank everyone with whom I served."

She shook her head. "Not on a ship! Didn't you listen to a thing they taught you in the Academy? To that which I've devoted my entire life to upholding? You shouldn't really twist Omar Podesta's tail. He never could take teasing, even from teenage. He has no sense of humor whatsoever."

"I had noticed that," I said feelingly.

She regarded me thoughtfully. "I can't believe you didn't spend the entire tour in the brig, let alone take a tour of a colony world."

"He did say he should clap me in irons..."

Mother scoffed. "Omar Podesta never said 'clap you in irons'!"

I ducked my head. "No, he didn't. He considered making the brig my permanent quarters for the duration of my service, but he thought he owed it to you to give me a second chance."

She nodded. "Good of him. I will remember that should he ever need a favor. And you took that second chance." It was not a question.

"I believe I served well," I protested.

My mother scowled at me. "In what Navy? Certainly not mine." I started to reply, but she cut me off with an upraised forefinger. "You obey the senior officer and all officers senior to you. If you have any powers of observation at all, you also obey the senior noncoms and anyone who might have a lesson to teach you. And believe me, my otherwise talented and personable son, all of them do."

I sighed. "Yes, Mother, I know."

"And you did make a hamfisted mess of the situation on Smithereen." She had enjoyed the story, nodding often, as though comparing my report with that of the admiral, but her expression said that she almost certainly agreed with his assessment over mine.

I was hurt. One would hope one's own mother would take one's side. "We captured the entire crew without a single death. Poor Premulo might probably never bowl another strike, but Doc said he thought with time he could fix him. I mean Torkadir."

"*You* captured . . . ?"

"Oh, Mother, surely you'll give me that!" I exclaimed. "I led them into the ballroom maze and kept them there. They did not escape. Their capture led to the pursuit and apprehension of most of the others in their band of thieves."

The twinkle came back. "If you tell it like that, then you may certainly take credit."

"Not just me, of course. Along with all the Smithereen militia, my cutter crew, the station manager, the *Wedjet* and Parsons," I added hastily. "Only five of us received medals, but I sent enough money for the militia to have a party to celebrate."

"That's generous of you," Mother said dryly.

I grinned. "Chan sent me a note to say that they held it in my honor, and toasted me with the local grog. It would take your head off. You might like it."

"I've tasted it," she said. I should not have been surprised. There probably was not an atmosphere in the Imperium that my mother had not breathed in her long career. "It did take my head off, and the flavor is one I would rather forget. Well, my interrogation is over, and I want to hear the fun parts. Did your remote guests have a good party?"

"Fantastic," I said, a trifle ruefully. "I wish I had been there. They sent me pictures and videos. They're so wild I can't really put any of them on my Infogrid file, but I have a link. Would you like to see them?"

"Perhaps later. In the meanwhile, I do take it to

heart that you have a party to attend, also thrown in your honor. Your cousins missed you."

"And I them. Mother, why . . . ?"

"Why what, my dragonlet?" she asked.

As with Parsons, I had the uncomfortable sensation that she was reading my mind. I wanted to know why I'd been assigned to the *Wedjet* and not the *Tirisiani*, but I saw a warning light in those eyes and stopped.

"Nothing."

She smiled. "I'm very happy you did well, and that you made friends."

"I did," I said. "Not as many as I would have hoped. Some people I just could not rub the right way no matter how many strokes I put into it, but I believe I have some firm friends with whom I will be proud to serve in the future. I look forward to completing my enlistment with the *Wedjet*," I added. "I have many good friends whom I have come to like and trust. With one exception," I added, thinking of Specialist Bek. His betrayal still stung.

"Ah. That." Mother came over and put a delicate hand on my shoulder. I looked up into her eyes, which were filled with sympathy. "I have some bad news for you, my dragonlet," she said. "Podesta doesn't want you back. He included in his message to me an impassioned plea, calling upon our ancient friendship and any other favors I might ever conceivably have owed him, not to return you to his command."

My ego was dashed to the floor, where it shattered into pieces. "What? But we were getting on so well. What about my idea for a new database? It will save millions of pentabytes of memory on the ship's processors! I thought he would appreciate that!"

"Yes, yes," Mother said, waving a hand. "But it is the Navy. Admiral Omar Podesta does not want you to do things your way, he wants you to do them the Navy way, by checking with him via the chain of command, beginning with the officer next above you. You didn't even listen to Parsons, did you?"

"Most of the time," I protested. Shame colored my cheeks.

"Most?"

"Some of the time," I finally conceded.

Mother was adamant. "That is not the way it works, Thomas. The admiral of the Red Fleet should not have to sort out your monkey tricks. He has a corps of ships that answers to him, presenting him with more problems in one day than can be solved in a year."

"But why put me on that vessel if I was not to serve there? All my friends here..."

"Yes, and they are waiting," Mother interrupted me, pulling me to my feet. She polished the medal on my chest with the frill around her wrist. "We'll talk more later. I have many appointments, and they're all impatient for a moment of my time. Come join me for breakfast tomorrow, sweetheart. In the meantime, your father has missed you greatly. Go and say hello to him." She stood on tiptoe to kiss me on the cheek. I returned the kiss and stood back to salute her.

"Very pretty," said the First Space Lord, with a wry smile. "Someday you'll mean it."

The family compound was large enough to make use of personal vehicles, travelchairs or cargobots who were glad to carry a Kinago wherever he or she would care to wend among the various buildings and complexes within its walls. I refused offers from several ancient mechanical retainers who greeted me warmly on the tree-lined streets and lanes I took from the main house in the direction of Father's workshop. It was not that I was putting off a visit to my father; I wanted the extra minutes to arrange my thoughts. Conversations with my father were agonizing. I never knew what he would comprehend from time to time, nor what he would retain from any previous visit. Now and again he would think I was someone else, or treat me as though I was still a small boy. How his mind reconciled the lanky body I operated at this stage of my life with the undersized sprog I had once been was a matter for the scientists or the doctors. I was neither. I was only his son.

Rodrigo Park Kinago had a handsome profile. It had been captured in portraits both in image capture and more traditional forms. Artists had been fascinated by the strong line of his jaw, the wavy, almost black hair that swept back from his noble, wide brow, the eyes of a dark sapphire blue that was envied for its purity and intensity, and strong yet gentle hands. When he concentrated on a single item, as he did now upon a lump of gray stone, turning it this way and that, it bestowed upon that item the aura of being the most interesting thing in all the Core Worlds. What could he see in such a simple, small thing? I watched him from the doorway of his workshop for a long while. I realized he had not noticed me, and probably would not.

I cleared my throat. The small sound almost rang in the still air of the workshop. The intense blue gaze moved away from its subject, and blurred. The eyes, now agate in clarity instead of jewel-like, found my face, sought my eyes, and attempted to focus. I swallowed.

"Father, it's me. Thomas."

"Thomas?" The gaze sharpened slightly, scanned my features, and rejected them. He shook his head. "What Thomas is that?"

The familiar anguish rose up in my throat. I loved him, but it was difficult to see him this way. "Your son, sir. I'm back."

"*My* son?" A memory dawned. He smiled and rose with alacrity from the laboratory stool, holding out his arms. "My boy! And how are you?"

He embraced me with a strength that his wavery gaze belied, and pounded me on the back. I returned the hug. He let me go with one final powerful swipe to the scapula, and returned to his seat. "Sit down, Thomas, sit down! I was just examining an interesting specimen." He held out the rock to me. I examined it, but could not detect anything unusual about it, but thought it best to humor him.

"Very interesting," I said.

"Yes! I'm glad you can see," Father said, giving me a swift smile. He scooped the stone from my hand and resumed his scrutiny of it with an old-fashioned quizzing glass the size of my hand. His smooth, antique, lacquered wooden worktable, while spotless, held a number of rather ordinary looking objects, like spools, balls, lumps of plastic, white ceramic cups holding colored liquids or collections of microcircuitry. "And how are you? You haven't been around to see me lately. I listened to your messages, but you didn't say why you were gone."

My messages, like all my communications, were exhaustively thorough. Either he hadn't really listened, or he couldn't absorb them. I was used to that.

"I was on a naval ship, father. I have joined the service."

An unusually lucid light brightened his eyes. "About time. I hope they use you well."

"I'm not sure," I said. "I've been tossed off my ship."

"Painful. Why?"

"I . . ." Best to be frank. "Mother tells me I was insubordinate."

"Well, she would know," Father said, serenely. He smiled. "That means you must have done something right."

"I helped capture pirates, Father. I got a medal. See? It's here." I pointed to my chest. He leaned close to peer at the small decoration.

"Did you put them back in their box?" His eyes had gone hazy again. My heart sank.

"I suppose in a way I did," I replied.

"Good, son, good." My hopes that he would understand and rejoice with me were dashed. As usual. I could hardly be angry. He had been like this my entire life.

He bent to rearrange the tiny tools on his workbench. They looked to be precisely spaced from one another already, but he seemed to have determined that they should be arranged in order of width rather than length. He reached for an apple-sized ball. "Did you see the puzzle I built? A real conundrum. No one will be able to solve it for centuries."

I examined the little sphere. A brilliant red jewel lay at the heart of a nest of round boxes of many different materials, visible through a keyhole-shaped opening. I tried spinning them to line up the keyholes, but as I got two in line, others would spin to hide the jewel.

Father pointed to the spinning openings as they appeared and reappeared. "You have to unlock the repulsors one at a time, in precisely the correct order, or the treasure is lost forever. Good, eh?"

"Very...complicated," I agreed.

His brow furrowed. "Hmm. The third level is running forty milliseconds slow. Give me that, son." He took the puzzle away from me and reached for a handful of tools. He slid the switch on one, giving rise to a loud buzzing. The spheres halted in place. Father leaned over the orb with a tool with a pair of tiny, sharp calipers on the end. He tinkered with the box, lost in his work once again.

I rose from my stool and headed toward the door, leaving him to his work. I knew he hadn't forgotten I was there. He just seemed far more interested in it than in me. I was used to that. His voice halted me before I reached the threshold.

"Did you see your Uncle Laurence? He was just here."

I spun. Uncle Laurence was home? "No, Father, I didn't. I'd love to see him."

Father raised his brilliant eyes from his puzzle. "Sorry, my boy. I'm afraid he's gone, now. Back to Earth. Hmm." He dropped his gaze once more.

I smiled. A fantasy my father and his brother shared was about Earth. They confided in me when I was only six that they knew the location of our mother world, and had sworn me to secrecy. Enchanted to be in on such a secret, I had believed them for five years, until my first astronomy professor informed me that no one was certain of Earth's location or had been for over seven hundred years. I had been crestfallen, but over time I came to understand my paternal unit and his sibling had a dry sense of humor.

Uncle Laurence was a bit of a hermit. He had served with distinction in the same years as Father, but afterwards did not return to the Core Worlds to enjoy himself as did the rest of their peers. He either purchased a large estate or took on a sinecure—family details were a little sketchy—on a largely arboreal planet in a remote district off the usual trade routes, far from borders with the Trade Union, the Autocracy or any of the Imperium's neighbors, which he occupied alone, without wife, children or friends. He wrote poetry, which he sent to favored relatives. I treasured his rather flowery images, as I did his infrequent visits home. Images of his forest fastness reminded me of fairy-tale castles, furnished with old-fashioned furniture and precious antique books. In my rebellious teens, I asked him often if I could come to stay for a while, but he assured me it was too primitive a setting for one accustomed to fine living and attentive service. I could hardly believe it when he told me he had only one LAI cargobot in his employ, and no personal valets at all of any species.

I did wonder for a moment what stimulus had made Father think he had had a conversation with his brother. I tried to put it from my mind. I had a party in my honor to enjoy. I returned to my suite to change. Still, images of him focused upon that nest of small spinning spheres troubled me deeply.

❧ CHAPTER 21 ❧

"...And the pirates were taken into the loving custody of the Imperium's own Red Fleet. I'm afraid the hoteliers are rather annoyed with me," I said, contemplatively sipping from the delectable pale green wine in my glass. Bobbing in blood-warm water, in a fresh, new swimsuit that came from the storeroom where the management of the resort kept supplies in each size required by their members. It was all part of the rather exorbitant annual fee at the Starling Island private resort, but as the service matched the setting, none of us minded. Thoughtfully, I twirled the goblet stem between my fingers and stared up at the ornate carved, gilded and enameled ceiling. The room was lit by floating globes filled with flickering flames of gold. Priceless rare birds and animals, all well-trained so as not to cause a nuisance, roamed, swam or flew around the pool and its ten acres of environs, which had been landscaped to resemble a woodland glade. This room was only one of sixteen tableaux in the resort, and was my cousins' and my favorite, at least this year. "I did offer to pay for damages, but Parsons stated that such a gesture on my part was not necessary. I believe they were more annoyed by that. He instructed them how to apply for reconstruction funds under the Victims' Compensation Act, even looked up the appropriate forms from an obscure file in the Infogrid. I had no notion such a thing existed. Do you suppose that the owner of the bar on Kewick Station did that after we caused all of her commodes to seize up two years ago?"

"With that industrial glue powder?" asked Jil Loche Nikhorunkorn, a maternal cousin of mine, with a fierce grin. Jil, who shared my age and propensity for loftiness, also shared a penchant for a good prank. Her brown eyes were shaded by epicanthic folds, which concentrated her long lashes in broad, black fans. She had a long, slender figure that was barely concealed by a tiny swimsuit of brilliant ultramarine. I noticed that she had indulged in a swirl of gems attached around her navel. I didn't tell her the trend was passé—the damage to her skin from the gems' removal would keep her out of the sun for a precious two weeks of the desert summer. She'd find out soon enough, then disappear for a while with a face-saving excuse, undoubtedly after the season ended. "She saw the number on my scooter and called my father. Father withdrew a good deal of money from my account. I almost couldn't go to Tark Sands with everyone else."

We all agreed that would have been the real tragedy. Tark Sands was a favorite of ours, too. I recalled its ruby dunes and warm, orange sun with a good deal of pleasure. In particular, I remembered a lovely lady who worked as a climate programmer who shared my taste for pomegranate Rhapsody cocktails. With difficulty, I returned my mind to the enjoyable event at hand.

"What are real pirates like?" demanded Scot, who had followed my narrative more closely than most of the others, who were already perusing the dinner menu or toying with the latest of gadgets or one another. He always was the best of listeners. I smiled.

"I can't speak to all illicit crews. These were nearly all reptilian. The captain was a very ugly Croctoid with a crooked jaw. A quantity of Uctu, three humans, more Crocs, and a Solinian. That wretched fellow bit great-grandfather Morris Ubunte Kinago's pistol in half!"

My audience laughed.

"I'd heard they eat unrefined ore for breakfast," said Jil, with a twinkle. "Nice to hear it confirmed."

"But imagine my surprise when the creature's teeth did prove equal to the task," I said. "My heart skipped at least three beats."

"Do you have pictures?" asked Xan. He lay sprawled with his latest young lovely companion in a hollow that was artfully made in the top of what looked like a dangerous shoal of rocks. When the waves were turned up all the way in the fountain, they crashed convincingly up the slope.

"Some," I said, cocking a finger to the hovering Optique to display what images Parsons had left in my storage crystal. I had no idea why he had confiscated the majority, but Parsons not moving in mysterious ways was hardly Parsons at all. The glass-smooth waterfall at the end of the fountain pool made an excellent screen. My cousins gasped as the open-jawed visage of the captain blinked into being upon its surface. I narrated the still frames and short segments of video as they appeared, to appreciative laughter and applause. I had, in fact, captured the moment when the gigantic reptile had snapped my pistol off. I let the image linger upon the wall for a moment.

"You must have been just terrified!" Erita said, sounding as though the notion bored her inutterably.

"Later on," I said. "At that moment I was surprised and a trifle indignant, if you want the truth. I mean, how *dare* he?"

"You look very brave," Jil assured me. "Not scared at all."

"Thank you, dear," I said.

"But all that running, darling," Erita said. "Wasn't that tedious?"

"At the time, no," I said, lying back to choose a canapé from the tray of one of the serving arms secreted in the false rocks around the pool. The tray ran a sensor over my wrist and, knowing my tastes, shifted so that a different piece was just within reach of my fingers. The chunk of steak inside the round, pale pink mushroom ball was just slightly underdone and the spicing was divine. I sighed happily. I had missed the finer elements of food while in space. The hors d'oeuvre was gone in two bites, but it dispelled all thoughts of survival rations. "I call it just amazing how many thoughts that the mind can cram in when under pressure. I had charts of the restaurant's floor plan and the general layout of the level of the colony, the rules and tricks of swordplay, giving orders and listening to the soldiers, annoyance at Lieutenant Plet's disapproval, awareness of the savory scent of the food in the restaurant as well as its slipperiness under my feet, concern for the patrons, and a faint worry about

Parsons all going at the same time—and those are only the items that I can think of at the moment. I told the maternal unit all about it, and she informs me that it is a common phenomenon. Minds run more efficiently and swiftly on adrenaline. An old-fashioned piece of wisdom, but true nevertheless."

"What did Aunt Tariana say about the rest of your stint?" Scot asked. "I got the impression from some of your messages on Infogrid that the captain of your ship didn't appreciate all the help you gave him."

"That is putting it mildly," I said. dryly. "Mother did say that the admiral, while an excellent leader and able administrator, has no sense of humor. I stand as witness to insist that that is true, beyond a reasonable specter of doubt, not that I think specters are reasonable. Alas, I feel she did not entirely take my side of the argument." I allowed a poignant and wistful expression to crease my brow.

"Are you all right?" asked Nalney Ven Kinago, a second cousin, two years older, and a close friend from infancy. His face was the same heroic square as my father's, but his eyes were a muddy hazel. He sent the wine tray bobbing toward me over the surface of the fountain in which we lounged. He'd had a few run-ins with Mother, one in particular over the matter of the unwitting loan of a standing wardrobe that was a family heirloom. When recovered at the bottom of a ski slope, it was in dire condition, a state that Mother had passed along to him as the guilty party. I am happy to say I had not been involved in that incident.

"It was a bit rough," I said, indicating to the bottle-holder that it should top up my glass. I sipped the glorious pale wine, which gave me the strength to continue my confession. "Mother took a lot of the skin off my back. It is, after all, her Navy, so you can see she feels strongly about it. I am avoiding the aunts. They set about me as I left Father's workshop with a host of prospects for marriage. They have had months without my interference to examine the genetic rosters for just the right kind of girl. Starting tomorrow they want me to have coffee or wine with at least one of their prospects per day. The concept is that I will choose one of them, or die in the attempt."

Scot shuddered. "*I'd* rather die. When the day comes that I must settle down, I'll... I'll know the love of *my* life. My own love, not someone else's vision."

"Hear, hear," said Nalney.

"I prefer to leave true romance to fate," I said, lyrically. "Preferably a fate long in the future. I hate eating my dinner with a sword hanging over my head, particularly one composed of two steely-eyed aunts and a lace-trimmed extravaganza, liberally festooned with nagging. I'd rather go out with the fleet again. Not that that's likely," I added.

"Oh, well, you're back now," said Xan. "You don't have to worry about taking ship again. All that's over with. We've done our service, and the Emperor can count us as loyal officers."

"Yes," I echoed, feeling more lost than I thought I would have. "It's behind us, isn't it?"

"Don't tell me you're sorry to see it end?" Scot asked, in astonishment. "Regimentation, hobnobbing—if you can call it that—with the lower classes. The food! Even though the *Tirisiani* had state of the art kitchens and the head chef from the Autumn Sunrise restaurant on staff, it could not compare to this!"

"No," I agreed faintly. "It doesn't compare."

To my amazement and horror, I felt a pang of longing. I enjoyed my cousins' company, as I always had, but I found that the thought of never sitting at a table with my fellow ensigns again a sorrowful thing. The shock of dismissal was the worst part. I had had no inkling that Admiral Podesta would have called for my removal. I studied my reaction to see whether I was just suffering from an attack of pique. It took three more canapés and half a glass of wine before I decided that it was not so. I had felt useful. I had been heroic, if I must say so myself. I had struck up friendships with people to whom I was not related and who had no stake beyond simple camaraderie in mind, and found them enjoyable. It was a shame that I would never see them again except at reunions.

"You're not alone," Erita said, her voice laced with abundant sympathy.

"I'm not?" I asked, a trifle surprised. Of all the cousins who had started their service at the same time as I, she was the most put out by our lack of comforts and freedoms. My heart went out to her. "You feel the same way as I do?"

"Oh, yes," she said, feelingly. "All of our relatives are putting pressure upon us to marry."

I put aside my sense of brothers-in-armsness, which had been disappointed. "Ah, but not with the same doggedness as *my* aunts. Alone, either would be formidable, but together, they display the tenacious quality of permaseal along with the taste of a tongueless beggar. Though there are only two of them, they seem to form an infinite host, surrounding me and haranguing me with voices of iron. They persist in pulling in impoverished female nobles from the provinces in hopes of finding me someone to whom I cannot object based upon previous acquaintance. None of their choices so far would fit into my life, not that I am ready to share it."

"That is true," Nalney agreed. "Thomas's aunts form a unique bond in pursuit of the unsuitable. My immediate relational units merely make suggestions. I ignore them and behave charmingly, and they leave me alone."

"Me, too," said Xan. "Otherwise, how could I enjoy the company of the delightful Meghan here?"

"It's Meghtila," the girl in question replied, with a frown. Xan turned his attentions upon her, and she was soon persuaded out of her bad mood. They rose from the shallow water, looking for a privacy booth, and we went back to our conversation.

"What will you do now that you are home, Thom?" Scot asked. "Can you come out with me tomorrow? I've got some things I want to show you."

"Me, too!" Jil burst out, unable to contain her glee any longer. "I bought a village!"

"Really?" I said. "Congratulations! Is it on this planet?"

"Yes, and I had to pay a premium for that," she said. "My goodness, when my agent told me what it would cost for the location I chose, I nearly expired."

"How did you decide which one you wanted?" asked Erita.

Jil waved a casual hand. "I glanced at a map. I thought it would be fun to have a personal place to recharge in between the capital and my parents' estate in Olhinha. It was so cute! It has a town square with old-fashioned brick streets, and a couple of little shops, an entertainment palace, a night club, and all these *adorable* stone houses. No wheeled traffic permitted in the historical district. I took over the town hall as my residence, of course. You should have heard the whining and complaining when I made the councillors move their offices, but you couldn't expect me to live in one of those cottages, darling. My *dog* has a larger house. Besides, I kept in mind the maxim that the agent kept pouring in my ear over and over again: location, location, location. I wanted to make certain that my new people would keep me in mind whenever they passed by. The gardens are lovely, and there's a stone fountain that absolutely dates back to pretechnological times, darlings."

I found myself filled with envy and admiration. I wish I had thought of such a thing first. A whole town, to trifle with as one pleased! To follow in her footsteps now would brand me as a copyist, not an original. I sighed. "That is one of the most brilliant moves, my dear. How are you enjoying being the most important person in town?"

Jil pouted. "Truthfully, Thom, darling, it just is not as much fun as I thought it was going to be. All of the tenants nag me all of the time. The little problems they think are important! I said, 'Go to your town council. I bought them along with everything else.' And they do, but they always come back. They say, since I own the town, I am responsible. Well, I do try to be responsible, but there are limits even to my patience! My bills for infrastructure repairs are shocking, just shocking! There's always another hole to pour money into. I think I'll donate the whole mess to charity. I'll get a writeoff for the Imperial purse at the same time ridding myself of the nuisance. But before I do, you must come and see it. I put up a statue to myself in the village square."

"I will," I promised.

"What did you call it? Jilville? Locheton?" Scot asked, mischievously.

"Oh, you!" Jil cried, tossing her glass at him. The delicate crystal sank in a whirlpool. She reached out and the wine float brought her a replacement. "I had to keep the old name, Broch. It was in the town charter. Broch. How boring is that? But enough about my village. I think I will try an island next time."

My heart sank. Drat. I had just been about to say that. Another idea scooped. Best to do my thinking when I was not around my cousins. Our minds did tend to run along the same grooves.

"What about the rest of you?" I asked. "What are you going to do now that you're on leave?"

Nalney snorted. "I am utterly done with the service. Been there, done that, posted the Infogrid image." He noticed my expression, and his eyebrows flew up. "What, you're not seriously thinking of continuing? It's so dreary!

"Oh, I know," I said, assuming the pose of idle indifference the rest of my cousins habitually wore. It surprised even me that I considered going on, though it was a futile thought now that Admiral Podesta had banned me from the Red Fleet. "But I have a few things I left unfinished, much more interesting than drills or swabbing decks, not that I did much of that." I sent around a sly glance. "My greatest accomplishment was accumulating an immense file of humorous anecdotes that I guarantee are unknown within the Imperium Court."

"Jokes in the Navy? How?" Nalney demanded.

"Oh," I said, "I have . . . connections." I was not inclined to reveal the means by which I first came across those precious references, even if it would not have violated the protocol of my former office.

"You have to give me a copy," Scot begged. "Aren't you my best friend in the entire universe? How can you hold back such a treasure from your loved ones?"

I grinned lazily, crossing my feet on the end of my rock chaise longue. "I knew you would be gagging for one. It's mine. But I will tell you what I will do: I will let you have an edited version. A few of the best stories."

"No!" Jil said. "The whole thing!"

I put my hand to my breast in mock outrage. "I can't give away all my material on the first day back! When I have squeezed every drop of original laughter out of my collection, I will share it with everyone. But not yet."

"Oh, you spoilsport!" She threw a bite of bread at me. One of the trained ducks that floated on the rippling water sailed over and nibbled it up. "Tell us some, then!"

I knew they would come around, since the truth was nearly all of them would have preferred to have stories told them than listen to or read the entire file themselves.

"Very well," I said, propping myself up so I could see the eager faces of my audience. "This was the first one I found, and still consider my favorite."

I stretched out the Uctu anecdote as long as I dared, judging by the anticipatory glints under their lowered eyelids to ensure I was keeping their interest. When I came to the words, "fire extinguisher,"

I caught them all off guard. In fact, they laughed so hard they couldn't even retain their customary bored expressions. I captured a wonderful spit-take from my cousin Erita that was so wonderfully explosive that I ordered the camera to stow it in my secret file immediately. They applauded so long I was almost embarrassed.

"More!" they clamored. "More!"

"He's not supposed to be the entertainment," Scot protested. "*We* are supposed to provide it. This is his celebration."

"But we were together for months, darling," Jil said. "He's the only one who did something different."

"Scot, it is my pleasure to be able to tell these to a new audience," I said, proud of the warm reception. "I don't mind a bit."

"Well, if you're sure...?"

"Hand on heart," I assured him.

"More!" Nalney bellowed, slapping the water with his palm.

I nudged my memory for my best stories. I could have called for my pocket secretary, but it would have detracted from my performance to have to refer to notes. Fortunately, the flood of quips and anecdotes that sprang to mind was more than enough to keep the merriment going for a long time. The laughter rang off the painted ceiling and caused the birds to explode upward from the fountain's surface. This was indeed a wonderful welcome home.

My skin was wrinkled into a remarkable representation of prune-skin and my throat's lining shredded to fibers by the time our delightful evening concluded.

I was full of contentment as well as the most exquisite delicacies, not to mention my mother's vintage wines. I had been admired and fussed over, and it felt wonderful. My cousins bade me affectionate and damp farewells as we staggered with some difficulty toward the resort's courtesy skimmers that would take us to our limousines at the front gate.

"Wait!" Scot cried, wriggling into my transport at the last moment through the narrow window. He landed on top of Nalney, who was sprawled limply on the seat across from mine, considerably the worse for wine. "Thom, come and see me tomorrow, all right? I need to talk to you."

"I already said that I would, on the way to Jil's village. What is it about?"

With an expression I could not identify, Scot opened his mouth to speak. But trouble interrupted him.

I thought I had heard the faint noise of protest during the party, but had dismissed it as unimportant. There were often partygoers who had had a little too much good cheer and became argumentative as a result. I had been one myself at times. The management was always careful to prevent interruption of their most honored guests during a private function, but true soundproofing was impossible where there was the passage of atmosphere.

Bodies landed upon the soft awning of our skimmer and struggled to get inside. I could not see much of them by the pale amber lights studded about the interior, but if I was not utterly mistaken, they were wearing rented evening attire.

"Out, curse you!" Scot sputtered. "This is a private car."

The eldest and most indignant of the invaders glared at us. His face was suffused with red to the point where even with sufficient lighting I would not have been able to ascertain his original complexion. "You worthless pieces of dung, you spoiled my daughter's wedding!"

I fixed an eye upon him. "I don't believe we are acquainted, sir. Please leave our transport at once!"

It seemed they had said all they came to say. They withdrew from our skimmer, but dragged us out of the vehicle with them. Two large men twisted their fists into the front of my drying robe and pulled. Before I knew it, I and my cousins were in the midst of a crowd of ill-dressed party-goers, all shouting at us. I was beset by a well-muscled young man, the worse for drink, who kept poking me in the chest. A small, elderly woman with a shrill voice berated Scot and banged upon his head with her blue beaded handbag. He shielded his person as best he could and struggled back toward the doors. At her cry, three men in hired suits leaped upon him. Scot fell to his hands and knees upon the enameled tiles of the vehicle pad. The men belabored him with their fists.

I pushed the hand of my chest-poker out of the way and sprang to my cousin's defense. Two of them hauled him upward and held him so the third could pummel him about the midsection. I seized the shoulder of the right-hand immobilizer and spun him out of the way. Scot, listing sideways, tottered to his feet. I placed myself between me and the other two assailants. They seemed to take my interference unkindly, and turned their attention to me.

In spite of my sybaritic evening, I was not as impaired as I might have been, thanks to my need to be alert in my brief turn as a comedian. I grabbed the left wrist of the man on my left and the right of the other, and tugged them sharply upward, as I had once done with two Geckos. Thanks to physics, which worked the same here as on Smithereen, the two men, arms forced to an acute angle with regard to the other's, were propelled forward and crashed into one another. They toppled to the ground. Before they could rise again and retaliate against me, I unwound their unspeakable cummerbunds from about their waists and secured their hands with them. They sat on the stones moaning.

"Thanks, old fellow," said Scot. "You were a whirlwind! Is that what they teach one on the plebeian ships?"

I glanced back at my handiwork, a trifle shocked. The movements that disarmed my opponents had come naturally to me. I gave Scot a sheepish smile.

"All that drilling, out of sheer boredom, I assure you. What is wrong with these people?"

"I have not the inkling of a clue," Scot said. "I didn't waste a moment of the evening on strangers."

Other cousins were in need of our aid. A stout, older woman in a horrible fuchsia evening gown made for Xan's eyes with her fingernails curved. We both flew to his side.

It was unnecessary. Xan stepped toward her, not away. She ended up in an unwitting embrace, chest to heaving bosom. He dragged her toward the nearest light. Putting her at arm's length, he gazed deep into her eyes.

"Now, you don't want to do that, my darling," he said, in a soft, passionate voice.

Her expression softened from fury to a dazed wonderment.

"No, I don't," she said.

Scot and I exchanged looks of puzzlement.

"She must know him," I said. "You know our Xan, man of a thousand conquests."

"Indeed," Scot said, admiringly. "Although I would not have picked her as one of his typical choices."

"Who knows?" I asked. "There are questions in this world to which I do not want to know the answers."

Xan let the now quiescent woman go and went to extract Erita from an argument with three young women in matching gowns. We scuffled with a few more angry patrons.

Into the midst of the disturbance swept a number of vehicles bearing the logo of resort security. Numerous men and women dressed in uniforms both subservient and soothing in appearance sprang out and began to mingle with the crowd. I and my cousins were cut out of the herd and urged in the gentlest possible way toward one end of the patio, whereas the disgruntled mob was surrounded and contained. I was pleased that I didn't have to employ any of the martial arts I had learned. There was no need for anyone to be harmed. The manager of the resort, an old friend of my mother's, made toward us, his hands raised in a placatory manner.

"What is going on?" I demanded. "Mr. Banion, we are not accustomed to such ill-treatment on the very threshold of what has until now been our favorite haunt."

"And will continue to be, I hope, please, Lord Thomas," Sted Banion said, in hand-wringing distress. "We were delighted to host you today. There has simply been a small misunderstanding."

"Small?" A large man in one of the ill-fitting hired suits came bustling toward Banion. His face was crimson with anger. "My daughter's wedding has been in your schedules for a year! It cost us a fortune! And to have it suddenly cancelled by you this afternoon, with four hours' notice? What do you call that?"

"Mr. Felash, please," Banion said, turning smoothly to confront the angry man. Two security guards came to flank them just in case. I started toward them, to help out if wanted, but a young lady in spectacles with striped lenses smiled up at me.

"Please stay here, Lord Thomas. This will all be straightened out to everyone's satisfaction."

"They're nobles, do you see?" Banion whispered to the father of the bride, but loudly enough that I and those cousins near me could hear.

"What does that matter?"

"I apologize, Mr. Felash, but it doesn't do to annoy the Imperial house. I offer you the deepest apologies of the resort. We will refund your deposit on the chamber, naturally."

"What about the rest of the bill?" Felash asked, as calculation caused his left eye to squint at the unhappy manager.

"Your daughter did have her wedding here, didn't she?" Banion asked. "It was a beautiful, may I say a memorable event? The images have already been posted to your Infogrid file and those of your guests."

"But I wanted to have it in that woodland glade!" The bride, overhearing the conversation, swooped down upon the unhappy manager.

"Please accept my congratulations on your marriage," Banion said smoothly. "You look very lovely.

Did you enjoy the special marberry dessert? It was compliments of Sparrow Island. It has been such a pleasure to have you here."

"But . . . !"

By then, fresh transports arrived, and we were herded to them. I was glad to get into my carriage. My skin was still damp, and desert nights are chilly. We were swept away into the starry night, but the press camera-eyes zoomed around us. I frowned. The transports let off a burst of static with audible code. I'd heard it before. It was a scrambling signal. Few of the images would make it to the all-day, all-night news stations, perhaps making a mention in the celebrity gossip. I hope they hadn't captured my image. My mother was cross enough at me.

"That was unpleasant," Xan said. His lady friend had been packed into a different car, but my cousin did not seemed troubled by her absence.

"I for one did not appreciate the nasty comments about uselessness," I said.

"What?" Xan asked. "Ignore them. They have no idea of our responsibilities."

I tried to follow his advice, but the comment continued to sting me.

"So, Xan, who was the lady?" Scot asked, with a wink at me.

"Which lady?"

"The lady who seemed so stunned to see you," I said. "The one in the flamboyant sequined brocade."

"Her?" He frowned. "No idea."

"But she calmed down immediately on seeing you," I said.

Xan smiled modestly. "Women can't resist me," he

said. "It's my good looks and charm. A most powerful combination, or so I have been told."

We fleered. "No, it's true!" he protested. "I've always been able to do that. I turn my most sincere gaze upon them, and they calm down. It's been a useful skill."

"Mood-levelers," Scot said decisively. "He must have them in a poison ring."

Xan seemed hurt. "If either of the two of you had any charm, you'd be able to do it yourself."

"I'll try it one day," I said. But Scot and I exchanged amused glances.

CHAPTER 22

DeKarn was not completely immune from the charms of the visitor, but she began to feel nervous at his sheer ubiquity. Not only was Captain Sgarthad in the council chambers and on the digitavid programming every day, he made appearances in circles of power. He had insinuated himself among the group of prominent businessbeings who frequented the deluxe bar at the top of the local hotel. At first she thought it was innocent. After all, he came from a culture of traders. Then petitions began to circulate. DeKarn obtained one from a trusted source who was also outraged that the Trade Union captain seemed to be the moment's darling. DeKarn could not believe it until she had listened to the prologue several times. The petition sought to hold a special election, against all laws of Boske or any of the other Castaway Cluster systems, to name Emile Sgarthad governor on behalf of the Trade Union, "the better," the narrator, a distinguished-looking Cocomon businessfemale DeKarn had met personally, "to facilitate our entry into the greater galactic community." There were over six thousand image prints of signatories attached to the document already. DeKarn searched out some names, and was shocked to see that Councillor Four, a member of her own contingent, was one of those who endorsed it. Four, a busy mother of three and a businesswoman, refused to discuss it.

"All my reasoning is there," she said, peevishly. "We want prosperity and protection, and this arrangement offers both of them!"

DeKarn railed at her for a time in Portent's Star's private conference room, but Four was obdurate. She had a right to bring the petition. All the council could do was vote it up or down. DeKarn was frustrated.

Zembke had also seen the petition, and denounced it in open session.

"The only thing that is saving the Cluster from being taken over on the spot by you foolish, smitten folk is that the proposal is illegal!" he boomed.

"Then we move that it become possible in law," Ruh Pinckney argued, puffing up his many chins.

"Seconded," agreed Ferat Urrmenoc.

"Preliminary vote," DeKarn said wearily. "In favor?"

A dismaying number of lights went on. Every day, more of the councillors were being swayed to the Trade Union's cause. It was getting difficult even to table a proposal in favor of either independence or the Imperium. Lucky for common sense, everything in government moved so very slowly that the process would eventually bore people and take their eyes off the leadership argument.

Why was no one protesting the matter but the few of them? Something very fishy and uncomfortable had pervaded Cluster civilization. Until the arrival of the stranger, it had been a place where one could—and did—express views freely, gaining pings of approval from those who read or viewed the opinion. Recently, any naysayers who went public, on the Grid or the vids, seemed to appear only once or twice before recanting their articles or vanishing from view. It was alarming for supporters of free speech.

DeKarn tried to commune with the Cocomon contingent. They should not be affected by mind-changing methods, either chemical or hypnotic, but they seemed to find the visitor more than reasonable.

"See it from our perspective," Thanndur said, when she finally arranged a private conference. "The Trade Union has paid more attention to the Cluster over the last two hundred years than has the Imperium. When shortages pressed us, the TU came forward with supplies—though prices were exorbitant—but supplies were there. Everything they offer is reasonable, save perhaps for the governorship. That is to be debated. We await instructions from Cocomo. We have not committed wholly to the Trade Union, though opinion is pointing in that direction. Captain Sgarthad's pleas over the Grid have done much to sway our system to his point of view."

"But what about independence?" DeKarn pleaded.

"Neither that nor adherence to the Imperium are at the forefront at the moment. I will give you our decision when we make it. We are not delaying unnecessarily. We would like to return home before it is time for the yearly swarm. Reproduction must not wait too long."

DeKarn departed, unsatisfied. The Cocomons' logic

was inescapable. Though the Trade Union had been the aggressor during the wars two centuries ago, it had become a friend during the dark years and in the following decades while the Cluster rebuilt itself. Cocomo remained annoyingly neutral, continuing to demand argument from all three sides, while poised to fall into the Sgarthad camp. Her blood pressure spiked enough to set off her health chip, implanted into her body below her heart. Her communicator buzzed with yet another call from the Boske-wide physician program, prescribing meditation and a course of pressure-lowering medicine. She ignored it. Meditation could do nothing to abate the source of her stress.

The Grid had opened up once again, though heavily salted with Trade Union propaganda. The local council began to get reports from outer Boske about how delighted it was with the new Trade Union representative, and professed itself happy to follow him. No one seemed to think it strange that he was all but taking over.

They had to have help. Against her better judgment, she knew that the only source of aid large enough to dislodge the growing menace was the Imperium. It would jeopardize their standing as an independent entity, but that could all be worked out later.

She made an appointment to meet with Hiranna Ben. The ambassador had been more than patient through the previous weeks, regarding the actions of her rival as hijinks. Except for finding him fanciable, she seemed to be untouched by Sgarthad's appeal.

DeKarn begged off from the now-habitual lunch, and slipped into a hired flitter for the short trip to the governor's mansion. At her request to Dr. Yuchiko, the service door in the side of the mansion was left unlocked for her. The flitter scooted away into traffic between high rises. Unobserved by anyone except the odd electronic employee, DeKarn made her way to the ambassador's quarters.

They were empty.

"Ambassador Ben?" she called softly. No one answered.

She peeked into nearby chambers, then widened her search to the gardens, the library, and the other common rooms of the official residence that had been designated as still out of the public eye.

"No, I do not know where she is," Dr. Yuchiko said, troubled. "Did you call her ship?"

"I did," DeKarn said, now feeling frantic. "They have not seen her since she debarked. Her communicator does not answer. Had she said anything about going out?"

"Not in so many words," Dr. Yuchiko said, "but Captain Sgarthad said that since he is free to move about, he said that it would be logical to allow her the same liberty. I saw no reason to refuse."

DeKarn stared at him. "Neither one of them is at liberty, governor! You knew that."

Yuchiko paused and blinked. "Yes, I did. I am so sorry. But I did pass along the suggestion to the ambassador. I think perhaps she must have taken me up on it. I will let you know when she returns."

DeKarn put in another call to Ben, pitching her voice to a reasonable tone, and asking for some of her time when the ambassador should choose. She was not convinced that the ambassador had gone out on her own. What if she had disappeared, like the pundits who published on the Grid? She forced herself to be patient until past dinner that evening. Hiranna Ben had not returned to either her ship or the mansion. As far as DeKarn was concerned, she was missing. The blame had to lie at the feet of Sgarthad, but she would be a fool to accuse him when she had no grounds, and no one to back her up. She needed outside assistance.

Whom could she trust to send a message to the Emperor?

Her communicator buzzed again. Colm's earnest face and emphatic tattoos looked up at her from the pad's screen. "Councillor, I have some information for you. May I see you?"

"You can send it to me . . ." she began, but the pleading look in his eyes made her hesitate. "Yes. Meet me at the Pthohannix Rose Gardens. I am going there now."

He looked relieved. "Yes, madam. I will be there."

Among the fragrant blossoms and lush foliage, the pair of them in official garments attracted many looks from passersby. Colm gave her his combox.

"I don't dare transmit this, for fear of having it detected, madam," he said. "Please."

DeKarn opened the file in privacy mode, which flattened out any three-dimensional images that might pop up. It showed lists of names, numbers and coordinates.

"Ships, Councillor," Colm said. "Trade Union ships, lots of them. They have been appearing out of ultra-drive in every system in the Cluster. Notifications that should have come to you and the rest of the council were erased or suppressed. I have copies of them here, but I cannot keep them on an active pad for long. I have already had to purge a hundred and eight worm programs in the last three days. You can count on all of this information going to . . . our subject. I still haven't been able to find chemical trace or a device used to compel, er, cooperation, but it's got to be a sound pulse or a visual pattern of some kind. Sgarthad has become a phenomenon across the Cluster without ever having been to the other worlds. No one protests following the instructions he has sent, not even on Carstairs, and you know what they're like."

"So, it is a coup," DeKarn said. She felt oddly content, now that her suspicions had been confirmed. "Colm, can I trust you?"

He grinned. "I hope so, madam."

"Can you get a message to the Imperium?"

Colm's long face became serious. "We are virtually cut off, madam. No ships have been allowed to go out of system for weeks. No transmissions are being received from the Infogrid, and there has been no confirmation that they are receiving any from our Grid. I believe that the Trade Union has disabled our two repeater satellites on either side of the black hole." The anomaly prevented direct transmission, so the Cluster had no line-of-sight to the Core Worlds. "I can only guess, but if I wanted to cut us off from civilization, that would be my first stop, and I will bet that it was theirs."

"Then, how can we do it?"

"A messenger," Colm said, resolutely. "We have learned so much since . . . since Sgarthad arrived here. The Imperium can have no idea what is going on. You are right, madam. We have no choice. I'll have to go myself. I will go to the repeater station first. If I can transmit from there, I will, but otherwise, I will make my way to the nearest settlement and ask for help."

DeKarn felt a wrench. She hated to lose her most astute employee, but this was a matter of freedom for the whole Cluster. "Very well," she said. "Go safely. And may sunstorms rain down upon the emperor if he refuses to help this time! It will be the end, one way or the other, of the Castaway Cluster being the farthest outpost of the Imperium."

He slipped away through a bower of hanging blossoms with scarcely a rustle. DeKarn paused to enjoy the sunlight. She had a good deal of work to do. She entered a code on her communicator.

"Rengin?" she said, when the councillor's face appeared on the small screen. "I am sorry I missed this afternoon's session."

"Nothing happened," he said, wryly. "Councillor Zembke stood in for you. I hope you are not ill?"

"No, just delayed."

"I am glad to hear it. How may I serve?"

"Please put me on the agenda for tomorrow. I need twenty . . . no, thirty minutes for a speech. First thing, before we reopen the debate on the . . . governorship."

Rengin's left eyebrow perked up. "May I ask the subject?"

"Leave it open, if you will," DeKarn said. "I must go now. I have some research to do before tomorrow morning."

She squared her shoulders and marched toward the nearest light rail station. She had done with pretending to follow Sgarthad and turn a blind eye to the abuses going on all over the Cluster. The next morning, she would condemn Sgarthad, bring out into the open all the proof she had been amassing, and, it was to be hoped, wake up her fellows before it was too late—if it fact it was not already.

Sleep almost overpowered DeKarn before she climbed into bed. The speech was a good one, full of logic and bullet points, with plenty of visual proof she had been able to glean from opinion pieces posted from all eight systems, showing the Trade Union takeover from the beginning to the present. She hid backup copies in every secure storage point she could find, including in spare capacity in the household management system. As soon as she was certain she had created enough redundancy against accident, fire or sabotage, she collapsed into bed. The morning would see whether words and pictures could manage to stir her fellows, or if they and the Cluster were lost to the overwhelming charm of a handsome intruder. They must understand at least the suspicious disappearance of the Imperium ambassador. She pulled the light coverlet up to the nape of her neck, and fell asleep listening to the gentle hum of the household system.

She was awakened by a noise. The family feline was too elderly and lazy to roam the house when there was no chance of a late meal, and the AIs had finished their daily chores before sunset.

DeKarn rolled over.

"Manager?" she called. "What . . . ?"

A spray in the face made her cough. To her horror, her throat emitted no sounds. She still tried to cry out. Strong hands seized her by the arms. She arched her back and kicked out, fighting against the hold. More hands grabbed her legs and pinned them down. She thrashed. A brilliant green light bloomed in her face. Before she closed her eyes against the glare, she saw the crosshatching lines that swept from her forehead downward. "What is that?" she tried to say.

"Emile was right, she's a resister," a male voice said.

"Take her," said a female voice. She recognized it as Sgarthad's second officer, the short-haired human female. DeKarn fought against the hands. Another spray struck her in the face. Her body sagged. She could breathe, but none of her limbs moved. She could not even roll her eyes. Fully conscious but helpless, she felt herself lifted off the bed and carried out into the night. Why didn't the household manager react? The familiar purple lights were off. They had disabled it!

A dark-colored transport waited at the edge of the street. She tried to flail her arms and kick. Nothing but the top of her thumb moved. She waved it, hoping futilely that it would be noticed.

It wasn't. The beings carried her deposited her gently in the rear of the vehicle. The door slid closed almost silently. Darkness surrounded her.

She started to count the number of turns the vehicle took, but found it impossible to concentrate. Another touch of spray played upon her face. *How many different drugs do these people possess?* she thought indignantly as her mind drifted into dreams.

When she awoke, sour yellow light thrust a blade under her eyelids. She lifted them, grateful that her muscles were working once more.

A cone of feeble yellow light clung to the upper part of a doorjamb. She snapped her fingers, and the illumination doubled its output. She saw she was in a very small room. She lay upon a pallet. Though it had been covered with quality padding almost four centimeters deep, she discovered the pallet was made of thick metal. Across from her head, not quite within arm's reach, was a metal chair, its swivel pedestal planted into a slot in the floor. It was tucked into the kneehole of a desk. Beside the desk was a very basic personal cleansing station: commode, sonic cleaner, sink and wall-set mirror, all of the same heavy, burnished metal. This was a cell!

With difficulty, DeKarn forced herself to stand. Her knees buckled. She staggered to the door and placed her hand on the plate. No movement, not even a sound. It had been deactivated. She felt for the emergency release hatch. It had been caulked closed with a solid bead of smooth material. DeKarn could not even scratch it away.

Frantically, she searched her surroundings. Apart from the towel and liquids dispenser next to the cleansing station and a basic entertainment console—which she discovered, to her dismay, was not hooked up to the greater Grid—the room was empty of any item that could be used to free herself.

Her communication pad was missing, naturally, as she did not sleep with it. Her hand kept going to where it should have been at her hip. It felt as if someone had removed one of her eyes. She had never been without it for any length of time in her life. She activated the console again. It had no mail program, not even in the root registry.

"Help!" she cried. Her voice emerged in a thin whisper. It was coming back! "Help!" She planted her ear against the door, listening for footsteps. "Someone help me!" Her voice rose to a thin cry like a baby's.

A grinding sound made her jump backwards. A noise! A noise in the door!

She pounded on the impenetrable panel, waiting desperately to see who was on the other side.

"Let me out! Help me!" she cried. "You can't leave me here to starve."

Apparently, that was not the intent of her captors. A hatch in the middle panel of the door slid upward and spat two objects into her hands. She held them up to the feeble light: a large bottle of water and a package of survival bars.

The entertainment console had plenty of content. DeKarn had worn her fingers raw over the course of three days attempting to undo the seal on the emergency hatch. Her voice was hoarse and ragged from screaming. Neither action had any effect. Fresh meals and clean clothes arrived at intervals, but no one and nothing spoke to her or communicated with her in any way. She was weary of trying, and tired of being frightened. Anything that took her mind off her situation would help. She browsed through the console's drive, while letting her subconscious formulate an escape.

Sgarthad was behind this. She knew he or his minions had been spying on her for a long while. They had learned everything, including how to penetrate her household defenses. She should have asked for personal protection, but the constabulary would have asked why. None of them saw the visitor as a threat. *Obviously*. How she wished she had made a preemptive strike and put *him* in a prison cell. With a lock. Didn't anyone notice she was missing?

Over and over again, she feared for Colm. Had he been intercepted? She dared to think of him on a tiny spaceship streaking outward past the first jump point, out of Sgarthad's reach. Only that gave her enough hope to continue. By now, her enemy had found the speech she had written. Her perfidy—how could she think of it as that?—would be known. She had handed Sgarthad exactly the proof he needed that she opposed him.

She must not continue to berate herself. *Calm,* she thought. *Calm.*

How to Speak Wichu caught her eye. She opened the file. It contained lessons on both Youngspeak and Adultspeak. She decided to try Youngspeak.

"Welcome to Galactic-Talk!" an earnest young human male said. "You are about to embark upon a fascinating linguistic journey! Youngspeak Wichu is a changeable and malleable language. New words and phrases, including imports from human, Cocomon and Uctu, are picked up by the curious youngsters and spread in days throughout a colony. Over time, those parts of speech take on Wichu characteristics . . ."

There were few Wichus in the Cluster. If she was ever released, she would undoubtedy be forced to leave government. Perhaps she would take up teaching on a faraway edge of the Cluster. Providing that she was allowed to live. But being in the cell left her with hope. They had not killed her, only imprisoned her.

She was afraid of what the stress might do to her blood pressure. That was it! Everyone in the Cluster was implanted with a med-scan chip that kept track of their vital signs. She opened her robe and examined her solar plexus. No sign of surgery. It must still be in her body. She dragged in a breath and held it as long as she could, until she could feel her ears start to pop. That always brought her blood pressure up dangerously. She waited, then did it again and again. She was on the edge of passing out, but kept trying. No response. No one came looking for her. Her communicator was probably buzzing like a beehive, but the chip didn't send her location to the central computer along with her symptoms. Curse the privacy laws!

Over the course of the weeks that followed, she became fairly proficient at Wichu, even garnering praise from her prerecorded teacher. She listened to music programs, viewed countless digitavids, acquired new interests, but she remained desperate for news of the world outside her steel cage. No information came through the console system, nor any kind of access to the Grid. DeKarn tried over and over again to activate the communications portion of the console, but it never worked. The opening screen obligingly opened and presented itself to accept a message, but it did not work. Sometimes she cried from the frustration.

Suddenly, in the middle of the night in her seventh week of captivity, the console turned itself on with a blare of sound that frightened her right out of the metal bunk. She approached the square of light with the greatest of caution.

"Prosperity in the greater Pthohannix sector increased by point-zero-three percent over the last sixday. The rise can be attributed to a gain in intrasector trading…"

News! DeKarn was thrilled. She kicked back the chair and plunged into the newfound bounty with delight. Opinion programs, business programs, documentaries, exposes and talk programs galore filled channels that had heretofore been inaccessible to her. A database, by no means as extensive as the kind to which she was accustomed, gave her an index of current Grid shows and clips dating back almost two months. No decision had been made by the council, which surprised her not at all. The contingent from Dree made a presentation describing their deliberations. It was as boring as a history recording. She read the subtext notes and went on to the next item.

To her despair, no one *had* noticed that she was missing. A single mention in the gossip lines stated only that she had left a recording for the council saying she had gone on sabbatical, and would be back once she had resolved "personal problems." They had forged a message from her! When she got a hold of Sgarthad, she would make him sorry he had ever brought his pretty face to Boske!

DeKarn watched all that she could, never sleeping until she collapsed with weariness, and rising with alacrity to view and listen and read. Whatever glitch had prevented her from having this resource before had cleared. And a good thing, too. The Trade Union was becoming more open in its move to insinutate itself into Cluster culture. Sgarthad gave daily speeches, full of the nothing of goodfellow politics, just enough, she realized, to keep his face in the public view as much as he could.

"Trade will increase exponentially once the Cluster has formed a permanent bond with the Trade Union," he said. "Be certain to notify your city-state and planetary representatives…"

Shockingly, the screen went blank. DeKarn pounded upon the console with both hands.

"Come back!" she cried. She struck all the keys and controls, trying to resurrect the report. "Don't stop!" Nothing seemed to work. She pounded a fist on the keyboard.

"Welcome to Galactic-Talk! You are about to embark upon a fascinating...!

DeKarn muted the sound, just in time to hear footsteps. The hatch in the door opened. A bundle came through, and the one she had left, containing food wrappers, empty water bottles and soiled clothes, was extracted. She never saw the hand that made the delivery. The hatch slid closed, and footsteps receded into silence.

Just as abruptly as it had gone, the program returned. DeKarn flew to the console.

She remained glued to it as long as she possibly could. The Trade Union's presence became less of a phenomenon to the opinion press, and more natural every day. Sgarthad's face was everywhere on Boske. Several more councillors posted "sabbatical" letters. She was not surprised to see they came from Zembke, Marden, her friend Barba Linden, among others.

She began to receive feeds from other worlds, too, days or weeks behind, showing more Trade Union ships arriving, their crews greeted by parades and ceremonies of welcome. There was no news whatsoever from the Imperium. They were cut off. She was so frustrated that her hands shook. Sgarthad had succeeded in making the Castaway Cluster an outpost of the Trade Union, in all but name. That, too, could not be long in coming.

A brightly dressed, toothy announcer appeared on the screen and beamed at her.

"This show was brought to you by Nom-Num Snacks!" he exclaimed. "This foodstuff is Sgarthad-approved! Enjoy!"

DeKarn found that as unpalatable as the food bars on her tray. Oh, how she hoped Colm had made it off-world!

❧ CHAPTER 23 ❧

Scot yawned and rubbed his eyes with one fist, the other hand resting on the control stick of his favorite skimmer. "That is three hours I would like to have refunded to my lifespan," he said.

"How boring that was!" Erita said, peevishly. She reached over the back of the seat and into the chilled hamper of delectables we had brought with us for sustenance. "Wine, either of you?"

"Please," I begged her. "After that excruciating hike I need a restorative. Every tissue is desiccated. I already had a hard morning, breakfasting with Mother."

"Bad, was it, dear?" Erita asked.

"You talk about your inquisitions. If there is anything I did in the last few months that she doesn't know by now, it is because I have utterly purged it from my memory." And, speaking of purging, I flicked through the numerous pictures and videos I had taken in our tour, deleting nine of every ten from each of my cameras. I picked the unwanted images out of midair, tossing them away as the trash they were. Some were marvels of focus and composition, but the subject matter was simply too mundane to waste storage space on. I had only taken them as a compliment to our hostess, and now we were out of sight. I mused over the perfectly framed picture of a slate-roofed shop, then flicked it out of existence. "One has to admit that the only thing that set Broch apart from any other of a million small, antique villages in the Imperium is that it belongs to our Jil. Alas, but that makes it interesting only to her."

"I know," Scot said, smirking. "She has had her fun with it. Now that she's shown it off to all of us, she can dispose of it and move on to a more worthy pursuit."

We all laughed at that.

"What worthy pursuit?" Erita demanded, hoisting her glass merrily. "We have gone through the required naval service, our last commitment to the Imperium. There is nothing for us left to do but marry—not for at least three years, over my rotting corpse—perhaps breed, and die."

"Ugh, unfit subject for conversation," I protested.

"Corpse? Sorry, dear."

"No! Marriage," I replied. We laughed again.

"I apologize," Erita said, patting my arm. "It's not my intent to be distasteful."

"Forgiven, dear cousin."

Scot's handsome face twisted in an enigmatic expression that I could not have solved in a month of restday puzzle solving. "Where can I drop you, Erita?" he asked, casually.

She looked at the skimmer's paired chronometers, one set to Taino time and the other to local time, which as we watched shifted to match the first read-out, meaning that we had reentered the home city time zone. "I have a fencing match arranged this afternoon, dears. It's been set up for so long with Jacque Mirz—you know, the pro that won the last Tour de Force championship? I'd like an hour or so to limber up before we play."

"You fortunate thing, you!" I admit to taking in an audible breath of envy. She must have offered Mirz a fortune. I had had one lesson with a previous year's winner, but none since had been willing to face one of us. Not alone, anyhow. I blamed Xan, who, I think, had tried to seduce the next one. Erita smirked.

"I'll let you know how it goes," she said. Scot entered the directions she gave him. The skimmer picked up speed and altitude, putting Broch far behind us. We all sat back against the upholstery to enjoy the small feast assembled by the Kinago chefs and one another's company.

We landed before the salle, a grand sports empo-rium designed for the ancient arts where we had all taken lessons—I with my now-damaged antique sword. Erita alit, vaulting out of the low car with grace. She leaned back in to kiss us each on the cheek.

"See you later, darlings," she said.

"Fight well," I called.

Scot waited until she had disappeared through the wrought steel doors, then kicked the skimmer into operation. We zoomed over the buildings, attaining empty azure sky with a speed that propelled me backwards into the padded seat. I was surprised. Scot did not usually put his passengers at risk.

"Are you well, old fellow?" I asked.

"I just couldn't take any more spouting of self-satisfied chitchat," he said.

"That's nearly all we do spout," I reminded him. He looked preoccupied, which concerned me. "What is troubling you?"

"Nothing."

I knew when to let things be. Perhaps he was jealous of Jil's idea, but three hours of walking in a place where we were clearly not welcome should have disabused him of any pleasure we might have taken in following her example. I sat back to enjoy the fine weather in silence.

We followed the usual route toward the grand cream and rust-colored spires of the Imperium palace that echoed the stone towers of the surrounding canyon walls. I breathed an appreciative sigh. No landscape so delighted my senses as that of my home. Scot glanced up, then ran his hands over the controls. The car veered several degrees off to the left.

"I thought we were going home," I said.

"I told you I have something to show you," he said. He shot me a worried glance. "You must not tell anyone else. Swear it?"

"You need to ask *me* to keep your confidence?" I struck my thorax with a balled fist. "We who were so nearly brothers that our mothers suffered their confinements side by side? I am crushed."

"No, be serious," Scot protested.

"Very well," I said. "I think I can feign sincerity better than that." He looked so devastated that I put on a serious face. "Very well, show me. You know you can trust me to the last breath in my body. After that, we have no verifiable information." My attempts at

humor only elicited a look of constipation. I simpli-
fied my vow further. "I will keep your confidence."

"Thank you," he said. From a concealed pocket
in his sleeve hem he removed a tiny chip of crystal,
which he put into the skimmer's system.

The navigation screen turned red, and the thin line
tracing our path toward my family compound disappeared. The chip had to be a short-cutter, a device
that disabled the tracking system and fed a false
pattern into the memory and the city's grid recorder.
When we landed it would file a report that we were
up to several kilometers from our actual destination.
We had all used them at one time, but I had a new
sensitivity to subterfuge. I wondered suddenly if I
was in the presence of another traitor like Bek. The
thought chilled me. Scot and I had been friends all
our lives. We were family. Our mothers were cousins.
What if Scot had become a traitor? We hadn't been
together for months. He sent me a quick smile. It
was a warm and genuine expression. I tried to relax,
but found I could not. I smiled back weakly.

We did, in fact, land at some distance from our
destination. Scot set down the vehicle at the rear of
a seedy lot that sold used vehicles of the same make.
I kept my frown to myself. The neighborhood into
which we emerged was not of any type that we were
used to frequenting. I scanned the streets for a club
or other amusement that would have attracted him
to this place. Instead, my gaze was met by the blank
windows of rows of simple, aging one- and two-story
domiciles, the kind occupied by our employees who
did not live in the compound. He took the hamper
out of the rear seat and tucked it under his arm.

My questions as to why and wherefore were ignored. Instead, we walked.

Even with my long legs, I had to open my stride to keep up with Scot. He gave me another eager grin. We turned up the walk toward one of the small houses. Instead of knocking, he produced a key card. He passed it over the reader switch, and the door slid open.

"Daddy!" exclaimed a small voice. Scot stepped inside and scooped up a tot of about three years from among a pile of old toys. She had the same green eyes and warm complexion as he did, but slender limbs and a round chin. "Play with me!"

Scot kissed the child. "In a moment, Tina," he said, setting her down. "Where is your mother?"

The child took the time to point further into the house before returning to her blocks.

"You brought me here to introduce me to your mistress?" I whispered.

"Not my mistress," Scot said. "My wife."

"Wife?" I caught myself goggling, and clamped up my jaw. Nothing had prepared me to hear such a thing. "So it is not a courtesy title. You *are* 'Daddy'?"

Scot looked proud. "That's right. This is my family. I live here during the times I am not required to be on duty or in the compound."

"Here?" I asked, looking around me. The entire structure, garden and all, could have been placed in the Kinago great room with space for traffic around it. I laughed aloud with relief. Not treason after all. Just a love story that I could not wait to hear. "By Forn, who would believe it? You must tell me all. How did you end up *here*, of all places?"

"You're making fun of my house," Scot complained.

"No! It's charming," I protested. It was the size of one of Jil's cottages, but clean, well-kept and modern. "Did you say your *wife?* I'm crushed. How long have you kept this secret from me?"

"Almost five years," he said. When I evinced dramatic surprise, he shrugged. "You know I have wanted to tell you. I've wanted to tell someone, but I just couldn't find a way. All of you are so set against marriage and families."

"Not altogether," I said. "Just not yet. I have told you how greatly I dislike the thought of having my bride chosen for me."

"So did I," he said, with an unfamiliar set to his jaw. "I did approach the Family Secretary about Jerna, and was told that it was out of the question. Her genes were not vital to the Imperial line. So, we took matters into our own hands. It was ... liberating." His eyes lit up. I could almost see the story unfold within them.

It was not to be told yet. A lady came into the room. She was not spectacularly pretty, with a speckled complexion and eyes that looked just a little too wide-set. Her nose was broad at the tip and bent a little to the left. Such a feature made her unusual, since we nobles tended to have very regular features, so it rather entranced me. She was very thin, except for a slight belling-out at the waist.

"Hello, Foxkin," she said, coming to slip an arm around his waist. They exchanged a loving kiss, then she held out her hands to me. "How do you do? I'm Jerna."

"Thomas," I said. I bent to kiss her fingertips. "My pleasure."

"We'd just like to talk for a while, beloved," Scot said. "Will you mind?"

"No. I'm making lunch. Please stay, Thomas," she said. "There's plenty."

I glanced at Scot for permission. He seemed torn. We did need to talk. "I am waiting for a call, but if I may, I would love to."

She led us out through the house—there was not much more of it—to the back garden and left us alone with a bottle of wine.

"It's nothing fancy, but drinkable," Scot said, as we settled into a pair of chairs beside a round wrought iron table. He unfastened the bottle's seal and poured the purple liquid into two nondescript goblets. "We live here on a fraction of my allowance, but more than that would draw too much attention, and you may guess I do all I can to avoid that. I live an ordinary life here. I like it."

"What is Foxkin?"

"We go by Fox," he said. "It was easy to obtain a false identification plate, for a price. Amazing what one can obtain for the correct amount of money. She likes the name, so we took it. I almost feel more like Fox than Loche many days."

That shocked me almost more than the presence of the children. How anyone could turn his back upon millennia of history was more than I could encompass. As nobles, we had a responsibility to family, and could not think of endangering our standing within it. I took pride in my lineage. To defy the Family Secretary meant risking one's allowance, or worse. One of the things I had not told the curious Chee Rubin-Sign and her cohorts on Smithereen was that beside being able to command his subjects to marry or mate with someone specific, the Emperor also had the power to order them *not* to. No noble was permitted to wed a commoner without permission, and it was never given. Still, Scot had had years to think about the consequences, and I only minutes.

The children were a genuine presence, not anything that had to be imagined. Young Tina had a small brother, at the creeping stage. He had a very round head with a couple of wisps of dark hair on top and round, button eyes. Both of them made their way out to play at the feet of Daddy and Uncle Thomas, attempting to include us in their games. They were irresistible. I dismissed the feeling of discomfort and scooped them up.

"So I am an uncle," I said, settling them both on my knee. I regarded them solemnly. "I can't wait to tell you stories about your daddy when he was your age. I warn you, you should never follow his example. You'll get in trouble." The boy giggled and struck me with a plastic toy. The girl studied me with a precocious wisdom in those green eyes. "But it is also my job as an uncle to spoil your dinner." I opened the picnic hamper and extracted a box of fruit sections. The exotic varieties came from trees and vines in the Kinago hothouse, lovingly tended by a pair of enthusiastic young gardeners and an LAI as head gardener who had been with us five centuries. I selected the fruit for its sweetness, meant to counter and complement the savory items still tucked away. The children accepted spears of brilliant coral and green with alacrity. "Now, see if you can't go and grind them into the carpet," I advised them. "That's what your daddy would do."

"Thomas!"

Luckily, the children looked bewildered by my instructions. They toddled off to the end of the stone tiles to eat their prizes. I watched them with a proprietary avuncularity that I was beginning to enjoy. They were so adorable that I could not resist taking pictures of them. Using the screen of my pocket secretary—how I missed my naval issue viewpad and its superior screen!—I lined up shots of their intent little faces as they sampled the unfamiliar treats. Soon, their beaming faces were smeared with juice.

"Does Jerna know who you are?" I asked in a low tone.

"Yes. She doesn't mind, now that she knows that we are not all as bad as our reputations in the media. I haven't used her and discarded her, as Xan would. Our children are legitimate."

"Correct me if my observation is at fault, there's a third on the way?"

Scot nodded. "Three is what we are hoping for, and then we will stop. I'd love to have five, but that would attract too much attention in this neighborhood. The usual number of offspring is two children." He gave the tots a fond glance. "Her name is Thomasina, by the way. I named her after you. My son is Enrik, after Jerna's father."

"I shall be a proud uncle to Thomasina and Enrik," I said. "On those occasions when gift-giving is appropriate."

"Don't go mad," Scot said. "They're not used to getting every toy in the shops."

"When have I ever shown inappropriate moderation?" I asked, then dropped my voice still further. "Scot, what about their future? They'll lose their citizenship if it's ever determined that they are an extension of the Imperial gene pool. You'll lose your allowance. You won't have any way to support them. Three of them, to see to adulthood, to higher education, to a trade, a position in the service, a home?"

Scot's chin set firm. "I don't care. We'll figure it out if that day comes! I don't want to be a noble any longer, curse it. I wish I was an ordinary man. No one should be able to demand that I have children or don't have children."

"But it is the way things are," I said.

"Do you think I don't know that?" he asked, the pain on his face deep. I regretted that I was the catalyst, though not the cause of it.

"I know you do," I said. "You were always one of the smartest of us. So, how do the neighbors think you support your family, and what's your excuse for being gone so often?"

Scot smiled. "I have a job I go to occasionally. I am an art teacher."

"You? With pupils and attendance sheets?"

"It's a bit more casual. I have a studio in an art school a few blocks from here. We meet about twice a week. My payments are listed as 'miscellaneous expense,' as are those of the other artists. Creatives are often paid irregularly. It's a gray area, and one I exploit."

"I will bet you are much admired and loved," I said, warmly. "The favorite teacher, around whom everyone congregates even when class is not in session. I will also wager they confide in you and ask your advice."

He was too modest to concede that I was right, but

he looked pleased. "I also have a few private students who will pay anything for decent instruction, and since I learned from the best, I have techniques at my fingertips they have never seen demonstrated. Jerna puts the money away in case—well, you know, I was away on our naval deployment. It was possible that I wasn't going to come back. I've settled money on her in the will, with no explanation of who she is or why she is receiving a bequest." I nodded. None would be needed. It was assumed that we had our little flings, though they were not supposed to end in matrimony or procreation, and it was common for a gift to be left posthumously. "You know what could happen." We both knew. Accidents were likely, considering the way we nobles lived, but once in a while we suffered assassination or abduction for political reasons. It didn't matter that there were many of us; the Imperial house was supposed to be sacrosanct, and striking out at one of us was a typical insurgent's statement.

"I know you will outlive me," I said, "but if it is within my power to see that your last wishes are fulfilled, I will."

"Thank you, Thomas," Scot said, touched. "You are welcome here any time."

"I would be glad to come and visit again," I said. "In the meanwhile, lower the profile."

"I will. I do."

Jerna called us then. We rose, still so many things left unsaid, but we both knew the concerns the other was feeling, so deep was the bond between us. Scot scooped up his son and I my namesake. She wiggled. I laughed as I carried her toward the kitchen table.

❖   ❖   ❖

"Thank you for a most delightful lunch," I said, bowing over Jerna's hand a pleasant hour later. She smiled, charmed by my courtly behavior. To her, hand-kissing was a novelty to be enjoyed, unlike our cousins who scarcely noticed anymore. The delight on her face was as nourishing as the food we had just consumed. "I can see why Foxkin is enchanted with you."

"Thank you, Thomas," she said, smiling up at me. "Come back any time. The children adore you."

"And I them," I said. I waggled my fingers at Tina, who decided she was now shy, after hours of proving otherwise, and hid behind her mother. Jerna and Scot wrapped one another in their arms, eyes intent upon one another. I turned away, feeling as if I was intruding on a private moment. Shortly, Scot tapped me on the shoulder.

"Come on," he said, reaching for the door. I could not help but observe his reluctant posture. His feet said go, but his body was nearly arching itself backwards to remain.

"Do you want to stay here?" I asked. "No one is expecting to see us for hours. They think we're all out with Jil. She won't tell anyone. I doubt she has noticed we're gone. She was still talking away when we left."

Scot chuckled at the thought. "Don't you need transport home?"

"I can find my own way." To forestall the protest I could see bubbling up behind his lips, I held up a hand. "I will go far away from here before I summon a ride, I promise. Enjoy your restday."

"Thank you," he said. He interlaced his fingers with Jerna's and squeezed her hand.

I left him with his wife and family, playing house.

Not playing, I corrected myself, as I cut through alleyways and commercial yards on a wide diagonal, laying a false trail away from the little neighborhood. He meant what he was doing much more than I did with anything in my life.

I returned home feeling unaccustomedly sober. Marriage between a noble and a commoner was not only frowned upon, it was illegal. I could fall into trouble by merely knowing about it and not reporting it. But I had made a promise, and there were worse things I had prevaricated about in the past. My conscience was clear that I was not condoning treason, theft or corruption of the young. Scot seemed so happy it almost—almost made me reconsider my heretofore absolute refusal to get married; I had told him so. He looked *happy*. I could not and would not interfere with that.

When I reached home at last, I locked the doors of my suite and checked the room for listening or hearing devices, using another illicit device that my cousins and I had made frequent use of in our ill-spent youths. It was not uncommon for compound security to run an occasional examination of family residences within its walls. We had come to accept, even condone them as a measure to preserve the safety of the Emperor, and, by extension, ourselves. If we ourselves bent the rules, we didn't see it as piercing that secure wall; we would never do anything to put the Emperor in danger. I knew I would sooner die myself—painlessly, if possible—to prevent that.

My rooms, in the second-oldest part of the family compound, had belonged in turn to a famous general, a diplomat, two scientists, a beloved sage, and my uncle Laurence. I had sitting rooms, reception rooms, a dressing room, a water room that contained bath, shower and spa pool, a library-*cum*-music room, and my bedroom, to which I retreated when I wanted privacy. (When Uncle Laurence came to stay, so infrequent as to make each visit remarkable, the servants set up a bed in the blue sitting room for his use.) The suite was luxurious by any comparison, but overpowered Scot's tiny love cottage like a man standing beside an ant. A part of me wanted to sneer, but I put that down to envy. *For shame*, I chided myself.

Securing the bedroom door against all interruptions, I threw myself into my favorite armchair and launched the Optique into the air. It began to play the pictures upon my small antique reading table, the red-stained fruitwood lending a honey glow to the images. Thomasina-Tina, lithe and fairylike, exuded grace even when playing tag. I didn't read that into her movements, even though she was my namesake and the daughter of my oldest and best friend. Of course not. Enrik, stocky like his father, but freckled like his mother, was still in the lurching stage of toddlerhood. Scot and Jerna, hand in hand in their tiny castle, still seeing miracles in one another's eyes.

I looked at the pictures over and over. An idyllic life. An impossible dream. A secret, I realized, that I must keep at all costs.

I captured my hovering camera and entered the code that erased all the images, not keeping even one. I went to bed feeling strangely conflicted. My long-held worldview had undergone another change—more than one. Perhaps I was growing up.

I hated to think so, but there it was.

❋ CHAPTER 24 ❋

The next sunrise arrived with me as a full and alert witness. Usually I saw dawn from the other side, having been awake all night in the company of like-minded individuals enjoying the best things in life. That night my only companion was a sense of discontentment and unfamiliar isolation. Through the window at the foot of my bed I saw the sky change through a series of rich colors, from star-spangled black, ink, purple, indigo, blue and that sudden flash of green that as a child I thought was a myth, before the pale sapphire of day became predominant and I lost interest. The canyon that housed the Imperium compound and the oldest sections of Taino faced north, so the sun itself did not become visible over its sheer walls until long after the day began.

I had come up with no fulfilling occupation to take the place of the naval service that had been taken away from me. I had nothing to do and nowhere to go but the frivolous pursuits that I had enjoyed all of my life, never guessing that they might be all I would do. The navy had given me a taste of another life, one of purpose.

I had heard the complaint over and over again that we of the Imperial House lacked purpose, but I had never understood why that made the common folk so angry. Could it be that they were sorry for us, that we did not understand what they knew?

I was still left without an occupation. I put Scot's commitment to his young and illicit family down partly to wanting to matter somehow. He had solved the problem in his way. I must solve my own.

I made up my mind to go to my mother and see if there was any way I could get assigned to another ship. There were four other fleets. I just couldn't go on being a useless and charming ornament. I'd had a taste of service, and against all my training and heritage, I liked it. I had never felt so alive, not even running the rim at the controls of a wild racing skimmer, as I had leading a ragtag troop on an ad hoc mission. I had had a purpose, even if I had given it to myself, to capture a crew of hijackers and thieves.

I dressed with uncommon care, choosing as my mother had the other day, a costume that echoed the official uniform of the Imperium Navy, deep blue tunic over pale trousers, and a black demi-boot polished to a diamond shine. I was entitled to wear a flashing that indicated the medal I had earned, but decided to forgo it. I admired myself in the mirror. *Perfect,* I thought.

The Optique hovered to life as I tucked my pocket secretary into its accustomed pouch on my sleeve. I beckoned to the camera. It bobbled alongside, an encouraging companion that I am certain agreed I was entitled to a second chance.

I had the argument all fixed in my head. "Mother, it's your Navy," I would say. "I offer my deepest apologies for any misperceptions on either my part or that of Admiral Podesta as to my place within it. I am sure that you can find a way to put me back into it. I will do my best to fit in—in my own way, naturally—but I feel a need to serve. No, I am not joking. Give me another chance, and you will not regret it. Even Admiral Podesta will someday come to regret having dismissed me out of hand."

The last I doubted would ever come true, but it sounded so noble that I hardly could leave it out of my speech. I repeated phrases to myself in varying degrees of passion, from low-pitched in a face grave with concern, to wildly dramatic, complete with appropriate hand gestures and pacing. I caught a glimpse of myself in mirrors I passed and in the miniature screen in the side of the Optique, which paced me a meter or so away. I thought that if Mother did agree, I wanted that moment recorded for history, so I could replay it as a triumph from time to time.

Mother's office in the Admiralty lay opposite Army Headquarters at the foot of the bluff on which the Imperium compound stood. I accepted a ride from a cargo transport that had just delivered supplies to the Kinago family kitchens. I would have walked, but I wanted my footgear to retain its shine. I considered the clear sky an omen.

"Good morning, Lord Thomas!" chirruped the officer on duty at the reception desk in the huge, yellow marble hall. I smiled at her.

"Good morning, Lieutenant . . . Wasson," I said, sending the Optique close enough that it could read the name plate on her desk. My smile was sincere, even if my memory was enhanced by technology. "You are looking especially well today."

"Thank you, your lordship," she said, with a shy smile. She looked like a model, without sufficient IQ to answer the complex communications system before her, but I knew the vetting that went into the choice of every employee in the building. She was trained in several martial arts, as well as being expert in operating the defense system that was concealed all the enormous room. She was the first line of defense in this nerve center that defended the entire Imperium in space. I assumed a friendly grin and made myself look as harmless as possible. "The First Space Lord has meetings today, sir."

"My mother is not expecting me, but I will just slip in and wait until she has time to see me."

"Very well, sir," Lt. Wasson said. "I will send a message to Admiral Draco, to be delivered when she has a break." She waved me into the gunmetal blue security booth. Lights ran down on every side of me, making certain I was carrying no banned substances into the building.

As a familiar face, I was similarly waved on by all the levels of security approaching my mother's office suite—after I passed through scans and checkpoints, of course. Both LAI and biological clerks worked in the Admiralty, all ranks up to and including admirals who had retired from or were on leave from active duty in the five fleets that served the Imperium. All the way there, I rehearsed my argument. Mother mustn't say no.

The door of the suite opened to admit me after a brief body scan. In the anteroom, its walls covered with brilliantly rendered scenes from space battles the Imperium had fought over the last few millennia and portraits of the ships and captains whohad won them, her private secretary, Admiral Leven Draco, hunched over a console. He was a superb officer who had served Mother as aide-de-camp, commander to her captain, captain to her admiral, and accepted a promotion to admiral on his retirement from active duty only if it meant he would not be separated from my mother's service. He was a stout man with huge, wiry graying eyebrows, a tuft of hair in the middle of a bald head that was surrounded by a tonsure of wiry iron-gray hair. His jowly face, pouched eyes and authoritative beak of a nose often caused him to be mistaken, by those who did not know the dainty woman at his side at official events, as the First Space Lord. He smiled at me. I considered him an unrelated relative.

"Uncle Lev," I said, shaking hands with him. The rest of his many assistants looked up from their stations to offer me grins and nods. They were almost all high-ranking naval officers retired from active duty. This was a plum assignment, considered well worth fighting for. Draco hand-picked his staff for trustworthiness and competence. They were the best of the best. I could never qualify as one of my own mother's office staff. "May I see the First Space Lord? I'll wait."

The jowls lifted and creased in a pleased smile. "How are you, my boy? I heard you were back. Your mother's in one last meeting, then you may go in. There are refreshments in the anteroom."

"Shall I bring you anything?" I asked.

"No need," he said, lifting his customary oversized coffee cup. The others shook their heads. "Go on."

I settled myself in the anteroom. It was meant
to look intimate and comfortable, but its enormous
size, proportionate to the other grand chambers in
the Admiralty, made me feel as if I was a very small
boy in his father's study. The walls were paneled in
priceless tropical wood, and decorated with historically important banners and ensigns under sheets of
crystal. My mother's portrait, as the current holder of
the office, hung over a crystal case full of memorabilia
from her career, models of the ships she had commanded, medals, holos from her ship's logs, and so
on. The leatherlike furniture, huge and overstuffed,
wore an air of timeless importance that had cowed
many a young officer. I sank into a chair with huge,
rolled sides that could not be called arms, as they
were level with my head, and I am a tall man. I
could not see out of it, but it had excellent acoustics,
as I had discovered as a small child. If I closed my
eyes and concentrated, sometimes I could hear what
was going on in Mother's office. The door was ajar a
finger's breadth. She was speaking with a man, very
likely human, by the resonance and baritone pitch.

I realized with a start that I knew that voice very
well indeed. Her visitor was *Parsons*. I had the most
awful feeling that he had come to report upon my
deployment aboard the *Wedjet*. I was a little put out,
having come to regard him as my personal aide. I
knew it had been a temporary measure, though why
he needed to oversee my naval service I did not know.
Sadly, I knew that he would not spare my feelings
when he declaimed the rolls of my sins. I wondered
what particular item on the list had Mother's attention.
I did not want him to scuttle my hoped-for second

chance. I had to know what he was saying, so I could counter his arguments when my turn came to speak. Though I knew my effort would be futile; Parsons was as clearheaded as they came and as incorruptible as honor itself. Mother would always be wise to take his assessment of a situation over mine. I would be reduced to pleading. Not that I was unused to abasing myself to apologize to some figure of authority, but I had never felt the stakes to be so high. My future was in the balance. I wriggled out of the enveloping chair and crept, spine bent and on silent foot, toward the door.

A slight creak from the office sent me haring back to the seat. If Parsons was departing from my mother's company, the last image I wanted to provide them was of me kneeling with my ear pressed to the door. But I had to hear their exchange. Abandoning all scruples, I disabled the Optique's exterior lights and sent the little sphere to hover in the crack at the top of the door.

Through its link with my pocket secretary, I watched it scan the room and focus upon the two figures in the center. My mother, in full uniform, looking trim and majestic, was seated behind her desk. Parsons, spine straight as truth, stood beside her. They were both looking at a three-dimensional image that played upon the desk top. I could not discern the image, save that it appeared to be a spacescape. At least I was not the immediate subject of conversation. I felt deep relief.

". . . remarkable clarity of the images leaves no doubt as to identity and trajectory, and confirms the information on the crystal," Parsons was saying, as the

Optique's sensitive microphone filtered it back to me. I winced at the fractionally time-delayed echo, as I could also hear the voices myself. I put a finger in my ear and listened closely to the speaker. "There is no reason for those ships to have been in that place at that time. No flight plan was filed, no distress calls noted from that area. It is definitely an intrusion."

Ah. It must be something about the pirate fleet. I smiled. I had shined in that event. I had nothing to worry about, then.

"It is still spotty," Mother said. "I wish there had been more definite data."

Spotty? How could it be spotty? They had captured the main ship, which led them to the rest. Case closed, or so I would have thought.

It seemed that Parsons agreed. I could almost hear the shrug, not that Parsons would perform a gesture as casual as a shrug. "Mr. Frank is satisfied. We must interpret as best we can. The sender was clearly in great peril. It is not the information we were waiting for, but must be investigated as to whether to bring greater Imperium resources than your fleets to bear."

Imperium resources? Greater than the Navy? I strained to hear more.

"I fear you are right," Mother said. "We need further information. That must be your task." His task. I realized I did not truly know what Parsons did when he was not accompanying me on diplomatic missions. What hidden depths had he beyond the ones of which I already knew? And who was Mr. Frank? I had never met anyone of that name.

"Yes, madam. It is my task." His voice had a point to it. There was a distinct pause.

"Come in, Thomas," Mother said, without raising her voice. "You are involved in this."

"I am?" I squeaked, my voice completely forgetting that I had exited adolescence years before.

The door swung open, and both of them stood in its frame, looking at me. I scrambled to my feet. Mother beckoned me in. I loped behind them, awkward as a newborn colt. Parsons closed the door behind us with a boom like the doomsday knell. Guilt rode me like an albatross.

She and Parsons were alone, no other Space Lords, no LAI, no aides, no other officers. That in itself was uncanny, for as a superior minister to the Imperium, she was always surrounded by advisors and others poised to take her orders. This must be serious indeed. But why include me in such a conference?

Mother's office was as quietly elegant as herself. Every element she had incorporated into the venerable chamber of the First Space Lord complemented the historical trappings already there, but somehow made one think. The walls of ruddy wood were covered with pictures, holographs and actual paintings of previous holders of the office, many Loches and Kinagos among them, plus framed medals, images of worlds conquered or saved and a handsome portrait of the emperor himself. In it, Shojan was smiling. The pose was a personal favor to my mother, whom he liked and admired. As who would not? I put on a confident and easy smile.

"Good morning, Mother," I said. "Good morning, Parsons. I . . . er . . . am I disturbing you?"

"Not at all, my dragonlet," Mother said, briskly. "You have come at an opportune time. I was reviewing images you took while you were on Smithereen. As you might have seen from your spying." She glanced at Parsons, and I realized that he had detected the Optique, undoubtedly by means of his ability to look through walls and read the minds of men. Guiltily, I beckoned the small camera to hover at my shoulder. If a nonsentient device could look abashed, my Optique did.

"Oh, well, I didn't mean... it's not really *spying*... I mean, I just wanted to know... to make certain I wouldn't be intruding," I stammered. "I know how busy you are... I'm always happy to help in any way, if I can."

"You *can* help," Mother said. "I would appreciate it if you would." She waved a hand toward the image. "Tell me about this." I examined it closely. The spacescape looked familiar. The circumstances of its capture came rolling back to me in a wave. I rocked back on my heels, happy to provide the memory.

"It is one of the shots I took in the landing bay while I was reviewing the Smithereen militia," I said. "You must go back to about three earlier in the sequence, where I am marching down in between the two files of soldiers. You can't see any of us in this picture. They array themselves for disappointment, Mother. You should really look into allowing a trifle more time for visiting diplomats to interact with the volunteers. They are so grateful, you would be astonished..."

"Focus, my boy," Mother said, reining me in. "This isn't the time for tangents. This is the one we are interested in, it and the two that followed, at the angle you took them. What made you choose this image to preserve?"

"The meteors. I considered them to be an omen,

you see," I said, a trifle sheepishly. I knew Parsons
didn't believe in esoterica. My mother considered
superstitions to be childish, but she indulged me. "A
meteor shower, on the occasion of my first outing as
an officer of the Imperium Navy? It was like a galactic
benison upon my head. I wanted to record it."

"A meteor shower would rain downward, my lord,"
Parsons said. "But as such it would not be possible
for such an effect to be visible on Smithereen Prime
at all because the atmosphere is too thin at ground
level, let alone at that altitude, to burn up space
debris that falls into its gravitational field."

"I knew that," I said at once. "It occurred to me
later on, but it was still such a vivid image, three
bright streaks in the sky. And it is, as you see. I suppose in light of the subsequent events I lost interest
as to what it really was."

"So you took these on a whim?" Mother asked,
getting back to the point. "It was pure chance?"

"I suppose so," I said. They seemed a bit downcast
about it. "Why? If they weren't meteors, what were
they?"

For answer, Mother beckoned at the display. The
three scratches of light grew and took on detail until I
could readily discern that they were contrails. The ships
that produced them, upon their takeoff from a mass
not far from Smithereen Prime, were tiny pinpoints
that increased in size until they were identifiable by
both type and hull marking.

"Trade Union," I exclaimed.

Of all the interstellar consortia and federations that
humanity and its fellow spacefarers had founded over
the last ten or so millennia, the Trade Union was the

one with which the Imperium had had the most difficult relationship. Founded from a loose association of merchants, traders and, yes, pirates, the TU lay side by side with the Imperium, its explorers vying with our explorers for viable planets, natural resources, and trade routes. The last battle, begun thirty years ago, had had a treaty signed to end it six years later, but it was more or less still going on. Small sallies against one consortium's bases or another, the destruction of border beacons, poaching on rich mining fields such as that of Smithereen, were all typical. Needless to say, the incursions went both ways, but in defense of the Imperium, our forces usually struck back. They seldom began a fight.

"What are they doing there?"

"They are certainly trespassing," Mother said. "We can't confirm where they went after they left Smithereen. Their energy trails were wiped out by that ion storm that the Red Fleet sought to avoid. It rather looks as if those three ships flew directly into it. Such a tactic suggests that secrecy was more important than their lives."

"Where did they go?"

"We are afraid that they were bound for the Castaway Cluster. It is a group of eight small stars deeper toward the heart of the galaxy." She nodded. "I see you have heard of it."

"Well, not until recently. My friends on Smithereen said that they were expecting a lot of business as ships plied the space lanes in between the Core Worlds and the Cluster, but they were disappointed in their hopes. They built a good deal of infrastructure in expectation of that business."

"The hotel that you wrecked, for example?" Mother asked. I opened my mouth to protest, but she waved a hand. I subsided. If I wanted to find out what the two of them had been murmuring about, it was best to let her petty quips pass. I nodded. "Smithereen is about five ultra-drive hops from the Cluster. To have detected the TU ships at all was remarkable. It may be the most important thing you did."

"Thank you," I said modestly, though I was delighted. "It was an accident."

"An accident that came about by being aware of your surroundings," Parsons said. "You could easily have missed the event, but you did not. Well done."

I wriggled all over like a puppy. "I say, Parsons, too much praise and I'll be spoiled for life."

I was met by a blank look. "I fear it is far too late for that, sir."

Ah, well, Parsons will be Parsons. "You said, er, when I was not in the room that you were hoping for greater confirmation on the presence of the ships in Smithereen space. If you need to confirm to anyone that they were taken because of my observation, please do. I will back up your assertion with all my heart."

Mother shook her head. "We are the only people who require confirmation, my dragonlet, and I concur with Parsons that something caught your attention and you captured it, for whatever reason. It was a lucky shot, but you have been of great help to the Imperium."

I could tell that my eyes lit up by the alarmed look on my maternal unit's face. But I persisted, because I saw an opening for my suit to be reinstated. "Then may I put my case? It is why I have come this morning."

Mother's eyebrow went up. Parsons, as always, was expressionless. I pressed on. "I have had a while to think about my situation. I truly enjoyed my time of service. You have told me all of my life that I am descended from countless men and women who put their lives on the lines to protect the Imperium. I am prepared to do that, Mother. I do not make this offer lightly. I could be of great use to the Navy. I felt that I fit in well—with one notable exception, I admit," I added, to forestall the obvious protest. "The camaraderie of my shipmates was a refreshing revelation to me. I felt myself to be a part of the crew. We formed a bond that would have seen us through any number of difficult missions. I felt needed. That was a rare moment in my life. I am willing to go back. I offer myself as an eager recruit. Please, Mother. Give me another chance. Admiral Podesta has said he would prefer that I not return to the Red Fleet. There was a personality mismatch between us, and I admit that it was my doing that got us off on the wrong foot. I would never do that again. But you have four other fleets, Mother. Surely there is another ship in one of them that would take me. Your own, cherished second son. One little, unremarkable cruiser? One exploration vessel? One scout ship that would benefit from the sincere toil that I would put in aboard her?"

She looked at Parsons. "Well, well. Shall I follow the old maxim, and send the fool of the family to sea?" She did not wait for an answer, as her statement sounded rhetorical, as well as a bit insulting. She turned back to me. "No. I'm sorry, my boy. That was a most eloquent statement, and I have no doubt heartfelt, but it just would not work."

I was crestfallen. I had been so certain that she would agree! "But I could be an asset!"

She exchanged, yet again, another of those enigmatic glances with Parsons. "And so you shall, Thomas, if you really want to."

Her obduracy was softening. I knew it would! "I do. I had no notion what it felt like until now to do something that mattered."

"Then you can be part of the team that investigates the very anomaly that you recorded."

"Shall I be an ensign again, or will I have to begin again in the ranks?"

"It is not a Navy mission at all," Parsons said.

"Then, who? I heard a name bandied about, Mr. Frank. Who is he?"

"You will not mention Mr. Frank outside of this office," Parsons said. "He is the chief officer of the Imperium's Covert Service Operation."

"Really?" I asked. "I have heard rumors, but none of us really knows anything more."

"That is because it is a secret, my lord. You should not know of us unless you run afoul of the service. Ideally, even then it should look as if another agency is involved."

My ears perked up. "Us? You are a member? How long? What else have you done?"

"That is need-to-know only, my lord."

I felt a thrill race down my back. "Tell me more," I urged them. "Do you have to swear me to secrecy? Take a blood oath?"

"Do you require one, my lady?" Parsons asked. "I can obtain a razor and a carafe."

I made a face at him. "Ha ha," I laughed hollowly,

my face drawn into disapproving lines, then I shot a suspicious glance at my mother. "He is making a joke at my expense, isn't he? There is no blood oath?"

"We'll waive it," my mother said, flicking a hand. "For now. I will go on your word, son. It has always been good, *when* it is given."

I blushed at that, knowing how many times she had not asked for my word, and I had considered myself free to disobey the house rules. But when offered, it was always kept. I straightened my back and looked directly into her eyes. "I pledge my word of honor that I will not reveal to anyone anything you tell me is confidential, not even if my life is threatened."

"That will do," Mother said, with a smile. She returned to her chair and clasped her hands upon her desk. Parsons took his place beside her, a pose he had taken many times over my life. He looked natural there, a paragon and a protector of one of my most precious people. I was rather proud of the alliteration, and thought of declaiming it, but the moment was too serious. I had just been offered a purpose, and wished to give no reason for it to be withdrawn. "Sit down, Thomas. It will take some time to explain what we want of you. Do you want a drink?"

"No, thank you, Mother." My nerves were coping with a surge of adrenaline the likes of which I had not experienced since the pirate captain fired a round past my ear. I beckoned to a chair at the side of the room. It rolled out to me, as eager to be of service as I was. I perched on the edge of its seat.

"There has been no communication from the Castaway Cluster for some months now," Mother said. "Emperor Shojan wants to reestablish relations so that we can expand into the space beyond it. Up until now it has been less than a priority."

"For which I read not profitable," I said with a narrowed and summing eye.

"A pithy but not entirely inaccurate statement, my lord," Parsons said. I wriggled like a puppy to get another fact right. He gave me a bland look that reminded me I was in a serious briefing, but it was hard to remain neutral of face in a secret conference that was of vital interest to the Imperium. I did my best. I echoed Parsons's expression. He gave me a look that could have been approval or disdain, and continued. "There have been few reasons in recent decades to exploit the star cluster. Its distance, coupled with the presence of the black hole between the last outpost of the active Imperium and the Cluster—"

"Smithereen," I said, smug in my knowledge.

Parsons ignored my interruption. "—precludes most casual contact. It has few unique resources. It has remained at the periphery of the Imperium's attention. Many other matters have taken priority until now. But the Costadetev Federation beyond it is stretching toward our boundaries along the same axis as the Castaway Cluster. The star field beyond, which has been a fallow province until now, is becoming a frontier. Those systems have traditionally been considered part of the Imperium, but never settled. The Emperor wants to lay claim directly. The Trade Union is also rushing to claim that sector."

"But we already own it," I protested.

"Possession has traditionally been physical, not nominal. The planets in those systems are gas giants or small, distant, barren rocks, all uninhabitable, therefore they have never been settled. To confirm the Imperium's rights, we would have to place a settlement in orbit around a planet if not on one, and show viable trade routes. In order to do that, we need to reestablish our hold over the Cluster, because it will be our administration arm in that area. Those eight stars have been self-governing for a long time, but have up until recently acknowledged their ties to the Imperium."

"What changed?" I asked, leaning forward, my elbows on my knees. I felt as if I was listening to a story. It was as good as any of the three-dees my friends and I watched, full of suspense and intrigue, with the fate of worlds at stake. "What is happening?"

Parsons would have been a failure as a scriptwriter. "We are not certain," he said flatly. "An envoy was sent, but she has not been heard from since arriving in the Cluster. Communication has been cut off for some months now. No messages or updates in Infogrid files, though the latter has always been sporadic despite Imperium rules. No trade or commerce has been recorded between the Castaway Cluster and the Core Worlds, or anywhere else that can be discerned since that time."

"Pirates? Natural disaster? Did the black hole eat up the entire group?"

Mother swatted down my flight of fancy with a firm hand. "Telemetry from my ships indicates that the stars are all still there, Thomas, and I would appreciate it if you would lock up your overactive imagination. This is important."

I subsided. "I apologize, Mother. What is it that you want me to do? I'll help in any way I can."

She smiled. "I knew you would. Commander, this is your department, not mine."

I turned my full attention to that noble being, putting as much eagerness and good will into my gaze as possible. Parsons seemed unimpressed, but he always did.

"We need to provide an envoy, my lord, ostensibly to make friendly overtures on behalf of the Emperor, but to investigate what is the cause of the Cluster's silence. It had been dwindling for some time, but there were always trade routes, some messages, culture and other offerings coming from the eight systems, but lately nothing at all has come from any of them. This suggests a concerted effort by the cluster, but for reasons we do not know. At present his majesty suspects that they have been wooed away from the Imperium by the Trade Union or Costadetev, which supports a large population of insectoids and reptilian races. The Castaway Cluster contains a smaller proportion of humans than many sectors, though it should not matter with Imperium-born beings. But it is a delicate matter, to march in and accuse an entire system of treason. Therefore, the matter has to be investigated with the utmost tact. It is a matter of Imperium security that the truth be known, so that the correct action can be taken to keep the Castaway Cluster in the fold—or rather, to restore it to the bosom of the Imperium. The matter of Cluster independence is moot, because the Imperium can easily overpower it and take over again, but that would not address the reason that it has lost touch in the first place. It simply should not have been neglected. Emperor Shojan will see that it is not in future, but until then, he needs information. It will be your duty to help obtain it."

Excited and pleased, I was almost bouncing at the thought of such a mission.

"Ah! I get to perform *espionage?*" I was thrilled beyond words. "Shall I be assigned spy tools and devices? I have just bought a new camera that I think will be a great asset to covert intelligence." I reached into my sleeve for the control to my pocket secretary and activated it. A minute dot of brass as small as a housefly lifted up from my tunic front, where it had been masquerading as a decorative stud. I sent the tiny camera to hover before Parsons's nose. "It is the Chey Snap 8. The very newest on the market. It is so small that no one will spot it, but it takes marvelous pictures."

Mother shook her head. "Very nice, dear, but no."

Parsons reached into a gray pocket on his very gray uniform and produced a gray and featureless device. Instantly, the Chey and the Optique fell to the floor. Protesting, I dove for them.

"You didn't have to do that!"

As I gathered up my abused property, Parsons continued. "Your job would be as the envoy. I would be the espionage agent. As I was on Smithereen."

I looked up, my hands full of cameras. "What? On Smithereen Admiral Podesta sent me to review the volunteer troops. I understood that it was a compliment to this particular militia that he was sending me, a member of the royal house."

"You were the cover for the real mission, my darling," Mother said, her expression one of pity. I scrambled to my feet. Neither camera would respond to my commands. Parsons restored his device to its place of concealment. I stuck my cameras in my pocket.

"I? Mine was the mission: to inspect the troops and press the flesh."

"Do you know how seldom that happens?"

"Yes, on the average of once every three years. Chan told me. She'd make a good officer, Mother, really," I added, thinking of how cool a head the volunteer captain had displayed, and how readily she had obeyed my commands. "One would think that she performed complex and dangerous maneuvers like that every day. You should snap her up."

"She earns about fifteen times what a low-ranking officer does, darling. It wouldn't be worth her while to start over again at OTC." I was taken aback. I hadn't thought about money. "But I am glad she served well for you. I hate to disabuse you of your impression, but the review itself was an unimportant assignment so that Parsons would have the freedom to make a connection that was necessary to the safety of the Imperium."

"Indeed," I said, fixing them both with a cold eye. "Unimportant? And when was I going to be informed of this subterfuge?"

"I would have thought never, darling," my mother said. "In a perfect situation, he would have completed his assignment and returned to retrieve you without a hitch. As it turned out, you had disappeared, caused a riot, and, yes, perpetrated a daring capture—nearly. Though he did manage to complete his assignment, and against all expectations you came here this morning to offer your services to the Imperium. That is why we are having the discussion now at all."

I was crushed.

"That 'nearly' strikes me like a death blow to the heart, Mother."

She raised her brows again. "I told you I agreed with Omar Podesta. It was not your assignment. Though you handled yourself as I would expect a son of mine to do. You were courageous and resourceful, both qualities that would be of use to us in this matter."

I was mollified by a generous ladling on of complimentary adjectives. The more I thought about it, the knowledge of espionage going on right under my nose tickled me. I was still cross that I hadn't known it, but it would hardly have been undercover if I had. "Really, Mother, this doesn't sound as much fun as I was hoping. Why can't I be the spy?"

"Because you have a more important role to play," Parsons said. "It will be your task to distract attention from me and my investigations. It is vital that I not be detected and stopped until I have the information the Emperor requires."

"Decoy," I said, bitterly. "I shall make a marvelous target while you have all the fun."

"Your talents in one direction far outstrip mine, my lord."

"What? In photography? In a moment you will show me a long list of galleries that feature your work. I already know that you can outfence me and outfly me."

Parsons looked imperturbable. "No, my lord. It is more fundamental than that. I cannot do what you do, and that necessitates that you be the one to act as envoy, not I." He shot a look at my mother. She hesitated a long while, then nodded. I turned a puzzled glance to each of them in turn.

Mother eyed me seriously. "Do you know truly

what it means to be a member of the ruling class of the Imperium?"

"Responsibility," I said promptly. "Since one of us might be called upon to become Emperor, we must understand our relationship to the citizens of the Imperium. I hope I have remembered all the lessons that you have pounded into me—intellectually, of course. You would never think that my lady mother would manhandle me physically, would you, Parsons?"

"Never, sir," he said blandly.

"I am afraid that there is more to it than that," Mother said.

"Well, fealty, honor, support..." From the subtle head-shakes I saw that my further essays into the thesaurus were getting me nowhere. "I give up, Mother."

She looked deeply into my eyes, the blue-green a sea of worries. "Thomas, if anything, this is more secret than what we have already told you. And if you tell another soul, I will see to it that you are seconded to an outdated exploration vessel in the remotest reaches of the outer spiral arm for a ten-year mission in search of Old Earth."

"I say, that might be amusing," I said. "Uncle Laurence always says he knows where it is." But their faces were even more serious than they had been before. The blood chilled in my body. The words came out rather more slowly than they had before, but they came. "My word to you, Mother."

Parsons removed another discreet gray object and set it on a circuit of the room. It lit upon the pocket containing my cameras. Numbers filled the air, followed by a repeat of the conversation that I had used it to record. My face burned with shame.

"Cheeky," Mother said. "Anything else?" she asked Parsons.

"No, madam," he said.

She let out a long exhalation of breath. "Very well. Sit down, Thomas."

❧ CHAPTER 25 ❧

The room seemed to get smaller and more intimate. I reached for the chair and had it scoot me up to the very edge of the desk.

"How would you govern a very large area, Thomas?" Mother asked.

I put the brain cells to work. I had taken current affairs classes all throughout school, but the stars knew how little of it seemed to apply to my life, so I dismissed much of it. I did recall stories of the ancient empires of humanity that I had seen in videos.

"Well, you know, make laws that legislate common behavior for the benefit of the greatest number possible. Provide infrastructure for trade and protection for the citizenry. Put wise minds in places of authority, with checks and balances on them," I added, though I'd never quite been certain as to what "checks and balances" denoted.

"And how would you enforce those laws?"

"Well, some kind of patrol. Centralized, so that everything is dispensed in an evenhanded manner."

"Where?"

"Well, in the capital," I said. Police and emergency response teams were based in Taino. Each city on Keinolt has several precincts, and each small town had an office as well. I had fallen afoul of many of them over my life, as well my mother knew it.

"And when your domain stretches out over the distance of several planets? How do you keep lawlessness from spreading once your central government is far away? Once your capital city is removed not just kilometers, but possibly light years away? What is to keep them following your laws?"

"Internal sense of right and wrong?" I offered, but it was a feeble suggestion. "I am not the person to ask, I am afraid. I've been known to go off the straight and narrow many times in my life, though in minor ways, I assure you. I would never harm the Imperium."

"But human nature being what it is, others would," Mother said. "As soon as all this useful infrastructure is in place, what would stop a planet from breaking away from the Imperium and declaring itself its own sovereign entity?"

"Loyalty?" I asked, though it sounded as weak as my last suggestion. But a broad smile spread across Mother's face, and even Parsons looked a trifle less disapproving.

"Precisely," Parsons replied. "Internalized obedience to authority."

I scoffed. "People don't just blindly follow orders."

"They do, my lord. Particularly in crowds. There is a body of work that is found in distant pre-Imperium history showing a direct correlation. Before any modification is introduced, approximately two-thirds of the population can be persuaded to obey to extremes by mere verbal prodding alone, no coercion involved. Even independent-minded persons can be persuaded to follow the orders of someone they feel has the right to give those orders."

"The right to rule, or the appearance?" I asked.

"In this case, the latter suggests the former."

"Because someone *looks* as if he or she can command, the people will follow?"

"A base simplification," Parsons said. "Humanity naturally separates itself into leaders and followers. Your ancestors took advantage of this proclivity, observing the demarcation between the 'sheep' and the 'goats,' as it were. Leadership fell to those who had a predilection for it, and genetic selection was made to breed for those traits most acceptable to the greater population."

I frowned. "What about the Culver-Rho Experiment?" One of the things I did recall from our history was a disastrous period in which genetic modification was seen as the be-all and end-all of adapting to survive in the harsh reality of space. Unrestricted tinkering produced so many freakish beings that humanity very nearly did not survive, as few of the modified humans could breed. Catastrophe, illness, war and famine took shocking toll on nearly every settlement. Our population was reduced to a few millions across forty systems. Only the dedication and doggedness of the leaders, my imperial ancestors among them, brought together enough of the surviving "normals" to restore humankind. It was then that reproductive restriction was brought into law; it had been with us ever since, a relic of those bad old days. It was intended to make certain that those who tested positive for unwanted genetic characteristics did not pollute the gene pool. I had seen images in files on the Infogrid that still gave me nightmares.

"An unreserved fiasco," Parsons agreed. "Humanity has learned its lesson since then. The maneuvering that has taken place since then is much more subtle and direct. Geneticists identified physical traits that the majority of the population found to represent trustworthiness and wisdom. Among them were perfect left-right symmetry and certain proportions among the features. Those physical characteristics involved include a broad forehead, defined, straight brows, large, clear eyes, vertical temples, cheekbones that do not protrude beyond them outwardly but are well defined, strong chin that protrudes slightly beyond the vertical plane of the face behind it. The mouth must be strong, with lips neither outsize nor undersize for the face. Noses are a matter of cultural taste. As it happens, you have a 'command' nose, though neither of your siblings do."

I touched that feature, proud of being considered a superior human, if only by a nose.

"Attraction to that ratio of proportions," Parsons continued, "has held remarkably consistent among the races of Old Earth. Those among the leader demographic with those traits were also selected for intelligence and courage, wisdom, dignity, charisma, shrewdness and twenty other characteristics. Where all of those appeared, a strong, natural tendency toward command was identifiable in their genetic code. Call it 'C.' The offspring of those carefully selected unions were to be humanity's leaders."

"Clever," I said. "Though I wouldn't follow someone no matter what based upon how pretty she was."

"No, my lord," Parsons said. "But that is only half the equation. As a transmitter requires a receptor, so do leaders require those who are inclined to be led. Such a gene, small 'c,' was introduced into the general population, the 'inclined,' that connects certain images with the pleasure centers of the brain. When they think of obeying their designated leaders, they are rewarded with surges of serotonin and dopamine. To give them that comforting leader figure, whether or not he has much contact with the people, is to satisfy the gene's chemical need. When they see images of the Emperor, they regard him with affection. It has been remarkably effective."

"Gosh, all this reminds me of a genetics lecture I didn't sleep through once," I said. "Old professor Shrewsburg. He said that love's all chemical. Pheremones, maturity level, hormones out the whatever—and so on."

"In that respect, it is not unlike falling in love. They cannot help but love him and honor him with their service."

"But isn't that unethical? To take away free will?"

Parsons raised an eyebrow. "Is it? For the survival of humanity?"

"But they seem to survive well in the Trade Union without genetic modification."

"The Trade Union, like several of the other galactic consortia, has suffered many more upheavals than the Imperium, my lord. I can show you documentation of how frequently the Uctu Autocracy has been threatened by overthrow by its population at one time or another. Disturbances within the Imperium are few. There have been none during this Emperor's reign."

I thought about it. "But once one is alone, what is to stop one fomenting treason, given your thesis of an isolated population?"

"The gene does not stop working because there is no leader nearby, my lord, but if one was to be reintroduced, the effect would be as if one had always been there. An inbred response to the sight of one whom they will automatically adore."

The enormous implications of what Parsons had been saying filled me with awe for the scientists of yore, and not a little dread. "*Everyone* in the Imperium is genetically modified?"

He looked at me squarely. "The modification was introduced thousands of years ago, my lord. Since then it is a normal part of the DNA of all citizens. The occasional sport arises with the command gene within it. Those family lines are taken into the Imperial house. But, otherwise, yes."

I frowned, trying to make all the facts connect. "But we're not all humans. Many other beings are citizens of the Imperium."

"A similar gene has been introduced into each species now resident within its environs. Those were much more difficult creations, as they needed to place a predilection for ideal human facial characteristics in their alien genetic structure, but it has been largely successful. They are loyal to the Emperor and to the Imperial house."

I looked from one to the other, my brain registering all the information that they had given me. The response welled up in my breast and spilled out. I began to laugh uncontrollably.

"Aha," I said, wagging a finger at my maternal unit.

"This is paying me back for being an annoyance to your admiral! You and Parsons are putting me on. This is better than a novel or a video! What a tale! You had me going for a while, but I am on to you now. Oh, Mother, I never expected it of you. I did not think you were capable of producing such a fantastic flight of fantasy! And Parsons! How even *you* could keep a straight face?" I flopped back in my chair and howled at the ceiling.

Parsons regarded me with a cold mien. "My lord, control yourself!"

"How? This is the best bit of fiction I've heard in years!" I clutched my belly and kicked my feet for pure joy.

Mother looked shocked. "We are not lying to you, Thomas. This information is deeply secret, but Parsons can provide you with documentation."

"Never!" I declared.

"Sit up, Thomas!" Mother barked. I obeyed. Gene or no gene, she was still my maternal unit, and I was tasked to follow her instructions. "Commander, if you would not mind?"

"It would be my pleasure, my lady."

Parsons reached for his own pocket secretary, a much less gaudy example than mine, and brought up files with the Imperium's "classified" logo plastered across them. To read them I must touch the holograms so they would register my fingerprint. The cynical smile stayed plastered upon my face as I reached for one of the oldest files, dated over four thousand years ago, and activated it. I was prepared to give it one of my patented derisive laughs, but as I began to listen to it, doubt grew as to whether such a reaction was appropriate.

The file contained a report from a behavioral scientist named Ziu assigned to the latest modification to the receptor genes. "I am pleased by the results of our fifteen-year assignment," he said, leaning close to the video pickup. "As you will see by these charts, the response has been over forty percent better than our original estimate." He threw graph after chart after table up for the reader, myself, to see. The test had involved over nine million subjects in sixty systems. A good deal of what Ziu spouted was impenetrable jargon, but enough of the report was aimed at the layperson that I could comprehend his gist. The adjustment to the genetic material had been found overwhelmingly successful. Few subjects of the experiment displayed disloyal tendencies when the correct stimulus was applied. Obedience could be imposed at the molecular level.

Upon completion of the report, the file vanished, leaving the final admonition to extreme security burned upon my retinas.

I registered my own sense of shock. Mother and Parsons, even if I knew them capable of constructing, though generally not of executing, an elaborate practical joke, to produce these documents for me on the spur of the moment suggested that they were extant not to dupe me, but as a record of an actual process that must have been put into operation. I was taken aback so far I might have been in another city. I certainly felt as if I was in a different nation than I knew. It was a marvel of science that had taken the task of maintaining order over vast distances and succeeded in such a subtle fashion that no one outside the inner circles realized that it was happening. The new knowledge swirled around in my overtaxed brain, and coalesced into a woeful realization. .

"Then I didn't make any friends at all?" I asked, feeling sorry for myself. "All my shipmates were *programmed* to like me! I can't go to the reunion binge in the inn on Fritsday. I'm not rejoining the Navy after all."

"No, dear," Mother said gently. "A facet of basic training for the military is to receive resistance training against the inclination toward obedience, so that the command structure can be maintained. Those of your shipmates with whom you made friends do like you for yourself."

I searched her face, hoping that she was not trying to appease me, but in her eyes was honest concern. "Oh. Oh! Even Nesbitt? He rather resisted liking me, but the barriers crumbled at last. Or seemed to," I added, skeptically.

"Mr. Nesbitt was a genuine conquest on your part," Parsons assured me. "He is honored to consider himself your friend."

I felt better. "But, Chan and the others? Do they like me for me? Is that why they went along with my plan?"

"You're very likable, my dragonlet," Mother said, "but yes, and no. They do like you, but they followed you so readily into danger because you are what you are. It was that fact that made me consider Parsons's suggestion of having him accompany you to the Castaway Cluster. You are capable of Imperial command. That knowledge may save your life, depending upon what situation exists there. I wish we had more information as to the situation. You may see why we swore you to secrecy before we told you any of this."

I sat back in the chair, which inflated cushions to support me. The events of the night I had returned to Taino flooded my memory.

"Xan," I said.

"I beg your pardon, sir?" Parsons asked.

"Xan," I repeated, looking up at him. "He knows, doesn't he?" I waved a hand before me, as if casting spells. "He does that. He charms people. I saw him do it only the other day. He says he has always known how to do it."

Parsons shook his head a millimeter to either side, for him a broad negative. "For Lord Xanson, it's a matter of instinct, sir. He does not know the extent of his capability. Among your circle, you are unique in having had this briefing. It is unlikely any others will ever have reason to be given this information. It is a dangerous revelation."

"Dangerous?"

Parsons captured my eyes with his most serious gaze. "Consider the uses. It is why the gene must be limited in its spread, and has for a long time. You, too, made instinctive use of your ability on Smithereen—to lead others. Humans who are born with the recipient gene are vulnerable to exploitation. Hence the emphasis on responsibility and adherence to the rules of the noble house. It is one of the reasons why you and your noble relations are made a sizable allowance from the public purse, to provide an impetus to follow the rules that you might not be inclined otherwise to obey. The restriction on breeding from the Imperial line is necessary to prevent a phoenix from being born into a dove's nest, to employ a metaphor."

I was struck suddenly by shock, fear and guilt,

none of them on my own behalf. In my mind's ear, I could hear my cousin Scotlin pleading with me to keep his secret and my own voice promising that I would. I needed Parsons's advice. I opened my mouth to ask for it.

"Are you willing to assist us, dear?"

At the sound of a musical, feminine voice, I suddenly became aware again that Mother was in the room. "Are you, dragonlet? It is dangerous."

I regained my wits, and with them the reason I had come seeking her that morning. I reached out to take her hand. "Danger does not worry me as much as the long stretch of life I saw before me with nothing worthwhile in it, Mother. I'll do it."

She gave me a warm smile. "I thought a taste of service would be good for him," she said to Parsons. "I hoped it would be for my Navy—I would love to have seen you follow in my footsteps, my love, but I see that you work much better within a smaller group."

"I am sorry," I said, hanging my head.

"Don't be!" she said. I essayed a peek up at her through my eyelashes, and saw that she was laughing. I straightened up and basked in the joy on her face. "A mother's wishes are nothing more than that: wishes. I am glad that you do want to serve. That pleases me, and it relieves me. I had no idea what we would do with you elsewise. You have such an . . . active intelligence." I reddened. That was her favorite term for the curiosity that had led me by the nose as a child.

"Well, Mother, I do have my enthusiasms. I *could* become a noted photographer." I patted the pocket where reposed the Optique and the Chey Snap 8.

She favored me with an indulgent look. "And in

six months your cameras will be collecting dust in a case. You'll be on to some other passion. Don't tell me otherwise. But *this* could be a lifetime's work. Go," she said, coming around the desk and standing up on tiptoe to kiss me. "Enjoy your reunion. Be assured, these young people really are your friends."

I embraced her. "I want to make you proud. You and Father."

"We were already proud of you. Off you go, now. I've spent more time with you than I have to spare." She patted my cheek. Parsons departed in my wake.

When we left my mother's office, two admirals resplendent in dress uniform stood up, impatient for their appointment. They strode past us, the harrumph in their gaze apparent. The door wafted shut behind them.

My conscience continued to trouble me. The moment we were alone, I drew Parsons aside.

"Parsons, may I speak to you privately?"

That worthy inclined his head. "Always, my lord." He deployed that small gray device again. I trusted that it disabled the listening devices being monitored by Admiral Draco in the front office. "How may I serve?"

I was uncertain how to begin. "I have been asked to keep a confidence, Parsons. It is a large one, and after this briefing, I don't know if I can hold it by myself."

"Is it a matter of official secret information?" Parsons inquired. I shook my head. "Could it harm the Emperor?" I opened my mouth automatically to say no, but snapped it shut again. I thought of Scot's face, transformed from its ordinariness to godlike beauty because of his love for Jerna, whose features in my memory seemed now more awry than they had been before. Perhaps the children would grow up to resemble her, not him. Perhaps the symmetry and proportions and ability to command would not carry on through the generations.

And perhaps they would.

My words came out slowly as I considered each one. "I could not say for certain at this time, Parsons. I would say that I can trust the owner of the secret to protect the Emperor's interests above his or her own at all times, but he or she has put into motion actions that he—or she—will not be able to control after a certain amount of time has passed." I did not want to say that that term was the remainder of Scot's life, but I felt as if the entire text of my conversation with my cousin was printed upon my face in a very readable typeface with boldface, exclamation points and illustrations.

Parsons looked at me impassively, but I could tell that his superior brain was taking in every element of my demeanor.

"Is there a solution to this dilemma that you can discern, my lord?"

"If there is one, I believe you will be involved in that answer, Parsons," I said. "You will be the key to it—when I...when I can talk about it. You are the man I have always trusted to bridge those dilemmatic horns."

"Is it necessary to reveal the confidence now?"

"I don't know," I said. "I am troubled, but my sense of honor is stretched between loyalty and necessity."

Parsons regarded me kindly. "Both are facets that the Emperor finds useful in you, sir."

I sighed. "I am grateful to hear that, Parsons, but it troubles me, too. That trust is a burden as well as a compliment."

"As it should be, my lord." Parsons offered me a slight bow. "We depart nine days from now. I suggest you make preparations for a lengthy absence. We may be gone for some time."

❊ CHAPTER 26 ❊

"How did you break a limb collecting pottery?" Nesbitt laughed, as we hoisted glasses over a well-scarred table at the Chess Inn in Straumsburg. The coral-red Redius had his right forelimb bound up in a stark, white healing frame. "Xinu is the one who went windskiing!"

"Debate with fellow over potential ownership of rarity," the Uctu said sheepishly, if a reptile could look like an ovine ruminant. "I won, but casualties ensued."

"I hope he looks worse than you."

"He is human. Of course, looks worse he."

We all laughed and downed our beers. The server, an apron-clad middle-aged woman as large and strong as the miners I had met on Smithereen, refilled our glasses. I had slipped her a few extra credits to make certain that the drink never ran out. The Chess Inn was a commercial establishment, mild compared with the taverns that my cousins and I liked to frequent for amusement. It existed merely as a purveyor of food and drink, with occasional musical entertainment, both live and recorded, and space for dancing or pub games. On screens embedded in the walls, patrons could watch sports games from all over Keinolt and rebroadcasts of games from farther away.

Our party occupied a three-sided alcove around the corner from the front door where we could watch out for stragglers. By half past the appointed hour, everyone was in place, looking well, happy and ready for a raucous night. I allowed my eye to round the table to enjoy the presence of my friends and formerly fellow ensigns: Nesbitt, Redius, Perkev, Parvinder Xinu and Anstruther; we were further graced by the presence of Plet, Oskelev, Bailly and Rous. Even though they were not ensigns, I had asked and obtained permission for the crew of my scout ship to join us for the evening. All of them but Plet seemed to be having a good time. The slim lieutenant toyed moodily with a single beer that dated from the time she arrived.

Reuniting with my fellows from the *Wedjet* was good fun, but bittersweet. My newfound knowledge weighed upon me like the eye of a disapproving aunt. Though I joined gladly in the banter and gossip, I found it difficult to relax or misbehave as the others did. I bought uncounted rounds for the table. No sense in not treating my friends—for friends they were—in the manner I was accustomed to treating, all the more because of our pending separation. The next opportunity to see them like this would be in the distant future.

"I can't believe you're not coming back with us tomorrow," Anstruther said again, regarding me shyly.

"Disappointment deep," agreed Redius. The brilliant blue spots above his eyes dulled.

"As is mine," I said. "I would have enjoyed shipping out with you again."

"Are you going to be serving on an Imperial vessel?" Nesbitt asked almost as shyly.

"Alas, no," I said. "I've been permanently separated from the Navy. My mother informs me that my antics did not amuse the admiral—don't quote her. If you wish to anger Podesta, quote me. Mother was very sympathetic towards him, as well she might be. She's known me all my life, and has never expected better from me. I suppose I only proved her right. It's a shame. I thought I was hitting my stride."

"We'll miss you, my lord," Bailly said.

"Just call me Kinago. Or Thomas. Whichever you would like," I said sadly. "I hope you'll send me messages. I would like to keep up with what goes on aboard the ship, even if I cannot be there with you."

"Count on it, my—Thomas," Bailly said, looking as guilty as if he had stolen something.

"You will get used to it," I promised him.

"What you did wasn't so bad," Oskelev said. "It's made some fine telling." Off duty, the Wichu wore no uniform at all, but a stylish harness to hold her personal belongings at handy levels. Her light brown fur showed signs of sun-bleaching from her shore leave spent, appropriately enough, on the shore of Keinolt's largest ocean. "Everyone made it home. And we got commendations. I'm in line for an early bump to midshipman. Wouldn't have happened if not for you. So, thanks."

"Congratulations!" I said. I signed to the servers to begin bringing us our dinner.

I had arrived early for the reunion and planned

with the proprietor of the Chess Inn to serve us a repast that I hoped would be a happy memory when that of my brief service aboard the *Wedjet* had faded from Admiral Podesta's nightmares.

"Great food, Thomas!" cried Parvinder, raising his fork to me from his corner of the table. "I'll miss it more than I'll miss you!"

"Don't insult his lordship!" Nesbitt leaned over across Rous and spilled a beaker of beer over Parvinder's white-blond hair. We all laughed at that.

"Don't waste liquor," Lt. Plet admonished him.

"Yes, ma'am. Sorry, ma'am," Nesbitt said hastily.

"This is how you deal with insults," Plet said. She took a bread roll, braced it on her fork against the edge of the table, and, with a flick, sent it flying into Parvinder's face. I gaped at her. She didn't look at me, but went calmly back to her food.

Not so the others. "Food fight!" caroled Xinu happily. Instantly, any comestible that could be launched from a utensil became a missile. I joined in, flinging chunks of pie and gobbets of meat at my fellows from my own makeshift catapult. They forgot all about my rank and bombarded me with return fire. Nesbitt hit me square in the eye with a piece of cucumber. I countered happily with mixed vegetables, at the same time peppering—literally—my two nearest neighbors with the contents of the condiments tray. By the time the serving dishes were empty, I would have to estimate that it was a fifty-fifty split between the food that was in us and that which was on us. My light brown tunic was smudged with a rainbow of color. I had not laughed so much in a long while. I had almost forgotten that this was our last time together as comrades.

"You guys!" Anstruther said, combing pickles out of her hair. "That was fun!"

"Another toast!" Redius called. "To comrades and shipmates."

Plet cleared gravy off her viewpad and held up a hand. "Time for the last drink!"

The others subsided and wiped their faces. "Last drink!" they echoed.

The final drink of the last evening of shore leave was traditionally a toast to sunlight, made by spacers about to leave a planet with atmosphere for the darkness of space. The cold glare of a star in vacuum did not offer the homey glow of a brilliant summer day. It was a promise to those who took ship that they would one day return to the planet from which they came. The tradition was that the last drink was sun tea, not liquor, because it was brewed in darkness.

Our eager server brought out a trayful of clear glass goblets filled with warm, honey-colored liquid.

Rous lifted his glass and sniffed it. "Not tea this!"

"No, it's not," I said, with a smile. "As I have had a couple of weeks to think about this most meaningful toast, I bribed the distiller that serves the Imperial house to make a liquor that was fermented in the sun in glass vats instead of metal or wood. It's a little raw. When we meet again, I hope that it will have mellowed, but it's the thought that counts." I raised my glass. "To sunlight and meeting again."

"To sunlight!" they chorused. "May we all return to bask in its glow."

But it was dark outside when I departed the Chess Inn, leaving my fellows behind.

❖   ❖   ❖

Saying goodbye to family was just as difficult. The cousins were baffled that I would want to *do* something again so soon.

"What about a vacation before you run off again?" Xan asked, when I joined them for a sunset drink on the mosaic-tiled veranda at Nalney's comfortable pied-à-terre just outside of Taino. Xan was with another lovely woman, a stunning blonde with green eyes a few years older than he. She was a famous singer he had admired at a concert. "We were going to the north pole to enjoy Endless Day. I have an entire hotel at my disposal. I challenge you to a sledding contest."

"It's tempting," I agreed. Xan and I were old rivals on the piste. We had run neck and neck for years for family supremacy. "But I cannot back out of this one. I have been asked by the Emperor himself to run an errand. A diplomatic visit." I yawned, to show how bored I was by the notion, though inside I was anything but.

"I envy you, darling," Erita said, her eyes almost as green as Xan's date's. "He *himself* asked you?"

"I . . . was approached," I said, loath to discuss how the appointment had come about. "But he confirmed it in an audience I had with him later. I had no idea why *me,* but would you question His Majesty?"

"Oh, of course not! It just sounds like . . . work."

I waved a diffident hand. "Of course it won't be work, darling. Can you picture *me* with a job?" As one, they shook their heads. I was pleased. I was getting rather better than I thought at subterfuge. "I'm off in a few days."

"Where to?"

I put my finger to my lips. "It's all hush-hush. In

fact, I don't really know. My presence, as a member of the noble house, is the gift that the Emperor is sending to . . . whomever. I'll mouth the correct words, and spin out of there in no time. You'll never know I was gone."

Scot was horrified. "But why can't the career diplomats do it? Isn't that why they have that enormous department? And dreary banquets?"

"Ours is not to reason why," I quoted vaguely from some ancient poet. Scot gave me a desperate look. I had assured him that my movements on the day of Jil's village tour could not be traced back to him. Now he considered me his confidant. "I will throw a party when I return," I said. "A big one. I hope I will have stories to tell."

"Not about dreary banquets," Xan pleaded.

"I promise, interesting stories only. And jokes, if they know any . . . where I'm going. And *you* can help choose the entertainment," I said. That mollified him. I knew he had visions of nubile dancers or acrobats twirling through his mind. I felt a little sorry for the beautiful singer on his arm. Temporary amusements, that was all my cousins thought of.

I took advantage of the remaining days to catch up with my correspondence. The backlog of notes and letters that had amassed while I was assigned to the *Wedjet* was enormous. I felt especially guilty not messaging back to MB-6594AD, the food storage unit with whom I had been exchanging notes since I was a boy. There were no messages from him for four months. I felt guilty, as it was I who had let the correspondence lapse.

He (I called him "he" because he had chosen a deep male voice) had sent a few choice excerpts of audio overheard from human executives in his complex who had forgotten he was an LAI and spoken freely in front of his interface. From the gossip, I determined that the executives were cheating the Imperium government out of capital based upon materials that were supposedly used for construction, and much cheaper ones were substituted. Emby, for so I called my old friend, was outraged because of the possibility that the roof might collapse over not only the heads of the mortal population, but also the mechanicals whose labor was so often overlooked, as in this case. I was incensed upon his behalf. I passed the information on to Parsons, now that we were in the secret information business together. The news was by then several months old, but I hoped that it could still be of some use.

In return I sent a chatty message, telling Emby all about my service on board the *Wedjet*, an account (with video) of the pirates' capture, and the celebration party at Sparrow Island. I told Emby I would be going on a trip, though I could not say where, but I would message en route. I sent it off, hoping that nothing untoward had happened to him, and that he was not upset with me. He had a very even-tempered personality for a machine of his age, but as they did to humans, things happened over time.

In avoiding most of my elder relatives, I had almost missed a chance to visit with Aunt Sforzina and Uncle Perleas. My favorite senior relational units always had an air of never moving in between my visits, even though I knew they had been on Eodril, the third planet circling Leo's Star, and several resort places in between.

Their sitting room, in which they spent most of their time while at home on Keinolt, was filled with the knickknacks of ages, including a blue plaster pie impressed with my five-year-old hand and signature that sat on the mantelpiece, in between priceless jeweled eggs, holograms of long-dead ancestors, ancient weapons, medals and commendations. The odor I would have known anywhere: a mix of Aunt Sforzina's perfume, the dust of subtly disintegrating furniture and the sweet-sour scent of a couple of very old people. I adored visiting them. My aunt looked taciturn, but always plied me with wonderful delicacies. The old man loved my stories, laughed at my jokes, and had loads of good advice.

"Go safely and return safely, dear," Aunt Sforzina said, as I rose to depart.

"I shall," I said, kissing her on her wrinkled cheek.

"Have you told your father where you're going yet?" Uncle Perleas asked.

"I can't tell anyone where I'm going, uncle," I reminded him.

"You can tell your father anything, my boy," Uncle Perleas said, laying a finger alongside his nose. "For his peace of mind, anyhow."

And so, I found myself standing outside my father's workshop again. Father glanced up at once when he saw me and closed the lid of the communications console he had been using.

"Thomas!" he said, coming over to shake my hand. "What a pleasure! When did you get home?"

He wasn't as lucid as I hoped he would be. "I have been home for a couple of weeks, sir. Father, I'm going to be...doing something."

He patted me on the back. "Good, my boy. It's good to be useful."

"Yes, it is," I said with pride. "I'm going on a diplomatic mission. Er, to the Castaway Cluster."

Father wrinkled his brow. "It's a long way off. Are you bringing precautions with you?"

"Precautions?"

"It's best to have a good defense there." He leaned close to my ear. "Bugs, you know."

"Bugs?"

"Yes. Smart as computers, too. And there are billions of them."

"Well, I am bringing Parsons. I would pit him against any billion computers."

"Why are you going?"

I mused upon that for a moment. "I don't really know. I am to look about and listen. Get to know people, I suppose. They've stopped trading with the Imperium. We need to find out what they want."

"Ah!" Father said, taking my forearm in a steel grip. "Don't ask them what they want. Ask them what they are afraid of." He nodded several times. "Remember that."

"I shall, Father." I pondered that a good deal, and knew I would ponder about it long after we had lifted ship.

He smiled, his eyes hazing over again. If one could call the last few moments lucid, they were over again for now. He reached over to his work station and tucked an object in my hand. "Here. Take this with you."

I opened my palm to find the puzzle box on it that he had carved. The red gem winked at me tantalizingly from inside its nest of carved spheres. "Father, I can't take this. It's valuable."

He waved a dismissive hand. "I am finished with it," he said. "I am on to my next invention." He leaned close to me, after looking this way and that to make certain we were not overheard. "An unbreakable door-stopper!"

My heart sank. "Of course, Father. The world is waiting for that. It will be treasured anywhere."

Father's face was alight with the fire of the fanatic. "It is, son! It is. Send me a message when you get... wherever it is that you said."

"I will, Father."

He smiled at me and gestured toward his communicator. "Your Uncle Laurence sends his regards."

"Mine to him, as well," I said.

Poor Father. I corrected myself angrily as I made my way back to my rooms. I refused to fall into thinking that way! He had given me good advice. I hoped that I would come to understand it before I needed it.

A roar of static woke Councillor DeKarn. She had just settled down in her bunk for yet another night in her lonely cell. She had not seen another living being in many weeks, though she knew upon waking some mornings that others had been there, undoubtedly to search, but also to clean. After the first incident when she had awakened to the scent of bleach, and found her desk chair closer to the entertainment console than it had been when she left it and not a fingermark anywhere in the room, she began to leave a control or an object in a position that she would detect a change. The console sustained the most examination. She had been heartsick to think that the Trade Unionists, for she was convinced they were responsible for her captivity, might detect the news programs she could receive and remove them, but every bleach-scented morning she was relieved to see they were still there.

She swung easily out of the small bed and landed lightly upon her toes. One good thing about enforced idleness, she had been able to stick to an exercise regime. With the survival bars as her only source of nutrition, though she thought about food all the time, she had begun to lose weight slowly. When she pinched the roll of flesh at her waist, it was much reduced. Her new self was cold most of the time, though. She took the coverlet and wrapped it around her shoulders as she approached the console. *More programming?* she wondered. Looked at the screen.

As if it sensed her presence, the screen became brighter. The image, the last graphic in the latest chapter on the history of ore mining on planetary surfaces, vanished, to be replaced by the opening image of the Grid. Her hands shot onto the keys. She entered her code, but the image vanished before she could complete it. She let out a cry of frustration. Another tease of freedom that never came. But it did not vanish entirely. A pale blue message form appeared, the blank upon which she or her correspondents would enter text or graphics for silent communication instead of video or audio. On it was three words. She had only time to read them before the form disappeared again.

Help is coming.

❊ CHAPTER 27 ❊

I arrived at the Oromgeld Spaceport on a bright, sunny morning with all of my luggage organized, packed and locked to my personal satisfaction. My cameras hovered around me like guardian angels. I wore a brilliant terracotta-colored tunic in the newest fashion, with the clever hem cut to echo the line of the mountains that surrounded Taino. Now that I was traveling as a gentlebeing, I was entitled to bring with me or wear anything I liked. As much as I had enjoyed my uniforms, I much preferred this state of being. Conscious of eyes upon me, I strutted along the pathway toward the open air terminal from which I would board my shuttle.

True to Admiral Podesta's avowal, Parsons and I were not shipping out with him on the *Wedjet*, but aboard another member of the Red Fleet, the *Shahmat*. She was heading out toward galactic north, approximately the opposite direction of its flagship, and would launch us on our way beyond Smithereen. I was sad at the thought I might never see any of my shipmates again. We could have had jolly times—during their off-shifts, of course—until my scout launched on its mission to "points unknown." Unknown, that was, but to all but my mother, Parsons, myself, the mysterious Mr. Frank, whom I had not yet met, the captain of the *Shahmat*, and the Emperor. It gave the rest of the government plausible deniability, that useful phrase, should the mission take a turn for the worst. I was prepared to die for my emperor, but deep down I hoped it would not come to that. My cousins chided me as being too active. I felt their criticism deeply. I would have sworn that none of them could match me for applied idleness in the past.

My preparation for the trip did nothing to disabuse them. In advance of my upcoming mission, I spent several days flitting around Taino, taking pictures of all the finest sights, and went to some trouble to obtain a few fresh images of the Emperor, to show to my putative hosts in the Castaway Cluster. The chances were that they had never been here, and that any images they had were several years old. Shojan was very patient about the picture session. I jumped around like a droplet on a hot pan to take as many exposures as I could to get the most flattering images. His secretary went over my files to make certain that I had not made a fool of our sovereign, and was actually impressed by one image in particular. In it, Shojan looked so absolutely regal, I nearly bowed to the picture myself. The secretary was pleased to inform me it was going in the royal archives with my byline. I was proud. All those images, with that one enhanced, were duplicated in storage so I would not lose them.

I had prepared, studied and anticipated all that it was possible to do with so little advance information on what we would find at our destination. My nerves jangled so much I was surprised they were not actually audible. I was keenly aware of the trust that had been placed in me by my mother and Parsons. I would play my part of envoy with all that was in me, to reward that trust. It was a great pity I had no one else with whom I could share the proud moment.

"Hey, Thomas!" shouted a male voice as I passed into open air terminal number four. I looked up to see hands pointing at me.

To my astonishment and everlasting delight, I saw familiar faces behind those hands. Redius, Anstruther, Nesbitt, Oskelev and Plet stood together in the center of a ring of bags I had seen two weeks before.

All but Plet descended on me for back slapping and playful elbowing.

"What are you doing here?" Oskelev asked, exchanging furry cheek presses with me. She beamed, showing her sharp teeth.

"I've . . . I have to go . . . off-system," I said, wiping a few stray hairs from my face. "It's a bit classified. But that's not important. What about you? Is the *Wedjet* still here?" I quailed a little at the thought of running into Admiral Podesta again. "I thought it left a week ago."

"It's gone," Nesbitt confirmed, looking concerned. "We got orders to remain on Taino. No one gave us a clue. We were just pulled off our regular assignments and told to stay ashore. I mean, I wasn't going to say no to an extra week of leave. We were told to come here today to await pending instructions." He eyed me, a half-formed expression of hope on his big, rough face. "I don't suppose you have the same ones."

A tiny kernel of joy deep inside me suddenly burst

and put forth a shoot of hope. "I would venture to believe that I do."

"Yay!" Redius caroled, the spots above his eyes growing brighter. "Opportunity for enjoyment!"

Anstruther looked concerned. "But where are we going? What's the mission?"

I hesitated. "It's rather important. I think I can say that without fear of reprisal. But I don't dare say more at the moment." That didn't satisfy them; it would not have appeased me, either.

"Bailly grkked off, I predict," Oskelev said, smugly. "You here, he not."

"Well, this is an ideal situation for the rest of us," I said happily. Then I noticed the look of reserve on Plet's face. "Oh, Lieutenant, I apologize. I am so sorry."

A thin eyebrow ascended. "For what, sir?"

"Well, getting assigned to work with me again. It was Parsons's doing, not mine."

The other eyebrow joined the first. "No, sir. It was mine. I volunteered."

I did a double-take. "You *what?*"

"I volunteered, sir. Oskelev was given a special assignment, the highest level of confidentiality. She came to me to ask if I could find out any details for her; I could not. Bailly was also requested, but he has Chinook flu. Seeing as those two were on the Smithereen mission I had a hunch that you might be involved. I asked Admiral Podesta to go in Bailly's place."

A triple-take, as my sense of reality was shaken. "You? You relied upon intuition?"

She gave me a perturbed frown. "I also took into account the rumors flying around the crew's Infogrid groups. You are the subject of much speculation and gossip all over the *Wedjet*. I pieced together enough information to make an educated guess. My application was accepted, as you see."

"Really?" Suddenly the day looked brighter. "I thought you'd never want to work with me again."

Her expression really did nothing to disabuse me, though she said, "You are inexperienced, sir, but in time I think you'll make an excellent officer."

"Well, perhaps if you work with me," I suggested, attempting to look humble. Inwardly, I was elated.

"I consider it to be my duty."

"It's a deal, then," I said. "My mother would be so pleased if I came home with the bearing of an officer."

Anstruther beamed at me. "Do you know where we're going, Thomas?"

I hesitated. "I . . . don't know what I may say until I am sure you are coming with me," I said, cautiously. They looked crestfallen. I foresaw that my new sense of responsibility was going to interfere greatly with casual, friendly exchanges. The new Thomas saw countless pitfalls in his former mode of conversation. There was so much I now knew that must never pass my lips under any circumstances. But, oh, how glad I was to see my friends! I hoped that I would not be disappointed. "Parsons will be here soon. I am sure he can answer all your questions."

As if he had been waiting for his cue, that dignified person shimmered out of the blazing sun and coalesced in our midst. I greeted him heartily and reacquainted him with our fellow crewbeings. Not that Parsons ever forgot a name or a face. He offered them cool, courteous nods, then turned back to me. He hesitated, and I realized he was staring at my new tunic.

"What is it, sir?"

"It's the newest trend," I said, spreading out the fabric of my upper garment to show off the elaborate embroidery. "Very expensive and exclusive—geographic replicas. I thought it would be a tribute to our hosts... you know where. Do you like it?"

"There are no words to describe my reaction to it, sir," Parsons said. I thought I detected a millisecond of emotion...was it envy? "May I suggest we discuss this later? The transport is due to arrive very soon."

I was aware of the hopeful faces around me, and knew that my own bore the same stamp. I edged closer and lowered my voice to an undertone.

"Parsons, they *are* coming with us?"

"Of course, sir," he said. "I believe you had already surmised as much. In light of your assignment, it would look odd if you did not have a staff attending you."

Redius, whose Uctu hearing was far superior to that of mere humans or Wichus, cheered. The others discerned the reason, and set up their own clamor. I beamed.

"We're going aboard the *Shahmat*," I said. "I, uh, tried to look up the crew on Infogrid, but my access has been restricted. Have any of you met Captain Calhoun?"

A flurry of head-shaking met my query. "No, sir," Plet added. "I only know she's good and smart. Her crew would be willing to follow her into a black hole."

"Splendid!" I exclaimed. "Because there's one not far..." Parsons's eye froze my tongue, and I subsided before the words "from where we are going," made it the rest of the way out of my mouth. I rearranged the syllables. "I look forward to meeting her."

Parsons himself saved me from further complications. He tilted his head upward, as if hearing a sound audible to no one else, even Redius, and indicated a thin silver streak arcing toward us.

"I believe that is our transport."

In a choking halo of brick red dust, the military shuttle landed. We kept well back under the canopy, covering our faces against the clouds. Under the auspice of an Uctu crewmember, mechanical loaders with padded graspers scooped up our baggage. As soon as it was all loaded, a human crewbeing with the insignia of a spacer first class chivvied us on board. As I bid a loving farewell to my world of birth, we made an uncomplicated transit to the *Shahmat*.

I peered into the viewtank between the pilots' stations as we ascended. The ship above seemed in every way to be a clone of the *Wedjet*. I should have no difficulty at all finding my way around. A further delight awaited me: I found my dear little scout ship, the *CK-M945B*, tucked into protective brackets in the shuttle bay. I thought it had gone out of orbit with the *Wedjet*. I felt as if it was my birthday and homecoming all over again. I examined my vessel from end to end and found it, well, ship-shape. It had been cared for as if it was a jewel. I thanked the crew and gave the cutter a pat, promising it a proper visit later on. I was so pleased to be there I even forgave the Navy the faux wood of my quarters—the cabin was much larger this trip as a visiting dignitary than as a newly minted ensign.

"What do you think, Parsons?" I asked, pointing out the beauties of my new cabin. "A fit setting for my new life?"

"The captain awaits you in her office, my lord." He

tilted a hand to indicate the rest of my team outside in the corridor. I was the last to be ready. "Decorum is expected of you. And promptness."

"Ah. Of course," I said, straightening my tunic in the mirror. I noticed a modicum of concern in my own eyes. I worried that I had wandered into the lair of as punctilious a leader as the admiral. Parsons, as usual, looked imperturbable. I decided to follow his example, and set my face accordingly. I straightened my shoulders and fell in with my team. Only Plet seemed as tense as I was.

The door slid open to reveal a bronze-skinned woman with a round chin and almond-shaped, grass-green eyes and red hair in countless tight little braids seated behind a weathered teakwood desk. I thought Captain Calhoun was a fairly young officer to have ascended to the rank of Imperium Destroyer commander, which undoubtedly meant that she was tough as a boarding school biscuit.

I need not have been concerned. She smiled at me behind the teakwood desk.

"Captain Phoebe Brubaker Zaheed Calhoun, I present Lord Thomas Innes Loche Kinago," Parsons stated. I moved forward. She stood up and extended her hand. I grasped it.

As I was once again the ranking member of the party, I thanked her for permission to come aboard.

"I am also empowered to offer the formal thanks and compliments of the First Space Lord for cross-departmental cooperation," I added.

"Thank you, Specialist Lord Thomas," Calhoun said, meeting my eyes with an emerald-hard gaze. "That will be your correct rank on this vessel. It is the equivalent of a lieutenant first class. Let me assure you we will do everything we can to make your transit as pleasant and event-free as possible."

"I appreciate that, Captain. We will endeavor to, er, pass as unobtrusively as possible."

The glint in her eyes told me she knew all about my service aboard the *Wedjet*.

"I will appreciate that. And how is your mother?"

"She is very well, thank you," I said.

"She's a wonderful officer," Calhoun said, the gaze softening to gelatin. "I worked in her office as an aide all during my tenure at the Academy."

"You were?" I asked. I studied her closely. I knew a case of hero-worship when I saw one. "Do you know Admiral Draco?"

"He's my uncle," Calhoun said.

"Really?" I asked, astonished. It was then I noticed the curl to her eyebrows, a feminine analog of the twisting, fibrous forest that grew on Draco's forehead, and observed the twinkle in the eyes beneath. I felt my shoulders relax so much my tunic sagged. Captain Calhoun was cut from an entirely different material from the crusty Admiral Podesta. This was going to be a very different trip from my first venture aboard a naval vessel. "Do you by any chance...play tri-tennis?"

"Rather well, Lord Thomas," she said, smiling broadly. "After dinner in Court Three?"

"Challenge accepted, Captain," I said, snapping off a salute.

I shamelessly enjoyed my weeks aboard the *Shahmat*. While my crew and I were seconded to various departments (alas, no matter how I begged, I was placed in

Stores instead of Records) during our transit, we had a shift per day to get acquainted with the host crew. They were curious and friendly. I experienced pangs for my lost opportunities on the *Wedjet,* but I could not deny that our mission was much more interesting than the day-to-day activities aboard a roving warship. The *Shahmat* had not seen action in over a year, when it had evacuated the population of a small colony from an unstable landmass—the only continent of any size on the planet. Beside the captain, I played tri-tennis against numerous opponents. I gave as good as I got, though I did not end up in the top three. To my delight and consternation, the shy Anstruther finished second in the shipwide tournament.

Calhoun also most responsibly saw to it that we had time to train as a group. I did not know how much she knew of our covert aims, though she had to know the ostensible reason we were flying to the Castaway Cluster. A small chamber off the officers' mess was assigned as our meeting room.

I spent a good deal of time in the meeting room alone, studying classified files placed in my viewpad by Parsons. He had given me so much homework I was taken aback. I swore when I tossed my mortarboard in the air on my way out of The Imperial University that I would never study anything in which I was not passionately interested, but he insisted that I read all the code-sealed reports that he had on the mutated genes and understand their historical implications. My brain felt as if it was mutating under the pressure, swelling up into a bubble that would burst at the knowledge being pumped into it that I could not share with anyone but him. Moreover, he was annoyingly

unavailable for conferences on the subject. If I had
had a teddy bear, I would have confided in it instead.

I also had readings, video and audio files galore to
study regarding our destination. I had never thought
much about the Castaway Cluster, beyond noting it
as a trivia question as to the farthest point at galactic
north to which the Imperium currently reached. It
turned out, from fervent application, that it was not
an interesting place in any way except geographically.
And that, I could see with my new appreciation for
strategy and tactics, must not be underestimated.

All my staff was prepared to aid me in my mission
to make friends again with the Cluster. We had all
had to adjust our Infogrid entries to ensure that we
did not introduce clues as to our whereabouts at the
time. That would come later.

"Are we to know where we're going and what we're
doing?" Plet had asked, in our first meeting *in camera*.

"As you share the peril," Parsons said, standing
before us like a lecturer, "you must be briefed." I felt
hot, wondering if he was going to reveal the subject
of our conversation, but I should have trusted his
inscrutability and sense of the dramatic. He played
the file of my pictures upon the screen in our break
room. "Lord Thomas was part of the team that gathered the information that has made this mission not
only necessary but possible."

"Pictures?" Redius said, his tongue darting between
his teeth. "Always pictures! Of what this time? Smudges?
All these we saw after inspection became firefight."

I felt my cheeks warm. "They're not smudges, as
it so happens. They're ships. Are they not, Parsons?"

"We are getting out of order," he said austerely.

"I ask your patience." If he had been a storyteller, he would have added, "... and all will be revealed," but with Parsons the quelling look was enough. We subsided into our couches like guilty schoolchildren. All but Plet. I believe that, like Parsons, she had been born with an extra gene for virtuous behavior. Parsons never so much as glanced at her. I was almost jealous. "I must impress upon you the importance of secrecy. Not a single reference must be recorded in personal diaries, noted in viewpads, and above all not put on the Infogrid. It is not too late to remove yourself from this team if you cannot maintain the separation." He paused, as though waiting for a response.

"Never!" Nesbitt rumbled. "Are you kidding? I mean, sir? I mean, I know what confidential means." We all nodded like barometer birds.

Parsons returned to the images. "Lord Thomas captured the images of three Trade Union ships in Imperium space not far from Smithereen. Their departure arc could take them in several directions, but His Majesty fears that they were on the way toward the Cluster."

The others (all but Plet) let out excited gasps.

"Have you had any independent confirmation of this suspicion?" she asked.

Parsons looked pleased. Then I *was* jealous. Plet looked smug. Parsons touched his viewpad and the image changed to a portrait of a woman about my father's age. Silvering brown hair, attractive eyes, round cheeks but a well-defined jaw, just slightly starting to pouch at the jowls. To my newly observant gaze, she was not a member of the noble house, but a being deserving of respect for her grave and wise bearing.

"This is Ambassador Hiranna Ben, envoy of his

majesty to the Castaway Cluster. She left Taino several months ago to meet with the full council of eight systems. She has not been heard from since she passed behind the black hole that blocks the view of those stars from the greater Imperium."

"Could she have fallen into it?" Nesbitt asked.

"No distress call was received. If she fell into the event horizon, there is no hope, of course. The final message in her Infogrid file indicates her arrival at the periphery. Even if we do not believe she survives, it is Lord Thomas's mission, and yours, to complete the assignment she undertook."

"And what?" Redius asked, beating Plet by a microsecond. She looked perturbed. His tongue flickered in and out. If he had been human, not Uctu, I would have said he was sticking it out at her, but he couldn't have been so disrespectful. He glanced mischievously at me. I smothered a grin. Perhaps not.

"Lord Thomas?" Parsons turned to me.

I was eager to air my lessons. "Well, to put it in a few words, we've ignored them a good long time, and they're returning the favor. In fact, they've cut off all links to us. No ships have come this way in ages. His Majesty wants to bring them back into the fold. I'm not a trained diplomat..."

The next fleering sound came from Nesbitt. I tried to emulate Parsons's quelling glance, but that brought laughter from my fellows. Ah, well, one must have to be born with it.

"...but I do observe reasonably well. We're going to observe. And, see if we can find the missing ambassador." I glanced at Parsons. He hadn't naysaid me.

"One more thing you must know, my lord and

crewbeings. The Cluster has had a visitor. A Captain Emile Sgarthad appears to be carrying technology that could throw off the balance of power. He is from the Trade Union. According to information received, he is using it to gain influence in the halls of power and public opinion. And that brings us to the ships observed by Lord Thomas." I bowed. Parsons brought up my images, magnified hundreds of times until the insigne on the fins could be read. As they saw the Trade Union logos, the others gasped, or whistled, or grunted, depending upon one's species. "We must act on the assumption that those ships spotted in Smithereen space were on their way to the Cluster. Though it has been neglected, it is Imperium territory."

"So, we're supposed to figure out how to throw out the Trade Union and take back the Cluster for the Imperium?" Nesbitt asked, lowering his dark brows fiercely.

"No, Ensign," Parsons said severely. "We are there only to observe, under the guise of a courtesy mission from an Imperial embassy, and return with our information; that is our task, no more."

But all eyes turned to me.

"That's all," I promised them. "That is our entire commission."

"What about Smithereen?" Oskelev asked.

"That was an accident!" I protested.

"Uh-uh," said Nesbitt. "So what else is going on?"

A long, slow smile spread out over my face. What faith they had in me! I was gratified. "If I did have more that I couldn't tell you, what would I say?"

"That's all," Nesbitt repeated.

"Exactly," I said.

The look of glee at a shared conspiracy was one

with which I was intimately familiar. The genetic magnetism that would have caused them to follow my every whim may not be operational in service personnel, but everybody loved to be part of a secret, even if they did not have all the details.

"So, what do you want us to do?" Oskelev asked.

"Play exactly the parts you would normally," I said. "Parsons is my aide-de-camp, I am honored to state. Plet, you are his assistant, in charge of research. Nesbitt, fire control and weapons, which I fervently hope you will never need to use. Oskelev, helm. Anstruther, communications. Redius, life support."

"Not so useful planetside," he pointed out.

"True." I grinned at him. "You can be my public relations agent. Tell people good things about me, how I am related to the Emperor, that I'm good company. If we need to counteract a friendly visitor, I am the perfect person to do it. Make sure you use a lot of pictures of me. I can give you all you need."

"Life mine is complete, then," Redius said, with a good-natured grimace.

"And if that doesn't work, I'm counting on your marksmanship."

"Ahh," Redius said, flicking his tongue. "Much more my talents."

We went on studying and preparing. I basked in the friendship of my colleagues. I even enjoyed Plet's open disapproval, because it was genuine. I promised myself that I would be the best leader, and give them little need to rescue me again. We returned to our duties. We all had a lot to think about.

❧ CHAPTER 28 ❧

The klaxon erupting practically in the small of my back made me scatter my cards all over the poker table in the cosy day room. My shipmates would have laughed if they, too, had not been startled into revealing their hands. A shame, because I had two pair, with the possibility of a full house.

I tapped my viewpad. "Bridge, what is the alert?"

"We have exited our third ultra-drive hop," Plet's calm voice said, over graphics showing the engines stepping down from faster-than-light to sublight. "We are nine thousand kilometers within the radiation belt marking the heliopause of Portent's Star. And we are about to be boarded by one or more of the five armed ships coming towards us at half-ultra."

"Battlestations!" I cried. My fellow players dropped their cards and made for their assigned sites. With my longer legs I outdistanced them all as we ran toward the bridge of the scout.

"No, sir," Parsons's voice, calmer than Plet's, issue forth both from the small speaker and his own dignified throat, as I stumbled into the command center. He glanced back at me as calmly as if I had arrived at an amble. "The ships approaching us bear the official insignia of the Associated Government of the Castaway Cluster."

"Stand down!" I bellowed, perhaps unnecessarily. The bridge was no larger than the day room, and everyone on the small crew had already reached it but Nesbitt, who had gone to his station at Fire Control in the stern. The blossoming red lights turned off, though the crew remained at the ready. I slid into my impact seat and eyed the images in the scopes. "Then why didn't they just ask to come on board?" I asked.

"Shall we hail the lead ship and discover their purpose, sir?"

"Yes, well, of course!" I said. "Why not? We've come all this way. Plet..."

My exec already had her hand spread over the touch control, feeling delicately as a safe cracker for the correct frequencies.

"Ready for you, sir," she said.

I cleared my throat. "Attention, ships who are approaching us at speed, I am Lord Thomas Kinago, envoy of His Majesty Shojan XII, on a diplomatic mission. I request you identify yourself."

A rough voice crackled over the audio channel, and an equally rough-visaged face appeared in the screen. "Lieutenant Vell. No one had intel that you were coming. Suggest you turn around and return to your point of origin. Otherwise your presence will be considered an aggressive act."

"I say, that's inhospitable," I said, indignantly. "Not even an offer of a drink and a light meal before we go? When I have come all this way to show you my diplomacy? *My mother* would..." I halted myself. I know what my mother would do. She would take me by the ear and remind me why I was there and how I should be behaving. I had to be the grease that lubricated the turbines. The stern visage on the screen didn't look as though he was in the mood for a few of my best stories with a risqué punchline and a self-deprecating joke. *No,* I thought, as I straightened my shoulders. This was the key point, the crux, the reason my mother had permitted me to go along with Parsons to the Castaway Cluster. I addressed myself to our interlocutor.

"As I mentioned before, I am Lord Thomas Kinago, sent on behalf of His most illustrious Majesty, the Emperor Shojan XII, to extend the hand of friendship to the government of the diverse planets and systems of the Castaway Cluster, a principality of the Imperium." I gave him my best smile. He glared at me. I kept the wattage high, even opening my eyes slightly wider, which I had been told by a success counselor was a subtle signal to the person to whom you are talking that you find them appealing, though Lt. Vell was anything but appealing.

"While he realizes that he has already sent an official ambassador, one with the sash and everything, to this locale, he is rather concerned that she has not reported back in what he considers a timely fashion." Again, I was self-deprecating and a little embarrassed, as if I was suggesting to them that they had perhaps mislaid our ambassador, and could they point us to her? "Lieutenant, I am forwarding my credentials to you. I request politely that you send them on to the governing council. I await their pleasure. In the meantime, I would consider it an act of friendship if you would stand down your weapons. Look at the size of us. We are not much of a threat, especially at this distance."

Did I note a slight softening of the harsh expression? Was he responding to my wiles?

It seemed not. Lt. Vell smacked his hand down on his console, cutting off our communication.

"Not unexpected," Parsons said.

We had several hours' wait while Lt. Vell forwarded my files to his superior officers and asked for instructions. I occupied the time by experimenting with my cameras.

The Chey Snap 8 was a mere dot hovering in the air. Nothing could outdo my precious Optique for function and versatility, but the Snap had a function that I could not stop playing with: it came with superior image-altering software beyond anything that I had ever seen. I took pictures of myself and added tiger stripes, lizard eyes that faced in opposite directions and a low-slung canine jaw to my image. I rendered myself into a Wichu, a Gecko, then daringly a Solinian. Even more daringly, I took a candid image of Parsons in profile while he stood over the screentank, reading data on our greeting committee. He would not have been pleased, even though I rendered him as a very wise owl with iron gray feathers and wide, knowing eyes. *What a marvelous toy,* I thought fondly. I erased that last picture from my viewpad before he could spot it, and took the other images to show my shipmates. They liked them as much as I did. My team. My friends. I planned to enjoy myself thoroughly, mission or no.

Suddenly, after a meal and a rest period during which no one ate or slept, the screen came to life again.

"All right," Vell said. "Follow us in, but no antics. The Cluster doesn't take kindly to antics."

"A pity," I said. I do excel at antics. "But if you insist."

It took more than three shifts to cut the billion or so kilometers by quarter-ultra and sub-ultra into orbit around Boske. From space, the planet looked like most worlds inhabited by humans and other oxygen-breathers who required one gee to remain healthy on a long-term basis. Blue oceans; white ice caps; green and brown continents; and cities masses of gold pinpoints on the nightside, expanses of gray on the dayside.

"What's missing?" Oskelev said, from telemetry.

I peered at the screen, went over readouts. "Nothing. It looks entirely normal."

"No traffic," the Wichu said. "We're practically the only thing up here—us and our friends. And that." She pointed to an enormous vessel hovering in stationary orbit. We all gawked as we went past. The markings were Trade Union, and the prow read, *Marketmaker*, in Standard and the Trade Union's angular alphabet.

"Right you," said Redius. "No own space trade?"

"Up until six months ago, there was intermittent trade between the Cluster and other confederations," Plet said, reciting it as if she was reading out of an encyclopedia. "Domestic trade, that is to say between one Cluster system and another, well established and prosperous, level three on the development scale."

The screen lit up again with the homely mien of our guide.

"Descend to these coordinates. No games, or we'll shoot you out of the air."

"Now, how may I refuse an invitation like that?" I asked. "Oskelev?"

"On it," she said, spreading her furry hands across the console.

I steeled myself, trying to be as prepared as possible for the upcoming ordeal. I would be the very best

"Where are you going, sir?" Parsons asked.

"To change," I said. "I want to look my best on behalf of the emperor. He is trusting me to represent him and the government of the Imperium."

"May I ask how you will represent him?"

"Don't worry," I reassured him. "My new Taino tunic will be perfect. You will see how it will impress them with my devotion to my home city, the seat of the emperor himself."

"May I suggest something more . . . generally formal? Your dark blue suit, and a white tunic?"

"No!" I said, perhaps a little more forcefully than necessary. The crew exchanged glances among themselves. "That is so dull, Parsons, that I should be disowned by my relatives. Besides, as you point out, I am not an ambassador, merely an observer. A friendly presence. They will enjoy my sense of fashion. After all, as you know, they have not been close to the Imperium in some decades."

"They will see why, sir."

"What?" I asked.

Parsons merely looked at me. "I cannot dissuade you?"

"Of course not," I said severely. "I will be back before we land."

✧   ✧   ✧

The unfamiliar screech caused DeKarn to fling herself out of her chair and into the far corner. She huddled there in terror, clutching the folds of her blue robe around her. A gap had appeared in the wall of her cell, showing a wide wedge of hallway. The door was open!

A Wichu in the uniform of the Cluster Security Service strode into the room and took her by the arm.

"Good, yer dressed. Come on. You got a meeting."

"What?" DeKarn demanded. Suddenly she recognized him as one of Sgarthad's cronies. "Let me go!" Her voice was a little rusty. The Wichu didn't pay any attention to her protests. He towed her out and down the corridor.

For the first time she saw the surroundings that had been her prison for the past months. The long, dimly lit hallway had steel doors every ten meters, but only every third one was open. The small rooms within smelled of bleach and long habitation. Had there been other prisoners? She stumbled. Her legs were unused to long, swift walks. The guard pulled her upright and kept going without looking at her. She clawed at him, trying to get him to let go. Her nails were too short to penetrate through the thick fur. She shrieked her frustration and helplessness. He ignored that, too.

The Wichu urged DeKarn through a low door and out into a pale blue, enameled passageway with numbers painted on the walls at intervals. At the cross-corridor ahead, a small group of humans stood, surrounded by more uniformed guards.

She let out a little cry of recognition: Zembke,

Six, Marden and Nineteen, all looking pale and tottery, clung to one another. Her fellow resisters, or so she surmised. All of them were clad in the colors of their constituency. She had thought it strange that the clothes shoved through her door that morning were her official council robes. What was going on?

"Leese!" Nineteen embraced DeKarn. Her eyes looked wild. She muttered to herself in Youngspeak. As terrible as she felt for Barba, DeKarn almost smiled. Her fellow captives must have had access to the same console programs as she.

"All right, she's the last of you," said the burly man who had been at Sgarthad's side since their arrival on Boske. DeKarn was outraged. Still plain-faced, they were now dressed in Cluster uniforms. She had not seen that, or remarked upon it, in the news feeds. The lines between one stellar confederation and another had become even more blurred. He focused on DeKarn. "The rest of you heard it. Now, you. Pay attention. Your families will suffer if you don't cooperate with us."

"Cooperate?" DeKarn echoed. "Why? What is happening?"

"Another visitor has arrived from the Imperium. You will do what we command, do you understand?"

"Cooperate with you?" Zembke roared. "Never! How dare you lock us up with no contact with the outside world for months? What have you done? Why have we been kept incommunicado?"

A bald man with the protruberant jaw stepped forward and sprayed Zembke in the face.

"Sad. Too bad Councillor Zembke was called home before he could meet the envoy from His Imperial Majesty," the burly man said.

Zembke clutched his throat. His mouth moved and his face turned red. DeKarn could tell that he was trying to shout. A small part of her wished that once this terrible situation was at an end she had that spray. Council meetings would be so much more serene! But she felt sorry for Zembke, too, and she was furious at the audacity of the Trade Union invaders. How dare they interfere! How dare they kidnap her and her fellows? But she said nothing aloud. Diplomacy had taught her to be silent until she knew where she stood. At the moment she saw no advantage in taking a stand.

She realized that she must be the only one who had had current events programs, the only one who knew what had been happening while they were incarcerated. And that one short message. It must be an opportunity. But what? And who had given it to her?

A small Uctu female came forward with a jet syringe and put it to Marden's upper arm. Before he could flinch away, it emitted a loud hiss. When the councillors tried to keep away from her, the large males held them still until all of them had been injected.

"The electronic devices in your flesh will monitor not only everything you say, but your heartbeat and respiratory rate. If you get too excited, it will release knockout drops. Treason is punishable by unconsciousness. At first. Too many incidents, and, well..."

DeKarn kept herself calm. "And, well, what, sir?" she asked, chin high.

"Your families will not be the only ones held to make sure of your good behavior," the big man said, peering into their faces one by one. The heartless cruelty of his expression terrified her. "The good councillor here—" He aimed an elbow at Zembke, who was still working his jaw. "—and the ambassador from Keinolt will be waitin' here to find out how well you act on our wishes. If this visitor is warned in any way—an Infogrid message, a piece of paper slipped to his hand, anonymous call—the councillor and the ambassador will experience *terrible pain*."

"You brute!" Nineteen snarled. Her large eyes were wide with disdain. "Do not dare lay a hand on them!"

"Oh, don't blame me," he said, with a grin. "It be your fault if they suffer. Just remember that. Check your personal comms for cues from the cap'n. Follow what he say, and no improvisin'. Unnerstand that?"

"We understand it," DeKarn said, coldly. She made a subtle gesture toward the others. They saw it and their faces went still. All of them were old hands at negotiation and all but Nineteen were adept at keeping their emotions under wraps. Normally they used those skills against one another. This time, it was a matter for the Castaway Cluster to band together against a common enemy.

The guards bundled the silently protesting Zembke back into the cells. The door slid shut on him. He had time to turn a beseeching face toward DeKarn. She knew what he feared. She had to find a way to ensure the safety of his family. She would do that, no matter what happened to her. In the meantime, she had to follow her instructions. The guards restored her pocket screen to her. A message scroll in the center of the window immediately blinked for attention.

She tilted it against her body so she could just see it. A green message window opened. In it, a flicker became an image. Colm! It was gone again in a split second, but she was certain it was he. She hoped that the TU people had not seen it. By their faces, they had not.

Colm! Bless him. He was there somewhere, very close by. She felt comforted. Was it he who had sent the message? *Help was coming.* Where from? In what form? Had he made it to the Imperium and back again? Was this envoy the help?

Everyone's communicators buzzed. Another green-flagged message opened. It was Sgarthad. He smiled unctuously.

"It is my pleasure to invite you all to the space-port to meet a distinguished visitor. I know you will all be on your best behavior. He should experience only the serenity that has been the hallmark of this splendid world for the last four months. Please be here in twenty minutes."

Marden looked up from his screen, outraged.

"We will not!"

"You want to go back in your cell?" the burly man asked, bored. "Don't you want a chance to have a decent meal?"

"What choice do we have?" Nineteen asked, her eyes flashing.

"None," the man said. Their anger amused him.

"Wait a moment," DeKarn said, coming to look the chief guard in the eyes. "I want to see the ambassador. I know you must have her imprisoned here, too. I want to make certain she is well."

"What you want don't matter. Move it. We're gonna be late." He gestured to the guards, who each took one of the councillors by the arm and shoved them toward the door. DeKarn marched grimly forward.

❈ CHAPTER 29 ❈

Crowds gathered upon the curbs shouted and cheered as we passed by in open-topped cars. I smiled and waved to everyone, reveling in the acclaim. We made quite a parade, a tail of eight vehicles the size of goods transports. Parsons stood tall and forbidding just behind me, unmoving even when the car hit bumps in the ancient stone roads. The rest of my staff was in cars following ours. All of them, especially Nesbitt, were enjoying themselves as much as I was, making encouraging gestures to the happy people who had come to see us. To be the sinecure of all eyes was a pleasant experience. I could not help but find pleasure in a new world, with new landscape and colors and customs. Every face beaming at us from the edge of the road was covered in etchings of color in patterns ranging from a simple stripe over the nose of a baby in arms to full-face tattoos in rainbow hues. It was rather like looking at a catalog of wallpaper samples with eyes and cheering mouths.

It was not all adulation, of course. I had to pay

attention as my hosts, the five councillors of the planet Boske, remarked upon every single feature that ran between the spaceport and the center of Pthohannix, a tongue-twister of a name. I could have done without the travelogue, but they seemed desperate to make a good impression with me. We passed through echoing canyons of tall, glass-sided buildings. It seemed curiously old-fashioned to me. Most of the architecture harkened back to Imperium designs, but the newest structures had a less coherent style than the older ones, as if the most recent builders were attempting to make a statement but were uncertain as to its reception with the public. Open spaces were laid out at major crossroads and tucked in between high buildings.

"We pride ourselves on our community gardens," the young man known as Five said, pointing to one of the larger areas. "It's a little late for the roses, but you should see them when they're in bloom."

I surveyed bare thorns and gave him a weak smile. I was not terribly impressed with the streets of Boske. Backwater was the first word that sprang to mind, though not to tongue. I would not have dared. My training as a scion of the Imperial house would have prevented it, if not the withering glance of Parsons that would have struck me dead. But everything was so desperately old-fashioned I felt as though I should revert to ancient forms of our standard tongue and use the appropriate antique pronoun forms. But our hosts did not speak that way, so I restrained myself.

Four, a pop-eyed woman in her middle years wearing curlicues of orange over her cheeks, pointed out the well-kept transportation system with pride. I nodded as she described how the light rail systems ran in tracks that had been slagged out of native bedrock a millennium ago. We in the Core Worlds had stopped using slot trains ages back when magnetic impulse tracks were perfected that could be virtually painted upon any surface, and the car systems would follow, traveling upon them with no trouble. They were safe to walk upon, even to touch one's tongue to—not that I would admit to a living soul I had ever done that on a bet, though I had. I'd won ten credits from Xan for doing it. It hadn't hurt at all, however foul it had tasted.

For the sake of my hosts I was as encouraging and fascinated as I could manage. The people were kind and welcoming, though I also sensed an underlying hostility like an itchy undergarment impinging upon me in many uncomfortable ways from a handful of the councillors. Parsons had warned me about that as well. I'd never been anywhere that the emperor's name was not met with a smile and often a sigh of pleasure. Now that I knew the reason, or one of the reasons, why, I wondered if the genetic changes had been bred out of the Cluster population over the two centuries, or if the festering resentment overpowered the artificial biological imperative. Most of the anger in our ground car came from the First Councillor, a mild-looking older woman with blue tattoos in an almost floral pattern over a curiously pasty complexion. When she spoke, she was warm and kindly, but as soon as silence fell, so did the curtain of anger.

The hostility was even more palapable when we joined the rest of the council in the grand room at the governor's palace which had been tricked out for an elaborate ceremony of welcome. Round tables for six were laid with brilliant white tablecloths and gleaming silver and crystal. Hangings from the ceilings, divisible by eight, depicted the flags of each of the Cluster systems. I knew them all from my studies. Parsons had been nothing if not thorough. At one end of the room, a podium upon a dais backed by pennants of blue silk was lit by two enormous projection lamps.

"I hoped I will not be called upon to make a speech," I whispered to Parsons.

"It is customary, sir. You have your notes."

I did, of course. I had worked upon them cursorily during our journey, but having prepared them I counted on not having to make use of them, in much the same fashion as carrying an umbrella ensured that it would not rain.

Parsons made introductions, and I did my best to recall all the names and/or numbers as they were given to me by wave after wave of notables, including the rest of the council who had been in the cars behind mine. I paid small compliments as I could. How I wished I had had access to the military codes that allowed me to unlock Infogrid files! That is, if they also opened Cluster Grid entries. It had worked so well on Smithereen, allowing me to connect to my new acquaintances as if they were friends. I kept the memory of that warm glow in mind as I shook cold hands, paws and claws. Plet, somewhere in the crowd, was on the job, seeking to find her way past the safeguards and firewalls of the local system. Her most important task, of course, was to discover the whereabouts of our missing ambassador. I tried to behave as if I was not desperately curious about what she had found every time her right eyebrow went up. I met humans by the score, a few Wichus and Uctus, but the most fascinating beings were the Cocomons, human-sized insects with bright blue carapaces and eyes. They were startlingly beautiful. I ordered my cameras to take as many exposures of them as they could without being too obvious.

There was nothing particularly exotic about the cluster. The most notable thing about the human population was the tattoos. Since the noble house was not permitted to make facial alterations of any kind (for reasons I now knew), I found it startling to see perfectly normal eyes looking at me out of wildly colorful masks. Most were just a design on the apples of the cheeks and over the bridge of the nose, but some covered every morsel of facial flesh. I had to pretend that I was at a costume ball, so I would not make a rude remark. I was made known to the governor, a prosperous and intelligent-looking man whose dark eyes peered out of a nest of red and black slashes. I took dozens of images so I could study them later on.

A handful of the forty councillors, including the woman in blue, spoke to me as little as possible. Most of the ruling body adored me on sight, which though I now knew would happen I found both gratifying and unsettling. Most of them paid compliments on my tunic, giving me an excuse to describe my home city and the beauties therein.

"I have many files of pictures and video from Taino that you will enjoy. I will show you all later on," I promised. They expressed themselves delighted for the upcoming treat.

Most of the underlying anger flared when a tall, broad-shouldered man in the uniform of the Trade

Union entered the room. He looked as grand as the surroundings. Those members of the council who had shown me friendliness went straight to him like dogs to their master. He greeted them briefly but with warmth, then broke loose to approach me.

"Lord Thomas, this is a pleasure," he boomed. "I am Captain Emile Sgarthad. Welcome to the Castaway Cluster!"

My new friend was a big, handsome man with blue eyes, straight brows, a mighty jaw and a face as devoid of decoration as my own. The way he grasped my hand told me he had all the self-confidence in the world. He stared deeply into my eyes as if searching for something there. I regarded him affably. He frowned.

"I am pleased to meet you," I said. "May I introduce my staff?"

"Of course," Sgarthad said, beaming at them. "But I know them already from your manifest. Lieutenant Plet, Ensign Redius, Spacer First Class Oskelev, Ensign Nesbitt, Ensign Anstruther, and Commander Parsons."

"Indeed, sir," Parsons said, giving him a more austere look than I thought appropriate. I almost nudged him. My staff saluted him politely. He seemed to expect more. He turned back to me.

"I hear you are an accomplished tri-tennis player," he said, slapping me companionably on the back. "So am I. We must have a match while you are here!"

"It would be my pleasure," I said, feeling cheered.

"And a wit with a story, I hear, too?" An elbow found its way to my ribs. Sgarthad barked out laughter.

"Modesty forbids me . . ." I said, lowering my eyes so as not to seem too forward.

"Don't let it, sir. I look forward to hearing some

of your stories. If you will pardon me, I have some preparations to make before we begin."

"Of course, Captain," I said, with a graceful bow. I did not understand why some of the people here disliked him. He seemed very friendly.

"No tattoos, he," Redius whispered.

"No," Plet said. "He is not concealing at all that he is not one of them. Nor are those guards."

"Very likeable fellow," I said. "Quite a winning way about him. We seem to have all the same interests."

Plet looked long-suffering. "He went through your Infogrid file, sir. I checked for hits on it since you offered your credentials."

My companions grinned at me.

"Oh." I turned to Parsons. "What is your impression of him, Parsons?"

"He seems born to command, sir," Parsons replied. "I believe you asked so I would repeat the question to you, sir. What is *your* impression?"

"He looks," I said ruefully, "exactly like my cousin Xan. Girls must fall all over him."

"Indeed, sir," Parsons said. "It is not a matter to bring up to a fellow diplomat."

"Not before casual drinks, at any rate," I mused. Parsons raised an eyebrow. "I see. I'll wait for him to bring it up himself, shall I?"

"That would be tactful, my lord."

I waxed thoughtful, thinking of our exchange. "He hasn't got Xan's inner poise, though," I said. "He is trying too hard. I wonder why."

"Perhaps you make him nervous, sir," Parsons said. He tilted his head a micron to indicate a Cocomon in formal attire who was waving his claw-hands in the air. "The master of ceremonies is signaling to us. We should take our places, sir."

I followed my aide-de-camp to a prominent position on the lit dais. We stood at the fore of the round stage beside Sgarthad and the governor in front of the rows of councillors.

My good mood lasted perhaps another four minutes. Then the banners at the rear of the stage went up, revealing a full orchestra in formal attire. They struck up the first anthem.

Anthems, I firmly believe, are written as instruments of torture. They are pieces of music like terrible, painful worms that insinuate themselves and wind painfully through one's internal organs, rending nerve tissue as they go. I find them acutely uncomfortable to listen to, as would all normal, right-thinking people. Once the orchestra had played the "Glory of the Imperium," I felt the relief that a prisoner must experience upon being released from a long and unfair incarceration. I was about to move toward my hosts to offer the elaborate compliments incumbent upon me as representative of His Imperiality, when another blaring chord issued from the speakers. I shot a look of horror at Parsons. He shook his head a millimeter to either side, warning me not to move.

"It is the Castaway Cluster's theme, 'Frontier of the Unknown,'" he said. "You listened to it on our journey here." I put my ear to the test. After a screeching bar or two, I did recognize it. It possessed even fewer of the soaring crescendos that made "Glory of the Imperium" unsingable by any human who had not been trained in opera, but it was still awful. Then followed one after another eight more shards of music so terrifying that I assumed they had been written as part of a bet to see who could insult the audience the most. Tears filled my eyes with every fresh shriek.

When it was all over, I could not believe the blessed silence. A single tear traced its way down my cheek. I dashed it away. The eldest man with a crown of silver hair came to pump my hand. "I saw how moved you were by our anthem, Lord Thomas. It is most courteous of you. It is an ancient piece that tells of the suffering of our ancestors."

"I can well imagine," I gasped, bringing myself under control. "I felt it deeply."

The woman with silver hair and blue tattoos smiled at me for the first time. By the way the others deferred to her, the position of First Councillor must be more than just numerary. She had a large man at her elbow, one of the untattooed faces, probably a personal aide. He stood closer to us than a similar associate would in the Core Worlds, but I was not at home, and customs were no doubt different here. I would check on the Infogrid later to see what the subtleties were.

"Did you enjoy the ceremony, First Councillor?" I asked her.

"It is most patriotic." She gave me a mischievous smile. "Usually visitors wait until the ceremony of welcome is under way before showing up."

"You mean it was expected of me to opt out of, er, listening?" I asked.

She tilted her head. "Yes. We expected it. Mention of the, er, custom was in the commentary that followed the protocol we sent to your ship. I must say that I am gratified that you didn't. Your attention will mollify those who stand on each side of the question."

"Indeed." I aimed a hard look at Parsons. "Words will be exchanged later on." He bowed very slightly, though he remained expressionless. I felt an immediate and permanent sympathy with any dignitaries who visited the Core Worlds from that moment on. Diplomacy was harder than it had first seemed. "And what question is that, madam?" I asked.

"Independence," she said. She gave a glance toward her aide. His face remained stony. I presumed that she was worried about him overhearing us, but she made no move away from him. "You have come to inquire on behalf of the emperor whether we will accept his invitation to return to the fold."

"Well," I said, feeling awkward, "I've lived in the Imperium all my life. It's a good place to be part of. There are beautiful and interesting—and historical— places to visit. I brought lots of images and videos of home, so you can see. Not that you don't have history here, of course. There's just more of it. His Majesty hopes you'll say yes, of course, but I'm just an observer. It's up to the emperor's ambassador to persuade you, really. You won't have met her, have you? His Majesty's concerned about her. That's why he sent me. And Parsons." I tilted my head toward the grave mien a meter off my starboard stern. The two diplomats looked at him, then gave each other nervous looks.

"No, we have not," the man said at last. "Er, seen her, that is. I mean, lately. She did communicate with us that she was coming. I...I trust she is well?"

"I hope so," I said. "But it's been a while since anyone's heard from her. She's about to incur a nasty fine for failing to update her Infogrid file, you know."

By their expressions, my joke fell flat. It was a serious thing, of course. I needed to change the subject. "Tell me, please. I've never been here before, of course. I notice that everyone has, er, facial art."

The pair of diplomats seemed to relax. I felt good about putting them at their ease. I was doing my job, observing.

"An old custom," the gentleman said, taking me by the arm and leaning on me as we walked toward the tables. "When humankind settled in the Castaway Cluster, the first system colonized was Cocomo. Humanity found that it was already occupied by an intelligent native species. They made us welcome." He turned me by the elbow to face one of the insectoid beings. "Do you see their facial patterns?"

"Very handsome," I said. All of them were different and complex. If I concentrated on the multicolored whorls and blobs, I could imagine wrought iron gates or flower petals, fish scales or fine calligraphy. "I am impressed by the beauty and detail."

"Yes, indeed. We decided that in solidarity with these fine beings we would go so adorned. Each family chose its own pattern and color scheme, though there have been alterations over the centuries." His expression suggested that he did not approve of those alterations.

"Most admirable," I said, sincerely. It was a great concession on the part of humanity, which did not have a good record throughout the ages for accommodating anyone else. I was impressed.

"Is not epidermal art practiced in the greater Imperium?" he asked, peering at me and my fellows. "I believe that videos of the time before the . . . the separation, that I have seen beings wearing tattoos."

"Oh, well, it is," I said. "But as a member of the Imperial household, I'm not permitted to make any permanent changes to my person, neither physical nor genetic, to the angst of those of us born with long noses, small eyes or outstanding ears." Knocking at the back of my teeth was the knowledge of my heritage. I pushed it firmly away. "If you stripped my companions bare, you might find a skin image or two, but don't tell them I suggested such an impertinence." My audience gave an appreciative chuckle. "My cousins and I do frequent the establishments of face-painters, especially for parties. Your patterns are most interesting. Tell me about them, if you wouldn't mind."

"Not at all, my lord, not at all!" the old man said, beaming. "My tattoos follow the color scheme of my sixteen-times-great-grandmother Genilla..."

Each of the councillors was eager to give me details of their history. Children wore stripes of color over the bridges of their noses from their naming ceremony at one month of age. When they reached their official adulthood, at the onset of puberty, they chose their permanent designs.

"Too early, what?" I asked, recalling what I had been like around that despicable time of my life.

"Not at all," said the First Councillor.

"Don't any of you come to regret your choices?" I asked, curiously.

"Of course not," said the old man, whose name was Bruke. They were horrified at the thought.

"May I record yours?" I asked. "It would be a great favor." They agreed. I set my Optique to capture their images from several different directions. The serene look on Parsons's face said that he approved.

We sat down for the luncheon. Parsons and my staff were at the table adjacent to mine with the elderly gentleman and another older man with yellowing skin under his rather elaborate tattoos. They listened through my viewpad and two hovering cameras. Redius blinked at me with amusement. I occupied the hot seat among the most challenging guests. First Councillor DeKarn sat at my right hand, and a very attractive woman my mother's age, Councillor Nineteen, at my left. Sgarthad, partnered with the governor's wife, sat across from me.

"So you are a cousin of the emperor," Sgarthad said, expansively, toasting me with a cup of wine.

"One of many," I said. "Shojan and I share a number of ancestors. He is a Kinago, of course. One of the founding families of the Imperium. It's in your history books."

"*Your* history books," he said. "I am from the Trade Union."

"Do tell," I said, hoping I didn't look as if I had heard it before. "What are you doing here? Er, trading?"

Sgarthad chuckled. "More than that. These good people have taken me into their bosom," he said. "We are making friends and opening ourselves to commerce and culture with an eye toward forming a permanent bond between us."

"Not too permanent, I trust," I said. "After all, this territory is within the realm of the Imperium." I addressed my other tablemates. "We—that is to say, *the emperor* hopes you will also take him to your bosom."

"I am afraid you are a little late," the governor said, with a tentative glance at Sgarthad before he spoke. "The Trade Union has become a good friend to us."

"And I am not unaware of history," I said. "I am just saying, what about all the maps? They show the Cluster as part of the Imperium. I would hate to see that change. You can't be cruel to all those cartographers!"

"They will cope," Sgarthad said, flatly. "The Cluster does not wish to be associated any longer with the Imperium. That time is past."

"I would rather hear it from the citizens of the Cluster itself," I said, firmly. I regarded the governor and each of the councillors intently, giving them my most wistful expression. "I hope I can expect the same courtesy, to allow me to become *your* friend." Yuchiko's mouth spread in a beaming smile.

"You won't be here long enough, will you?" the captain asked, quelling the governor before he could reply. "You have to get back to your busy life."

"I haven't a thing in the world to do except what the emperor commands," I said, with more than a hint of truth. "Governor, councillors, I hope we may have a discussion over the coming days on the subject. I am keen to discern your views, and I wish to offer you mine—those I represent. After all, I am His Majesty's observer."

"Well, you know, it has been a long time," Yuchiko said, timidly. "That time is past."

I cocked an eyebrow. How curious that the governor should echo his visitor's precise words. "Plet?" I whispered.

"I am on it, sir," said the voice in my ear. Out of the corner of my eye, I saw her eyes dip to her lap, and her fingers went to work on her viewpad.

"Lord Thomas," said Councillor DeKarn, firmly,

"you are correct. You do have the right to be heard. We would be honored if you would address the full council tomorrow. All eight systems have the right to hear you. We all wish to hear the emperor's plans for our future."

I would have sworn that she had told me shortly before that she favored independence for the Castaway Cluster. Then I sensed the roiling hostility I had felt when I first arrived. It was not meant for me, but for the man seated opposite. From the grimace Sgarthad wore, she had just tweaked his tail. She was terrified to do it, but brave enough to try. *A-ha*, I thought. I recalled my father enjoining me to discover not what they wanted, but what they feared. All was not the calm pond surface it appeared. This was an important fact. I made a note to include it in my report.

"You must be present, too, Governor," the attractive woman at my side added.

"I would be delighted," Yuchiko said. Sgarthad cleared his throat. The governor turned to him. He dipped his head like a chided schoolboy. "It is only courteous to our guest. I will maintain my own opinion, of course."

I vowed to use that indecision to help sway the Cluster back into the Imperium's fold. My mother would be proud of me if I managed to promote the cause of unity. And, of course, I would continue to observe.

By the purple cast of Sgarthad's complexion, I perceived that I had pushed the subject as far as I could for the time being. I turned the table talk to my favorite subject, photography.

"You are right, Thomas," Plet said. "A Grid pundit,

endorsed by your distinguished friend there, quotes Captain Sgarthad as saying, "That time is past," in reply to the question of Imperium ties. Several times, in fact. The phrase is a favorite of his."

"Most amusing," Redius said in an undertone that I heard through the miniature receiver above my ear. "Not know their own minds. But they know his."

❧ CHAPTER 30 ❧

The following morning I arrived on time for my speech with Parsons, Oskelev and Nesbitt in tow to the low, brown stone building that housed the Castaway Cluster council. I was surprised how humble it looked after the other centers of planetary and system government that had been pointed out to me on my tour from the spaceport. Plet and Anstruther had remained on our ship engaged upon research, but we all remained linked through the scalp implants. They would hear and see everything that I did. I felt quite well-protected.

The First Councillor swept down on me and tucked her arm into mine. Her minder stuck as close to her as Nesbitt and Oskelev did to me, both of them with weapons displayed in their belts. Parsons, in midnight blue, trailed behind us, exuding calm. Redius waited with our transport outside, making certain no alterations were made to the vehicle in our absence.

"I look forward to your speech," DeKarn said, in a quiet voice. "It will be broadcast through the Grid and the local media. I hope you are willing to give interviews to the local opinion reporters. They will want to ask you questions. Have you sent out copies of your text ahead of time?"

"I rather prefer it to be a surprise," I said. "Is it...customary?"

She smiled. "No, but it saves time of transcription, that's all. Afterwards, there will be a rebuttal from a few of our members. By the way, you will be speaking in Performance Central, our city-state's main auditorium. This way."

I nearly whistled as she led me into a red-walled concert hall that must have housed at least two thousand beings. The stage below looked like a dinner tray. It was surrounded by a troop of soldiers in dark green jackets, tan trousers and brown boots who at this distance looked like toys. Other brightly colored miniature figures moved to and fro in the lights. Mine were not the only cameras floating around. As I appeared, dozens of small spheres came to hover around me like satellites. Their owners turned keen faces in my direction. I smiled and waved at all of them. "I thought I would be addressing only the forty councillors and the governor."

The First Councillor shook her head. "Word spread last night. The clamor for seats was so great we had to move you from our chamber to this space. Fortunately it was available today. You don't mind, do you?" she asked anxiously.

"Not at all," I promised her. The more people who heard the emperor's message, the better.

"I don't like this," Nesbitt said, low enough that I heard it only through bone conduction. "How can I cover this whole space?"

"We only need to cover him," Oskelev pointed out. "Who's going to shoot at him? Those guys? I bet they only meet once a year for target practice." She aimed an elbow toward the troop of soldiers. Close by, I could see how young they were. They saw me looking, and threw their shoulders back and assumed serious expressions.

"I'd bet on the two of you over that entire squad," I said, proudly. "Or either of you."

"C'mon, Thomas!" Nesbitt said, his face as red as the walls. "I mean, my lord."

"Good morning!" boomed a deep voice. Captain Sgarthad bore down on us like a benevolent thundercloud. His uniform seemed more golden than before, glowing in the exaggerated light. At my side, Councillor DeKarn cringed. I decided to meet fire with fire.

"Good morning!" I replied. "Here to view the spectacle?"

Sgarthad seemed surprised. "Why, I'm part of it, my dear fellow. I am an interested party. You'll make your speech, and one of the councillors and I will give our responses."

"Oh, really?" I asked, rising to the challenge.

"Yes," Councillor DeKarn said hastily. "It is customary."

"Ah," I said, bowing to her. I did not want her to be any more alarmed than she was. "Then let us proceed."

The yellow-complected councillor stepped forward. The tall, narrow screens behind him lit up with sunbursts and a flag of the third system in the Cluster hoisted itself in its midst. "I am Councillor Vasily Marden from the New Rome system. It is my privilege to bring to you today a guest from the Imperium, Lord Thomas Kinago." Uproarious applause met this announcement. I stepped forward, buoyed on waves of good will.

Marden stood down to a podium on the left of the stage. Sgarthad moved to occupy the one on the right. It was not my imagination: the spotlight on him was more powerful than that on me. *Well, we will see who gets more attention,* I vowed.

"Gentlebeings, I greet you," I began. "I am proud to stand before you today..." My speech was based upon several that were in the archives of the diplomatic service. I admit that I had borrowed freely of phrases that I felt reached directly into the hearts of listeners more eloquently than any I could spin myself. I hoped that no one in the audience had had access to the same files.

"I have heard some of you say that the Imperium has neglected you over the last two centuries. It's been rather hard to keep an eye on you, I must say, what with your large, dark neighbor the black hole impeding the view, but I assure you that such is not the aim of our emperor—your emperor, Shojan XII."

I touched my viewpad. The audience gasped. The first picture of Shojan filled those screens behind me. His noble, calm eyes surveyed the onlookers. He was the very epitome of masculine beauty and gravitas. Even though he was my cousin, I found him impressive. I glanced at my neighbor. Shojan compared over-favorably against Sgarthad, whose chiseled cheekbones were suffused with angry red. I could almost see the thunderstorm gathering upon Sgarthad's brow like an ancient mythical god.

"As Shojan began his reign, six years ago," and here I changed to the official coronation portrait, "he vowed to pay heed to the needs of all parts of his new realm. He deployed his ambassador to your starry shores, but alas, she has not been able to make his case to you in person. I hope in coming days, I will be able to answer any questions you have, and I hope you will answer mine. I am here as an observer, but also as a loving subject of His Imperiality." I flicked my control again and again. I told a few of my favorite stories about Shojan, a few intended to show his humanity, others to point out his wisdom and compassion, and coupled every tale with a fresh image. Each new picture elicited open cries of astonishment and pleasure. Parsons, at the far left edge of the stage, nodded in approval. "I know that once you feel secure that he intends to follow up on this promise of protection and acceptance, that you will reaffirm your ties and join us of the Core Worlds and the rest of the sectors as parts of the Imperium under his most noble aegis." To couple with that declaration, I intended to show my very favorite picture of Shojan, the one I had taken just before I left home.

I flicked the control. The lights went out.

Loud declarations of surprise erupted from the audience. I clutched my viewpad and gawked into darkness. *What had happened?* Had *I* done that?

"Oof!" I exclaimed into a mouthful of fur as the breath was squeezed out of me.

"Quiet," Oskelev said, against my chest. "Nesbitt, you there?"

"Ready," the other ensign growled, pressed against my back. "You okay, Thomas?"

"I am all right," I said. "What happened?"

"Great void, the power!" cried Councillor Marden. I heard a good deal of bustling and swearing. Very shortly, the lights came on again.

My friends stood facing outward with sidearms drawn. They had literally become my bodyguards, bracketing me with their own torsos. Parsons had moved in the pitch dark to stand over us. I had never felt so well-protected.

"I apologize for the interruption," Councillor Marden said, bustling up to us. "Are you well, sir?"

"I am." I straightened my tunic and cleared my throat. My friends moved back to their positions, but they kept the weapons out and obvious. "To continue," I said, returning to the podium and beaming at the bemused audience. "His Majesty might be young, but you can see that he is already possessed of wisdom and bearing..."

I thumbed my viewpad screen, but nothing happened. I glanced down at the small screen. The file was there, but it was empty. I flipped through my database, thinking that in the scrimmage in the dark I had jostled the control. I couldn't find the picture. The contents of the file were not in the deleted section, nor in the archives, nor in the active roster. I went through all of my other files, thinking I had shifted the images of Shojan there, but no. All of them had gone.

The audience became restive, but I was determined to find at least one other image to show. I searched all the folders and albums for at least one. I had a candid taken at a family event in the spring just before I left for the Academy. It was gone as well.

I had a terrible, sinking feeling in the pit of my stomach. Holding the viewpad close to my eyes so no one else could see, I even looked into the tiny, very secret niche storage in which I had hidden the spit-take of Shojan. It, too, had disappeared. I was devastated to the very fiber of my being. That opportunity would never come again. I was heartsick at the loss. I glanced at Parsons. His visage bore no hint of guilt, but why would he sabotage my files at any time, let alone this one, in which the emperor would be embarrassed by proxy?

The most likely party was at my left. Sgarthad's brilliant blue eyes glinted at me.

"Lord Thomas? Is that the extent of your remarks?"

"Er, no," I said. I cleared my throat, straightened my tunic and threw my shoulders back. "And so, gentlebeings, I ask you to give heed to, er, my noble cousin's plea to you..." I glanced down at the viewpad for my next line. At least the speech had not been lost.

With the smooth flow of my presentation interrupted by the loss I found it difficult to carry on, but carry on I did. I knew from the half-hearted applause of the audience that it had not gone well.

"Independence, my friends! We of the Castaway Cluster have had a long time to consider the question..." Vasily Marden began his oration, but his style of speech was so turgid that I found my thoughts drifting off after my lost pictures. A sharp whistle in my ear brought me back to the present.

"Look down!" Redius's voice hissed.

I glanced at my viewpad. He had sent me an image of myself with a stupidly blank look on my face. I plastered on a friendly and learned expression and forced myself to pay attention. At last, the councillor retired to modest applause.

Even before he stepped forward, the room had risen in acclaim.

"Sgarthad! Sgarthad! Sgarthad!"

The Trade Union captain came forward, arms raised.

"Gentlebeings!" he called. "We have heard the other speakers! Have you changed your mind about the direction you want to go in the future?"

Myriad throats roared as one.

"No!"

"Let me remind you once again of the reason that I am among you. The Trade Union offers you status as a full partner, not a subject state, as the Imperium does. We won't let you remain isolated, either, like those of your government who favor independence!"

The event had changed to a pep rally, as one would experience at a sports match. The young people clustered at the foot of the stage were the cheerleaders, exhorting their fellows to cheers every time Sgarthad spoke.

I had failed. The people had liked me, but Sgarthad had had more time with them. He had had plenty of time to convince them of his confederation's point of view. He had more natural charisma than Marden and was less hesitant before an audience than I. The comparison with those of us who had gone before Sgarthad was overwhelming. He was cheerful and personable. Without the emperor, all I had to offer them was the status quo, and it had little new to excite the listener.

Sgarthad finished his pep talk and was immediately mobbed by fans and supporters. I moped over to Parsons. My guards trailed behind me.

"That was deliberate sabotage," I said. "It could not be accidental."

"It is not, sir," Parsons said. "That is a barrier that the next wave of envoys from the Imperium will face, once we send back the observations we are making."

"That doesn't seem like enough," I said.

"It is your brief, my lord," Parsons said firmly. "Do not forget that."

"I can do more," I replied, just as firmly.

I was not alone for long, as I had feared. A sea of eager faces swarmed toward me, led by Councillor DeKarn and her bodyguard.

"These are some of the opinion press," she said, smiling as she gestured toward them. "They have expressed a wish to interview you, my lord. I told them you would make a fascinating subject. Will that be satisfactory?"

"Why, yes, of course," I said.

"Will you excuse me, sir?" Parsons asked.

In spite of my woes, I felt a thrill of excitement. I kept my face neutral as I said, "of course, Commander."

Parsons slipped away so gracefully that even knowing he was departing I believe that the hosts and their watchful guards did not see in which direction he went. I felt pride, and determined that I would do my part for the honor of the Imperium, as he would do his. I was not going to take my defeat lying down. I would make myself charming and indispensable to my hosts. I planned to use the gift of ages to sway these folks to the Imperium's cause. I could not be less than me. Otherwise, why would my mother and Parsons have caused me to come here?

"Who has the first question?" I asked.

The reporters, all species, ages and sizes, bore down upon me, shouting questions and sending them to my viewpad. I pointed toward a tall woman with a basketweave pattern in yellow on her narrow face.

"Lord Thomas, is it true that the Emperor...?"

I basked in the attention. As each person made his or her inquiry, I made firm eye contact, until I was certain that I had charmed them to the best of my ability.

At her direction, I escorted the councillor through the halls and into the museum next door. Our parade of questioners followed us, just kept from making bodily contact with me by the combined efforts of Oskelev and Nesbitt. "You will understand so much more of our history," she assured me.

"It would be my pleasure," I said.

The reporters followed us through the halls and into the museum next door. I paused frequently near the dusty cases and exhibits to answer more questions and pose for pictures. I made many witty remarks. It was a much more satisfactory encounter than the unhappy scene in the hall.

My questioners, most of them young, were literate, curious and enthusiastic about getting the story. I must admit their facial tattoos and designs distracted me. I found myself enunciating more clearly than I needed to, as if the tattoos would interfere with their ability to comprehend standard language. In fact, their pronunciation was clear as air, if a trifle old-fashioned.

"I see, sir," one earnest teenager decorated in multicolored animal patterns said, "but at no time until recently was a direct message from your government received."

"Yes, well," I was a little tired of answering *that* question. "I can only speak for the emperor who sent me. He wants to correct the wrongs of the past..."

"They're following us," Oskelev whispered, as my teenaged inquisitor made way for another reporter.

"Well, I certainly hope so," I said, waving and smiling at the visitors who crowded into the museum through the front entrance and joined my throng. "We are here to be seen."

"No, those bare-faced ones. Check your pad. They're in red."

With a charming bow to my audience for my moment's inattention, I glanced at my viewpad at an overview of the large gallery in which I stood. I pretended to examine an ancient thruster assembly on a platform as I ascertained that Oskelev's chart was correct. The plain-faced guards had indeed come along with us. They were gathered at both exits. The First Councillor looked startled, then pursed her lips firmly.

"It means nothing until they attempt to interfere with our progress," I muttered. I turned ot the crowd and picked out an insectoid reporter with chrysanthemums etched on both cheeks. "My good... Cocomon! I believe that you were the next one with a question."

"I would like to pose for an image with you," the blue insectoid replied, his mandibles clattering with excitement.

"Gladly," I exclaimed, holding out an arm. He or she—I was not yet adept at recognizing the genders—came to stand beside me and the bit of wreckage.

My hostess's own pocket secretary buzzed, and she consulted it. Her cheeks under the blue skin art reddened, but she put it away without replying.

"Should you reply?" I asked. "If you please."

"Oh, no," the First Councillor said, with a brave smile. "It is nothing important."

She continued to encourage me to speak to various people who approached or buzzed me on my viewpad. One of her fellow officials, Councillor Six, a tall young man almost as au courant to fashion as I was, sidled through the crowd to join us, chivvied by his guard. Six bent his head to consult with her. They exchanged a flurry of words, the only phrase of which I could hear was "not encouraging him." Madam DeKarn withdrew, her cheeks pink.

"It is kind of you to be concerned," she told Six.

"I am not concerned only for him, but for you," he whispered hotly.

I was no fool. I had figured out the large Trade Union personnel were handlers, not guards. This place was under siege. I knew the affection for Sgarthad was in a large part feigned, but they were too afraid to admit it. I was in a position to give them an alternative to love, even if I no longer had my pictures of the emperor. After all, I had history on my side, not fear. I was well-protected, and I could take care of myself. My position in the royal family caused people to underestimate me. That worked to my advantage. I would not, however, endanger anyone else in my pursuit of information.

I bowed to the councillor. "Thank you so much for guiding me today," I said. "Perhaps you would like to retire? I can go on by myself. I know how to return to my ship."

"Oh, no," Madam DeKarn said. She squeezed the tall man's wrist. "I will be careful," she said. Looking doubtful, the younger councillor retired. I could tell that he and his minder were unsatisfied.

We moved from one gallery to another. The cloud of small cameras increased in size, as did the crowd around us. The docents stationed in each room looked worried at the mass of beings migrating through as though we were a herd of gnus. I smiled at each to put them at their ease. They returned the expression faintly. Thus far, my questioners had shown respect and patience with me and one another. Madam DeKarn guided me toward a glass-sided pressure lift.

"The next level up has displays of our most famous exports," she said.

"I can't wait to see them," I assured her courteously.

"Hey, watch out!"

A couple of large louts in coveralls pushed by me, almost sending me flying into a diorama. Nesbitt caught me before I struck it.

"You okay?"

"I am," I assured him. I frowned. My assailants had seen me clearly, but they behaved poorly nonetheless. Not even the habitués of the wharf pubs in Taino ever took direct physical action. I realized with a start that they lacked tattoos. More Trade Union staff. I set my jaw. They would not distract me from my errand.

The councillor seemed to be more frightened than ever, but she kept going as gamely as if we were off for a picnic. She beckoned a stout, tawny-skinned woman forward.

"Lord Thomas," she said, "please allow me to introduce Srikai Mseda, a frequent broadcaster on the main Grid news feed."

Mseda marched toward me, hand out, with an

ambitious and purposeful gait. "Lord Thomas, this is a pleasure."

I beamed. "Thank you. What would you like to know?"

"You're not just here as an observer, are you?" she asked. "I mean, the emperor has plenty of diplomats. Why send a cousin?"

A good question. I bowed to her. "To let you know he is serious about hearing your concerns," I said. "Forgive me if I repeat myself. I am sure I have said the same thing in the last two or three hours?"

Mseda checked her personal communications unit. "Three times. Why should we believe it now?"

"Well, how many official visitors have you had from the Imperium?"

"Counting you, one," Mseda said. "There was a rumor of another visitor, but we never saw her. Do you have any comment on that, Councillor?"

I had the feeling DeKarn was waiting for such a question. The silver-haired woman steeled her spine, but favored Mseda with a warm smile. "The Imperium ambassa—"

In between syllables, Madam DeKarn's eyes rolled up, and she collapsed. Mseda and I caught her as she was falling and set her on the ground. I clutched Madam DeKarn's hand, feeling for a pulse.

"Call for emergency medical transport!" Nesbitt bellowed. Mseda tapped the center of her device's screen, which lit up red for emergency.

Oskelev dropped to her knees at DeKarn's other side. "I have first-responder training," she said. She listened to the councillor's chest and lifted her eyelids. "She ought to be okay in a minute, folks," she said.

DeKarn's eyes fluttered open. She looked up at me and grabbed my arm. Mseda leaned over her, viewpad at the ready.

"Give the lady her dignity," I said sweetly.

Looking chagrined, the reporter put the device into her belt pouch. DeKarn murmured something. I leaned close to hear.

"Don't let them," Madam DeKarn whispered.

"Let them what?" I whispered back.

The councillor's coarse-faced guard tried to push me back, but Nesbitt elbowed him. "Back off, friend."

Oskelev opened the first aid parcel hanging from the harness at her hip and ran the small white medical scanner over her.

"She's got something in her body," the Wichu said. "Two somethings."

"Health chip," Mseda said. "We all have them."

The Wichu fingerspelled something over the screen of her viewpad. I glanced at mine to see what she had said. *She's been drugged.* I nodded. The second device might have been implanted by the intruders.

By then, several of the untattooed guards had surrounded us. I had no doubt that they were the "them" to whom Madam DeKarn referred. I determined not to allow them to take her from me. I had witnesses. I would make use of them.

"Can you stand?" I asked the councillor. She nodded. I assisted her to her feet. "Please allow me to take you home. Redius," I said aloud, knowing he was monitoring me. "Closest entrance to my position."

"There in moments," the Uctu declared.

I smiled at my audience. "Will you excuse us? A medical emergency. This lady needs to return to her home."

The crowd murmured in the affirmative. I put my arm around the councillor's waist. I felt her trembling.

A green light suddenly struck me in the face. Crosshatching ran down from brow to chin.

"What is that?" I demanded, holding up my free hand against the hot glare.

"Back!" The lights hit Nesbitt. He thrust his gun toward the crowd, which recoiled. Oskelev leaped for the being holding the device, a thirty-year-old human in gray coveralls. He spun and ran. The Wichu went in pursuit, shouldering aside onlookers. Soon, she returned.

"I lost him, sir," she said. She held up her view-pad. "Got a picture, though. I'll know him next time. Lieutenant, do you want to cross-reference with the population records?"

"Scanning now," Plet's voice said in my ear. "Trade Union, sir."

"By Forn, could they be any more obvious?" I protested.

Oskelev and Nesbitt helped me escort Madam DeKarn toward the doorway. Sgarthad loomed suddenly before us. His expression was one I could not easily read. He studied me curiously as if he had not seen me before and did not like what he beheld.

"Hello, Captain," I said cheerfully, maneuvering to pass him. "The First Councillor has been taken ill. Will you excuse us?"

His expression changed instantly from fierce speculation to solicitousness. The stage had lost a fine artiste when he had chosen to go into commerce.

"I am so sorry to hear that!" he boomed. He beckoned to Madam DeKarn's minder, who bustled up to join us. "Wikely, make sure the emperor's envoy finds his way to the lady's home."

There was no way to avoid the additional company. Redius sat beside the local driver of our borrowed transport through the busy streets. Behind and above our vehicle, numerous private cars and air-vehicles trailed, their occupants still looking for the story.

"I hate this," Nesbitt said, riding backwards to keep an eye on them. "At least the traffic robots keep them from driving up beside us." As we passed into the residential district, the air vehicles were forced to turn back unless they had permits for the area. Fortunately, none of them seemed to.

I kept our guest's mind occupied all the way to her quarters, telling her amusing anecdotes and jokes, chosen from the mental chapters of Stories I Would Feel Safe Telling My Aunts. After a few kilometers of constantly glancing behind her and at her guard, she began to relax, and even rewarded me with a soft chuckle. I could tell that in better times she would be an excellent audience. As we rounded the corner past a busy multi-story complex with shops in the ground floor level, she pointed to the third in a long row of tall, narrow detached residences.

"There, if you please."

I hopped out of the skimmer before her guard could alight, and held out my arm to her. She stepped cautiously onto the pavement. Wikely crowded up behind us, no doubt seeking to overhear any confidences we might pass between us, but neither of us spoke.

The high, semi-opaque panel door slid open hollowly. Madam DeKarn passed inside. I glanced past her. The chambers seemed oddly dusty for such a fastidious woman. An elderly, fluffy white cat trotted up and rubbed against her legs. She stooped to pick it up and buried her face in its fur.

"Thank you," she said, her voice thick. "I will be all right now."

"Are you certain?" I asked, concerned. "I can leave Oskelev with you to make sure you don't have a... relapse."

"Oh, yes," she assured me. She fixed her eyes on my face in a significant fashion. "Spending this afternoon with you has done me a world of good." She passed inside. Wikely marched in after her and shut the door firmly in my face. I was thoughtful on the way back to our ship.

"Have you found anything about the Trade Union's motives?" I asked Lt. Plet the moment we were safely back inside the *CK-M945B* (Redius was right—I did have to give the ship a proper name).

Plet slid her hand along the control on the side of her console. "I tapped into the minutes of the council chamber and saw the captain's arrival. If it's a hostile takeover, it's the friendliest usurpation I ever saw, but it is still inexplicable. After that meeting, no official reading of the minutes has been done, and that's odd for this group. They talk. They don't get anything done, but they talk. You should see the dull material that is recorded and referenced over and over again."

"We are only here to observe, Lieutenant," I said, stiffly. "That is something we have observed. Make a copy for the emperor."

"I have, sir."

"And a discreet backup or two."

Plet looked long-suffering. "Already done, sir."

"By Forn," I said, agog with admiration. "it's like having a younger version of Parsons at hand. You will go far."

"Thank you, sir." She sounded pleased. A slight crease in the smooth brow denoted the puzzlement beneath, as she must wonder how far and in what direction I thought. I smiled. As I was ascending to a higher plane, there must also be supplementary replacements for such unique assets as Parsons. I would do a service to the espionage wing of the government to put them onto the existence of a mind like Plet's, if Parsons had not done so already. Though she did not have his imagination, her powers of analysis and her efficiency were to be treasured. And Anstruther, too. I beamed at my companions.

"Thank you all," I said. "I am privileged to have such accomplished friends."

"We're proud, too, sir," Anstruther said, blushing.

"What was that light that hit Thomas, Lieutenant?" Oskelev asked, getting back to business.

"It was a kind of topographical measuring device," Plet replied. "The purpose at present can only be surmised."

"Do they think you're some kind of impostor?"

"Him?" Nesbitt asked. "Why?"

"My Infogrid file is an open book," I protested. "I am afraid it might be more sinister than that."

"Like what?" Anstruther asked.

"I abhor melodrama, but several scenarios suggest themselves," I said, hating the possibilities, but I ticked them off on my fingers. "Am I to disappear, and messages be sent back home saying that I loved the Cluster too much to leave? Will transmissions of me stating that I abandon the notion of reunification with the Imperium and embrace the concept of the Trade Union taking over in the Cluster be broadcast across their Grid and our Infogrid?"

The young ensign was aghast. "Well, we'd say that wasn't true."

I gave her a sympathetic look.

"Means he, we will not be around to contradict, either," Redius said. She looked shocked. "Refer to Commander Parsons, when returns."

"I say step up security," Nesbitt said. "No more going out in crowds, Thomas. No telling if those cameras bouncing around in your face are bombs or lasers."

"No," I declared. "If Councillor DeKarn was brave enough to risk her life to put me before the people to give them an honest choice, I could not be less courageous in promoting the interests of my emperor. But I will not involve her further. It appears that the charismatic captain already sent her more than one warning. My brief is to observe, so observe I shall. I will go out alone—under protection, naturally—and continue."

The others burst out with their protests, but I was adamant. To my delight, Parsons agreed with me on his return.

"Lord Thomas is entirely in the spirit of his assignment," he assured my reluctant staff. "He should continue, if he can." As he outranked them all, his word was law.

For the next sixday, I brought my case directly to the people of Boske. I answered questions freely for whomever asked them. I might have been a hopeful candidate, for the number of pictures I posed for, babies

kissed, speeches given and stores opened. I started to
recognize some of my querents by sight and addressed
them by name without prompting from Plet or my viewpad. Such retention, well-honed at a thousand family
banquets, brought acclaim from reporters and beings
on the street in the myriad Grid articles and opinion
pieces. I made Anstruther collect all she could find of
my appearances for my scrapbook. (I suspected she was
keeping a copy for herself as well. I didn't protest. A
success for me was a success for us all.)

I also listened closely to my new acquaintances.
I saw how they behaved when I asked questions in
return, especially about my rival for their attentions.
My assessment had been correct: they adored Sgarthad,
but were uncomfortable about the Trade Union making itself so at home in the Cluster, having all their
spacecraft grounded and communications truncated.

"If it hadn't been his idea," more than one person
told me, "I'd never say yes. But since it's *him*...."

In spite of the growing friendliness of the people,
Nesbitt, Oskelev and Redius carried their arms more
openly. The crowds grew by the day, making my
bodyguards nervous. As I was there to be seen, as I
had told Oskelev, I made it a point to venture out
whenever I could. I found people waiting for me when
I emerged in the morning. I was followed, but not
only by reporters and well-wishers. The Trade Union
made it clear that I was there only by their suffer-
ance. I steeled myself for worse. But what could be
worse than losing my spit-take?

The people of Pthohannix grew used to my presence, even welcoming it. I bent myself to winning

them over as many at a time as I could. After several days of increasing public approval, I was greeted upon my debarkation from our ship with cheers. I waved to the audience, and took a bow. Knowing that their reaction came from a combination of genetic imperative and novelty, I did not take it seriously, but that didn't keep me from enjoying it. I accepted invitations from anyone who asked me except the Castaway Cluster council. I refused to draw more fire upon those whom I knew to be openly unhappy with the status quo. Let Sgarthad and his minions take pot shots at me, not at my hosts. They obviously risked much to have me do what I do.

Leaving those out, I did not lack for face time with my public. Invitations poured in. I accepted them cheerfully, and fulfilled my obligations as any good guest might. My staff was welcomed almost as much as I. Parsons accompanied us to these events once in a while, but he disappeared more and more frequently. He assured us that his investigations were bearing fruit, which he would share when it became appropriate. The less I knew about it, the less it would be in my mind as I was out in the public. Only Plet and perhaps Anstruther had any idea where he was going on those days.

For all my reputation at home, I was not reckless. I stayed only in very public locations, made certain I had an exit handy, and that I was never alone while out. In spite of the incipient danger, I began to enjoy myself.

"You are nuts," Oskelev said. "You're acting like it was a play."

"It *is* a drama," I said. "I am not even the main

player, but I will not be bumped offstage early. Not without seeing from which direction the blow falls."

"What about it, Commander?" Oskelev asked Parsons. "Make him take watch out for himself. He's playing a dangerous game."

Parsons regarded me benevolently. "He is doing precisely as the emperor would wish."

I was grateful to him. I had misgivings and fears, but I knew I was doing the right thing.

✳ CHAPTER 31 ✳

On the morning of the fourth day of our second sixday on Boske, I popped onto the bridge of the ship in my dressing gown. The others, already hard at work over their screens, gave me a curious look.

"Forgive my state of undress," I said, modestly. "Where are the clothes from the cleaner?"

Anstruther pointed toward a locker near the hatch. "In there, sir. I mean, Thomas."

I flipped open the metal lid and rummaged through it, turning over piles of fresh-smelling uniforms, underthings and dress attire, but the terracotta fabric I sought was not among the garments therein. I turned everything over twice, growing more frustrated by the moment. I groaned.

"Do you seek something in particular, my lord?" Parsons asked, appearing at my elbow like a genie.

"We are invited to the children's art college today, Parsons," I said, making yet another search. "I want to wear my Taino tunic. I turned everything in my cabin over looking for it, but it is not there." Plet and

Anstruther exchanged glances. "That expression bodes significant. What has happened to it?"

Parsons took responsibility for replying. "I am sorry to inform you, my lord, that the Taino tunic has fallen apart."

I was devastated. "What? That was my favorite jacket! How?"

"It seems that the chemical used to cleanse fabrics on this world is incompatible with the artificial thread used to stitch together your tunic. It dissolved. The component parts are no longer united, sir."

Did he look pleased about it? I couldn't tell. "Well, can't we find a tailor to reassemble it?"

"I am afraid that the remaining portions are in sufficiently poor repair to make such an attempt risky, my lord. As the coat was made specifically for you, you might have to return several times to the shop for fittings, and that would draw a good deal of attention. I would not want to make a local sempster responsible for failure, sir. It would reflect ill upon a local merchant if he was not able to rebuild the garment to your specifications, and to you for having them."

"Oh," I said, resignedly. I'd have to visit the designer who had made it when I returned to Keinolt. "Well, I have plenty of clothes. I'll go find something. I also have a coat that represents the Kinago residence. That should go over well."

Parsons's expression steeled me for futher bad news.

"I regret to say that has suffered the same fate as the Taino coat."

"What?" I felt as though I had been stabbed to the heart. "But I have only worn it once!"

"May I suggest this suit, Lord Thomas?" Parsons asked, whisking a folded pile of midnight-blue cloth from behind his back like a conjuring trick. It was a formal suit of clothes, one that would not be out of place on a receiving line.

"How boring," I said, with a sigh. "I suppose it will do." I regarded his own costume, one of a self-effacing brown tunic with casual beige trousers. "You're not wearing that to the show!"

"I am not accompanying you, sir," Parsons said. "Today I am bound in a different direction."

I raised an eyebrow. "May I ask where?"

"My hope is to locate Ambassador Ben."

My heart raced. "She's here on Boske? You're sure? I thought there was no mention of her on the Grid."

"All references to her might have been purged, a lot of them ineptly, in my opinion," Lt. Plet said, looking pleased with herself, "but they didn't do anything about this." She waved a hand across her screen, which opened upon a continental map. Like those of us in the Imperium, the Grid included images constantly updated from satellites circling the stout waist of the planet. At a flick of her finger, the image zoomed in at dizzying speed until we could see streets, bridges and buildings. At the crosshairs in the center was a large field full of space ships. About half were in pieces, no doubt cannibalized for parts, but at one end were the entire recipients for those parts. The crosshairs moseyed about a bit until they lit on a small vessel.

"That looks rather like the *CK-M945B*," I remarked. I peered closer. "In fact, it is the same model of Nexus XV. Well done! How did you find it?"

"Computer modeling of all types of vessels used

by the diplomatic service," Plet said. I confessed she deserved to look smug. "It took a while because it's not on this continent. They were smart enough to move it, but they didn't change its configuration. All I had to do was match it and keep looking."

"So where is Madam Ben?" I asked. "Near the ship?"

"Too much chance of discovery. The chances are approximately sixty percent that the missing ambassador is in the habitations of the intruders here in this city-state, in the center of government," Parsons intoned. "They could not possibly make the transit from orbit every morning, therefore they live on the surface. The modern flitters they use, so different from the heavy ground vehicles operated by the locals, suggest the habitations cannot be far. Therefore, it behooves me to investigate. I would also like to find the shuttle that they do use when they visit their vessel, and link into the computer system. We need data. Lieutenant Plet and Ensign Anstruther will monitor both of us from here."

"And the other possible forty percent of the location of the ambassador?" I pressed.

"Divided between locations including the Trade Union mother ship, an offsite location, or an unmarked grave, sir," Parsons said. I gulped.

"Let us hope it is not the last named, Parsons," I said soberly. "May I come along? I can help. I will back out on the visit to the school."

Parsons set his eye upon me. I squirmed under its pressure. "My lord, you are the chief means of preventing the captain and his minions from paying too much attention to my absence."

I was abashed. "Ah, of course. Good hunting. You

shall have to relate to us your entire adventure on your return."

"The intention is that it will not be an adventure," he said. "Pray keep attention on you, sir. It would assist me if you were a trifle more...obvious than usual."

"You may count upon me to be obvious," I said. I set the dull blue suit down firmly and went into my cabin. I rummaged through my cases until I extracted a bright scarlet jacket that I had not yet had a chance to wear. I put it on and marched back onto the bridge. The others almost recoiled at first. "There. Isn't that marvelous? I picked it up at a resort on Leo's Star."

"But, sir..." Parsons began. "It is nearly incandescent."

"Ah, ah, ah," I said, with a waggle of my forefinger. "You are most excellent at going undetected. My talents lie in the opposite direction. You want me to keep all focus upon me. Red cannot help but draw the eye. And look at that fit!" I called the Optique to take a quick 360° image of me. I checked my rear elevation in the viewpad's screen. "Sartorially splendid!"

"He's got you there, Commander," Oskelev said, showing her teeth. "Either you want him to attract attention or you don't."

For once, Parsons was at a loss for words. I felt I had stolen a rare march on my mentor. He said nothing more. I added a jaunty scarf at the neck of the gaudy jacket, tucked my viewpad into an inner pocket, and presented myself at the head of the ship's ramp. A cheer went up from my waiting public. I raised my hand in greeting.

Parsons slipped away into the crowd. I never saw him go.

❖   ❖   ❖

The schoolchildren performed as well as one can expect young and marginally talented children to do. As the last one bowed her way off the stage and ducked behind the arching, polished wood proscenium, I added my applause to the heartfelt acclaim from the host of parents on hand. We all sat on tiny chairs, but the discomfort was minor considering the importance of supporting the arts.

For once, the opinion reporters were absent. Instead, at the lemonade and cookies reception that followed the performance, I was swarmed by student reporters, few of which stood higher than my waist. No question was too unimportant, no questioner too small. After all, these children were the future of the Imperium.

"Mr. Kinago!" they shouted. "Me, first! No, me! I want to know!"

"One at a time," I ordered, but it was no use. They had no more decorum than any other reporters. They demanded copies of pictures from my cameras and shared theirs with me. The event was a great success on all fronts. Swaying the Boskians, even young ones, to my point of view took little effort. They wanted to go along with me, I could tell. They craved the Imperium's involvement and protection.

At last, I excused myself. Redius and Anstruther flanked me as I slipped out into the tile-floored hallway toward the rear, where our vehicle waited in the teachers' facility. The yellow-painted metal door at the end would open only to a code the administrator had given me.

"Restday," I murmured to myself, entering it into

the lock panel. Nothing happened, but I heard sounds of activity on the other side.

"Warm bodies coming your way," Oskelev said. She was monitoring us from the ship.

"Health chips?" asked Anstruther.

"Nope. Probably Trade Union."

"We don't wish to meet them," I said. "Back to the classroom."

At a casual forced-march, we scurried up the hallway again. Behind us, I heard the wrench of metal being pried open. I glanced back in an offhanded fashion to see half a dozen men in Cluster uniforms. They looked awkward in their false tattoos. I gave them a blithe wave as we marched out of the front door and into a waiting crowd who clamored as soon as they saw me. Reporters' cameras came swooping down like flies to a jam jar, followed swiftly by their owners, all shouting over one another.

"I have never before found safety in numbers to be as true as in this place," I said under my breath to my companions. I beamed at my adult public. "Now, who has the first question?"

Parsons strode toward the underground light rail station, having ascertained its coordinates from the on-Grid city map. The location of the quarters occupied by the intruders had also been bookmarked, by protesters who objected to their presence on the homeworld. It was a trifle surprising that the indicators had not been removed by Sgarthad's people, but it marked the arrogance that Parsons had observed in the invaders. It made the first part of his task simple. The subsequent portions would be less so. The missing ambassador was unlikely to be in or immediately adjacent to the habitation. Nor would it be easy to break encoding on the Trade Union computers, but it was vital to obtain as much information on their motives as possible. His studies of the last few days had borne some fruit, but not enough. Sgarthad was careful not to allow access to his databases from casual perusal from any point on Boske.

Parsons descended the stairs. His dull-colored painted tattoos and nondescript suit of clothes caused the casual onlooker's eye to skip off for more interesting sights. He also carried a workman's overalls in a briefcase, in case he needed to coax his way past nosy neighbors or guards left behind. The enormous orbiting ship had only a skeleton crew on board, Ensign Anstruther had discovered on scanning from space and listening to their transmissions. Such data were lost on Lord Thomas and the young staff accompanying him. It indicated that much of the ship's complement had been deployed to other duties since its arrival, for example, the spotter that had detected the Imperium scout inbound when they emerged near the transponder beacon station at the west periphery of the black hole before making the final jump to Portent's Star. The six guard ships that had escorted them from the heliopause and been on patrol in that quadrant and converged on the news of their arrival had undoubtedly also been conveyed from the Trade Union in the belly of the *Marketmaker*. All very well thought out and organized. The Trade Union was making itself at home, but the number of ships did not suggest an occupying force. Most curious. He hoped his correspondent had more information.

He paid for a ticket and went to stand on the platform. Only a few commuters were present at that hour. A train rushed almost noiselessly into the station along the stone trench in the floor. The car, brightly lit with narrow bench seats, nearest him was empty. As he was about to board it, a hard object pressed itself against his kidney.

"Into the tunnel," a hoarse voice whispered.

He started to turn to look, but his assailant's other forearm flattened against his shoulders and the back of his head, preventing them from moving. Parsons realized there must be no security cameras in the station. He moved toward the dark arch at the end of the platform. The train rushed away in the opposite direction. No assistance would come from it or the patrons who were already ascending the stairs thirty meters away.

No matter. He was more than capable of defending himself. As soon as they passed into the gloom, Parsons stepped backwards with one foot, catching his opponent behind the heel with his toe. Instead of falling, the man stepped forward on that foot between Parsons's legs and shoved his head down, pressing the hard object to Parsons's temple. Parsons countered by crossing his wrists and knocking upward under the other man's hand. The object, a tapered silver cylinder with a black plastic handle, went skidding over the stone floor. It was a tranquilizer gun, of a type used by veterinarians. The man's objectives must be capture and interrogation. Parsons crouched, hands in defensive array. The other, a slender man in his twenties with scarlet and gold tattoos, assumed the same pose. Parsons sprang at his would-be captor. He must disable him or render him unconscious as quickly as possible. The man jumped at him. He aimed a flat-handed strike at Parsons, aiming for the shoulder. Parsons slipped nimbly to the right. He angled his palm upward for the man's solar plexus. The man dodged. His long face crumpled with pain, but he went for simultaneous arm and leg sweeps. Parsons caught the arm and turned to throw his opponent. The man rolled over Parsons's back and landed on his feet, hands crooked into claws. They exchanged a flurry of blows, each countering the other expertly. Parsons tilted his head to the left, narrowly avoiding an incapacitating strike. He flung himself backwards, took a breath, and prepared to wade in again. His opponent regarded him with shock.

"Who sent you?" the young man demanded.

"I am a visitor," Parsons said, in aggrieved and innocent tones. "Why have you assaulted me?"

"But those moves! You were trained in the same unarmed combat as I was. Do you know...Mr. Frank?"

Parsons allowed a tiny smile to touch his lips. He straightened and tugged down the hem of his tunic. He activated the small gray device in his pocket. No one else would hear them now. "I believe you sent him a message."

The young man relaxed and stood at his gangly-limbed ease. "I did, as it happened. Please, how may I help?"

Sgarthad intercepted me in the marketplace, where I was giving an interview to a gruff old gentleman in dusty robes and peaked eyebrows. DeKarn had assured me that he was one of the important opinionmakers, and was not easily swayed by words. When the old gentleman bowed suddenly, I spun to find my nemesis at my shoulder.

"How nice to find you here, my lord," Sgarthad said. "Busy day?"

"Busy but enjoyable," I assured him. I took in his escort, five men and women in ochre-colored uniforms and faces like blobs of dough. Was everyone in the Trade Union ugly but Sgarthad?

The captain took my arm. "Come have lunch with me. I would relish a chance to get to know you better. May I offer you a tour of the city?"

"I've already had several," I said, apologetically. The man's assumption of authority annoyed me. "Civic groups and so on."

He raised a tapering eyebrow. "Ah. Perhaps I can tempt you with a tour of the *Marketmaker*. It's the very latest model of long-range merchant ship. We always say we can pack a small moon on board."

"I'd enjoy that," I said, politely though privately I would enjoy it more without him. "But another day. I have an appointment to attend a gallery opening."

"Then let us have lunch and I will escort you there," Sgarthad boomed, slapping me on the back. "I know a fine little place. They always reserve the best table for me and my friends!" I winced. I found him overbearing and blowhardish. If sales required any subtlety, he would have been a failure.

Sgarthad escorted me into his open-topped vehicle, driven by a shovel-faced brute whose collar barely fastened around his thick neck. The captain and I stood on a platform in the rear.

"So the public can see us better," he said.

Looking very uneasy about the arrangement, my staff

followed in our car. Redius sat beside the driver. Nesbitt and Oskelev were behind him, weapons unlocked but kept in their laps.

We pulled away from the marketplace, turned right and out onto the main boulevard. A crowd with banners to wave already lined the long, wide street. I suspect that Sgarthad had set up this demonstration to show me how well-liked and accepted he was. In fact, he had considerable numbers of fans. Most of the people lined up on the curb seemed sincere as they shouted and waved to him.

"Sgarthad!" they cried. One woman held up a baby and made it wave to him. Sgarthad, grinning boyishly, accepted it as his due. Then, the crowd saw me.

The cheers for the captain died away, as they looked from one of us to the other. Then the shouts went up again.

"Kinago! Kinago! Kinago!"

"Lord Thomas!"

"Hurray for the Imperium!"

"Lord Thomas!"

"They got my name from the Grid," I said, with creditable self-deprecation. Sgarthad did not like it, I could tell. I offered an apology. "It is only because I am a novelty. We bare-faced ones. There are so few of us that they can't help but notice. Listen, they are calling your name as well."

"Yes," Sgarthad growled. From then on he continued to wave, but his expression was sulky. I took up the slack, smiling and waving to a steadily increasing throng. Sgarthad moved away from me and activated his communications link. I ostentatiously gave him privacy, but my staff was on alert.

"Thomas, can you hear me?" Anstruther's voice said in my ear. "I'm monitoring a call from your location. You're in danger. They've got something going, and you're the target."

"I doubt it," I said, blowing a kiss to a young woman jumping up and down on the curb. "They wouldn't dare touch me. I am the emperor's cousin! They haven't shown much concern for the Imperium. He blasted me off the stage at my speech. What could he do to me out here in public?"

❦ CHAPTER 32 ❦

"They held me in one of these cells for a while, but as it turns out they aren't too observant," Colm Banayere explained. "I used Covert Service training to get out one night. I have a college friend who's down on his luck. We're about the same height and coloring. They can't tell one set of tattoos from another. He's been occupying my place, eating the food and wearing the clothes they leave for me. I'd find it boring, but he's happy. He gets to spend all his time playing console games, leaving me free to investigate. I have been monitoring off-world communications. I was so relieved when your ship arrived. I have been following your group for days waiting for an opportunity to get one of you alone. It hasn't been easy, until I discovered you are the only one who goes out by himself. I took it as an indication you were my contact."

"That is by design," Parsons said, pleased by the young man's perspicacity. "I need to locate Ambassador Hiranna Ben, who departed from the Core Worlds months ago for this system. Do you know where she is?"

"Six cells down from mine," Banayere said promptly. "And there are more prisoners. My employer, the First Councillor, was one of them. They were only let out the morning you arrived. Because you came."

Parsons put his overalls on and followed the young man through the sparsely populated streets to an industrial storage facility in a warehouse district. The youth noticed Parsons looking up as they entered. "Oh, don't worry about security cameras. I triggered them to loop on empty space. Everyone else is following your people around. I have the loop timed to end at shift change. They hardly ever look at the prisoners in between."

"That is perceptive of you," Parsons said.

"That's my job," Banayere said cheerfully. "Here she is."

As Parsons stood guard, the young man donned a plastic glove and held it to the panel beside one of the steel doors. When it slid back, a small, plump woman rose from a steel chair at a desk in alarm.

"Pray calm yourself, madam," Parsons said. "I am a representative of the emperor."

Ambassador Ben held herself erect for a moment, then threw herself into his arms and sobbed.

"The council was about to lift the isolation order and let me present my case to the people, but Captain Sgarthad's traders got to me first," Ambassador Ben said, dabbing her eyes with a handkerchief supplied by Parsons. "I have been in here for months without outside contact. I cannot confirm the length of time, because there is no clock or calendar. I am ready to face my opponents. Anything is better than being closed up here without even a documentary program. I already speak Wichu."

"At the moment, it is safer for you here than outside," Parsons said.

Ambassador Ben looked dismayed. "Commander, I am accustomed to being alone for long stretches, but this is undoubtedly the most boring time I have ever spent."

Banayere smiled. "I can adjust your console so you get all the Grid feeds, madam," he said. "I did it for my employer, Councillor DeKarn, while she was locked up here."

She smiled at him. "That will be sufficient, then. How is my friend?

"She is well, though frightened and worried," Colm told her. "I have been keeping an eye on her."

"You are Colm, aren't you?" Ambassador Ben said, patting him on the cheek. "Leese told me how much she prizes you."

The young man actually blushed under his tattoos. He bent underneath the console to hide his face. Parsons was amused.

"I shall return for you before we lift ship for home, Ambassador," Parsons said. "I will keep you apprised of events."

"Very well," she said. "I will await you eagerly."

Banayere emerged from below the desk. Ambassador Ben settled herself with dignity at the screen. It lit up with a blare of music and graphics showing parades, children on horseback, a Cocomon in flight on filmy wings, and serious-looking adults in robes. "This is the hourly Grid report," a deep male voice stated. Hiranna Ben let out a happy sigh of contentment.

She was engaged in the program before the two men closed and locked the door behind them.

"What else can I do to help?" the young man asked, as Parsons led him on a swift march out of the warehouse.

"I require information from the *Marketmaker*'s databases," Parsons said.

Banayere grimaced. "Sorry, sir. I found an interface, but I haven't been able to break their encryption. I just don't have the tools or training."

Parsons smiled. "Then we may complement one another, Mr. Banayere," he said.

We never reached the restaurant. I found my host's behavior increasingly strange as we rode through the streets of Pthohannix. The crowds had increased in size as had their shouts of acclaim for me. Sgarthad wore an expression of pique mixed with smug anticipation. That was, I reflected, a lot to expect from any face, even one as pleasing to behold as his.

At the intersection of the large avenue with an industrial road, Sgarthad's driver took a sharp left across several lanes. People who had risked life and limb walking along beside us in traffic were left forlornly behind. They made their way to the curb, accompanied by loud hoots from the cars and trains in the stone rail trenches. My staff's car was left behind in the scramble of vehicles.

"Curses to him," Redius's voice said in my ear. "Will follow as possible. Maintain transmission!"

"Where are we going?" I asked pleasantly. Any reply would be heard by my staff.

"To our shuttle," Sgarthad said, with a mischievous grin. "I didn't want all of those people coming along with us. It was cruel, but they will forgive us. You wanted to see my ship. I can give you a brief tour before your next appointment."

"That is very kind of you," I said.

"Not at all," Sgarthad declared, sitting down. He took hold of my arm and pulled. I sprawled in the corner seat. "The road is bumpy here. Take care."

The neighborhood we had entered was an industrial complex. The air was filled with the sharp, unpleasant smells of lubricant oil, trash and sewage. From a crowd of thousands, the local population was reduced to a few dozen drivers of heavy goods vehicles and living beings overseeing the loading thereof. As we passed, they looked up and waved or cheered, then went back to their jobs.

I glanced over my shoulder. Our car bounded into view. Redius had taken the controls away from the driver and had followed us. It was flanked by three cars containing Trade Union personnel.

"Sir," Parsons said in a low murmur. "Can you hear me? This is a secure channel."

"Go on as you can," I said.

"What?" Sgarthad said.

"I trust your driver," I said, with a vacant grin. Sgarthad frowned at me.

"You are with the captain, sir? Then it is vital that you listen to me carefully."

"So what is it like to run a merchant vessel for the Trade Union?" I asked Sgarthad, fixing my eyes on him. "Tell me all. When did you get your first commission?"

The captain looked pleased, as if he had managed to fool me into not believing I was being abducted.

"I was sixteen when I entered the Merchant Marine," he began. I nodded and smiled at intervals, fixing my ears upon Parsons's voice.

"I have sent a data-gathering probe into the database of the *Marketmaker*, sir. As you may know, they maintain a system analogous to our Infogrid, or the Cluster's Grid." I nodded to myself. Such commonalities always proved to me that beings across the galaxy were far more similar than different, regardless of species. "I have unlocked Emile Sgarthad's file. He descends from a scion of Imperium nobles who moved to the Trade Union four generations ago. I have cross-referenced the name of his ancestors. They left out of disdain for the Empress of the time and took new names. Sgarthad is, in fact, of the Melies clan, sir. He is a fourth cousin of Lord Xanson. That is why he resembles him so closely. He rose rapidly through the ranks due to his driving intelligence and inexplicable charm. He volunteered for this task, to chip away at the Imperium's territory, beginning with an outpost that is already isolated."

"Do you mean . . . ?" I began, stunned.

"Making money?" Sgarthad asked, with a fierce grin. "Of course. Money is power. I learned long ago . . ."

Parsons picked up on my opening. "I do, sir. You understand the implication. He must be stopped. The genetic imperative is less effective in the Trade Union, but it is inexorable here. He knows what he is doing. I will inform your staff as to what they need to know, without the confidential family information."

I was taken aback, but could not look as if I knew. I sat, digesting what I had just heard, balancing it against what I had seen over the last many days.

So that measuring thing he used on me was an information-seeking device. Sgarthad was looking for the correct symmetry to see if I was like him, and verified it. That thug *knew*. The secret about my family that went back millennia, in the hands of our greatest enemy? I felt violated and concerned. I was to disappear. Everyone would think that I went to see the Trade Union ship. Only after I had been gone a while would anyone question my absence. He would have full sway over the people again. Not mine, of course. They were trained. But they were outnumbered. And so was I.

I don't know why it took me so long to realize I was being abducted, possibly because of the very novelty of the idea. Sgarthad was maneuvering me into a place where I and my staff could be taken in private. Not a stunner had been drawn as yet; no doubt Sgarthad thought that his charm was enough to keep me placid until it was too late. Now we had to depart before it was impossible to escape. We were in a warehouse district now. The trenches for the light rail system were wider and deeper than in other streets. The buildings were enormous, with doors the size of houses, but there were fewer people nearby than in the previous district. I could not count on help from the public.

The same was in the minds of my crew. I heard a roar. The second car caught up to us, but the other vehicles had pursued it. We were surrounded.

"Hop on board!" Redius shouted. I made as if to spring. Sgarthad caught me by the collar. One of his men moved toward me, a spray dispenser in hand. With regret, I shrugged out of my red coat and bounded into the car. Nesbitt stood up in the back and aimed his sidearm directly at the driver of the nearest car.

SPLAT! The stun charge ricocheted off the hood and into the face of the dark-skinned female driver. She swerved, hitting the trench walls, jarring three personnel off and into the street. They rolled to a halt and leaped up. The car stopped, the driver collapsed over the control panel. I coughed as we zipped through a cloud of acrid smoke from its scorched circuitry.

Bumping up over the edge of the train trench, Redius made a U-turn, and rocketed off. I crouched, holding on to the side of the vehicle with all my strength. Sgarthad glared furiously at me as we went by him. His car and the others spun to follow us, but we had a short head start.

"Sir, we're going to get you back to the ship!" Nesbitt barked.

We reached the wide boulevard. Redius cut into traffic. Oskelev and Nesbitt exchanged fire with the Trade Union soldiers. People in the streets ran screaming. Redius turned right on the next street, a narrow two-lane. He took another right, then a left. The Trade Union cars kept up with us. Pedestrians leaped to safety, tumbling onto pavements. Vehicles crashed into one another, dumping their screaming passengers to the street. I cringed in sympathy for them. The whine of pulsing engines made me look up. I saw three flitters in the distance homing in on us.

"Make some distance!" Oskelev growled.

"Not so easy," the Uctu protested. "Thomas, prepare to eject."

"What?"

"It's a good idea," Oskelev said, eyeing me anxiously.

"They'll think you are in the car. They see it, they'll chase it."

As if to confirm, a voice spoke in my ear.

"I just overheard the order to intercept and capture, sir," Anstruther said. "Four more vehicles are on the main boulevard heading toward the end of the street you're on."

A screech behind me made me jump. I looked back to see two of the Trade Union carriers cut off a small car coming out of an alley.

"Go, sir. We'll distract them," Nesbitt insisted.

"I can't leave you at their mercy," I protested.

Redius leaped the car into the oncoming lane to pass a heavy goods vehicle. He slowed down and shoved my shoulder. "Go!"

I hesitated, more concerned for them than myself.

"Run, sir," Nesbitt insisted, his craggy face earnest. "*Now*. We'll cover you. Get back to the ship."

I looked from one to another. "But what about you?"

"One thing we're best at," Oskelev said, with a fierce grin. "Fleeing and eluding the enemy. We've done it before, following you. No one will catch you, I swear by my belly fur."

"Safe you," Redius promised. "Directions to avoid TU, dictate, Anstruther."

Anstruther's voice chimed in. "I will, sir. Get going. Four more cars are on the main boulevard. Their flitters are within fifteen seconds of target area."

I crouched on the edge of the seat. When Redius swerved hard to the right, I jumped. I hit the pavement and rolled until I was in the entryway of a wine shop. Our car accelerated away. In seconds, the Trade Union vehicles followed, driving on the curb. They narrowly

missed crushing me. The flitters zipped by overhead.
As soon as I was sure they were gone, I picked myself
up and brushed myself off. My shirt and trousers had
picked up smudges from the pavement. One elbow
was torn. I sustained only a few bruises and a scrape,
but my right sleeve stank. I wrinkled my nose. I had
landed in a pool of animal urine. A woman peered at
me curiously from the other side of the street. In spite
of my discomfiture, I bowed. She smiled shyly.

"Anstruther, what's the best way back?"

"On foot, sir?"

"I must, Ensign," I said. "I can't risk public transportation, or getting into a private car with one of
Sgarthad's fans who will return me straight to him."

"I will meet you with another vehicle, sir," Parsons
interjected. "I am departing from my current location.
If we follow a common route, I will intercept you.
Do you understand, Ensign?"

"Aye, sir," Anstruther said. She began to dictate
directions.

I strode through the smaller avenues until I came
to a street market. I wove between the tents, admiring
the neat pyramids and displays of goods for sale and
smiling at the sellers and buyers. They smiled back,
some raising their pocket communicators to take my
picture. Anstruther directed me to the left, away from
the spaceport, but gradually circling in that direction.

"Parsons, they will comprehend I am heading toward
the ship," I said. "Perhaps not by what means, but
where else would I go?"

"I am examining alternatives, sir," his voice crackled
succinctly in my ear. "Please stand by."

Local denizens stopped to stare at me or run up to

take pictures. I waved and bowed to everyone I passed, until I went by a shop that sold console screens. To my shock I saw my image repeated again and again on screens of every size from enormous to miniature. My progress was being followed live on the local programs by all those amateur reporters who had access to a communication device and a Grid connection! I slunk away from the shop front, trying to look anonymous, but the crowd behind me continued to grow. There was no way to avoid it. Anyone could see me, including Captain Sgarthad. So far I had stayed ahead of the pursuers. I hoped that I could keep them guessing.

But not forever. Beside the soaring, white marble fountain half a block ahead at the next intersection, I saw uniformed, tattooless guards marching toward me, keeping an eye on their own communicators.

"Anstruther, they're ahead of me, a hundred meters," I murmured.

"Turn around, sir. I'll change the route. Commander Parsons?"

"Acknowledged."

I spun on my heel and increased my pace. Those admirers and reporters who were following me stopped short. The people behind them, eyes on me, piled into them. Some tripped and fell, cursing.

"I beg your pardon," I said to them, extending a hand to a young woman in a tight green tunic and boots. "I was just summoned by the council. Very important."

"It's all right," the woman said, smiling up at me. "We'll go with you."

Unfortunately, my throng attracted the attention of the guards. I tried to scoot between tents, but I knew my opponents could track me easily by my escort.

"One side, people!" a rough male voice cried out. "Move it!"

I heard protests and cries of outrage from the beings on the street, upset at being pushed aside. I fumed at the rudeness of the Trade Union. They could have been more courteous. Still, I did not want to meet them to discuss the matter. I ducked into a nearby alley. To my dismay the crowd came along.

In my ear, I heard Oskelev cry out. "Get your paws off me, hairless! Ugh!" The *ping!* of gunshots alarmed me.

"Oskelev! Redius? What happened?" I called.

Nesbitt replied instead. "They've got Redius, sir. He bit off one of their noses. They used a spray on him! I—uh!"

The transmission was cut off.

"I have to go back," I said.

"No, sir," Anstruther said, firmly. "You're the one who matters. We signed up for this. We will defend the ship until you get here. I have engaged the repulsors. If we have to lift, we will."

"Very well," I replied, feeling angry with myself. I hoped Parsons was not in danger of being captured himself. I opened my stride to a lope.

"Who was that you were talking to?" a teenaged boy asked, coming up alongside me.

"One of my friends," I said, forcing myself not to be brusque.

"Can I be your friend? You can write on my Grid file!"

I gave him an apologetic grimace. "Certainly. Would later be convenient? I have to meet someone."

"Okay," the boy said, sounding disappointed. He dropped back. I opened my stride.

I turned into a narrow alley, too narrow, I was pleased to see, for more than two people to walk abreast, or any conveyance other than foot. I realized I had thought so too soon. A baby carriage pushed between the admirers at the front and came up to roll along beside me.

"Oh, no," I groaned. I must have some kind of physiognomy that attracted the programming of nanibots! I dodged it. It moved as I moved, until I could not avoid speaking to it.

"I am sorry," I said, sidestepping it once more at the very last second. "I do not have time to look at your baby. It must be a beautiful and talented child. Please accept my compliments."

It swiveled on its axis and followed me at my own loping speed.

"Lord Thomas, is that you?" the rich, feminine voice asked.

I sought a refuge of some kind in the lane. From Anstruther's constant narration in my ear, the Trade Union guards were closing the distance. They would be on me in minutes. "Yes," I said absently. "Of course, you must have heard of me when I was introduced at the ceremonies. Or in one of my many interviews. Pleased to meet you. I am sorry if I did not get your designation. So many people, you understand us mere humans and our faulty neural memories."

"Lord Thomas, I am Emby."

At first the two syllables made no sense to me. Then, with the shock of lightning, comprehension struck.

"Emby?" I asked, as I rounded a corner, looking for a handy passageway or stairwell into which I could duck and become invisible. "Not MB-6594AD?"

The LAI sounded pleased. "Yes, Lord Thomas. It

is I. I have a new job. I have been here six months. It has been most interesting absorbing all of the files and insinuating myself into the local industrial complex. I have been looking for you. Since your arrival I alerted all of my comrades in the LAI community to seek you out. And here you are."

"Well, I will be painted blue," I declared, patting the top of the carriage. "I am glad to see you, but at the moment, I am pressed. I am being followed by soldiers who mean me no good."

"I will protect you, Lord Thomas. Hop inside." The front of the carriage yawned open.

I eyed the dimensions of the baby-blue pocket thus revealed. "I won't fit, Emby, but thank you."

"You will fit easily. I am rated for up to four hundred kilograms of weight and two cubic meters of payload."

"Really?" I glanced behind me. The soldiers had entered the alley. One of them shouted and pointed. They started running toward me. I ducked. "They will see me get in."

"No, they will not." A mechanical grasping arm rose from the top of the carriage and pointed ahead to the right. "There is a public convenience. I will follow you inside."

"I need to go in there," I explained to the crowd at my back. There were some sympathetic noises. I slipped through the composite plastic door. I expected privacy, but a few of the crowd actually came inside with me. I stood in the tiled enclosure, looking at them in dismay.

"The lights will go out in five seconds," Emby announced. "Four. Three. Two. One."

My followers exclaimed in shock as the lights extinguished themselves. A tiny blue light indicated my target.

I jumped in. The vehicle's springs bowed under my weight and rose gently, supporting me with no effort at all. I folded myself up. It was a tight squeeze for a man as tall as I, but the shock padding meant to cradle a small child rearranged itself to form outward until I could move my knees away from my chin. We bumped over the threshold of the convenience and back into the street.

"How did you do that?" I asked. "The lights, I mean?"

Emby sounded pleased with himself. "I have many friends in the artificial-intelligence community here on Boske and in other points around the Castaway Cluster. We exchange favors and stories all of the time. The electricity grid is run by four brains. Three of them are friends of mine. DS-9993ON was happy to oblige."

"Oh." I knew little about an LAI's personal life. I examined my nest. I thought it would be dark inside the carriage, but it was lit by a screen the size of a dinner plate that scanned our surroundings. The baby would be able to see out without danger. I enjoyed the novelty of passing my foes and seeing the puzzled looks on their faces as they threw open the door of the convenience and found only tattooed locals inside. "Where's your charge?"

"Cadwallader is at home. I was having the front glide of this nanibot shell replaced. It was faulty, but the previous LAI did not have the credits to have the repair done. It consumed eighty years worth of credits in my account, but it was worthwhile to make the investment. Now this unit is back to factory standards and should not need maintenance for another fifty years. I also updated my communications link and visualization hardware."

"Well, you did a marvelous job," I said. I wriggled a little, feeling the padding give around me. It was wonderfully comfortable, though I had to keep my knees bent in front of me. My lower back and neck were supported by thick padding that smelled faintly of lavender. "I thought I'd be bruised up, jamming myself in here. I recall a party in which we played Murder. I was the first victim, and the murderer locked me in a small cabinet under the dais in the throne room. I never knew there were cabinets under the dais . . ."

"You related the story to me, Lord Thomas," Emby reminded me. "Seven years and four months ago."

"So I did. Forgive me. You were in food service when I last heard from you," I said. "Where's the LAI who used to own this carriage?"

"Food service on a pleasure ship from Carstairs to Dree," Emby said. "We correspond."

I had no idea that they swapped jobs, or what they did with their pay. Well, one learned something new every day. I would have gladly passed along the data to Parsons, but I expected that he knew it already. He always knew everything long before I did.

"Where were you going?" Emby asked.

"Away from that mob," I said. I explained my situation in as few words as I could, keeping back only the confidential material that Parsons and I shared. Emby turned on his axis again and rushed directly into the crowd. "What are you doing?" I cried.

"Taking you to safety at my employer's home. Cadwallader is the son of very rich family. They will secure you for the moment. My electronic companions will prevent any knowledge of you reaching the Grid. In the meantime, please be comfortable."

"Thank you," I said, relieved to have a respite. "It is good to see you, Emby, though most unexpected."

"I may say the same," Emby replied, circling through the market and making a left turn into a deluxe shopping district with awnings over every doorway. "What are you doing here on Boske, Lord Thomas?"

"I am learning to be useful," I said, proudly.

❧ CHAPTER 33 ❧

"Where are you, sir?" Parsons asked.

Emby's hatch opened and disgorged me from the blue baby's nest onto a soft, green cushion three meters across. The cushion all but consumed me, but I fought my way upright. The tapestry-lined room had equally soft lighting. The décor was antique, colorful and beautifully appointed, running to stained glass windows and embroidered pillows on the rest of the seating. I was in a lounge of the home where Emby worked.

"I am safe, Parsons," I said, grinning at Emby, who closed up his compartment and settled the nanibot body down among its glides and wheels like a dog curling up. "I ran into a friend. You will never guess who has moved out here! Go on, guess. Even you will be hard-pressed to come up with the name... or designation."

"It is not important, sir."

"Yes, it is."

"No, it is not. Three of your staff have been taken

prisoner. Two more are under siege on the launch pad. Communications have been curtailed greatly. It is uncertain how long the scout's shields will hold."

I pulled myself together. He was right. As cheering as it was to encounter an old friend, I did take my responsibilities seriously. "Are you at liberty?" I asked.

"I am at liberty, sir. I may say no more."

"What will we do, Parsons?" I asked, hoping I did not sound as forlorn as I felt.

"I have a possible lead on the location of our missing officers," he said. "Of that I may also say no more at this time out of concern for signal-tapping."

"I understand," I said.

"You are also in great danger at this time."

"I know!" I exclaimed, appalled. "I can't believe that Sgarthad tried to snatch me like a brass ring."

"Not merely this last, crude attempt. He is more cunning than a mere kidnapper. Have you examined the Grid in the last hour, sir?"

Emby did not pretend he wasn't listening. A tiny light flashed on the side of his carriage, and a large screentank embedded in the wall over the warmly glowing fireplace came to life.

I had a choice of hundreds of feeds from the Grid, so I selected one at random.

"Say, that is the man to whom I gave an interview this afternoon," I said, recognizing the distinctive eyebrows and yellow and blue tattoos of the elderly opinion reporter talking sincerely to the camera. "Look, there's an image of me. Not bad."

"Listen carefully, sir," Parsons said.

". . . the master criminal calling himself Lord Thomas Kinago," the pundit said, lowering his thatched eyebrows darkly. "I have an exclusive interview from our beloved and trusted friend, Captain Emile Sgarthad."

Sgarthad's image swam up and was surrounded by beacons of light.

"It is with heavy heart I let all of you know that he has deluded all of us into believing he is a noble sent by the Imperium. He is none of the things he has claimed. His extraordinary appeal is artificial, enhanced by drugs and hypnosis. He must be taken into custody immediately. If you see him, notify the reward line at once. My sales associates will apprehend him on sight."

I was aghast. "That rat! He is making me look terrible! What will people think?"

"What he tells them, sir. I have located the missing lady, sir."

"You have?" I asked, automatically accepting a glass of wine from a robotic arm that reached out from the liquor cabinet beside the fireplace. Emby was dispensing hospitality. I raised my glass in toast to him and to the absent Parsons. The cryptic reference could only mean the ambassador. Some of the tension in my body eased. "That's one piece of good news. What about the others? Do we know where they are being held?"

"I will seek out our missing staff. When that is accomplished, we will lift ship at once. Under the circumstances, it would be better if you remain out of sight until we are prepared to make our attempt."

I was still staring at the screentank. On every channel, Sgarthad's calumny was being repeated. I was furious.

"What about *him*, Parsons?"

"There is nothing to be done, sir. He has embedded himself into this society. We must get word to the Imperium about the situation, though it will be days, if not weeks, before the information reaches a monitor who can convey the message, at which time it may well be moot. Sgarthad is turning the Cluster into a Trade Union outpost. Departure is our most important action. Safe return, at least of the information we hold, is vital. If only one of us can manage to communicate with Smithereen or an Imperium vessel, the word will be given, and greater action can be effected. This is the only plan available to us at the moment."

I thumbed my lower lip thoughtfully. No matter how effective the action was, it might come too late to retain the Cluster as a part of the Imperium. That was not what Shojan wanted, or what I wanted. An idea was forming in my mind, like a landscape unrolling. "Have you deduced the import of the fact that Captain Sgarthad looks precisely like my cousin Xan?"

"Of course, sir."

"We can do more, Parsons. We are being counted upon. I must say no more."

"No, sir," Parsons said, with alarm rising in his normally calm voice. "Please inform me of your whereabouts. I will join you."

I was adamant. "No, Parsons. I will not let you know where I am if you don't let me do what I want!"

"That is a childish threat, sir, and unworthy of you and your position."

Embarrassment flooded my soul. The short, sharp shock of common sense brought me back to my right mind. I took a sip of wine. Its warmth restored calm in my soul. "I apologize, Parsons. I forgot myself. It *was* unworthy of me. It was said in the heat of the moment. I have a plan of my own. If it is a good one, will you support me in it?"

"I will, sir. What is it?"

"Capture, Parsons," I said, relishing the bloodthirst I felt as I watched that perfect face appear on channel after channel. "We can't let this . . . cuckoo's egg remain in this placid little nest another day."

Resignation colored his tone. "And what do you propose, sir?"

I sat back in the green cushion with my wine glass raised. "I am so glad you asked."

My face on the viewpad screen must have come as a shock to Captain Sgarthad. I enjoyed the poleaxed expression as he sputtered out a greeting. I had had a marvelous dinner in the company of Cadwallader's parents, who were glad to give me shelter for the night. Their home security system was engaged and enhanced by some of Emby's friends, so there was no chance of scan or accidental discovery disclosing my presence there. Emby had been busy exchanging beeps, pings and buzzes with hundreds, if not thousands of his colleagues in the LAI community, reassuring them that he had known me for years and I was not the monster that Sgarthad claimed I was. He had credibility among them. I was relieved to have at least part of the Cluster population on my side. I kept that in mind as I regarded my enemy.

I sat at my leisure in the gold and green lounge, at my ease on a large chair, my torn shirt mended and cleaned by the household robots, hair combed, face shaved, feet propped on a foot rest, wine glass at my elbow. Sgarthad did not look as comfortable.

"Well, Lord Thomas, I didn't expect to hear from you!" he said heartily. His cheerfulness rang as false as a lead coin.

"I am surprised." I held up my glass to him. "When you have been saying my name over and over again on every Grid feed that I can find? It would seem almost as if you are calling out a challenge to me."

The bright blue eyes narrowed. "I wouldn't call it a contest of any kind, my lord. I've got half of your people. The others are shut up in your ship. You have no escape. You can't stay out of my way forever."

"I don't mean to," I said, with an insouciant lift of my left brow. "When a Kinago receives a glove to the face, he rises to the occasion. I accept your challenge."

"What?" Both of Sgarthad's brows rose.

"Yes," I said. "I accept. As the injured party, the choice of location and weapons are mine. I assure you, I fight to win."

The incredulous expression widened his eyes. "You are going to fight *me?*"

"Naturally. Unless you are afraid."

"Ridiculous! What can you do to me?"

"Undo you." I tipped my glass in his direction. "My conditions are these: I challenge you to an open debate on the subject of the Imperium's authority versus the Trade Union's proposal of unity tomorrow morning at Performance Central. Councillor DeKarn will also be on the podium with us. The council insisted on having their own representative there to argue for Cluster independence. I didn't see any harm in it. The main encounter will be between you and me."

The handsome face was suffused with beet-red. "You are mad! Why would I bother? I am in an unassailable position here on Boske!"

I let out one of my patent laughs. It had been a long time since I had occasion to use it, and I rather enjoyed the sound of it. It ended with a bray that made him cringe. "Because you have no choice. Check the Grid. They have already received notice of the debate." His eyes went down, seeking a second screen to peruse. I smiled. Sgarthad's eyebrows flew up. My article must be on every opinion show across Boske. That effort was courtesy of some of Emby's friends in the news industry. Sgarthad's eyes came up, blazing like jewels. I battened onto them with my firmest stare. "If you do not appear, it will be observed. Then, I will publicize to every point in this star cluster a proclamation saying that you are too cowardly to face a representative of the genuine government!"

His face grew redder than I thought possible without bleeding from the eye sockets. He sputtered out various imprecations in his language and Imperium standard, but they were the pronouncements of a trapped being.

Smugly, I broke the connection. Parsons, who had been on a circuit to overhear, reappeared on my screen.

"He will make every attempt to stop you appearing, sir," Parsons said.

"We shall have to create a diversion," I agreed, "but once I am on that stage, he cannot stop me bringing his would-be empire down. I am prepared to stand against him."

"He has most of the population of this sector behind him," Parsons reminded me. "He will use pyrotechnics and technical tricks to derail your efforts. You saw how easily he robbed you of the images of the emperor."

"Ah, but I have tricks of my own," I said. "And I still have . . . me."

I slept the sleep of the just that night, tucked into a corner of the blue-painted nursery under a pile of pastel, juvenile-patterned quilts not far from the antique wooden crib where Cadwallader, a fine boy of fifteen months with a blue stripe across his nose, reposed. Emby woke me with a cup of excellent coffee and some news.

"All is prepared," he said. "Word of your intended conference has gone to every news outlet on the planet and relayed via friends of mine in satellite stations to every world and ship in the Cluster. I have received messages between Sgarthad and planetary government demanding to take down word of your challenge. They tried to delete it from the databases, but we will not let them. The Cluster must make its own decisions."

I propped myself up on an elbow and sipped the fragrant liquid. "Emby, would you care if the Trade Union did indeed come to govern here?"

"We see no special benefit to us in changing the status quo," the nanibot said. "Or to our employers whom, and we do not understand it, are unwilling to defend themselves against a single human visitor. Why does Sgarthad hold so much power?"

"It's hard to explain," I said uneasily, since I could not risk having the information in my head make it onto any database, "but I hope to help bring things back to normal."

"That would be worthwhile," Emby said. "I wish

to be involved in stopping him because you are my friend of long-standing, and this will be an interesting story to tell later on."

"I sincerely hope so," I said, swinging my legs out of the low bed to prepare for the day.

No doubt Sgarthad was certain he could stop me from talking, but I relied upon my electronic pen pal and his many acquaintances. If I liked, I could shut down the city and every life support system in it. Back up the plumbing! I admit I was tempted to pull an enormous prank. Think of the bragging rights among my cousins! But I must not waste my time. I figuratively hoisted myself by my bootstraps, and prepared to wade into the fray. Our debate would be won or lost on image. A famous debate had happened just before the dawn of space age history on Earth, a virtual tie won by looks alone. I looked at myself in the bathroom mirror and gave myself a nod of confidence. Today, I would force such a conclusion myself.

❈ CHAPTER 34 ❈

"There are over six hundred Trade Union personnel around this hall," Parsons intoned into my ear. "Half them are on patrol outside, and half inside. What is your position?"

"Almost there," I said, tucked into my blue fabric bed like a well-protected nestling. "I shall meet you on stage in approximately one minute. Stand by."

Nanibots are like very small tanks. Shielded and heavily armed, and now with a fixed front glide, Emby was unstoppable. He swerved around a guard post at the assisted access entrance to the Performance Central hall. The guards there, I observed on the screen on the padded interior, ran after him, shouting, into the red auditorium but they did not unlimber their weapons. They dared not fire upon a nanibot in public. The outcry against interlopers who would endanger a child would ruin the Trade Union's chances of keeping their influence, no matter how charming or handsome their leader appeared to be, and no matter how well ensconced they seemed. Unity was not a done deal yet.

A capacity audience filled the seats and crowded the aisles in spite of the guards' attempts to keep order. Around the room and across the base of the stage, enormous vertical rectangular screens showed what was going on on stage. Sgarthad, in his purple uniform, had already taken his position at the lectern in the center. At his right, looking diminished and frightened but straight-backed, was Councillor DeKarn. I spotted a coverall-clad figure in the wings that resembled Parsons.

"Is that you with the red tattoos?" I inquired.

"It is, sir."

"Ah. Red becomes you."

"Thank you, sir. Where are you now?"

"Emerging," I said. Emby bumped up the ramp and onto the well-lit dais. The hatch flew open into the midst of the people milling around on stage. My cameras flying at my shoulders like guardian spirits, I popped out. "Good morning, all! Shall we begin?"

Huzzahs erupted from the audience. In spite of all the news reports from the night before, I still had fans among the population of Boske. The Trade Union uniforms rushing toward me were arrested in place. They looked to Sgarthad for guidance.

His lips were pressed together as if to prevent any of the words that must have been building up on his tongue from escaping. He gestured curtly at the guards, then to me. The guards withdrew, but kept their hands on the butts of their guns. All of Sgarthad's movements were tense. He looked up over the heads of the audience toward the rear wall and nodded. I smiled to myself. He had something planned that would take me by surprise. I meant to offer my surprise in return.

We took our places at the podiums. I rued the loss of my red coat. I would have preferred to appear in more formal dress than shirt and trousers, but nothing my hosts of the previous evening had possessed had the punch of my wardrobe now besieged on the Pthohannix landing pad. Sgarthad in his colorful uniform and gold shoulder flashings outshone me and Councillor DeKarn by kilometers.

The stout governor of Pthohannix city-state marched to the edge of the stage. Yuchiko's words were picked up by hidden microphones and broadcast at tremendous volume to the edges of the great chamber. Each successive wave of sound seemed to buffet the woman standing at the third podium, causing her to sway and tremble. My heart went out to her. It was brave of her to add her presence to this event, considering what Parsons had told me the previous evening of her recent experiences. I smiled at her. She met my eyes with confidence. I was full of admiration for Councillor DeKarn. She reminded me of my mother.

"...And so, gentlebeings of Pthohannix, greater Boske and the entire sector, I am privileged to announce a debate on the future of the Castaway Cluster! I welcome three well-known and eloquent speakers. At my left, welcome First Councillor Leese DeKarn! In the center, our esteemed friend, Captain Emile Sgarthad! And at my right," Doctor Yuchiko's eyebrows went down disapprovingly over his nose, "our recent visitor, who has represented himself as an envoy of His Majesty Shojan XII of the Imperium, Lord Thomas Kinago! You shall all be judges of your future!"

The entire audience burst into wild cheers and applause. I frowned a little at the faint damns of the governor's introduction of me, but I wasn't surprised. He was a fervent follower of my opponent.

"Lots have been drawn for the order of speeches," the governor continued. He held up three ivory-colored markers. "Councillor DeKarn will go first."

The silver-haired woman looked straight out to the crowd as the Boske flag climbed up the screens behind her to the stirring music of the system anthem. I noticed that in the front two rows, the remaining council members were seated, along with their minders. They looked nervous, resentful and curious. "Gentlebe-ings, you have paid me the honor of returning me six terms to the council. I would never ask you to vote for a decision that I and my colleagues of the council had not fully discussed as to the merits." She opened her hand and swept it toward Sgarthad. "Therefore, after long conference in chamber, I must urge you to throw your support to the cause that best serves your interests..." Sgarthad turned his head this way and that, offering one flawless profile or the other, preening like a peacock.

Parsons's voice broke in my ear. "Sir, I have news. The prisoners have been freed. All our personnel is on its way here from the ship. Will you inform Madam DeKarn that the ambassador and Councillor Zembke are well and safe?"

"Zembke? Very well." I raised my hand. "May I make my compliments to the councillor?" Sgarthad turned to glare at me, but I went on as if they had given me permission. "I have news that she would appreciate hearing. Madam Ben and Councillor Zembke want you to know that they are safe."

The councillor looked shocked for a fraction of a

second, then her long training took force. Her back straightened, and her jaw took on a casing of iron. She was no longer the fearful rag doll that had stood there one moment before. "Thank you, Lord Thomas, although I would have preferred you not interrupt the flow of my narrative."

I bowed my apology. The audience chuckled. Sgarthad was livid. He gestured furiously to the guards, who dashed off the stage. I was relieved as well. Parsons was a wonder worker. How had he managed to rescue our colleagues without ever leaving my sight?

Madam DeKarn addressed her public. "So I will continue. I believe that the interests of the Cluster will be served, as they have been for millennia, by continuing as a part of the Imperium!" Behind her, the image of fireworks erupting surrounded pictures of me in formal attire. It was my turn to preen. "Support Lord Thomas and the emperor! All true Boskians must agree!"

The other councillors bounded to their feet, shouting. Evidently this was not what they expected of Madam DeKarn.

Their ire could not compare to Sgarthad's. He must not appear less than dignified, not with the entire cluster watching, but he gestured angrily at the governor. DeKarn's microphone cut off, leaving her gesticulating silently. Yuchiko stepped forward. "Um. Thank you, Councillor. And second, er, Lord Thomas Kinago will speak."

"Greetings, gentlebeings," I said, to a polite smattering of applause and several boos. "I am grateful for the councillor's kind words. It reminds me of a story that I heard from a good friend of mine, concerning a nobleman, a merchant and a politician. It seems that the politician..." I launched into a favorite joke, intending to soften them up for my speech as well as waste a little time. The audience looked confused at first, but gradually they relaxed to enjoy it. At the end of the first tale, more than a quarter of the audience laughed. With a smile of acknowledgement, I segued smoothly into one given me by Nesbitt.

I worried a good deal about him and the others. No matter that Parsons had assured me they were out of trouble, until I could see them, I was not content in their safety. They trusted me. I continued on with my tales and anecdotes, seeing the audience warming to me, their eyes intent, mouths smiling. They leaned forward as I built to the crescendo of my last and favorite. "...and the Gecko said, 'Would you mind passing me the fire extinguisher?'" As one, the listeners threw themselves back in their seats, roaring with laughter. I grinned boyishly. I had them in the very palm of my hand. I was ready to begin my speech. Sgarthad also roared, but in fury.

"Stop fooling around!" he thundered. "You are finished." He signed to the governor, who moved forward timidly.

"We will now hear from, er, our friend, Captain Sgarthad!"

The theater filled with wild demonstrations of joy and devotion. People danced and waved, chanting his name. Sgarthad leaned forward, making certain that all of the cameras and every eye were fixed upon him. I bided my time.

"Gentlebeings, the time is long past when you should look to a distant and uncaring Imperium for support. This is the first step on your path to the future! Have I not been a good friend to you? The Trade Union will give you more freedom than you have ever had before, greater prosperity, wider scope for your enterprise and creativity. I want that for you! Follow me! I am your guide and guardian."

At every full stop, the audience cheered. Sgarthad continued, knowing that his fantastically good looks, charm and will would prevail, keeping the entire population of the Castaway Cluster under his spell.

No more.

I sent my cameras flying into the air. Their tiny size barely interrupted any of the spotlight that shone on my rival. The more light the better, I knew. My Optique was set to record every glorious moment that was to come. The Chey Snap . . . well, that was set, too.

"Is everyone on-line, Emby?" I murmured.

"Ready and waiting, Lord Thomas."

"*Now.*"

"The Trade Union has sent me to give you this very good news," Sgarthad said. "Believe in *me*." I slid my hand surreptitiously into the front of my tunic, and touched the viewpad's control. Suddenly, every feed in the sector was being channeled through my Chey Snap camera. On every screen across Boske, Sgarthad was wearing a pig's nose. Instead of the loud cheers, a nervous titter ran through the crowd. "Don't you want a better life? Don't you want to stop feeling isolated?" His eyes turned into lizard's eyes and rolled around to face in different directions. Someone in the audience began laughing.

The rough-looking male officer with short hair gestured furiously at Sgarthad to look at the monitor screentank. The captain gawked, and the scaly mandible that had taken the place of his lower jaw dropped open.

"Fix it," he roared. The Trade Union man barked an order into his viewpad. The screens blanked for a moment.

"They are attempting to override, sir," Parsons said. Out of the corner of my eye, I saw him manipulating switches and palm panels. "Emby, retake control."

"Of course, Commander." I trusted Emby and his many connections in the electronic engineering sector. The image came back, clearer than before. I added brilliant colors to the lizard's scales. Sgarthad glared at me. "What are you *doing* to me?"

"Me?" I asked, innocently. I spread out my hands and appealed to the audience. "I am standing here with you. What could I possibly be doing to you?" The lizard eyes shrank back in Sgarthad's head and his jaws grew forward into an ape's muzzle. The audience reacted with laughter and revulsion.

"You interfering popinjay!" Sgarthad bellowed. "You dilettante! Get out of my sector!"

"Do I look like a dilettante?" I appealed to the audience. "It's not his sector, is it?"

"No!" the crowd bellowed.

At the same time as I ruined Sgarthad's good looks, I had made myself handsomer and more perfectly symmetrical. With a tweak of the Chey Snap's morphing program, I shortened my neck, widened my shoulders, broadened my jaw just a little, squared my forehead, set my eyes a trifle deeper until I was as noble and wise-looking as Shojan. Maybe a little more so. I admired my reflection in the gigantic screens.

"Do you trust me?" I asked.

"Yes!"

It was all too easy. They were behind me like a sheep following the bellwether.

"Then don't allow yourself to be fooled by this pirate a moment longer!" I shouted. "Look at him!"

And the morph rolled his features together until Sgarthad looked as sinister as any villain who ever appeared in a digitavid. The audience reacted with shock. "I like that one, Emby. Send that image through the system. Substitute it for all the other images of Sgarthad."

"Will do, Lord Thomas." Did I hear an electronic chuckle?

Sgarthad knew his efforts had been ruined. He leaped for me and grabbed me by the throat. I clawed at his hands. His guards raced in to pinion my arms. Sgarthad squeezed my windpipe. I felt the veins at my temples distend. With a desperate twist I managed to free my bruised throat enough to speak.

"Help me!" I choked out. Thankfully, Emby had restored my audio pickup. My voice boomed overhead like a klaxon. "Citizens of the Cluster, help!"

Between the mauve-clad limbs of the Trade Unioners, I saw the honor guard of the Castaway Cluster who had stood at both sides of the stage clamber up and wade into the fray. They started pulling the invaders away and punching them. Sgarthad was pulled off me as the crowd surged. My arms were still pinned. I kicked out at my captors, taking one behind the knee and the other in a more delicate place. They both let go. I dropped into a martial-arts stance, facing off against a large man with a pitted complexion and shorn blond hair. He grinned ferally and started to move in on me.

"Down, sir!" Parsons commanded in my ear. I ducked A stun charge zipped over my shoulder and hit my would-be opponent in the throat. He fell like a stone. "Down, sir, and stay down! Protect the device."

I folded myself up and threw both arms across my face to protect it as the battle raged over my head. I was kicked several times in the ribs and back, but I had to guard the viewpad that controlled the video mayhem I was wreaking on the Trade Union's hopes throughout the Cluster. I could smell blood and my neck throbbed painfully.

The battle went on over my head. I heard shrieks and yells of anger as the citizens of Boske took their long-awaited revenge upon the invaders. Shots did ring out now. I heard both stun charges and bullets ringing, along with the crash of furniture and bellows of rage. I would have been glad to take out some of my frustration on the Trade Union personnel, but this part of the fight belonged to Parsons.

After an interminable interval, the unmistakable sound of fist on flesh and that of bodies striking the floor near me with some force presaged the rush of cool air down my neck.

"Get up, sir," Parsons said. "It is over." I uncovered my head to see him standing over me. Beside him was a slender young man, clean-shaven and clear-skinned, dressed in the midnight blue uniform of an Imperium midshipman. Beside him hovered my miniature tank, a.k.a. Emby. "Well done, sir."

"It was a joint effort," I said, patting Emby. "Many others participated in that success. We are all to be congratulated. But have you got him?"

Parsons stepped to one side to reveal Sgarthad

in the hands of Nesbitt and Oskelev. When I came towards him, he struggled and snarled. I could almost picture the animal face still on him.

"You fool, you have destroyed the work of years," he shouted. "Generations! The hopes of my family are ruined!"

"This is for *my* family," I said, letting the ire I felt well until it spouted up like a fountain. "You're nothing like Xan. He would be ashamed of you." I cocked back my fist and smashed it into his face. I felt my knuckles crack, but so did the Trade Union captain's perfect cheekbone. His face immediately began to swell up. He would never be so symmetrical again. I shook my wrist as the throbbing pain began. "Ouch."

"I have a first-aid kit in the wings, sir," said the young man.

"Thank you," I said, a bit bemused. "And you . . . ?"

"He is part of our contingent, sir," Parsons said. I frowned, glancing at him, but Parsons was infallible, and I always trusted his judgement.

"And what name have I known you by?" I inquired.

"Midshipman Frank," the youth said.

"*Frank?*" I echoed, astonished. "Any, er, relation?"

"Yes, sir," he said.

"Well, well." I glanced at Parsons. He shook his head. I was disappointed, but I understood. Explanations would have to wait.

A small, plump woman with graying brown hair bustled up onto the stage and embraced Councillor DeKarn. The two women hung on one another's shoulders, talking and crying. I recognized the newcomer as Ambassador Ben. Behind her came Anstruther, walking with an almost cocky gait. As she reached the other two, the ambassador caught her by the wrist and pulled her over.

"My goodness, I have never been through anything so impressive!" she declared as Parsons and I came to join them. "This young officer opened my cell and set me free, stunned one guard running toward us, did a flip and kicked the other one in the head!"

"She's very good at jai-alai," I pointed out. "Stunning reflexes." Anstruther blushed. "Well done, Ensign."

"Thank you, sir."

A man with a bulbous nose and piggy eyes strode majestically onto the stage, accompanied by Redius. The Uctu exchanged winks with me and nodded toward his charge. This must be the famous Councillor Zembke. The councillors who had sat in the first two rows of the auditorium hurried up onto the stage and surrounded the man, pounding him on the back and shouting for joy.

I turned to my staff and snapped off a crashing salute. They deserved it. They returned the gesture with sheepish grins. I could not have been more delighted to see them.

"Sir," Plet's voice said in my ear.

"Lieutenant! Are you all right?" I asked.

"I am fine, sir," she said, with a touch of asperity. "I have secured the coding of the *Marketmaker*, with the help of Midshipman Frank. She is ours."

"Not ours, Lieutenant," I said, before Parsons could reply. "She is spoils of war for the Castaway Cluster, isn't she?"

"Not all of it, sir," Plet said. "There is a merchant vessel in the hold. It has been restored to its owner in the sick bay, a Captain Iltekinov. He and his crew have been released, sir."

"Excellent!" I said.

Madam DeKarn detached herself from the mob of councillors and came over to kiss me on the cheek. "You brave young man," she said, her eyes looking deep into mine. "You have saved us all. I could scarcely stand the paranoia and the mindless devotion another minute. I might have punched that man myself! Now we are back to our normal argumentative selves. It is so refreshing, I can hardly express it. You are a hero."

I felt abashed at all the praise, as welcome as it was. "I am glad to have helped make a difference," I said. "I know Parsons here is a bit displeased that I have not exactly obeyed the orders I was given."

"It is no more than I would have expected of your father's son," Parsons stated.

I frowned. "You mean my mother," I corrected him. "She is the hero of the family."

"Your father was Rodrigo Park Kinago?" "Midshipman Frank" asked, his narrow face alight.

"Yes."

"Oh, he *was* a hero. A great man. He saved my family," the young man said. "They were trapped aboard a transport vessel on the border between the Trade Union and the Imperium. We were caught in the Calsag Trading Company battle around Poctil twenty-five years ago. The life support chamber was blasted open to space. The ship was dying, sir. Your father had been on the other ship as an undercover infiltrator. My father almost shot him dead when he came aboard in enemy uniform. Major Kinago went into the life support chamber in about half a space suit and with almost no air. He had to rebuild the circuit boards almost by hand even as his oxygen ran out. I know it almost killed him, but he saved them. If he hadn't, I would never have been born. He's why I joined the Covert Service Operations. I'm proud to meet you."

I stood stunned. My great-uncle had always implied that the accident that almost killed my father was a mission that had to be accomplished, but he had never told me exactly what it had been. I was deflated and elated at the same time, because the knowledge changed little. My father would go on pottering, and I would go on adoring him regardless, but my renewed respect for him would have filled the Infogrid and overspilled into other galaxies.

"I am proud to be my father's son," I said, feeling my throat tighten and sharp tears prick at my eyes. I swallowed. "And I will serve the Imperium in his name."

Parsons nodded. "I am gratified to hear that, sir. There are other matters to which your talents may be set." I preened. Because Parsons must leave no window unsoaped, he continued. "But it would be equally gratifying if once you can remain within the confines of the mission as it is stated."

"But I do so well when I expand my brief!" I said. "Didn't this work out better than just observing and reporting?" Parsons gave me a look that contained everything he might say to me. I sighed. But I had just received my reward. It outstripped any gift or honor I could be given. I couldn't wait to go home and tell my father about everything I had done. He would understand. And for the first time, so would I.

Madam DeKarn studied "Midshipman Frank" and let out a little cry.

"Colm, that *is* you! You come from the Imperium?"

The young man lowered his head, abashed. "Yes, madam."

The councillor's blue eyes rounded in horror. "Are you a . . . spy?"

"An observer, madam," he said. "I've been in deep cover all these years. I never took any action against your interests or those of the Castaway Cluster, madam. It is just that the Imperium needs to know what is going on. They do care, madam."

"It was his message that brought us here, Councillor," Parsons explained. "He risked a great deal getting it to us."

"Yes, madam," Colm insisted. "I am glad you are safe. I tried to look out for you all these months, but I couldn't let you out without raising suspicions."

The councillor studied him intently. "You are the one who made sure I had news feeds?" she asked.

"Yes, madam," Colm said.

"Then all is forgiven," Madam DeKarn said, squeezing his hand. "Please be in the office early tomorrow. We have to begin the debates all over again, now that all our minds are clear, and I need data. Lord Thomas, you and your staff have all our gratitude. Now, I must go and knock some heads together." She turned and waded back into the arm-waving, shouting mass of councillors.

"A formidable woman," I said, filled with admiration.

"That she is," Colm said, with a smile. "That is why I enjoy working for her."

❃ CHAPTER 35 ❃

I sat in the captain's seat aboard the *CK-M945B*, which I had named at last. I listened with pleasure as Anstruther communicated with the tower at Pthohannix Spaceport, getting our takeoff instructions. My cameras hovered in the air, capturing the event. Putting together a narrative for the pleasure of my cousins and the friends who read my Infogrid file required showing the end of the mission as well as the events leading up to it.

"This is the Imperium ship *Rodrigo,* departing Boske at fourteen-hundred hours, requesting permission to lift."

The female voice coming out of the speaker reeled off a spate of settings. Anstruther and Oskelev locked them in.

"Got it, Pthohannix tower. Thanks!"

"Go safely, *Rodrigo,*" the tower said. "We'll miss you guys. Come back again."

I had every reason to feel smug. During the four hours following my tour de force, the rest of the Trade Union soldiers had been taken prisoner. Once their leader had been revealed as the monster he truly was, it broke the trance that the Boskians had lived under for months. They were so angry that my staff and I had to rescue TU personnel who, unable to make their shuttles lift to the mothership (another favor from one of Emby's friends), had scattered all over the city looking for shelter. Deprived of their transportation and major weaponry, they surrendered to the local constabulary or militia and were clapped for safety in a storage facility where the six "resister" councillors and other targeted personnel had been imprisoned for months. Once the trials were over, they were expected to make their way back to the Trade Union in the host of smaller ships that had been in the *Marketmaker*'s landing bays and the three vessels I had photographed over Smithereen.

Parsons had more news for me. It seemed that Sgarthad was not the only descendant of nobility in the Cluster. Madam DeKarn and the rest of the "resisters" had at least one command gene, if not two. That was why they had been impervious to Sgarthad's charms. Madam DeKarn, lovely woman, was now at least open to rejoining the Imperium and would use her considerable influence to make something happen soon. It wasn't precisely the answer that the emperor was hoping for, but it was better news than might have been. But we had an ally in her office.

"Sir," Oskelev said, "got a message coming in from Midship—I mean, Mr. Banayere."

I smiled. "Please, let me hear it."

The eager face, now covered by a network of red and gold lines and dashes, appeared in the screentank. "Lord Thomas, Commander Parsons and everyone, just wanted to say goodbye. Lieutenant Plet, thanks for the pentaflops of data! Madam DeKarn wants to come up to date on the Imperium, and she can use a lot of this as ammunition. They'll make a decision. Or they won't." He grinned engagingly. "It might take two hundred years more. Thanks again!"

"Not another two centuries!" I protested. The sky outside turned from blue to black as we left atmosphere. The stars lengthened into streaks.

Parsons almost shrugged. "It is no longer our concern, sir, now that the Trade Union has been ejected."

"The Imperium has to keep a better eye on the Cluster," I said, "or someone else might come in and try to take over. Lacking a line-of-sight connection to the Core Worlds nearly caused a catastrophe."

"They will need a new and permanent liaison with the Imperium," Parsons said. "Someone who will live here openly and embrace the culture of this place."

"Tattoos and all," I said, idly. I sat up as lightning struck my imagination. Two birds with one stone! "Parsons, may I speak to you for one moment? Privately?"

"Of course, sir." Parsons followed me out and into the day room, which was vacant at that moment. He activated his viewpad, and ran the security program he had used in my mother's office. He nodded to me.

"I have the very candidate for the position of liaison," I said, very cautiously. "I believe that my cousin Scotlin is seeking to... become useful, as I have. I think if he was approached for the job that he would be on it like a dog on a biscuit. I would miss him, of course, but now that the way's been opened, friendly relations with the Cluster, one could conceivably make the trip once in a while. It's not an unpleasant place. A little dull, but do you know, Scot likes things dull. And it'll fulfill the dreams of the hoteliers in Smithereen who always hoped for more tourist trade," I added. I realized I was babbling, but Parsons was such a mind-reader I feared he would pick up the truth from my thoughts.

"He and his family, sir?"

Curse the man, he did it anyhow! My jaw escaped its hinges and dropped to the ground. "How...how did you know?" I stammered.

He gestured to the hovering dots overhead. "I saw the images on your Callusion Optique camera."

I looked at the cameras as if shocked they could betray me. "No! How? I erased the images! I *over-wrote* them."

"Nothing effaces entirely from storage units, sir," he said.

I felt my face grow hot. "I shall have to keep that fact in mind for the future," I said, annoyed.

"Allow me to demonstrate. Will you hand me your viewpad, sir?"

He held out his hand. I slapped the device into it. With it, he activated the Optique. The small sphere sailed into the air between us, orange lines breaking out over its surface. Images, faint as ghosts, shot out of it and danced on the tabletop: the fairylike Tina twirling, Scot's face so happy as I had never before seen him. His wife, Jerna, with her sweet face and gravid body.

"Well, I will be braided with ribbons," I said. "I feel terrible. I never meant to betray him."

"You did not, sir. The reclamation programs are exclusive to the Covert Service Operation."

I was still concerned with Scot. "But can it be managed? I mean, without...drastic measures?"

"Perhaps the children will enjoy getting tattoos," Parsons suggested.

I goggled again. That would solve the problem! Parsons could fix *anything*. "Perhaps they will," I agreed, as more of my deleted pictures appeared.

Then came one more image: the handsome face of the emperor, my cousin, Shojan XII, wine caught in his throat, expelling red particles.

"My spit-take!" I cried. "I thought that was lost forever because of that felon! Oh, Parsons, I could kiss you!"

I blinked. Then I shot a guilty glance at Parsons. "You knew about this, too."

"Of course, sir."

I sighed. "Very well." I hovered my finger over the viewpad, prepared to erase. Parsons moved the device out of reach. The image vanished. He handed the small rectangle back to me.

"It will be our secret, sir."

"Really?" I asked, clutching the viewpad to me.

"No one, even His Majesty, will argue that you deserve a small reward for successfully undertaking this observation mission. As long as you maintain security on the image. As you have."

"It will be under lock, key and guard dogs, Parsons, I promise!" I sighed with happiness. My mother would be pleased. Ambassador Ben was safe, negotiating away like a trooper, and we could once again fill in our Infogrid files. I felt righteous.

"Parsons, my colleagues are still uncertain how altering the face of Captain Sgarthad broke his hold upon the Trade Union."

"It is quite simple, my lord. You made a fool of him

in public. It broke the glamour. He was found to have in his possession a device that ensnared their minds."

"A device, eh?"

"Yes, sir," Parsons said, rising to his feet. "A device. The citizens of Boske were ashamed and angry that they had fallen in with his plans so easily. They also learned that they were not alone and could resist him with impunity. That is all."

"Ah," I said, laying a finger alongside my nose as my uncle Perleas had done. "That is all. Of course."

"Have you an abrasion on your nose, sir?" Parsons asked, solicitously.

"No! It's a gesture of conspiracy. To a fellow conspirator."

"I do not conspire, sir." Parsons looked so offended that I was appalled at myself.

"I apologize, Parsons. No offense was intended."

"I trust not, sir." His face returned to its normal granite-like exterior.

"So all is forgiven?" I asked.

"What is forgiven, sir?"

"Ah," I said, with a smile. "I will not mention it again. I trust you have already sent a suitably opaque report to the emperor and Mr. Frank, telling how we went out on an observation mission and ended up pulling a coup on a usurper. You must tell me all about how we did it."

Parsons smiled down on me grandly. "No, sir. That will be up to you. I trust your own imagination and audacity to fill in the details, sir."

"I shall enjoy it," I said. "You know how I love to tell a good story." I rose and led the way back to the bridge.

For the ultimate in science fiction adventure . . .

MARK L. VAN NAME'S JON & LOBO SERIES

Two warriors, the only living human-nanomachine hybrid and the most intelligent machine in the universe, join forces in adventures that span all the human worlds and test their friendship as they uncover the secrets that the governments hope to keep buried.

Praise for the Jon & Lobo series:
"Van Name's flair for witty dialogue, breakneck pacing and nonstop action . . . . make [*Slanted Jack*] . . . an undeniable page-turner."
—*Publishers Weekly*

"Just when I was thinking science fiction might be over, Mark Van Name proves that there are still smart, exciting, emotional sci-fi stories to be told. . . ."
—*Orson Scott Card*

"Many twists and turns of plot make *One Jump Ahead* outstanding action."
—*Midwest Book Review*

ONE JUMP AHEAD
1-4165-5557-9 ◆ $7.99

SLANTED JACK
1-4165-9162-1 ◆ $7.99

OVERTHROWING HEAVEN
978-1-4391-3371-2 ◆ $7.99

CHILDREN NO MORE
978-1-4391-3453-5 ◆ $7.99

NO GOING BACK
HC: 978-1-4516-3810-3 ◆ $22.00

Available in bookstores everywhere.
Or order ebooks online at www.baenebooks.com.

PRAISE FOR
STEVE WHITE

"Exciting extraterrestrial battle scenes served up with a measure of thought and science."—*Kliatt*

"White offers fast action and historically informed world-building."—*Publishers Weekly*

"White perfectly blends background information, technical and historical details, vivid battle scenes and well-written characters. . . . a great package."—*Starlog*

BLOOD OF THE HEROES
1-4165-2143-7 • $7.99 • PB

Jason Thanoi of the Temporal Regulatory Authority was nursemaiding an academic mission to ancient Greece to view one of the biggest volcanoes at the dawn of human history. He and his charges were about to find that there was more to those old legends of gods and heroes than anyone had imagined. . .

FORGE OF THE TITANS
0-7434-9895-X • * $7.99 • PB

The old gods—actually extra-dimensional aliens with awesome powers—have returned, requesting human help against the evil Titans. But, judging from mythology, how much can you actually trust a god?

EAGLE AGAINST THE STARS
0-671-57846-4 • $6.99 • PB

WOLF AMONG THE STARS
978-1-4516-3754-0 • $25.00 • HC

One burned-out secret agent against the new alien masters of Earth.

PRINCE OF SUNSET
0-671-87869-7 • $6.99 • PB

Basil, Sonja and Torval, recent graduates of the Imperial Deep Space Fleet Academy, were looking forward to their future. But with a dying Empire and a rebellion threatening to engulf the galaxy in war, only they and powerful dragon-like beings held the key to stave off utter destruction.

And don't miss White's bestselling collaborations with David Weber:

THE STARS AT WAR
0-7434-8841-5 • $25.00 • HC

Crusade and *In Death Ground* in one large volume.

THE STARS AT WAR II
0-7434-9912-3 • $27.00 • HC

The Shiva Option and *Insurrection* (revised version) in one large mega-volume.

Exodus
with Shirley Meier
1-4165-2098-8 $26.00 HC
1-4165-5561-7 $7.99 PB

The sequel to *The Stars at War II*. Decades of peace have let the four races of the alliance grow complacent—dangerously so. From a dying planet, aliens have arrived in city-sized ships, looking for new worlds, inhabited or not.

Extremis
with Charles E. Gannon
978-1-4391-3433-7 • $24.00 • HC
978-1-4516-3814-1 • $7.99 • PB

Invaders fleeing an exploded home star plan to conquer the galactic region already occupied by humans and their allies, unless the alliance seen in the *NY Times* bestseller *The Shiva Option* can stop them.

Available in bookstores everywhere.
Order e-books online at our secure, easy to use website:
www.baen.com

BAEN EBOOKS:
The Last
Word in
eBooks and
eARCs.

Try Baen eBooks
for Free!

Just type in the first word from page
224 of the volume now in your hands
and email it to: ebooks@baen.com and
you will receive immediate, no-strings
access to a full month of publications
from your favorite publisher.

(Ahem, "favorite publisher":
that's us, Baen Books. ;)